Betrayers of Magic

Lynette E. Creswell

D1332175

ALSO BY LYNETTE E. CRESWELL

Sinners of Magic

Published in 2013 by Lynette E. Creswell

First Edition

A CIP catalogue record for this title is available from the British Library.

This book is dedicated to all the sons and daughters who have served or who are serving in our Armed Forces.
We are all so very proud of you and the courageous work that you do.

Acknowledgements

My journey as a writer never ceases to amaze me and the support from my readers, family and friends has been truly astounding. So many people have given me valuable encouragement and so I would like to thank everyone on Facebook who took the time to support my pages and an even bigger thank you goes to the people below without whose help I would still be trying to write the trilogy. My thanks go to:

My dear daughter-in-law to be, Hannah Clark, for proofreading a manuscript yet again and for loving the characters as much as I do. To Andy, my husband, who also proofread my story and got so involved with the plot he forgot to proofread it! Lisa Atkin, my fellow colleague, for helping to get those first few chapters spot on. The NHS staff at the Diana, Princess of Wales Hospital, Grimsby for cleaning me out of books! Liz Lane who not only helped me find an editor for this story but also gave me a real confidence boost. Karen McUrich for her friendship, loyalty and for driving around with posters in her car for the last nine months! Ann Gipp for being a true and dear friend. Lisa Brighton for her belief in me. To all my sons for their continual encouragement and for being proud of their mum. To Sue Christelow for being the most talented editor and who put my story straight. And last, but by no means least, Phil Moss, whose cover for *Betrayers of Magic* excelled way beyond my wildest dreams.

Prologue

The word swept across the city like a harrowing disease. The Wanderer was to be set free from prison and the paid watcher waited not a moment too soon to tell the world of his imminent release. As the morning sun glowed with an orange-gold light, the deadbolt was drawn back inside the prison and the strong timber door thrust open. The gaoler, guarded and alert, shot his eyes in the direction his prisoner should take if he wished to taste his freedom. He felt his lips tighten when he saw someone draw an arm close to his face. It was caked in a layer of dried dirt and he watched the prisoner block out the streaming rays of sun with the back of his filthy hand.

'Ger up with ya,' the gaoler snapped, pointing towards the corridor, 'or I'll 'ave this 'ere door shut faster than ya can say – filthy, dirty scavenger!'

Muscle cramped from sleeping on a cold, damp floor, the prisoner forced himself to his feet, wincing when he threw his shoulders back to help ease the ache in his lower spine. He dragged his dark hair, lank and covered with lice, behind his pointed ears, feeling it heavy with months of grease and ground-in dirt. He dropped his hand, shifting towards the door and he pushed it wide, forcing the gaoler to take an involuntary step back, revealing to him the row of prisoners who were locked inside adjacent cells.

On hearing a disturbance the prisoners rushed to their feet, scurrying like rats to see who was being set free and in seconds, desperate shouts were ringing along the cold walls and a deafening drumming perforated the chilled air. With a sudden fury the inmates started hitting the metal bars and bare stone walls with their dented plates and battered cups, their despair at being locked away and forgotten momentarily heightened by the unexpected release of the Wanderer.

The Wanderer stepped out into the corridor, his lips pursed at the commotion and he slid his gaze to the floor, pretending he could neither see nor hear the din which followed him when he left the stinking hellhole behind. Concentrating only on his freedom and what he would do next, his thoughts drifted to a certain accommodating maid who worked at the local inn that he'd used before being incarcerated.

Hope she's still working there, he mused, scratching his backside and then wiping his nose with what was left of his torn shirtsleeve. *It's not like she'll have been busy with me being away ...*

The gaoler turned towards him, a look of distaste clearly visible on his old, leathery face and he shouted to the prisoners to be quiet or face the consequences of their actions once he returned. The noise died in their throats when the gaoler flashed a menacing grin. He gestured for the Wanderer to take the lead until they reached the end of a second passageway where their exit was blocked by a thick oak door, rimmed with rusty steelwork.

'Stand back and wait 'ere,' the gaoler ordered, pulling out a heavy set of iron keys and inserting one into the lock. The Wanderer did as he was told, eager to be set free without further delay. The door gave a loud screech when the crude bolt protested, forcing the gaoler to give it a sharp tug and light flared once again inside the corridor. The Wanderer shielded his face but appreciated the warmth of the sun when it touched his cold skin. He had been in semi-darkness for many months and his dulled retinas hurt from the bright light, but his arrogance had seemingly not dimmed. He followed the gaoler, rubbing his burning eyes and walking between two marching columns of soldiers, most of whom he knew only too well due to their own underworld connections. Their faces shone with amusement when they caught his eye and their lips curled mockingly at him, for they knew he would return, it would just be a matter of time.

He passed a narrow archway which led to the lower set of dungeons and felt himself stiffen, for those prisoners who were held deep inside their belly would never live to see the sunrise and he gave an involuntary shiver. He trusted no one either inside or outside of the prison walls, for there had been a small bounty placed upon his head and some would not yet know he'd paid the price at the hands of the sentinel. He knew he had no more chances, yet he could never change his thieving ways and his mind drifted to his trial. The council had spared his life, of which he was still stunned. King Gamada ordered for him to be executed, yet after his untimely death the council proclaimed a reprieve, forcing the Wanderer to accept a further sentence of hard labour instead. He'd worked in the charnel house, stripping the continual flow of dead of nothing but their rags and dignity. Disease ridden and half starved, the pile of mounting bodies lay waiting for a paupers' mass burial. The stench of their rotting flesh became his own personal torment as with every passing day his enslavement ate at his soul, destroying what was left of his already pathetic attempt at humanity.

Pushing these dark thoughts aside, he found himself exiting the compound and stepping out on to the streets of the city. His heart was pounding so hard when he heard the prison door slam behind him that he thought it would burst and kill him there and then. His shifty eyes observed his surroundings and he moved to a darkened corner where he could take a moment to get his bearings. When he felt it safe, he stole towards a set of four small cottages. His pace quickened when he reached a ginnel, the darkened passageway beckoning to him like a beacon in the night and he rushed forward, eager to be swallowed by the darkness. His feet were silent as he made his way through and once he reached the other side, he headed straight towards a common flowerbed.

After checking to see if he was being observed, the Wanderer scraped his foot along the soft, brown dirt until the heel of his ill-fitting boot stuck on something hard. Crouching low, he brushed the last remnants of dirt away with his trembling fingertips to show a secret gateway where he found the quick-release mechanism and pressed it. A portal sprang open and he closed his eyes, bringing his hands to his chest in silent gratitude. He turned on his haunches, pulling close the thin, tattered cloak which he'd been given by the gaoler and without a moment's hesitation jumped from one loathsome place to the next.

His eyes were sharp and his wits sharper still when he turned his head to focus on his whereabouts. The Wanderer moved like a slick cat over broken debris and rotting vegetation when the exposed portal sealed immediately above his head. The chamber was foul smelling and damp. The dulled walls dripped with a constant stream of stagnant water, creating a stench within the air which would have made any normal being caught within its belly retch, but not the Wanderer because this was his home and to him the smell brought only contentment.

He was met by a score of archways and twisting tunnels branching off into a sequence of passageways. He knew each destination would lead within the city walls and that on more than one occasion this knowledge had been his salvation. However, after some time he paused, checking for signs of being followed, his eyes already accustomed to the gloom. With caution burning in his eyes, he sieved through the darkness, searching the shadows for any clear warnings of danger and once he was satisfied he was alone, he turned his attention back to the moment at hand.

Wiping away a patch of fungus and slimy mould, he mumbled an enchantment which caused a series of twisted cracks to shoot along the wall. Like a zigzag of long, bony fingers the solid fractures reached out across the outer surface. Then small hairline cracks appeared, and he reached out, pushing hard against the stone. He stepped back when a rush of rubble and fine dust fell at his feet and he shook his dirty boots clean. He took a shuddering breath, concerned that the sudden commotion might alert someone to his presence and he listened intently for any approaching footsteps. When the dust settled and only the echo of silence rang inside his head, he drew away from a society he had learnt to hate and took back the life they'd tried so desperately to take from him.

Once inside his domain, the loneliness which he'd endured in prison returned but this time he embraced the isolation with an unexpected shiver of excitement. However, his many months away had seen his den grow dilapidated and neglected and mushroom-shaped organisms grew in several moist patches in the damp, mouldy earth. The stench of their musty aroma was overpowering, yet to the Wanderer it smelt like sweet perfume. His bed, covered in a simple blanket made of homespun yarn, lay thick with a layer of soft, green mildew. His meagre belongings stacked in the corner awaiting his return looked pathetic and rather inadequate for someone who boasted having infinite wealth.

Gripping a candle, he threw his hand and a small flame shot from his fingers, setting it alight. The candle's glow illuminated a small, hollow cave revealing misty vapours which were hanging like fluffy clouds high above the roofline. They floated in odd shapes between the flowstone, clinging to the lime deposits which grew in sharp, pointy horns, creating a wondrous valley which allowed the mist to nestle between its colourful towers of stalactites. It was bitter cold inside his den and the air was thick and stale. The Wanderer moved with haste to where a firepit had been carved centuries earlier deep within the stone. Another flick of his hand and a burst of fire blazed with a flurry of golden embers, causing the vapours to dance in a heat-filled frenzy until, one by one, they each dispersed.

He gave a thankful sigh when the room filled with warmth and golden light and he strolled to the furthest corner, letting his hands touch the cold walls as he travelled. His fingers brushed the different contours of rock, touching the rich colours of green and white which were threaded through the limestone.

Bending down, he dug his fingers in the soft earth, tearing at the layers of dirt until the palm of his hand touched something solid. His fingers curled around two further objects and he immediately drew his hand to his chest. He straightened, opening his fingers like a careful child and revealed three small, shiny pieces of quartz; these minerals were his very own Lodestones. He played with them like toys until they left the sanctuary of his palm, hovering unaided in mid-air, spinning like a sun with two moons. They were coated with petrified coral, making them stones of immense power. He had stolen these magnetised minerals from King Gamada's treasury and the reason why he'd been dually punished, but even after his arrest the Lodestones had somehow managed to stay in his possession. Unbeknown to him the orbs were enchanted with a dark spell and their true powers never unleashed – so far. The stones not only protected those who had accumulated a notorious large fortune, but they could also find rare and exquisite treasures, leading any gluttonous immortals who were foolish enough to wish to pluck more riches from the hidden depths of obscurity straight to them.

The Wanderer mumbled an incantation which allowed him to see through the solid rock face. He grinned as only the greedy do when his eyes saw the overwhelming display of shiny gold, stacked high against a mountain of sparkling jewels. Piled high from floor to ceiling, his treasure was hidden in every conceivable nook and cranny and the pyramid of shimmering gems glistened like polished stars each time they caught the glow from the flickering firelight. The orbs spun faster and faster whilst they cast their spell of protection and this caused his desire for more riches to intensify. His wealth and valuables were vast, yet he lived like a common hermit, unable to stop himself from hoarding everything he stole or allowing a single piece of ill-gotten gold to ever leave his fingertips.

A thunderous blow exploded on the outer surface of his den, causing him to freeze like a frightened rabbit. He pulled a hand across his forehead when tension shot across his brow, unable to comprehend how someone had managed to hunt him down so soon after his release. Aware of his sudden vulnerability, he cursed aloud, feeling a numbing sensation rise through his body and he shot his hand to his mouth to stifle a cry. The continuous boom of an agitated fist grew more and more intense and the Wanderer's resolve started to slip away with each shuddering vibration.

He cast his mind, enabling him to speak to the intruder through the stone.

Who are you and what do you want? he demanded, noticing his mouth was turning dry as he tried to stay in control. He swept the Lodestones into an inner pocket, forcing them to lie still inside the lining, his heart hammering in his chest at the mere thought of losing them to another.

I command you to open the door at once, replied an authoritative voice inside his head, yet the Wanderer didn't recognise it and his worry grew.

He snapped his fingers to disperse the spell that revealed his hidden treasures and felt a trickle of cold sweat run down his cheek. He wiped it away with the back of his hand and then searched his forehead for more. He found his brow to be drenched and he rubbed the rest away with the cuff of his torn shirtsleeve.

11

Be gone stranger, he commanded, *for I am sure I have never had dealings with you in the past and I wish for none with you in the future.*

I am here with a heavy purse of gold, the voice bellowed, sounding infuriated at being made to wait outside. *However, I will not stand here all day and discuss my business for all but the rats to hear!*

The Wanderer took a step forward, interest flaring behind his dark, narrow eyes and he managed a crafty grin. His insatiable hunger for wealth was starting to override his need to be cautious and he thought perhaps his visitor to have simply heard of both his talented reputation and recent release. This episode was unusual though, for any work he'd been offered before had always been through his strong underworld connections, reaching him via his favourite drinking hole, the Stumble Inn, and although this thought niggled at him, he chose to ignore it.

For the first time in his life he felt trapped within his own den, yet a shiver of excitement betrayed his fearful judgement at the mere mention of a bag of gold. He sensed his visitor had not come through some idle whim. Indeed, he had earned the reputation of being a dangerous and notorious thief, yet here was a stranger banging at his door with a confidence he would not have expected from any living soul. Evidently his visitor was unafraid of any retaliation from such an unsavoury character or fearful of suffering a painful repercussion at a much later date ...

The Wanderer pondered these facts for a moment longer, sensing that the intruder would not leave until some kind of bargain was struck between them. With growing anticipation he called for the intruder to stand aside, mumbling the spell which would open the entranceway and make him vulnerable to whoever stood on his doorstep. With the spell cast, the doorway broke open to reveal his unexpected visitor, giving the Wanderer cause to regret his somewhat impulsive action. He stood open-mouthed, staring at the tall, dark silhouette which blocked his doorway and felt his heart miss several beats. He heard the figure speak and enter his domain without being invited in. The Wanderer forced himself to bow and listen intently to the strong, dominant voice which revealed to him a terrible, dark secret. The visitor appraised him for stealing the Lodestones and the Wanderer's face turned white. His visitor ignored his look of anguish, choosing instead to explain what he had in store for him to do and all the while the Wanderer nodded, mindful that his own outrageous fantasies and unscrupulous ideas for the future had just shattered like glass before his very eyes, only to be replaced by the perfectly moulded structure of someone else's dreams ...

Chapter 1

Bright, early morning sunlight bathed the frost-coated windows with shimmers of shiny gold. Inside, the heat from the open fire made the room feel devilishly warm and the soft crackles as the flames licked at the pyramid of firewood forced the bitter cold to stay outside.

Crystal sat, curled like a lazy cat, in her favourite armchair. She observed Beatrice pour milk into a cup of hot tea before readily accepting the drink when offered, with a warm, grateful smile. Taking a slurp, she studied her mother who was busily fiddling with an awkward packet of custard creams. It seemed to take her ages to get into the packaging but once opened Beatrice fussed about, arranging them on a rose-patterned plate and then offered them to Crystal, who simply declined with a wave of her hand.

'So, what are your plans for today?' Beatrice asked, placing the biscuits untouched on the tea trolley. She reached for the sugar bowl and dropped two cubes into her cup, absent-mindedly watching the white, snowy crystals disintegrate under its milky surface.

Crystal shrugged and took another slurp of tea, but then an unexpected dark shadow shot across her face and she turned away to try and hide it. Too late, Beatrice had seen it and she raised a quizzical eyebrow, registering the protective shield which dropped like a newly sharpened guillotine behind her daughter's eyes.

'You seem to be hiding yourself away from the world these days,' Beatrice mumbled, looking rather sour faced. However, her eyes had grown shrewd and Crystal knew her mother was constructing a plan behind those darkened lashes in which to extract whatever it was that was bothering her secretive daughter.

'Are you seeing that boy again?' Beatrice asked, a little too casually. 'It's been a while since you've met with him, hasn't it?'

Crystal groaned.

'His name's Matt,' she snapped, rolling her eyes in consternation. Jumping up from her seat, she almost threw her teacup onto the small mahogany table which was placed right beside her. The cup clattered when the fine china made contact with the hard wood surface, startling Beatrice.

'What on earth's the matter with you?' she retorted, placing her own cup firmly on the trolley. 'I only asked you a simple question.'

Crystal stared into her mother's wide eyes and saw the hurt there, ripe and clear, but how could she explain to her that she was miserable because she wanted to go back to the Kingdom of Nine Winters? Her body ached with longing at the mere thought, yet she feared returning too, aware of the wave of controversy that swept every realm because of her.

'I'm so sorry,' said Crystal, hanging her head, ashamed of her unexpected outburst. 'I didn't mean to take my frustrations out on you.'

'What's with you these days?' asked Beatrice, looking rather bewildered. She unconsciously rubbed the back of her neck with her hand. 'Ever since you got involved with Matt you've changed, you seem more secretive, more distant somehow?' Crystal felt her cheeks burn scarlet. A twist of guilt tightened in her gut, forcing her to break eye contact and she stared instead at the sickly green swirl pressed deep in the pattern of the carpet. The cool touch of shame slithered down her spine because she knew she was allowing Matt to take the blame for her recent change in behaviour.

I miss you, called Amella inside her head, *when will you return to us?*

The sound of her natural Elvin mother calling to her sent a wave of astonishment to surge inside her already overloaded brain. The maternal pull knotted itself around her heart, causing her to feel like she was being stung by a large swarm of angry bees. Her eyes shot towards Beatrice and she jumped from her chair, confusion flaring inside her startled eyes. She manifested stillness, wondering if Beatrice could hear the voice too. She had never expected something like this to happen and when Amella's voice faded, it became obvious Beatrice hadn't heard it at all and so she rushed from the room with a river of tears streaming down her face.

Beatrice merely watched with unmasked surprise when Crystal ran from her sight. Clearly concerned, she rose from her chair and hurried to the bottom of the stairs. She clutched the balustrade as she contemplated climbing the stairs and following Crystal to her room. She allowed her foot to take the first step, but faltered. She shook herself, trying to regain her composure and her eyes shot to the top of the landing, willing Crystal to materialise. A solitary clock ticked somewhere behind her and after a couple of tense minutes it was clear Crystal was not going to reappear. Beatrice bit her lip, unsure what to do, afraid that she might spark a scene or, worse, a fight if she confronted her daughter and so with some reluctance she returned to the drawing room to sit alone, comforting herself with a cup of tepid tea and an abandoned plate of custard creams.

In her bedroom Crystal reached for her mobile phone and rang the first number programmed into her list of contacts. A gruff male voice answered, causing her to force a weak smile.

'Hi,' she said, dabbing her eyes with a soggy tissue and throwing herself on her bed, front first. She glanced towards a poster of her favourite artist, Adele, and her pose, both happy and relaxed, made Crystal feel all the more miserable. She kicked her legs behind her and allowed her slippers to fall from her feet and she unconsciously played with a luscious, stray curl, her gaze still fixed upon her idol.

'Hey,' said Matt, sounding surprised to hear her voice on the end of the line. 'What's up?'

Crystal flung herself onto her back and stared blindly at the ceiling, sniffing loudly.

'I heard Amella calling to me,' she said, pulling the phone closer to her ear, 'just now in my head, she asked me as clear as if she was standing in front of me when I would be returning.'

Matt's voice sounded tight. 'We've only been back five minutes, isn't it a bit soon to be thinking of returning?'

'I guess,' she said, blowing her nose down the receiver, 'but it's all I can think about.' Matt let out a deep sigh.

'Look, I'll meet you in the library in about twenty minutes if you like, we can talk more there. I've got Camilla hovering and you know how her ears burn when she knows I'm talking to you.'

'Okay,' said Crystal, grunting sourly when she thought about his meddlesome sister, 'but make sure you come alone.' Matt chuckled to himself.

'Don't worry, Camilla's not in the habit of making the same mistake twice. You really freaked her out the last time you met, so I think it's safe to say she won't be tagging along this time.'

Crystal pushed the red button and ended the call. She liked how he always made her feel better and rushing down the stairs, she ran into the kitchen and grabbed her coat from off the peg. Beatrice swiftly followed.

'Are you alright, dear?' she asked, looking at her daughter's swollen eyes.

Crystal ran over and gave her a big hug.

'Really sorry about earlier,' she said, relaxing her embrace and kissing her mother's cheek. 'I don't know what came over me.'

'Hormones!' said Beatrice, returning the hug with a tight smile. 'Well at least that's what I've put all this strange behaviour down to.'

Crystal forced a smile.

'Do you really think so, mum?'

'Yes, of course, love, what other possible explanation could there be?'

Crystal nodded, recognising the need for her mother to analyse her erratic behaviour. 'I'm off to the library to meet Matt,' she said, catching a glimpse of her mother's immediate look of disapproval. 'I'm not sure how long I'll be,' she added, grabbing her bag, 'so please don't make me anything for dinner.'

Beatrice's lips pulled back into a tight grimace.

'Fine,' she snapped, reaching for her glasses from off the breakfast bar and placing them abruptly on the end of her nose, 'but just be careful and remember boys are only ever after one thing!' Crystal was taken by surprise at her exasperated comment and immediately burst out laughing.

'Oh mum,' she said, searching for her purse and checking she had enough bus fare. 'It isn't like that between us.'

'It's always like that,' Beatrice insisted, her chest rising. 'Just you mark my words; Matt isn't any different to any other boy, you'll see I'm right in the end.'

*

Later, sitting on the back seat of the *Red and Rapid* town bus, Crystal stuffed the earphones from her MP3 into her ears in an attempt to block out the world. The loud music hammered inside her brain with only her tangled thoughts to interfere with the noisy melodies. Her mother's warning about Matt had needled her and she tried to brush her unfounded comment aside, trying hard to forget what she'd said.

As the bus made its journey along the high street, she glanced out of the window, watching the busy town bustle with its day-to-day activities. She loved people watching and the sweet face of a Chinese girl held her fascination when they stopped en-route in the town centre. The girl was about seven and she wore long, bright socks and girlie bunches in her hair. She was talking very fast to her mother who was trying to ignore her and browse through a popular fashion magazine. Crystal wondered, what would it be like to go back to knowing only one woman as her mother instead of two? She felt herself take a sharp intake of breath. Two different mothers in two separate worlds, how did she ever find herself in such a situation?

She soon met Matt as planned in the furthest corner of the library away from prying eyes. He was already there when she arrived, breathless from hurrying through the rain which had begun to pour.

'You're late,' he chided, his eyes lighting with pleasure at seeing her. 'I was beginning to think you might have changed your mind.'

She gave him a warm hug and felt his keenness to mould her body into his melt over her. Her mother's warning rang loudly in her head and she pulled back, suddenly afraid of where their relationship was leading. She gave a nervous chuckle, diving into an easy chair which greedily enfolded her small frame. Matt plonked himself next to her, the soft light of the library showing the slight fleshiness of his jaw, allowing flashes of light to infiltrate his perfectly formed green eyes.

'So, what have you been up to?' he asked, pulling his foot to sit comfortably on top of his knee. She deliberated an answer, switching her gaze to a large-framed man, dressed in uniform, who was walking by. She nodded an acknowledgement to the security guard when he shot her a wave, momentarily distracted.

18

'I've been practising some magic,' she whispered to Matt, once the guard passed by, 'but I don't appear to be very good at it.' Matt's brow creased.

'I thought you weren't going to practise magic anymore?' he replied, giving her a look of disapproval.

'I know, but I couldn't help myself,' she giggled, turning shy. Her beautiful face lit with pleasure when she told him her secret and her sapphire blue eyes shimmered with an excitement he hadn't seen since they had embarked on their perilous journey to the extraordinary world. She looked so much like her father ... yet she had her mother's delicate features and thick, luxurious hair. He had never met anyone like Crystal and he knew he never would again. Even before he realised she was a magical being, banished to live with the plain folk because of her parent's crimes against the realm, he knew she was more than special.

His mind wandered to Amella and Bridgemear. Her parents' sins had been to simply fall in love and create a child. In their enchanted world, loving another from a different realm was forbidden, yet Bridgemear and Amella had fallen foul to true love. Their relationship had been ripped apart by those who saw them merely as traitors of the realm, punishing them dearly for the love they had tried to keep so desperately hidden. The Elders had been cruel when deciding their fate, punishing them both to the extreme so as to be a warning to others who may have thought to dabble with such sins of the flesh.

Amella had been forced to give her newborn babe to the Elders to save Bridgemear from a life of eternal purgatory. Overcome with grief and despair, she had taken a life of exile, hiding deep within the enchanted forest as a simple dweller, living a desolate life away from prying eyes and judging faces. She had never been able to bear the loss of her only child and the betrayal of her lover who had seen their daughter as merely a terrible burden. Yet in the end when they had been forced together through events of which they had no control, she had forgiven him everything without an ounce of regret.

Crystal gave an exaggerated cough and Matt shook his mind clear, focusing on the present day instead.

'I said,' she insisted, raising her voice and trying to snap him out of his daydream, 'that my mind seems to have become more powerful since we got back. I have millions of strange incantations and spells running loose inside my head and I find myself trying to create these spells, just so I can get rid of them to make space for more.'

Matt uncrossed his foot and moved closer, grasping her tiny hands in his.

'You're going to have to be very careful not to draw unwanted attention to yourself,' he said, remembering Abbadon the Destroyer and worse still, Forusian. He closed his eyes and pushed the painful memories of what both he and Arhdel had endured at the hands of Forusian to the furthest corner of his mind.

'You must understand my concerns for you are genuine. Haven't you learnt there are those who might visit our world who are evil? You've already tasted some of their hospitality in your own world and you know you're still extremely vulnerable to people like that who torture, maim or, worse, kill your kind for your powers. Doing magic willy-nilly certainly isn't going to help keep you safe; don't you remember how easily Tremlon found you?'

His statement made her think about the shape-changer, causing her to pout. Her normally radiant blue eyes turned dim at his reprimand. She dropped her gaze, her mood changing to one of gloom. Matt saw the pain in her eyes and felt a sudden stab of regret.

'Look, all I'm saying is don't go doing any spells or enchantments unless it's really necessary,' he said, squeezing her hand in an attempt to reassure her.

'I just can't help it,' she moped. 'You know I hear voices in my head, spells are at the tip of my tongue and at night when I sleep, I have the strangest dreams. It's all so overpowering and it's eating away at me day after day. I think I need to go back to Nine Winters and find out what I'm actually capable of. All this hocus-pocus is just becoming too much for me to bear, I think I'm going to end up as mad as a hatter if I carry on like this for much longer.'

Matt stiffened.

'But college has started,' he insisted, trying to sound logical and hoping it would be enough to change her mind. 'Why not wait awhile, get back into the swing of things here, there should be enough projects this term to help keep you occupied or, at worse, distracted.' Crystal shook her head and pulled her hands from his.

'No, Matt, it just isn't going to work. I can feel the pull towards my real world growing stronger every day. It's like having invisible fingers trying to drag me back. I love it here and I love Beatrice too, but I need to be where I belong, I need to be with Amella and Bridgemear.'

'I'm not sure I can face going back,' said Matt, jumping from his chair, his face lined with despair. He took a step towards a column of books, resting his hands on a half-empty shelf, his body racked with sudden tension. He didn't want to lose her, yet how could he go back so soon after what he'd endured?

'You don't have to come with me,' she whispered, unable to look him in the eye when he spun round and stared open-mouthed towards her.

His wide eyes searched deep into hers.

'Is that it?' he asked, sounding flabbergasted. 'Are you saying you don't want me to come with you?'

'No, that's not it at all,' she blurted, stumbling over her words and realising the conversation could easily turn into a full-scale argument if she wasn't careful, and she turned to him tight-lipped, unsure of how to ride the wave of uncertainty.

Matt looked grim and gave an involuntary shudder.

'I'm not ready to go back,' he said, his anger deflating. 'But I can't stop you, even though you know it will be dangerous for you to return.' His eyes searched her face for a hint of her intentions. 'Well, what is your decision?'

Crystal leapt from her chair, her mouth opening and closing like a suffocating goldfish and, because she believed he wouldn't understand, she ran from him instead. She fled down the stone corridor, the heels of her shoes sounding hollow against the huge flagstones. Hot tears burst from inside her, flowing down her cheeks as free as a bird, her mind whirling with distress. She thought of the price she must pay to return to Nine Winters and decided if losing Matt was what it took, then she would do so willingly. She felt a stab of betrayal slice through her heart, yet she was unable to think of anything else but her own people. She called

21

to Amella, opening her mind portal and searching for the connection.

I am ready to return, she messaged, feeling the extra-sensory link unlock. *Come for me, Amella, please, I beg you ...*

'Why can't I make you see sense?' Matt yelled after her. He was astonished that she'd reacted by running away from him. He felt his anger reignite as she crashed through the double doors and out into the throng of strangers who were rushing like unstoppable ants along the main street. He spun on his heels, fury burning in his chest, her stubbornness fuelling his resentment of her other life to the point where it started to overwhelm him and he kicked out at the nearest bookcase in retaliation. The unexpected crash when the case keeled over, scattering its precious cargo all over the floor, sent a shock wave straight down his spine. The noise ricocheted through the building and brought an alarmed librarian running to his side with the security guard close on her heels. Her face changed from one of concern to one of dismay when she realised the books had been knocked over on purpose.

'What do you think you're doing?' she demanded, taking in the disarray of books lying dishevelled on the floor. Gasping, she crouched down and began picking up as many of the books as she could into her sweeping arms. Matt dived down to help, but she lashed out, smacking his hands away as though he was nothing more than a naughty child.

'You've done enough,' she hissed, holding the books to her chest and trying to protect them from him.

'Frank!' she bellowed towards the security guard. 'Get this ignorant young man out of here; it's perfectly obvious to me that he has no respect for these books or for the library.' Matt tried to protest, his anger diminishing and in its place sat embarrassment and shame.

'I'm really, really sorry,' he said, when Frank put a firm hand on his shoulder and then tightened his grip. 'I honestly didn't mean to knock these books over.'

The librarian ignored his apology. Instead she checked each spine for damage, already selecting those she thought may need some kind of repair. Her fingers caressed each cover with nimble dedication, seeking out any hairline splits they may have sustained.

'I'll be sending you an invoice if I find any of these books need restoration,' she snorted when Frank frogmarched him towards the exit. Matt tensed at her words, feeling Frank's grip tighten all the more.

'And I don't want to see you in here for at least a month,' she added for good measure, watching Frank open the main door and push Matt out into the street.

Matt hung his head when the guard released him, but then he was raising his chin and glaring at him when he saw a smirk touch the corners of his mouth. 'I'll be seeing you, son,' the security guard said, and his eyes held his for a second too long, but then he was turning away and locking the door behind him.

Matt, feeling deeply confused and bewildered, stared blindly at his feet. His thoughts turned to how he had managed to get himself into such a mess? He knew he was not the most mature person in the world, but to get himself thrown out of a library, well ...

He kicked at a loose pebble, sending it skimming down the path. His mind raced along with it, until the small stone bounced and hit the kerb. He wondered how long Crystal would wait for him to change his mind or whether he would simply become like the stone, worthless and insignificant. He pondered over whether she would really go back to the Kingdom of Nine Winters without him, especially after everything they'd gone through together and decided, surely not. With this thought in mind, he brightened, heading for home with a lighter step. He would give her some breathing space and enough time to realise they were made to be together and then perhaps she would stop all this silliness. He continued through the busy streets convincing himself she would never leave this world without him by her side, never in a billion, zillion years.

Chapter 2

By sunset Crystal had readied herself with stunning speed for her journey back to her mother's realm. The decision to stop Matt from travelling with her stung her brain like a cornered wasp, yet she could not honestly say she regretted her hasty decision. The longing to return to Amella strengthened with each solitary tick of the clock. Time would stand still here; Matt would never know she had abandoned him and this thought gave her some much-needed courage.

She didn't have a clear idea of how she would travel back to Nine Winters, all she knew was that someone would have to come and fetch her. She expected Tremlon to appear at any moment, unsure of the time structure from one world to the next and she worried herself for being ill-prepared.

On leaving Amella, she had given back the *Spirit of Eternity*, the necklace which her mother had given her as a gift when she'd been taken away to live as a mere mortal. Crystal believed it was more dangerous for her to keep it, especially after the incident with Forusian where he had been able to use it against her, almost killing her. Her mother had seemed unhappy with her decision and made it very clear that she could have the amulet back whenever she felt ready.

Crystal watched with growing anxiety for the darkness to descend, unsure if anyone would arrive that night or any other night for that matter. When she finally went up to bed she stopped outside Beatrice's door, unsure how to say goodbye without her mother growing suspicious. She pressed her ear to the door and heard Beatrice's soft snoring; she smiled and let out a sigh, thankful she had been unwittingly released from her quandary.

There was the sound of a creaky floorboard somewhere behind her and she turned to see her bedroom door being pulled open and Bridgemear standing right before her. His eyes flashed with uncertainty and he quickly beckoned for her to follow him, swiftly moving into the seclusion of the shadows. He looked strangely out of place in such a modern world and his clothes looked like something from the pages of a sixteenth-century novel.

'I've come at the request of your mother,' he whispered, when she entered her room and closed the door softly behind her. 'She sensed that you were not happy and insisted I bring you home at once.'

Crystal's reaction was to burst into tears, causing Bridgemear to look quite startled. Unable to hide her emotions a second longer, Crystal hurtled towards him like a raging bull and she felt his stomach muscles tighten when her chest connected with his. She snaked her slender arms around his waist and pulled him tight, happy to have her father so close, but Bridgemear wavered momentarily, his blue eyes widening with sudden alarm. He wasn't used to such open displays of affection and it showed, but Crystal persevered, refusing to let go until he found himself returning her embrace and whispering soft words in her ear in the hope that they would help to soothe her.

'Look, I have brought you a special gift,' he said, finally pulling away and placing his hand inside his dark robe. She watched him draw his hand from an inner pocket and reveal a flash of gold.

'It's an Elvin bangle,' he explained, seeing her eyes grow wide with wonder. 'It was forged by my own hands when I was a mere apprentice to your grandfather. It's entwined with the symbol of the butterfly which means you are deemed immortal and the magic spell held within the butterfly allows you to keep one precious memory locked inside the centre stone.'

Crystal's face glowed with pure delight when Bridgemear clasped the bangle to her wrist. Overwhelmed by his unexpected show of generosity, tears filled her eyes once again and she touched the band of gold, marvelling at the sparkling purple amethyst set in the centre of the butterfly's abdomen.

'It's so beautiful,' she gasped, unable to believe this treasure was really hers. 'Please, tell me, how do I get it to work?'

Bridgemear chuckled and his eyes danced with amusement.

'Why it's very simple to use. When you're ready, rub the stone with your finger and remember a moment in time which you never want to forget; it could be a memory from the past or something happening right now. Anyway, once you have captured your moment in time and you wish to relive it, simply heat the stone with your breath and the memory will reappear before your very eyes like a ... picture on a movie screen.'

'Wow, this is just the coolest present ever!' Crystal marvelled, touching the stone with her fingers and watching it glow. 'And I promise you, I will treasure this gift forever.'

Bridgemear flushed, his eyes sparkling and he swallowed, but all too soon he was pressing his lips into a tight line and turning serious.

'My dear Crystal, now your tears have dried, will you not tell me what troubles you so? Is it that you don't actually wish to go back to Nine Winters so soon?'

Crystal looked shocked.

'No, of course not,' she blurted, and her eyes flashed in surprise. 'It's just that I'm leaving here without Matt and I feel as though I'm abandoning him.' Bridgemear nodded and drew her close. He placed his hand on her shoulder and squeezed it tight.

'It is better for him to stay here and live his life as a mortal,' the magician acknowledged, clearly understanding her distress. 'It's far too dangerous for his kind to come to our world; you know how much he suffered the last time. He cannot live the same life as you and deep down you know this fact to be true.'

Crystal wiped the last of her tears away with her sleeve, her own thoughts on their visit to the extraordinary world sending her emotions into another flurry of activity.

'I know you're right,' she sighed, moving away from him and plonking herself on the bed. 'It's just that we have become such good friends and I always feel safer when he's with me.'

Bridgemear followed her, gripping both her hands in his. He looked simply lost for words and when silence dropped between them he released his grip and walked away from her.

'You have a very nice place here,' he said, inspecting her surroundings. Crystal nodded, watching him more closely. He was right; although her room was fairly small, it was comfortable and clean and it was decorated with a lavish border of bright, pink stencils drawn around the upper coving. All four walls were plastered with posters of the latest pop idols and she could see by the look on his face that he thought they looked rather hideous.

With his curiosity ignited, Bridgemear swept around her room, brushing his hand over an assortment of paperback books and a few of her odds and ends, and then he hesitated when something caught his eye and he reached forward, gripping a large, framed photograph perched high on her vanity dresser.

'Is this your earth mother?' he asked, staring accusingly at the picture. Crystal nodded, sensing a sudden bout of tension between them.

'Her name's Beatrice and I have to say that she has looked after me very well.'

Bridgemear's jaw flexed and Crystal watched his grip tighten around the frame, realising he was finding it hard to look away. He then let the picture slip from his fingers and it landed with a clonk on the soft carpet. He moved towards the window, the picture and the frame abandoned on the floor, and then busied himself by inspecting the wooden frame as though he was looking for signs of woodworm and, without a sound, grabbed hold of the latch and pushed the window wide open. A mirrored reflection in one of the glass panes caught Crystal's attention and she saw her father's eyes glow for just the briefest moment; then he whispered a magic spell and swept his hand across his chest and the whole window and its surround dropped away, allowing the cool night air to flounce inwardly and take her breath away.

Crystal gasped, waiting for the glass to shatter when it hit the ground and the commotion which would follow and ultimately cause Beatrice to run outside to see what dire emergency had sent her there. But there was no crash of glass. The only sound Crystal could hear was the cool wind blowing gently through her hair as she waited to see what Bridgemear would do next.

'We must be on our way,' said her father, turning his attention back towards her. 'We have a long journey ahead of us and the sooner we leave here the better.' She saw the moon cast a silvery glow across his handsome face, making his features shimmer in the light and she watched him jump onto the window ledge, the moon now shining on his feet, his balance nothing more than perfection.

'Quickly child, climb on my back,' he urged, raising his arms like he was contemplating suicide.

Crystal's eyes gleamed white with panic.

'You've got to be joking!' she muttered under her breath, but she found herself grabbing a sweater and forcing her arms inside the tight sleeves.

'Crystal, let's go,' Bridgemear urged, glancing over the hills and beyond. 'We must hurry, for we haven't got all night. All too soon the darkness will lift and then we risk the chance of being seen by the plain folk.'

'Will I be staying in a tavern, like last time?' Crystal asked, picking up the photograph and putting it back in its rightful place. She looked down at the duffle bag she'd packed earlier with what she thought were essential items.

'No, you will have no need of any mortal clothes,' Bridgemear replied, looking with distaste at her baggy, orange jumper and skinny jeans. 'Anything you need during your stay with us will be rectified once we reach home.' Crystal looked up at him in surprise.

'Are we going straight to Nine Winters?'

'Er, well, no, not immediately. I will need to rest from such a long journey. I thought perhaps we could stay a day or two in Raven's Rainbow, so we could get to know each other a little better, whilst my strength returns.'

Crystal looked at him with a surprised expression, but before she had time to comment they both heard Beatrice cough, get up from her bed and then open her bedroom door, heading for the toilet.

'It's now or never!' said Bridgemear in a sudden panic, gesturing for her to come to him. 'We must leave before I am seen.'

Crystal nodded, sensing his urgency, her own thoughts of being caught making her hurry to where he stood waiting and she climbed on his back as easily as a monkey climbs a tree. Her long, slender limbs held him tight and she trembled when she felt him push off with his tiptoes.

There followed a rush of air which brushed past her senses and she let out a squeal when she realised they were still falling. Squeezing her eyes tightly closed, she waited for the ground to swallow her, but then she felt a violent shudder course through Bridgemear's body and when she was brave enough to peek, she opened her eyes to see she was resting on the back of a magnificent, golden eagle.

Crystal was in awe of what had just happened and watched completely mystified as the ordinary world slipped away and another began to materialise. The night sky was lit with a million bright stars illuminating the darkness to form a stadium of light. With a cool breeze blowing against her skin, she felt exhilaration flood through her, she had never felt so alive and she laughed happily when they both soared higher and higher up into the sky.

The eagle let out a high call to the very beyond, flexing its talons and beating its huge wings against the gentle force of the wind. The call of the wild pulsated deep within both their hearts, causing her to realise she would never be able to stay away from her natural world for too long.

Over mountains and valleys they flew as one and when the weather grew cold, Crystal burrowed deeper into the gilt-coloured feathers to help keep warm. His magnificent plumage was soft and thick, keeping the bitter chill well away from her fragile bones. She snuggled into the fluffy clusters until she was hidden in a thick layer of down. Eventually her eyes could no longer stay open and she fell asleep, her body moulded to her father in such a way that anyone who had seen her ride would have thought she had journeyed on the back of a golden eagle at least a thousand times before.

Chapter 3

In the Hall of Light, the Order of the Guild made their way in stony silence to where their ancestors were known to have sat long ago. The night was unusually dark and thick clouds were spinning themselves into a heavy curtain, suffocating the bright, silver crest of the moon. It is said, in Raven's Rainbow, that on nights such as these, devils ride on horseback and the dead have nowhere to hide.

Elveria stood on a large raised platform, waiting for the murmur of excited voices to finally die down. The room crackled with anticipation and the atmosphere was dark with hidden doubt and cunning curiosity. As the huge doors closed behind the last Guild member, all faces turned expectantly towards the eldest sorcerer of Oakwood.

'Welcome, good men of the Order,' Elveria began, facing the Elders and bowing low. 'It was not so long ago that the Order of the Guild was *the* most powerful council upon this earth; my, how times have changed.' He heard a deep rumble of acknowledgement pass throughout the assembly and he shook his head, opening his arms towards the heavens in sympathy.

'I solemnly stand before you as one of the highest council members. It has been an honour and a great responsibility over the years to serve you, but now I find myself in a situation which causes me great pain and I feel it impossible to allow what I have learned go without consequence, for I have a duty to these fair lands and to the laws I have held dear for far too long.' He stole to the side of the room where he grasped a piece of parchment, newly signed and dated.

'I hold in my hand a document explaining the new constitution of the Kingdom of Nine Winters. A few of you may be aware of what is written here in fine ink and, alas, most of you will know what has happened since last we met. King Gamada has been murdered at the hands of the evil tyrant Forusian. It was indeed a sad day when we lost this prestigious ruler, however, his daughter, Princess Amella, has returned to her kingdom after years of exile to claim her throne. The coronation has already taken place; she is now Queen and has therefore seen fit to change the laws of her land, allowing Bridgemear, a mere wizard, to reign as her Prince Regent and therefore acknowledging the freak of nature she produced as her daughter.'

A roar of outrage filled the grand hall, causing Elveria to pause for a moment. Many members of the Guild were openly condemning what, in their opinion, the new Queen had foolishly seen fit to do. Elveria secretly revelled in their damning words of discontent and savoured the moment when an angry fist flew in the air, demanding justice for her people.

'Silence!' bellowed the Inquisitor, forcing his staff to the floor to command order. When he was ignored and the roar continued, he propelled his staff at a structured angle, sending a shock wave of authority in the form of a beam of light to encircle the disobedient members until silence blanketed the room.

Elveria placed his hands to his lips as though deep in thought, before turning to face the stone wall situated directly behind him. His voice rang out when he broke a spell against its cold exterior; immediately ancient text appeared on its surface, inscribed in the old language and written by an invisible hand. The antique laws procured from the Elvin Bards unravelled before the captivated audience, bold and clear the evidence unfolded before them.

The members of the Guild began feeding their loathing of this new Queen whilst they each studied the laws, unable to digest the devastating consequences of what Amella's new constitution would inevitably achieve. The words of condemnation flowed clearly and concisely upon the stone, evoking a tremble of unconscious fear to rise amongst the assembly.

'I too am appalled,' said Elveria, turning to face the bickering crowd. A subtle flicker of triumph ignited behind his watery eyes when their hushed tones grew fierce. 'These laws were violated by the very person who now changes them to suit her own purpose

31

and thinks nothing of the consequences of these actions, nor if it's the will of the people.'

The Guild shook with despondency, their faces ashen.

'This selfish act will alter our future forever and put us all in great danger, for if the realm of Nine Winters can now have mixed breeds and produce legitimate children, then what is to stop the other realms?' We have already suffered at the hands of the Nonhawk - should this outrageous behaviour be allowed to continue?'

'No!' shouted a unison of voices, 'but what can we do?'

Elveria straightened, his thick robes rustling softly when he walked the breadth of the hall. Not a sound was made when he passed each council member, staring at each one in turn, his dark eyes piercing their own.

'I'm known to be a practical mage, yet I find myself wishing to see this parchment burned, banned or eradicated, outlawing what is written upon it for all eternity. Of course, there are ways of making amends for what Queen Amella has seen fit to do, but there will be a cost to us all if we should fail.'

'We must at least try,' said the most noblest of Elders when Elveria shifted closer. 'This whole situation is nothing more than an abomination.'

Elveria nodded, the frown lines on his old, leathery face deepening.

'Then we have no alternative but to take matters into our own hands. For we have ruled the realms for over five centuries and the likes of Queen Amella must be forced back into her rightful place.'

'But she has the right to make her own laws,' protested a further member. It was Lord Kane, low in both status and power. Elveria shook his head, his face turning sour, clearly unimpressed at the stupidity of his young associate.

'The ancient laws from the Elvin Bards and Imperial Elders should never have been broken. Each ruler must live within the handwritten scrolls, changing only what is agreed by the council. She should have come to us, yet she chose to play the devil's advocate. Indeed, it is true, she can change whatever laws she wishes in her own land, but if the other realms follow suit it could create chaos and total anarchy. These laws were created to protect our kind, to make sure we could all live in peace. If children are born having been mixed with goblins or, worse, the Nonhawk, then they will have produced a world full of evil, evil which we will no longer be able to contain.'

Elveria's eyes closed to mere slits when the elf took his seat and fell silent.

'Are you with me, council?'

'Aye,' they roared, the noise almost deafening. 'We are with you all the way.' The Inquisitor was caught up in the flare of hysteria, allowing the howl to continue without any interference from his stave this time. The noise grew intense but Elveria simply rejoiced in his moment of victory.

'Then so be it,' said the mage, with an excited glint appearing in his right eye. 'The die has been rolled and the cast set.'

The great doors were pulled open, ending the meeting and exposing the cold, dark night. The air outside was thick with yet another evening of drifting snow. Elveria stepped out into the swirling flakes, his cloak dark against pure white. A snorting horse was brought to his side and a young stable boy's back used as a step for the elder mage. Once mounted, Elveria hurried away, the horse's hooves silent in the thickening snow. With the wind howling around him, Elveria melted away into the forest, the darkness swallowing him from sight and he soon became a memory to those who still waited inside the shadowy building.

Chapter 4

When the morning finally dawned, Bridgemear felt the weariness drag like lead at his tired eyes. His body ached from the hours of flying and a terrible thirst gripped his dry throat. It had been a long journey, one which could have been fraught with hidden dangers and terrifying consequences had the Guild known of Crystal's intentions to return so soon. Thankfully it had at least been a peaceful flight and now he was almost home he was secretly relieved. He called to Crystal, who had fallen asleep when the world turned pitch-black, burrowing deep within his thick plumes to warm herself and shield her body from the cold and icy wind which tried to tear at his feathers and her tender flesh.

He attempted to wake her using her mind portal. The gateway was easily opened whilst she slept, his voice penetrating her mind like a soft wave pushing against the sand until she stirred, momentarily confused when his words floated like wisps of smoke inside her mind.

Is that your stomach I hear growling or is there an avalanche somewhere close by? he teased.

He felt her awaken and she rubbed the sleep from her eyes, and lifted her head in response, enjoying the sunlight which streamed onto her face, washing it with the glorious colour of yellow.

No, it's not my stomach which rumbles like thunder, she answered inside her head, *it's merely the terrible vibration produced from your own hungry belly!*

Bridgemear grinned inwardly at her grumblings, happy in the knowledge that she was showing no signs of having suffered any trauma from her unusual mode of transportation. He soared higher and higher, also enjoying the benefits of the warming rays which were penetrating through his feathers and down onto his back and he watched the bright orange ball rise alongside him. His piercing eyes espied two familiar specks sitting on horseback on the distant horizon and he gave a thankful cry, watching with contentment when both riders raised a magician's staff towards the heavens, acknowledging his welcome return.

In response he flapped his huge wings faster, gaining momentum before he descended through the thickening cloud. He dive-bombed to earth, pinning his giant wings back to give much-needed speed and then he was swooping and dipping over soft terrain, his taut wings outstretched in a flurry of feathers and gentle undercurrents until his gigantic claws flexed outwards and he finally landed on the top of a large, mossy bank.

He bent his neck, allowing Crystal to slip down his back and over his head as easily as rain down a drainpipe and once she was at a safe distance he gave a violent shudder and transmuted into his human form. He felt the flush of energy cease through his body and once he could no longer feel the effects of his transformation he straightened his clothes, regained his composure and moved to his daughter's side.

Mordorma and Amafar had not lingered when they'd seen the golden bird prepare to land and instead urged their horses into a soft canter, taking only minutes to reach the spot where Bridgemear stood waiting.

'Perfect timing as usual,' called Amafar, dismounting. He threw his reins around a leafy bush and took several strides to reach the powerful mage, patting Bridgemear on the back and grasping his hand in a strong, welcoming embrace. He turned his attention to Crystal and, without ceremony, hugged her tight.

'It's good to see you back so soon,' he grinned, his smile broadening when her face lit up with embarrassment. 'I'm guessing you enjoyed riding on the back of a golden eagle albeit that it was only your father and no one special!'

'You both look tired,' interrupted Mordorma, jumping down from his horse and pushing his fine, woven cloak over his shoulder. He eyed the exhausted magician with the concern of an elder brother. His jaw set in a serious frown.

'I trust you had a safe journey with no incidents along the way?' he asked, flicking Bridgemear's robe to one side to check there were no signs of injury. Bridgemear slapped his hands away.

'Yes, as you can see, I'm fine and still in one piece. You will also be pleased to learn that everything went according to plan, although I must admit I'm tired to my very bones.'

'Then you must rest,' insisted Mordorma, turning his attention to Crystal and sweeping his arm around her shoulders. He guided her towards two large boulders which were spilt between a formation of rock. Dark green mosses and lichen covered most of the huge stones, making them look like soft, gigantic pillows and she instinctively reached out to touch them, convinced they would feel like velvet.

'Welcome to Raven's Rainbow,' Mordorma whispered softly in her ear, causing her eyes to sparkle. 'I hope you enjoy your stay here with us far more than you did the last time you visited.'

Crystal nodded her appreciation at being made so welcome and her gratitude showed in her eyes.

'Where's Elveria and Voleton?' she asked, dropping her hand from the stones, their softness momentarily forgotten. She raised her fingers to her forehead, shielding her eyes from the wintry sun, as she searched the distance for a glimpse of the other magicians.

'Both Voleton and Elveria will be with us on the morrow,' Mordorma explained, shifting his eyes and stealing a wary look at her father.

'Oh, I thought you all lived together in a close commune?' she said, somewhat confused by his sudden revelation. 'I always believed you lived in a brotherly kibbutz, so to speak.'

'On the contrary,' Mordorma added dryly, a smirk twitching at the corners of his mouth, 'we each have our own domains within Raven's Rainbow and you will find we have never lived in each other's pockets.'

Crystal accepted his explanation with a nod of her head and left his side, already distracted by the abundance of rich, lush greenery which surrounded her, becoming overwhelmed by the beautiful paradise her father was lucky enough to call home.

She found his domain to be truly amazing. The whole valley was surrounded by majestic fells which were filled with dozens of woodland paths scurrying beneath the tall, lush trees, reminding her of long, milk-chocolate fingers. The view of the snow-capped mountains far away in the distance was utterly breathtaking, but the most impressive feature to catch her wandering eyes was the magnificent waterfall. Its powerful cascade of fresh water was the most fantastic thing she'd ever seen, although she found the roar of the falls as it blasted from the highest ledge to be almost deafening to her ears when she approached. It was at least sixty metres high and its powerful surge was nothing less than colossal. Although the waterfall was quite broad at the top, its anger abated halfway down when it broke into five smaller falls before finally resting in a large, glistening pool, the water flowing away like a forgotten memory.

It is the waterfall of Valandil, Bridgemear whispered inside her head, *come, we must go inside and get some food.*

Crystal lingered, finding it impossible to tear herself away from the cascading falls and drew closer instead, breaking out into a radiant smile when a colourful rainbow appeared above her head. She felt the wonder of Valandil melt into her heart and she watched as the rich, luscious ferns such as horsetail and club mosses danced softly against the cool breeze. She looked down at her feet to see rarer species creeping into the lush undergrowth, clinging to the slippery rocks and tree roots, their fronds no thicker than a fine silken thread.

Eventually Crystal was persuaded to enter Bridgemear's den, wary that this was a place that belonged solely to her father. The thought gnawed at her conscience, making her feel as though she was some kind of intruder and she couldn't help but drag her feet.

She found herself guided through a cool, dark passageway. It smelt of nature and the fresh outdoors, yet she tensed further when the darkness enfolded her like an unwanted black cloak and for the briefest of moments her thoughts flew to Forusian's underground lair where he'd held her captive and a shiver snaked down her stiffening spine.

She forced those frightening thoughts to the back of her mind when sunlight lit her face and she glanced at her father who was showing them a small room set well back from the stones. Crystal was pleasantly surprised to find his den was full of bright, natural sunlight, but when they entered into another room, she was startled to see living creatures leaping in a frenzy of fear, scared by the group's unexpected arrival.

Two horn-headed green toads were bounding around in a most distressed state of affairs. Their long, skinny legs and fat, slimy toes were jumping from one direction to the next, narrowly missing Mordorma's stony face before he managed to dive out of the way. To make matters worse, several purple and green oysters were singing in a gurgle of high octaves, having realised their master had returned. Their obvious joy became rather alarming when they started to jump up and down in a feverish dance. The oysters, hidden deep inside their pods, forced the rims of their shells to open and close, creating such a clatter that nothing else could be heard over their din. The noise was almost deafening, but Crystal couldn't help being amused at such a strange display from a cluster of shellfish. Watching the three magicians chasing the slimy toads and try to pull the oysters' lips tightly closed caused her to giggle in amusement.

The toads' croaks grew more distressed as the minutes ticked by and Mordorma's patience began to wear thin until his level of tolerance finally disintegrated and he forced the bottom of his staff to strike the ground. A powerful boom made the earth shiver and the walls shake with a deep vibration that made Crystal's teeth chatter. She opened her mouth to protest, but found her speech was slurred to the point that she sounded like she had just suffered a debilitating stroke and she raised her hand in the air to grab the three magicians' attention instead. To her surprise she found her movements were as though she was swimming underwater and it was then that she saw everything was moving in a kind of slow motion, everything that is except for Mordorma.

When one of the toads sailed past his upturned nose, its mouth agape and its golden brown eyes wide with fright, Mordorma's arm came forth, like a cobra striking its prey, and grabbed the toad in mid-air. He appeared to look the toad straight in the eye before his hand flashed and then he was throwing the amphibian to the ground. Crystal's eyes widened and her mouth dropped open in shock, concerned at the mere thought that the toad would suffer any injury at the hands of the furious mage, but as soon as the toad made contact with the floor it exploded into a puff of yellow smoke. The magician moved swiftly and caught its partner. His powerful grip held the desperate toad fast, smashing it to the ground until it too became nothing more than a wispy trail of yellow.

Amafar stood with his back against the wall, a look of perplexity spread over his young face. He seemed somewhat confused at Mordorma's attempt to restore calm and carried on watching the mage with obvious bewilderment when he collected all of the oysters and then shoved them into a large pail of water to drown out their incessant singing. Finally satisfied, Mordorma struck the staff on the ground once again and normality was restored. Bridgemear, however, did not look impressed with Mordorma's theatrical performance.

'Do you have any idea how long it took me to find those horn-headed toads?' he snapped, tight-lipped.

'Then you should have taken better care of them,' Mordorma snapped back. 'Having toads flaying themselves around your den as though they are domestic pets isn't acceptable. I mean, what kind of an example are you setting your daughter for goodness' sake?'

'And what is all this mess?' Amafar interrupted, moving from his resting place and beginning to pick up several abandoned scrolls lying strewn across the floor. He walked over and placed them with care inside a deep caddy already overflowing with ancient manuscripts. He pushed them into place and tried to close the outer case, clucking his tongue like an old mother hen when the clasp refused to close.

'Bridgemear, were you conceived in a pigsty?' he grumbled, when his eye spotted more disorder. 'I just don't know how you can live like this!'

Bridgemear rolled his eyes in consternation and before Amafar could say another word, his hand shot out towards the casket and the lid closed with a snap, only narrowly missing Amafar's fingers.

Amafar looked like he'd just been whipped and Bridgemear couldn't help a smirk touch his lips. His attention was quickly stolen by Mordorma who was whinging about being famished and so Bridgemear set to work on finding enough fresh supplies to produce a suitable meal for his hungry guests. He was still clearly irritated by his brothers' interference and he stomped about his den like a spoilt child. Eventually, when his temper cooled, a fire was lit and food prepared. Although he couldn't help grunting his displeasure, Amafar helped Bridgemear turn a table hidden underneath a pile of old spell books into some place where they could eat without getting a mountain of dust in their mouths. Bridgemear ignored his whining, working hard to clear the mess that had gotten out of hand and set to work laying the table, which enabled him to watch Crystal out of the corner of his eye.

Crystal was oblivious to him, too absorbed in learning about her father and it was clear by the look on her face that she was openly surprised to see that in every nook and cranny huge, voluptuous volumes of magic were stored as tight as a drum. Old, unintelligible maps and musty manuscripts were scattered on chairs, unstable ledges and even piled so high in places that they were almost touching the ceiling.

'You really need Amella to come here and sort out all this mess,' Crystal said suddenly, wiping the dust from her fingertips and giving him an unexpected scowl.

Bridgemear caught her fierce expression and winked.

'Your mother would skin me alive if she ever saw how unkempt this place had become,' he said, sounding somewhat relieved that she did not. 'I think we should all agree not to enlighten her either for I fear for certain parts of my anatomy should she ever find out.' He couldn't help grinning at his own exaggerated remark and then he started to laugh, the mood in the room changing to one of hilarity.

Once the table was set, Bridgemear waved his hand over the cloth and a hearty meal was set before his guests. Without ceremony, they all sat together in a somewhat contented group and Crystal sat close to the three magicians, eyeing them each with open fascination. They were all so very different, yet they were each part of a powerful band of mages which made them as close as brothers. She watched her father eat with his closest friends, relaxed and happy, their laughter spilling like wine, overflowing enough to touch her heart and fill her with a welcoming bolt of belonging.

Bridgemear's eyes shot towards hers and she sensed, when his brow creased, that his somewhat calm exterior was not quite so composed deep inside. Then he looked away, his attention

40

returning to Mordorma and Amafar, and her moment of worry dissolved, dispersing any niggles of anxiousness which tried unsuccessfully to linger. She felt a strong wave of fatigue wash over her, forcing her to admit she was still bone-weary and her judgement therefore clouded.

Bridgemear's face returned to hers and she noted the anxiety knitted around his eyes and she smiled sleepily.

'Come on, little one,' he said, placing his empty goblet onto the table. 'I think it's time you got some well-earned rest.' He moved to her side and with a firm hand lifted her elbow to guide her towards a chamber he had made ready for her. He linked their arms together like two precious chinks of unbreakable chain mail and they looked so natural together that no one would have ever suspected they'd been apart for sixteen years.

Once inside the chamber, Bridgemear tilted her chin and smiled down at her.

'It's time for us to grab some sleep,' he advised, when dark circles appeared to gather around her already tired eyes. She nodded her agreement before turning and eyeing her bed with appreciation. It was covered in a soft, silken bedspread, seemingly handmade and spun with delicate threads of shiny silver and shimmering gold. The design had been made into a picture, the completed design was elaborate and extremely detailed and she laughed lightly when she recognised the representation of her dear parents holding her proudly as a newborn baby. The rich, colourful tones used to help make the picture look so vividly real were also amazingly accurate.

Whilst she watched, her own image in the centre of the bedspread began to change before her very eyes from the small infant she once was to what she had become, a young woman. She gazed in wonderment at herself, depicted tall and proud between Amella and Bridgemear, their arms wrapped protectively around her waist and shoulders. She felt a lump rise in her throat when she digested the look of immense happiness in her mother's eyes, realising it was a chapter of Amella's life which had been stolen from her, the precious years of her daughter's childhood. She left Bridgemear's side and allowed her fingertips to brush the silky material, admiring the delicate stitching perfected by the person who had woven it together.

'This is so beautiful,' she whispered gruffly, unable to hide the raw emotion in her voice. She glanced back towards her father with questions dancing in her eyes.

'Who ...?'

'Amella had it made for you,' he explained, drawing back the sheets. 'You will also find something appropriate for you to wear under your pillow, your mother has been very busy in the short time you have been gone.' He grinned, looking genuinely happy.

'She is itching to have you by her side again,' he added, kissing the top of her head. The light from the morning caused her to pull a face until he drew his hand and the room suddenly went dark. A small halo of light formed above his fingers and he flicked his hand to allow the small glow to hover just above her head.

'Say the word '*out*' when you are ready and the light will diminish,' he explained, watching a flicker of fascination dance in her eyes. 'It should last until you are tucked up safely in bed.'

Crystal watched him close the door, proud to be able to say that this magnificent magician was actually her real father. It had been tough growing up without him in the ordinary world but she could tell he was trying to make amends for all those empty years she'd endured without him. She heard his footsteps melt away and so she undressed, and within minutes she'd snuggled deep within the warming sheets and very soon fell fast asleep.

Bridgemear headed towards Amafar and Mordorma who waited with unexpected stony expressions on his return.

'This world is turning bad,' said Amafar, when Bridgemear offered him a fresh goblet of wine. 'Amella and Crystal could be in grave danger.'

Bridgemear sighed.

'What are you saying?' he asked, taking a gulp of his own. 'Tell me, what have you heard?' Amafar appeared to hesitate, allowing the atmosphere to crackle with anticipation and it was Mordorma who spoke up.

'There are dark times ahead,' he said, when the fire snapped and hissed at his feet. 'We have heard rumours that the Guild is furious with Amella for changing the laws to allow half-breeds into her

42

realm knowing what repercussions could occur if the other realms decide to follow.'

Bridgemear felt his chest tighten.

'It's what I expected,' he said darkly. 'But you know we had no choice.'

'Indeed,' said Mordorma, turning towards the fire and allowing the hot glow to warm his chilled bones. 'Yet we all fear a reprisal. Our spies tell us the council has met and we are not yet clear as to the outcome, but mark my words, dear brother, it would not have been favourable to either you or Amella. There are those who live in the dark ages and fear change, the future for them is to stay as we once were.' Bridgemear looked lost as he stretched the weariness from his shoulders.

'So what do we do?'

'There is nothing we can do, except wait. There is none yet to fight, yet a fight will come. We must simply protect Amella and Crystal when the time arises. It may take years, who knows? It all depends on the Elders and what they have decided and of course if any other half-breeds are born, then they could be in serious peril especially if the trolls or goblins decide to take matters into their own hands; after all, look what happened when the Nonhawk were created all those centuries ago.'

'No one will want to have their children,' said Amafar, pulling a grotesque face and then gulping the last of his wine.

Mordorma winced.

'No, perhaps not, but what do we do if they start raping our women or if women who have fallen on hard times eventually agree to have their children for money?'

'It won't come to that,' said Bridgemear, hitting his fist hard against the table. 'That's just sick!'

'Don't you be so sure,' Mordorma interrupted, breaking his stare. 'Because you know as well as I do, people will do absolutely anything for power or gold, indeed, absolutely anything.'

*

When Crystal awoke she found it to be early afternoon and she worried that she may have slept longer than intended. She quickly washed and dressed, finding a crisp, clean gown and matching accessories set out for her on a bedside chair. Her fingers wrapped around the soft, cool fabric and she toyed excitedly at the many sparkling jewels which were sewn with invisible stitches around the neck and waist. She had to admit she loved the clothes her mother had so generously had made for her; they were always so exquisite, woven in fine detail and cut from the best quality cloth. She eyed the narrow waistline appreciatively and without hesitation put the garment on. It was a beautiful shade of emerald green and it instantly drew out the vivid redness of her hair, allowing the deep copper tones and shades of amber to flash when it fell in a thick mass around her neck.

Once dressed, she hurried to join the others, disappointed to find Bridgemear to still be sleeping. Amafar and Mordorma looked pleased when they espied her heading towards them in her full regalia and the many goblets of wine they'd consumed in her absence made them look rosy cheeked.

'My dear, you look every inch the grand princess in that gown,' said Mordorma, gesturing for her to come and join them by the fireside. She smiled shyly at his compliment before taking the drink offered to her by Amafar.

'We were just discussing the feast which we are all to attend tomorrow,' Amafar explained, plumping up his cushion before sitting back down. 'It's the day of the Four Quarters Festival, a truly marvellous day when all the realms come together in Raven's Rainbow to choose this year's apprentices.'

Plonking herself next to Mordorma, Crystal forgot all about her drink when she asked, 'What do you mean by a festival? And what kind of apprentices are you looking for?'

'Well, magical ones, of course,' boomed Mordorma, pulling out a pair of wiry spectacles from thin air. His large hand pushed them roughly onto the end of his nose and then he unfolded a battered poster which he'd kept hidden inside his pocket, pushing it along the table to show her what it was he was talking about. Crystal was intrigued, glancing at the eye-catching headline proclaiming an exciting event soon to arrive in Raven's Rainbow, an event which apparently happened every year.

She read the notice and her eyes grew wide with excitement.

'So what actually happens at these festivals?' she asked, sliding the poster back to the mage.

Mordorma's eyes danced with merriment.

'Well, let me get this right,' he teased, giving her a playful nudge and pushing his drooping spectacles further up his nose. 'Each village will send their best contender and it has to be someone who has shown some natural magical ability. Once chosen, they will join the Supreme Circle of Mages which is held within the realm of the Kingdom of Nine Winters. There, they will learn the most sacred gift of all, how to become a sorcerer. You see, a magician's journey will most likely take several lifetimes to complete, as in one life you can never truly learn everything so this is just the start. However, once a magician is deemed supreme, he can then make a life choice. He may perhaps decide to become one of the Queen's own magicians or perhaps become one of us, an Oakwood wizard *if* they were born within the realm of Raven's Rainbow.'

'Wow, does that mean you were all once apprentices?' Crystal asked, staring intently at the slightly inebriated mage and giggling with amusement when he unexpectedly let out a loud hiccup. Amafar couldn't help but snigger and before Mordorma could breathe a word he was answering her question for him.

'Indeed we were,' he said, his brows rising high towards his hairline. 'Although I have to say that both myself and Voleton did not learn to be magicians within the Supreme Circle of Mages, why no, we chose a very different path by which to get here.' He smiled wistfully at Mordorma, still grateful after all these years to his elder brother for teaching him the art of such powerful and intense magic which enabled him to continue on his life's journey as a dominant sorcerer.

'So, are you telling me that my father also had to learn how to become a wizard?' Crystal pressed.

Mordorma let out a low chuckle and mischief danced behind his eyes.

'Why, yes my dear, even Bridgemear had to learn the art of controlling his magic.' But Amafar let out a contradictory yelp.

'That's not strictly true, more like he had to learn how to control his temper,' he said, in good humour. 'Your father never needed to learn how to become a magician, that came naturally to him for he

45

was born with the knowledge, but it was the self-discipline and self-control which was his failing as a boy.'

The roar as the magicians argued over the reasons why Bridgemear became an apprentice caused him to awaken from his turbulent slumber.

'Can't a magician sleep in his own bed without being woken by hoodlums?' he shouted grumpily, entering the chamber and pulling his evening robe close to his bare chest.

Amafar gave him a guilty stare.

'Sorry, Bridgemear, we were just discussing the feast of the Four Quarters Festival and got a little overexcited. We were explaining to Crystal that you, Mordorma and Elveria were once royal apprentices and how you all became at the mercy of the Kingdom of Nine Winters.'

Crystal's face broke into a huge smile.

'Is that how you met Amella, through the Supreme Circle of Mages?' she asked her father, her eyes glistening with open curiosity. Bridgemear looked at his daughter, reading the hunger in her eyes. He could see she so desperately wanted to feed on their history, to devour and finally understand how it all began. He sighed when distant memories came flooding back. The palace had a lot to answer for and yet he would never have changed a second of his life within the palace walls. Amella had been his only true love since the first time he clapped eyes on her, a love which had been doomed from the very beginning and was now watched closely by those who wished for nothing else but to see it fail.

He lifted his glass and held it in salute to his daughter.

'To the Four Quarters Festival,' he said, with a wiry grin. 'Let's just hope you don't lose your heart to a young, talented apprentice, just like your mother did all those years ago.'

Chapter 5

It was mid-afternoon when Crystal and the three magicians rode their stately horses into the arena of the Four Quarters Festival. The wind was blowing fiercely but the sky was clear and blue.

At the main entrance two huge, black jaguars stood on guard, each with eagle wings jutting from their powerful flanks and a short, enchanted chain ensuring they were fixed securely to the outer wall. They roared and bared their teeth when each horse passed by, allowing their magnificent paws to claw at the softened dirt, a warning to those who may wish to cause trouble of what consequence stood waiting if they chose to do so.

Crystal felt herself tremble as she passed them. The huge animals looked angry and overly keen to break the magical bonds which held them tight and she felt the hairs on the back of her neck rise in fear; she immediately pulled the reins tighter, forcing her horse to move closer to her father's.

A few curious looks were exchanged when Bridgemear rode through the centre of the arena. He wore a superbly crafted ceremonious robe fit for a king and his royal daughter dressed in her emerald green gown looked equally distinguished Colourful flags flew high in the sky and a cheer rose from the milling crowd when the crest of the Oakwood wizards was finally recognised.

Mordorma looked magnificent with his own robes of exquisite deep scarlet and he clasped his highly decorated staff with such pride. The staff held the image of a golden horse's head. Inside each eye socket sat a meticulously polished opal and the elegant mane had been made from hundreds of tiny silken threads which had been woven together with the smallest specks of black diamonds, creating a long, flowing tress which shimmered like jet. Amafar, riding at the rear, sat both proud and erect and his long, dark cloak of purple and black swirled mysteriously around his body; his staff, however, was nowhere near as elaborate as those of his elder brothers'.

A sudden shout made Crystal turn in the saddle and she beamed with delight when she espied Voleton making his way to her side. His horse seemed skittish and overexcited, yet the magician held her fast, showing the crowd his superb handling and equestrian expertise, causing an enthusiastic cheer to erupt when he finally grounded his horse to a dramatic halt.

'Where's Elveria?' Amafar shouted over the continuous din from the excited crowd, 'I thought we would ride as one?'

'Elveria is already in the royal box,' exclaimed Voleton. 'His days of riding with the lower classes have long since ceased.'

'Lower classes indeed,' mocked Bridgemear, smoothing his hand over his royal cloak. He shot a fleeting glance in the direction of the gallery and felt his gut tighten when he saw the smug face of Elveria sitting close to his Queen. A fanfare rang out when they drew close and the huge crowd of spectators roared wildly in return.

'Quick, we must take our places because the tournament is about to begin,' Voleton urged, reaching out and grabbing Crystal's reins. His strong hands guided Crystal's horse to where an eager boy of about twelve stood waiting for her to dismount. He bowed in respect before helping her to the ground and then trotted her horse away. Crystal was left feeling somewhat conspicuous as she waited for her father to dismount and a wave of nervousness invaded her body at the thought of greeting her mother with so many people watching.

All will be well, Bridgemear suddenly whispered inside her head. She turned towards him and felt his arm encircle her waist as though he was protecting her. *Just kiss her lightly on the cheek and take your place at her side, we will have time later to catch up on what we have missed since being apart.*

Crystal felt a rush of relief wash over her, reassured by her father's words. They strode to where the Lord High Chamberlain waited to show them to their seats. The stuffy man with his broad-brimmed hat and dark expression reminded Crystal of a dreary school teacher she had once had the misfortune to meet in junior school. She remembered setting his cheap, polyester tie on fire when he had scolded her for being late for his lesson. She couldn't remember who had been more alarmed, however, after that day he refused to teach her, stating she was psychologically unstable and a child of a demon. This childhood memory caused her to laugh aloud, realising what consequences would have arisen if he'd known what was really wrong with her. Bridgemear turned his face towards hers, throwing a quizzical stare as he pushed her forward to receive her mother's hand, unaware of how close she had been to revealing her true identity to an undeserving mortal.

'My darling Crystal, you're here at last,' beamed Amella, hugging her daughter fiercely in plain view of all the spectators, therefore breaking the rules of protocol as easily as threads which bind a web. Crystal fell shy.

'Mother, it's wonderful to see you,' she blurted, when Amella guided her with care to sit on her immediate left and Bridgemear took his rightful place by her side. She noted Elveria shift uncomfortably in his seat and she dropped her gaze once she had nodded her head in greeting. He acknowledged her by doing the same before turning his face stiffly towards the centre ring.

'What happens now?' murmured Crystal to Amella, expecting someone to call for the lions to be released and a sweat-stained gladiator to run from a tunnel brandishing a heavy sword and an equally mighty shield. Amella's happiness at her daughter being by her side made her eyes sparkle with joy.

'Well, let me see, firstly, it will be the opening of the ceremony and then the Trial of the Apprentices,' she explained, casting her gaze amongst those who already stood waiting for the ritual to begin. She continued by telling Crystal how she admired the determination of the young men who worked so very hard each year in the hope of becoming one of her apprentices and had yet to meet anyone who applied to the games to enter without total dedication.

'Then what?' asked Crystal, becoming more and more intrigued.

'Well, once we have chosen our new students for this year's Academie we will move on to the Grand Meadow where we will enjoy an enormous feast with lots of music and dancing.'

Bridgemear nodded, showing his own enthusiasm and he scanned the excited audience who waved bright coloured banners to support the many contestants. He enjoyed this day immensely too for it brought back pleasurable memories of his own trial for an honorary apprenticeship.

The main gates were forced closed and many of the budding apprentices were ushered along by the Queen's royal court magicians. Some stragglers were congregating on the sidelines, each waiting nervously to be placed in their prearranged groups, but soon they were seen to be herded like sheep into their rightful places.

The Lord High Chamberlain scurried to Amella's side and she rose from her seat, causing the audience to fall quiet as she eyed the arena with obvious pride.

'Let us give thanks for today,' she said to the hushed crowd. 'People from the realms of the Four Quarters, let us celebrate the seasons we share and for the good life we have been given. We praise Spring, Summer, Autumn and Winter and although not everyone has their fair share of sunshine, let us still be grateful.' There was a titter from the crowd when those from the realm of Nine Winters, voiced their displeasure at rarely having any sunshine to speak of for nine months of the year.

Amella found it easy to ignore them and continued with her opening speech and she watched flower girls enter the arena, scattering rose petals all around the ring. The young girls, perhaps no more than sixteen years of age, tossed them from their brightly decorated baskets, happy for them to meet the earthy, red soil. The petals lay still for only a few seconds before an enchantment changed them into what looked like large, translucent baubles; light and transparent, they bounced along the breeze, for the fierce wind had long since died away.

A priestess, dressed in black and suffering a jagged silver streak through her long hair, walked to the centre of the ring and stood in front of the Queen, curtsying low. She started to bless the wind and its earthly treasures as the bubbles bounced and bobbed recklessly about her, catching the sunlight which altered the many different spectral shades held inside to slithers of silver and white. Then the colours transformed again, this time Crystal thought it was simply the wind vibrating through them, making them shimmer but when the bubbles blew closer, she was delighted to see moving images inside them as though she was looking down into the surface of a shimmering pond. The pictures were of dark green forests, of magnificent animals and exquisitely bright coloured birds, of yellow cornfields and golden barley, all the things Mother Nature had always willingly provided the extraordinary world. The aroma of the fresh outdoors mixed together with the rich, sweet scent of wild flowers attacked her nostrils and she took several deep breaths, enjoying filling her lungs with the sweet-smelling fragrances, whilst the distinct, sugary perfume of violets lingered, creating an instant sense of calm throughout the whole assembly. Crystal shuddered, feeling humble. She had always taken everyday pleasures such as food and water for granted much like most young people and consciously made a pact with herself to respect where her food came from in future.

Once the opening ceremony passed and the priestess had finished blessing the seasons, it was declared time for the Trial of the Apprentices. Amella and Bridgemear looked on eagerly along with the other guests in the royal box, which included Amafar, Voleton and Mordorma. Each magician appeared to strain his neck in the hope of getting a better look at this year's sets of hopefuls.

The Queen's healer, Sawbones, was the first to assemble the contestants for their opening assault. Senior to most and skilled at making potions and elixirs, he strolled calmly to each contender and gave them a beautifully decorated magic wand.

'I thought magicians had staffs?' whispered Crystal to her father, watching every young man graciously accept the silver wand from the favoured physician. Each wand was examined closely by all of the participants, their pleasure shining like the sun on their bright faces. They stared mesmerized at the intricate designs engraved mainly at the base of the wand, embossed with an eight-pointed star both influenced and inspired by the talented silversmiths who had created the main formation. The star was not whole as each point was individual with a carving of a fire-breathing dragon inside each prong which was entwined by trailing vines such as Moonwort, Adders Tongue or Maidenhair. These eight symbols would be shared between all the apprentices as they were put into their 'bands' and therefore used as their own team emblems once they entered the Circle of Mages.

Bridgemear turned to her, grinning broadly.

'You're right in what you say, but they don't get staffs as students,' he explained, seemingly amused. 'All apprentices work with wands until they mature and earn the right to be called magicians; only when they graduate from the Academie are they given their staffs of honour.'

His attention returned to the respected shaman who made the two hundred boys, who had been put into groups of ten, line up so that each candidate would face his opponent, their wands poised and at the ready.

'What's going on here?' asked Crystal, feeling excitement build in the pit of her stomach, 'what are they going to do next?'

'They will each conjure spells until their rival falls to the ground,' explained Bridgemear, sitting back in his seat. No sooner had the words fallen from his mouth when one of the contenders fired his wand. Dazzling stars and blue-green smoke rose above the ill-prepared opponent, his frazzled hair standing on end and his clothes blackened and sooty. Bridgemear chuckled when the unsuspecting individual tried to retaliate, but the other apprentice was far quicker and he immediately shot his wand again. This time the boy fell like a stone to the ground, smoke leaving his body and two royal aides ran to his side. A red flag was held above his head and a sharp hand signal suggested his time as a viable contender was well and truly over.

'That's one down and a few more to go,' laughed Amella, turning towards her daughter. 'Don't worry,' she added, seeing the look of alarm on Crystal's face and patting her hand. 'Only his pride is hurt.'

There came a sound like sparks flying from a metal grinder as the other hopefuls used their wands. A cloud of thick smoke filled the air and when it finally dispersed only a hundred apprentices were standing, just as expected.

'Good gracious!' said Elveria, deciding to make an informal appearance, popping up from behind Crystal like a jack in a box. 'I'm sure it gets easier to get into the Circle each year, why at this rate we'll be savouring luscious treats and enjoying lots of merrymaking before we know it.'

Amella smiled but her smile did not reach her eyes.

'Indeed, Elveria,' she said, her voice tight, 'I'm sure it was all so very different back in your day.' He caught the bitterness in her voice and shrank back to his seat, clearly irritated.

'Take it easy,' Bridgemear warned, catching her intense glare. 'You know you mustn't make your dislike for Elveria so obvious.' Amella clicked her tongue in the roof of her mouth.

'I can't help it,' she admitted, checking to see who might be listening. 'Especially after all that he has been a part of.' A sudden rapturous applause from the crowd brought Bridgemear and Amella to their feet. They jumped up, each applauding the finalists with sudden gusto, their thoughts of Elveria momentarily forgotten.

The remaining one hundred apprentices were soon dressed in mail and royal livery, then given a horse and prompted to make their way, two at a time, to the centre ring, but Crystal looked confused.

'I don't understand any of this,' she said, pointing to the battle dress and shrugging her shoulders.

'They must show their skill at arms,' explained Bridgemear, looking serious. 'You see, all magicians must be able to fight and look after themselves; contrary to what you may believe, we cannot live by magic alone.'

Crystal felt a shudder run down her spine; she had hoped no one would be seriously hurt during the fighting but by the way the contestants were attacking each other, it was highly likely. She hadn't expected to see anything so brutal in the arena and she was annoyed at her own naivety.

With their wands strapped to their sides, the remaining finalists showed their courage as a warrior. Crystal watched the contestants fight for their place within the Circle of Mages with their bare hands. The competitors grabbed at one another, pulling their opponents straight off their horses, forcing them to the ground. Blows to the head by a heavy implement were forbidden, but each contender tried to strike the other with their fists, punching and kicking their rival until blood was spilt and cries for submission were heard above the cheering crowd. Brute force appeared to be the winning factor for this trial and Crystal closed her eyes and winced each time one of the contenders surrendered. The trial continued and the grunting and swearing grew louder until the finalists were beaten down to fifty, but only forty apprentice places were on offer at the Acadamie.

Suddenly, the Lord High Chamberlain appeared from behind a dark curtain, the weight of his robes obviously too much for him to bear, his brow sweaty with exertion. He came towards the Queen and to Crystal's astonishment, he merely pointed towards the heavens where a thick, black cloud was forming on the horizon.

'They have arrived at last, Your Majesty,' he puffed, looking clearly relieved. Amella smiled her congratulations and nodded her head, her eyes shining bright.

'Well done,' she said, flashing a look of appreciation. 'This will bring something special to the tournament this year, just like we'd hoped.' The cloud was growing closer and as Crystal watched, she realised the dark haze was moving in formation and had sprouted wings.

'Are they giant birds?' Crystal gasped, placing her hand to her eyes in an attempt to shield them from the bright sunlight.

'No, not at all,' Amella laughed excitedly, 'why, they're dragons and the apprentices will be expected to ride them. You see, those who are still standing will be entered into a race and the first forty finalists to cross the finishing line will gain their place at the Acadamie!'

Crystal stared in utter astonishment. She had never seen anything as fantastical in her entire life and when the dragons grew close, she watched them turn and rotate thirty degrees before diving towards the main arena, their magnificent black and green bodies shimmering like highly polished gemstones against the backdrop of the sun.

Mordorma slipped to Crystal's side.

'You're looking at a bunch of Western dragons,' he explained, smiling when he saw her eyes sparkling. 'They are the smallest species of ethereal dragon and therefore easily broken to ride. You can tell they are Western dragons by the Drakon beard under their chin, which turns red on maturity. They live in caves not far from here and are relatively friendly unless you try to steal their eggs,' he added with a chortle.

Crystal was enthralled, her eyes following each dragon as it entered the circle, watching their strong wings flicker and shake as they grounded to a halt, followed by heavy snorts when they eventually calmed themselves. Crystal thought in her opinion that none of them looked domesticated or easy to ride and secretly admired anyone who thought to try.

'Don't they breathe fire?' she asked, noticing how one or two of them appeared a little restless.

'No, not these,' said Mordorma, shooting her a broad grin, 'that's the beauty of this particular dragon.'

'Are you sure?' she persisted, clearly unconvinced, 'because they all look more than fairly capable to me.' Bridgemear and Amella burst into laughter which seemed to be infectious, causing most of the other magicians to join in.

'No darling,' giggled Amella, sliding her arm around her daughter's waist and giving it a quick squeeze. 'These creatures are deemed as celestial beings therefore they can do no harm, only the ice dragon and the evil red dragon born within the Valley of the Green Witch can breathe fire.' She turned to Bridgemear and reached for his hand and he took her hand in his before turning to his daughter and saying, 'you really do have a lot to learn, my dearest Crystal. I think perhaps it may be a good idea for you to become an apprentice in your own right. There is indeed a lot for you to learn, you're both completely untrained in the art of magic and ignorant of our ways.' Crystal dropped her gaze, shifting from one foot to another, suddenly uncomfortable at her father's unexpected suggestion.

'What an excellent idea,' cried Amella, removing her arm from around her daughter's waist. She glanced around the royal box looking for signs of approval; catching Elveria's cold stare she pulled her jaw tight.

'Why Crystal, you could start with the new apprentices,' she declared, watching Elveria's face turn purple with smouldering rage. 'After all, you are the Princess of Nine Winters, therefore it's the perfect opportunity for you to learn your rightful skills so that one day you will be able to reign as Queen.'

Bridgemear followed her stare and saw the other mages stiffen; his good mood instantly washed away. The knowledge that Elveria could never be able to threaten them on this soil gave him some comfort, but a threat he still remained. Whilst he contemplated their situation, the last fifty apprentices took their places on the dragons' backs. Bridgemear turned and looked at the cold face of Elveria who, in turn, caught his stare, the corners of his mouth turned down in an ugly grimace.

'Then it is settled,' said Bridgemear, flashing a warning glare to the elder mage. A sudden gasp came from Elveria as though he was unable to contain his outrage no longer. His jaw clenched at the biting mockery in Bridgemear's voice and he jumped to his feet, unable to listen to another word.

Amafar gave an unexpected snort.

'Sit down and enjoy the rest of the tournament,' he said, pulling at the elder mage's cloak to try and make him stay. 'Crystal becoming an apprentice isn't the end of the world.'

Elveria flicked Amafar's hand from his cloak as though he was an irritating fly; realising several watchful eyes were upon him he tried to keep his composure. He couldn't make a scene, not here, not when so many of his enemies sat waiting for him to fall.

'It would appear anyone can become an apprentice these days,' he sniffed, gazing at Crystal's face with contempt. 'However, she is your only daughter so I'm sure you will do whatever pleases you regardless of the consequences,' he added, sounding churlish. Amella turned in her chair and pursed her lips angrily.

'How dare you!' she hissed, causing her mouth to twist with distaste. 'I order you to leave this gallery this instant,' she snapped, pointing towards the exit, 'before I have you arrested for treason.' Elveria paled, realising his costly mistake; he bowed and tried to apologise, but it fell on deaf ears. Like a scalded cat he rushed from the royal gallery, his face crimson with overwhelming fury and Amella's eyes widened when she saw his raw hatred displayed for all to see. She quivered, believing Elveria was undoubtedly about to become a far more dangerous thorn embedded deep within her flesh and wondered what she was going to have to do to dig him free from her side.

Chapter 6

The Grand Meadow was exactly that. It looked like something from a picture postcard because it was smothered with a lush carpet of pretty bluebells, soft sweeping grasses and white clusters of baby's breath. The sea of flowers was a colourful distraction to the sprinkling of evergreen trees which looked like frosted cake decorations along the distant horizon and the ice-peaked mountains standing prominent in the distance made the wintry scene look truly exceptional.

The meadow was already being transformed to celebrate the festival with a multitude of outdoor trimmings and rich ornamental garlands, by royal command. Three huge maypoles, decorated with delicate ribbons of deep russet and soft saffron shades, had been erected in the centre of the meadow and their rich autumn tones were spectacular amidst the mesh of wild flowers which had been woven between the long poles and many decorative streamers. A mass of pretty circlets which had been made from the dark leaves of evergreens and entwined with both vibrant winter berries and delicious citrus fruits were now placed on the heads of the busy imperial servants. The feast looked magnificent and the sweet scent that wafted along the breeze was powerful with a rich yet tangy aroma of oranges.

Sawbones and the High Priestess stood waiting to greet the royal entourage and Crystal was surprised to see all the apprentices already seated in anticipation of their arrival. The Queen and her family made their way to where five decorated tables were filled with the most delicious foods imaginable and Crystal felt the connection to Mother Nature ripple down her spine when her feet trod over the soft, lush grass. She filled her lungs with sweet, fresh air and marvelled at the abundance of beauty displayed before her very eyes whilst she took her place.

Each novice rose respectively when the Queen approached, bowing their heads towards her when she also took her place at the centre table. A dutiful hush fell over the distinguished guests and newly appointed apprentices, and then the Queen cleared her throat, ready to give a royal declaration.

'It's time to announce this year's head apprentice,' she said, rising from her chair to look into the many faces who stared back at her with expectation glowing in their eyes.

'I must say I feel we have a most talented group of apprentices this year and you all worked very hard today to earn your place within the Supreme Circle of Mages. I will look forward to watching you all as you continue to make your journey towards a life surrounded by magic. However, I must tell you that there is one amongst you who showed great courage and outstanding commitment today, and with this in mind I wish to announce that our new head apprentice for this year will be ... Niculmus DeGrunt.'

Amella clapped her hands vigorously when a fair-haired young man jumped from his seat wearing the biggest grin she had ever seen. A thunderous applause followed by wolf whistles and loud cries of 'well done' preceded Niculmus in a deafening roar as he made his way to the Queen's side.

His bow was over-exaggerated and rather theatrical when he accepted the royal scroll which sealed his place within the Supreme Circle, causing Amella to smile at him in amusement. She recognised the long garment he wore, a jet-black robe with the emblem of 'The Circle' embossed colourfully on his left breast pocket. Bridgemear had worn the very same ceremonial robe, many years before. His blonde hair had looked almost white against the dark robe and his large blue eyes had danced merrily with both pride and exhilaration.

'You did extremely well today,' Amella whispered in Niculmus's ear, gesturing for him to join her. He eagerly took his place at the Royal Table of Nine, placing himself at Crystal's side. He bowed to her in a mark of respect and a ruby glow of triumph was seen to burn deep within his eyes. His long robe rustled slightly when he made himself comfortable, but once settled he appeared to ignore the princess, enjoying the feast of the Four Quarters Festival instead.

Crystal wasn't the least bit bothered, but then she spotted Mordorma and Voleton whispering to one another and saw Mordorma signal to the imperial servants to remove something. She glanced over to Elveria's empty chair and shuddered when she saw it was being taken away.

Breaking her gaze, Crystal turned to focus her attention on the countless young men instead who were enjoying the wonderful bounties and delicious drinks on offer to them. She observed them tucking into the magnificent platefuls of sizzling meats and deep-filled pastries whilst busily shaping new friendships and strong allegiances and she felt a sudden twinge of loneliness twist around her heart, forcing her to admit that she wished Matt was here with her. She remained silent when a sudden bout of isolation bubbled to the surface and, heavy-hearted, she turned her head and caught Niculmus's eye and as she did so she smiled, longing for the apprentice to turn into her dear friend instead.

*

'I believe you will go far within the Circle,' Bridgemear said, suddenly grabbing the newly appointed apprentice's attention and shaking his hand. Niculmus smiled with genuine appreciation, his cheeks glowing red with embarrassment.

'Thank you, my lord,' he said, lowering his gaze. 'However, I have to tell you that having a place within the Circle of Mages is all I've ever dreamt about,' he blurted.

'Yes, it showed,' laughed Bridgemear, flashing a dazzling smile his way. 'I'm pleased to see how hard you worked to gain your place and I will be watching you closely in future, for you showed great potential today.' Niculmus was predictably silent, but Bridgemear could not contain his pleasure. He roared heartily with the other magicians who each agreed on the excellence of the young apprentice's outstanding abilities. The ceremony continued and Bridgemear watched the rest of the apprentices being given their scrolls of acceptance, until the Lord High Chamberlain stood at the head of the main banqueting table and demanded the immediate attention of all its participants with a mighty boom from his staff.

'It's time to thank all the noble men and women of Raven's Rainbow who have worked so very hard to organise today's events, and to also give thanks to your families for their support by asking them to join in the feast.' He turned towards the horizon and pointed to where a crowd was seen to be gathering in the distance. Everyone followed the Lord High Chamberlain's gaze to see a stream of horses, decorated carts and excited revellers pour into the meadow. Many were waving the banners they had taken from the tournament and their lively shouts and insatiable laughter travelled along the breeze to reach everyone's ears. The apprentices grew excited as they waited for their close family members to greet them, their scrolls of acceptance held tightly in their sweaty hands, ready to share their first real achievement with the ones they loved.

When the crowd grew close, enormous toadstools sprang up in compact clusters, close to where the apprentices sat waiting. The 'shrooms', as they were better known, forced their way through the softened earth, creating tables and chairs for the expected guests, allowing the royal servers to fill their unusual arced centres with refreshing drinks and mouth-watering treats.

The atmosphere throbbed with happiness. The newly appointed apprentices, continuing to enjoy the generosity of the Queen, boasted of new rewards yet to come within the confines of the Kingdom of Nine Winters. However, after a time, the merrymaking grew mellow and the afternoon shifted closer to dusk. Once again the Lord High Chamberlain called for quiet.

'It is time for the ceremonial dance,' he declared, turning his attention to the royal guests. Bridgemear twisted his body towards Amella and gently took her hand in his. Smiling broadly, he guided his Queen towards the centre of the meadow and as they walked a magic faerie ring began to bloom around them, including an arc of mushrooms which were relatively small compared to the larger shrooms. The invisible faerie folk worked tirelessly when the royal couple prepared to dance, twisting and weaving the meadow's abundance of colourful flowers together to form a huge faerie ring. Once the circle was set, the grass shrivelled away, disappearing into the deep earth, stopping only to allow the soft green moss which had begun to spread to create a spellbinding carpet on which to dance. The ring was at least ten metres in diameter and mycelium gave it a silvery edge. Faerie music flowed against the breeze and Bridgemear took Amella in his arms, whilst the faeries who were completely unseen, busied themselves in creating a colourful explosion of beauty worthy of a Queen.

The charm of faerie music filled the air and Amella and Bridgemear started to dance, but when the tune spiralled to dizzy heights, every apprentice was ushered into the ring to join the royal couple and Crystal rubbed her eyes in surprised fascination when a womanly apparition materialised in the arms of every young elf. Each smouldering vision was of a graceful and most alluring maiden. Dressed in bright pastel shades of gentle pinks, light greens or delicate blues, the apprentices danced with the most beautiful girls of their dreams.

'They're all so gorgeous!' cried Crystal to Amafar who had shifted from his seat to come and sit by her side.

'Yes, they are,' he agreed, unable to take his eyes off a particularly stunning maiden who was gliding past his nose. He caught her eye and gave her a smouldering stare. 'I have to say, it's truly amazing what your imagination can create,' he added, seemingly in two minds whether or not to chase after her.

Crystal nodded, but she was really listening to the beat of the music. The melody was starting to change to a rather fast pace and delight blossomed on the faces of those who danced. Crystal watched each and every couple swirl and bow to the powerful beat of the music, the apprentices holding their illusory partners firmly around their waists, their steps as light as the ghosts they held so closely.

'How is it everyone knows how to dance so well?' asked Crystal, sounding rather impressed at how each step was performed to perfection.

'Most children learn from an early age,' Amafar explained, smiling dolefully when he spotted a couple of young elf children trying to copy the complicated steps shown by the more experienced grown-ups. Their feet were light and nimble as they mimicked their elders, an obvious sign to those who watched of their deep Elvin blood. His eyes fell back on to the young men who were literally dancing their feet off and he pointed to Niculmus when he swirled on by.

'The apprentices such as Niculmus must know how to dance when they enter the competition, for they must be able to dance when they are received at court,' he explained. Crystal nodded, clearly impressed at how much the fine young men knew of life before it had really begun. Suddenly Amafar jumped to his feet and held out his hand.

'Would you allow me the pleasure of this dance?' he asked, his eyes sparkling with mischief, but Crystal pulled away like a shrinking violet.

'Oh no, I don't know how,' she protested, hoping he would see her embarrassment, feel sorry for her and therefore leave her alone. Her heart began to hammer in her chest at the thought of humiliating herself in front of all these people.

'Nonsense and poppycock!' clucked Amafar, ignoring her whimpering and he reached out, pulling her roughly to her feet. 'All elves can dance, even you, and I won't take no for an answer!' he declared.

Reluctantly, Crystal dragged her feet towards the faerie ring, her face clearly flushed with predictable discomfort. A flute started to play and she felt a shudder of relief when she realised she might just be able to disguise her inability to dance within the light flow of music.

She curtsied to the magician and caught her father's surprised stare which he tried to mask with a forced smile of encouragement. Then Amafar took her in his arms and before she knew it, she was dancing as though she had been gifted her entire life. The steps came so easily, she looked down at her slippered feet and watched each foot take a calculated step without her brain telling them to do so. She grinned, allowing her stiffened body to melt into the soft rhythm that followed. She was soon gaining confidence until Amafar abruptly stopped dancing mid-flow and she saw his arm drop down to his side. She blinked in confusion, but then Niculmus came into her eye line and he was asking her to dance ...

'Will you do me the honour?' he asked her softly. She nodded, taken aback by his sudden appearance and then she felt his arms entwine around her waist, twirling her around the velvety green carpet of moss. She noticed he was slightly taller than her, his frame was broad and strong and she could feel the thrum of magic pulsate from his body as he guided her with a confidence and poise usually only seen from those with years of experience.

'You look very beautiful in that gown,' he told her, when her eyes eventually found the courage to find his. She smiled shyly, unsure how to respond to his compliment, her mouth having gone dry and she felt her parents' watchful gaze burning on her back. 'May I continue by saying that green really suits you,' he added with a slight grin.

She felt herself blush right down to her toes and she dropped her lashes accordingly. He had such a powerful charisma that she felt drawn to look back into his dark brown eyes, and she became captivated as flecks of silver flicked teasingly around his large black pupils. Surprised, her light smile broadened until she managed to look away when the heat from her blush grew too much to bear. She was overpowered by his unexpected charm, finding his strong personality somewhat alluring. She felt her heart racing, but allowed the music to pulsate through her body and she let Niculmus swirl her faster and faster amongst the many friendly faces, making her slightly light-headed. She was finding it all so intoxicating and as she danced in his arms she decided she never wanted the evening to end. Finally the music died away and everyone, still feeling exuberant, walked unwillingly back to their places. Niculmus bent forward and kissed her.

'Thank you for making my evening perfect,' he told her, but she found she couldn't answer, his gentle kiss still lingering, there, on her sweet lips. She watched him walk away, her mind stunned at what had just occurred between them. Feeling very conspicuous standing in the middle of the meadow all alone, Crystal rushed back to her chair.

Darkness was descending and ferocious beacons were soon lit, conjuring both warmth and golden light. The crackle of fire when each beacon was ignited caused the flames to hiss like vipers, sending handfuls of bright sparks to fly into the night sky, creating a dazzling array of light, golden embers. Glow worms and glass lanterns filled with fireflies were added to the maypoles giving them an eerie luminosity against the darkness of the night. The meadow looked ablaze with fire and light and the stars twinkled down from the sky in appreciation.

Crystal noticed that there was no sign of Niculmus and, feeling slightly confused, drank the rest of her wine a little too fast, the heaviness of the day wielding its way into her tired bones. She paused to toss a smile, the side of her mouth quirking up when she saw Amafar heading towards her prancing like a circus horse, his hat skew-whiff and his cape dangling off his shoulder. Crystal blinked at the scene before her and then burst out laughing.

'Are you drunk?' she giggled, when he fell over his feet and flat on his face. She jumped up, concerned he had hurt himself. He lay on the ground in a stupor, his hair in disarray and his clothes wet with spilled wine. Most of the apprentices and their families were also the worse for wear and hadn't spotted Amafar's impressive attempt at disgracing himself. Rushing to his side, Crystal linked her arm into his, forcing him to his feet; he rose with an exaggerated leap, immediately smoothing his tousled hair back into place with his fingertips and grabbing his hat. He gasped, opening and closing his mouth like a stunned goldfish, seemingly unable to form any words which would aid a conversation before spinning on his heels and running somewhat drunkenly towards the sanctuary of the other mages.

'Princess Crystal,' Niculmus whispered from somewhere behind her. 'I hear you are to become an apprentice and to train with us?' Crystal spun on her own heels, not recognising his voice and she felt her heart beat violently in her chest when a picture of King Forusian came from deep within her sub-conscience and placed him to the forefront of her mind.

Niculmus's broad silhouette loomed out of the darkness and towered over her like a menacing shadow, catching her completely off guard. A sharp stab of fear pierced straight through her ribcage and Niculmus threw his hand out to steady her when she almost slipped, trying to get away from him.

'What's the matter?' he asked, pulling himself from the shadows and refusing to let her go. He shot a look at Amella and tried to open a mind portal. The party was noisy and his concentration wavered when someone accidentally bumped into him, disconnecting his link. He regained a connection, still holding Crystal's arm, but his message became intercepted by the Prince Regent instead. A whoosh of air and Bridgemear was stood beside him with Crystal wrapped in his arms so securely Niculmus thought she would snap in two if his grip got any tighter.

Bridgemear rocked his daughter to and fro until the fear left her eyes.

'Are you alright?' he asked, finally holding her at arm's length. Crystal's eyes filled with tears and she immediately covered her face with the palm of her hands.

'I'm fine,' she blurted, though her throat sounded constricted, 'I just feel such an idiot.'

Niculmus raked his fair hair away from his serious brown eyes. His mouth was drawn tight as he stared openly at the distraught princess. Bridgemear shook his head when Amella approached.

'What happened?' Amella asked, sweeping her gaze from her daughter to Niculmus.

Niculmus shook his shoulders and Amella was seen to pull a face.

'Let's get you away from here,' the Queen announced to her daughter, putting her arm protectively around Crystal's shoulders and drawing her close. Hugging her tight, the Queen glared dangerously at Niculmus.

Niculmus stared back at her in disbelief.

'But, I ...'

'Leave it,' ordered Bridgemear, pointing a firm finger. 'I think you've done quite enough for one night, young man.'

Niculmus was clearly lost for words and he watched Bridgemear bend down and whisper something in Crystal's ear. She looked upwards and opened her mouth as though to argue but before she could utter a sound, both Amella and Bridgemear were rushing her away with a flurry of servants and drunken magicians hot on their heels.

Niculmus looked down at his feet and gave a heavy sigh. It wasn't so much that he had somehow gotten the blame for the princess's distress, but that she, Princess Crystal, had been so deeply afraid of him when he had merely thought to surprise her. He tried to think of a reason why she would react in such a way and came up with no reason at all. He thought about his home and how his determination to succeed as a royal apprentice had meant he had little knowledge of the outside world. The Kingdom of Nine

Winters had almost been a mystery to him whilst working in his small hamlet. Perhaps when he reached the Kingdom and started his apprenticeship he would learn more about the princess and be able to put right what had happened tonight? He felt himself relax at this thought. Watching the many drunken men and women with growing distaste he decided he could no longer tolerate their exaggerated laughter. Shifting to the darkest shadows of the meadow, he transmuted into the body of a large, sleek fox, his four black paws falling silent on the ground when he eagerly scurried away. The dark tip of his bushy tail swished to and fro when he broke through the long grasses, his small, golden eyes sharp and alert, prepared for unexpected danger.

Under the cover of moonlight, he travelled for many miles until he reached a foxhole, buried deep within a large copse of hardy trees. He stopped, lifted his paw and sniffed the air for any intrusive scents. His sharp eyes shot towards the distant moon when he finally felt he was safe and, without hesitation, he dived into an earthly burrow, vanishing from view when a solitary owl hooted a warning as it too descended into the world of unsuspecting darkness.

Chapter 7

Professor Valentino was a fussy old wizard roughly aged around three hundred and sixty two. He had been ready to retire from the Academie this year, but one of the new faculty lecturers had decided to take a position within the realm of the dwarves instead, leaving the Academie understaffed and in a position where they had no one qualified who was willing to teach water magic or the art of modern witchcraft at least twice a week.

He wandered the majestic palace corridors already cursing his days without the benefits of early retirement. The majority of the palace was buried deep within the mountain and although a strong wall, a few common turrets and a large courtyard had been recently constructed on its outer rock face to reinforce the city, most of it still remained hidden to the naked eye.

He clicked his tongue whilst he wandered the elegantly cut marble corridors, the perfectly smooth and incomparable design mixed with the many slabs of gleaming gemstones turned the whole palace into a rich treasure trove of beauty, yet he saw none of this as he worried about the apprentices who were scheduled to start at the Academie the very next morning.

The new left wing which was housed on the outer rock face had fallen into mindless chaos due to the lack of organisation from those who had waited until the last minute to prepare for the new term. He felt a pain in his stomach. He had not long finished his lunch and the extra portion of juicy mutton was giving him severe indigestion. As he walked along the bright corridors, he rubbed his tummy as though to aid his digestion, his concentration turning to passing the painful gases which were building up deep inside. He wiped his mouth with his long, white beard which had grown thin with age and his rheumy eyes only held the odd sparkle when he became unexpectedly amused, which didn't happen very often these days.

A moment later Magician Phin, the new specialist teacher of transmutations and animal magnetisms, turned a corner and collided straight into Professor Valentino who was carrying an armful of books and a selection of first year exam papers. He snorted loudly when his own books flew high in the air, neither magician young enough to cast a spell to stop the inevitable accident from occurring. Both cursed aloud before the professor garbled a common spell which placed his books firmly in his ridiculously long arms. Magician Phin shook himself, turning red, before he too mumbled a spell enforcing his own books to slide into a small, orderly tower, creating a very neat pile. Still flushed with embarrassment, Magician Phin hastily picked up his books and Professor Valentino raised his brow in concern when he saw his hands were shaking.

'Are you alright?' he asked, running his watery eyes over the magician, checking for any superficial cuts or sudden bruising. He looked at his comrade's dishevelled robes and saw they were old and the colours faded and Valentino realised from his own smart attire that this magician had perhaps at some point fallen on hard times.

Magician Phin nodded in reply.

'Yes, I'm fine, really, it's just bumping into you has just added to my distress. Everything within the palace to do with the apprentices appears to be at odds and ends and my classroom still isn't ready after weeks of negotiation and I hear the casting room has yet to be repaired from the students who almost destroyed it last year!'

Professor Valentino gave a hearty chuckle.

'Welcome to the Palace of Nine Winters,' he said, casting yet another spell which allowed his books to leave his aching arms and float instead by his side, hovering as though they were nothing more than particles of fresh air.

'You will find everything will eventually calm down in the next week or so, it's always rather hectic at the beginning of term, but I'm positive your classroom will be ready in time. If you're concerned, why don't you speak to Madame Orlanna? She is our resident black witch and is absolutely superb at laying

68

enchantments. I'm sure she would be most happy to help you iron out any discrepancies within your department.'

Magician Phin's look of distress appeared to ease a little.

'It is very kind of you to offer me your good advice,' he said, forcing a broad smile, 'because up to now I just haven't been able to get any help from anyone.'

The professor's chuckle appeared to deepen.

'Well, it's the least I can do after causing our collision,' he said, straightening his robe. 'I realise it isn't easy taking on a new position and settling into a new realm in such a short time,' he added, reaching up to stroke his beard absentmindedly. 'However, I can assure you it will all come together, eventually,' he added with a slight grin.

Magician Phin eyed him with genuine gratitude and nodded.

'You're very kind,' he said, bowing to show his appreciation. 'I will indeed seek out Madame Orlanna and speak to her regarding my concerns, especially as I feel I am getting nowhere fast.'

The professor gestured for him to come closer and he put a friendly arm around his bony shoulders.

'It will all get worse before it gets better,' he explained, pointing in the direction Phin should go to find Orlanna. 'Mark my words,' he whispered, almost to himself when Magician Phin disappeared around the corner. 'You're going to wish you never set foot in this damn place, just like I do year after year.'

*

Flushed with his success, Niculmus entered the Kingdom of Nine Winters like a battered soldier returning victorious from his crusade. His horse was old but strong and his few meagre possessions were strapped securely to his side. He held the ceremonial scroll of his apprenticeship tightly in his gloved hand for he would have to be dead for a thief or vagabond to take it willingly from his grasp.

He stopped, turned in his saddle and pulled at his water bottle. His journey had not been a long one, but the dust had dried his throat all the same. He straightened, eyeing his surroundings with caution, conscious of the fact he had unwittingly upset Princess Crystal and therefore he was not as confident as one would have expected, especially after his recent triumph in the arena.

The black cob he was riding threw her ears back and snorted her impatience, causing her breath to stream from her nostrils, creating a warm cloud of white. Niculmus rubbed her between her ears and stroked her neck with affection. She had been his mother's horse, but now she was his and he calmed her with his reassuring touch.

He nudged her stomach with the heel of his boot and she broke into an exaggerated trot. The local villagers were milling around the outer palace walls, their day already starting before the wintry sun had time to rise and only a few glanced his way when he rode on by. He had only ever been to Nine Winters once before, when he was a small child. It had been a day just as this, when the apprentices rode through the royal gates, waiting for their lives to begin in a kingdom renowned for its incredible service to the art of magic and sorcery. He had watched those boys with hidden envy and then decided that he too wished to walk the uncertain path of a magician. His mother showed him a few magic tricks which she'd learned from the local shaman and his taste for magic increased as he grew and his senses heightened when he forged an unusual friendship with the local witch, endorsing a strange friendship which helped to teach him the basic skills to aid him in the art of magic. He was born with 'the gift', the witch forewarned him, and when he turned sixteen his mother (for he had never known his father), rather begrudgingly gave her permission for him to enter the Trial of the Apprentices.

A gentle snow was falling when he made his way to the stables and he was thankful they'd made it to the city before the icy wind had forced its way through his thinning shirt. He recognised a few of the faces assembled in the courtyard from the trial and when he dismounted, a cry of welcome ran in succession throughout the small crowd as they too put their horses into the awaiting stalls.

All the apprentices entered the courtyard once their horses were fed and watered, surrounded by hissing torches and a multitude of colourful flags and banners worthy of the royal emblem. The young elves were approached by one of the many lecturers who had come to round them up as though they were nothing more than uncooperative sheep, requesting they congregate by a tall, stone tower.

Whilst Niculmus was busy digesting his surroundings, a doorway flew open within the tower itself and the first shots of a fanfare blasted out from the highest turret. Amella stepped out onto a balcony set on a small frame way, followed closely by Bridgemear and what Niculmus learned later to be three of the Academie's oldest and most trusted magicians who were held with the highest regard within the confines of court. The magicians' faces were as grey as the stone which surrounded them, but their trained eyes were sharp and clear. Niculmus felt a shudder run down his spine when one of the magicians turned and glared directly at him and he cursed himself for looking so conspicuous.

'Welcome,' Amella called towards the misshapen circle of young elves. She took a step forward and laid her hands on the small balustrade held up by two solid plinths of rock. Her gown of royal blue sparkled when the snowflakes turned to water and trickled over the gemstones sewn onto her gown.

Biting his lower lip, Niculmus tried to hide his sudden bout of nervousness. He had always been so confident but his recent incident with the elf princess had clearly rattled him. He threw a watery smile towards Amella hoping he could bluff his feelings of impending doom, but soon realised when her eyes connected to his that she had not forgotten the incident. A boy standing close to him poked him sharply in the ribs.

'I see she's got her eye on you,' he teased, his voice filled with mockery. Niculmus glared angrily towards the pock-scarred lad, but before he could raise a comment the large oaken doors to the lower gate began to swing out and the apprentices were each called by their full names to enter the royal Academie.

Professor Valentino kept a watchful eye on Niculmus when he entered. He'd already been privy to the incident concerning Princess Crystal and he was no fool to those who imposed self-importance to hide their own weaknesses. He watched the young apprentice make his way through the gate; his stride was long and confident, his eyes blazed with a raw determination and Valentino knew he'd seen that look once before. There was something almost alluring about the boy's mannerisms and the professor found himself taking a step forward to take a closer look.

71

His sixth sense told him the boy had a good heart and his aura oozed an unusually high magical strength. He stood back, his mind clouded with confusion. He wavered momentarily against the Queen's decision to ensure Niculmus stayed low within the ranks of the Circle of Mages. He realised this would be near impossible with an apprentice showing as much power in his semblance as Niculmus. He touched his index finger to his lower lip when the Queen and her entourage stepped back inside to the warmth of the palace. He dallied outside for just a few moments longer and saw the skies erupt with unexpected clashes of thunder. He turned his face towards the heavens, his eyes blinking rapidly as the snow fell on his wrinkled face. Then a streak of lightning criss-crossed through the sky, breaking up the thickening cloud to create a towering figure in black which stood menacingly before him. Another flash lit up the magician's face and he saw the warning was gone as though the spirits of his forefathers were defending their rights to protect their own, heralding the young apprentice's arrival to those who were wise enough to realise this was indeed a sign not to be ignored.

Professor Valentino fell back inside, the sanctuary of the palace walls felt thin and insignificant when he closed the door abruptly to the outside world. His breathing was shallow and he turned his attention towards the small, delicate drinking fountain made from a miniature ice floe which held various sharp icicles in a frozen cluster. He guzzled the water which, once melted, dripped into a long, pear-shaped bowl but no matter how much he drank, his unquenchable thirst brought on by his newfound knowledge would not leave him. He cursed again for his lack of retirement and hiked his thumb to his throbbing temple. He felt himself quieten and smoothed his beard to help steady his nerves.

The Queen suddenly appeared before him.

'Are you all right?' she asked, her brow knitted with concern. All he could do was nod and Amella looked about her, as though she had misplaced something.

'Tell me, what's wrong?' she pushed, reaching for a small cloth and handing it to him so he could wipe his mouth. Valentino dropped his head, it was impossible to lie to her.

'There is something I must tell you,' he said, dabbing his lips and then returning the cloth to its rightful place. Amella's beautiful eyes immediately welled with tears and she unconsciously bit her lip.

'I saw *the sign*,' she rasped, her voice sounding hoarse with despair. 'Tell me, Valentino, what must we do?'

The ageing magician pulled himself to his full height. His robe, smooth and shiny, swished against the floor when he walked with purpose to her side.

'It pains me to say it but we must prepare ourselves for darker days,' he acknowledged, his eyes clouding with dread and uncertainty.

'It's as I feared then,' Amella said, clinging hold of her gown. 'Yet again I find myself in a position where I have no choice but to wait and see what hand fate deals me.' Professor Valentino looked sad and he drew closer to the Queen.

'Then we must make the best of a bad situation,' he insisted, reaching out and patting her hand like a doting father, 'for if anything is true at least we have the light on our side which will force the darkness away for a time.'

'But what will become of my daughter? Crystal is neither wise enough nor experienced enough to save herself let alone our kingdom should we come across troubled times and I should fall,' Amella gasped, pulling her hand away. The professor's shoulders appeared to sag but then his eyes glowed with clear insight.

'She will be ready, my Queen, of that I promise you. When the times comes and she has to fight for those who depend upon her, she will know what to do, mark my words, dear Queen.'

I pray you're right,' said Amella, still fighting her tears, 'for not only this kingdom would become lost without her.'

Chapter 8

'It's not fair! Why should I be the one who has to be segregated and made to learn my skills with the princess?' Niculmus snapped in utter despair. He had been called to one of the lower chambers as soon as he entered the palace and when Magician Phin suggested that he should help Crystal become an acclaimed scholar, he felt his blood boil. He had never anticipated this happening to him, not in a million years, and he folded his arms against his chest, his jaw clenched in defiance.

Magician Phin looked rather pale and drawn. It was obvious his first day on the job hadn't quite gone as expected, his eyes were red rimmed and bloodshot as though he hadn't had a decent night's sleep in weeks and he continually flicked his tongue over his lips, unable to suppress his nervousness.

He walked over to a crystal decanter floating in mid-air on a fluffy, white cloud and poured two goblets of deep crimson wine. He offered a goblet to Niculmus who eyed him with caution whilst the cloud, soft and light, swirled about the magician's cup in broken wisps of silver and white.

Once Niculmus accepted the drink, Magician Phin went to take a gulp of his own, but said instead, 'well, tell me boy, what is your answer?' Niculmus, still furious at the thought of having to babysit the princess over the next few months, threw the goblet to the ground. The cup crashed to the floor, spilling the ruby-red contents lying within and creating a rich, watery pool of what looked like his own sweet blood. Magician Phin shook his head in dismay and simply stared at Niculmus who stood firm, his face flushed with humiliation and a trickle of sweat produced by his growing frustration slid silently down his cheek.

'No, I won't do it!' Niculmus declared, watching the last of Magician Phin's confidence ebb away. 'This was supposed to be my chance to shine; I don't want any distractions, especially from her. I should be with the other apprentices as promised, not hidden away in some dark, forlorn chamber whilst she tries to learn the basics of magic. Don't you realise what this means? I'll never live it down!'

Neither of them heard the shift-click as Bridgemear entered the chamber and it was his voice not Phin's which penetrated Niculmus's stubborn skull. Niculmus felt himself take in a large gulp of air, his eyes wide with unexpected surprise when he turned to see someone lurking in the dark shadows and when Bridgemear pulled himself into the light, Niculmus noted that his face was pale like Phin's.

He gulped again and glanced towards his tutor, hoping for some moral support, but Phin merely turned his face away and replaced his untouched goblet back onto the swirling cloud, his drink momentarily obscured by a billowing silver haze. Phin took his leave and left Bridgemear alone with the uncooperative apprentice.

'This is not what I expected from you,' said Bridgemear, placing his hands behind his back and beginning to pace the floor.

'My lord,' said Niculmus, becoming subservient, 'I did not hear you come into the room.'

'Indeed,' said Bridgemear, raising an eyebrow, 'yet, am I to assume this is how you would normally speak to your superiors?' Niculmus sounded flabbergasted.

'No, my lord, of course not. It's just, well, it's just that I feel I am somehow being punished for what happened at the festival.'

Bridgemear raised the other eyebrow.

'Really?' he said, sounding incredulous. His eyes suddenly sparkled and a slight smirk reached the side of his mouth. 'Do you really think this is all because you upset the princess the other night?' he asked.

Niculmus burbled with confusion, his mind racing ahead with thoughts of unsavoury punishments and he watched Bridgemear step towards the cloud and poured himself a rather stiff drink.

The snow had finally stopped falling but the sky was still grey and the light from the small crescent window held high in the stone wall gave enough light for Bridgemear to see the bewilderment displayed on Niculmus's young face. The mage took a sip of his wine and unconsciously reached for the hilt of his sword. He was known these days to carry the Sword of Truth at his side at all times. Ever since Elveria went missing on the day of the Four Quarters Festival he would no longer venture outside without it. To make matters worse, at the opening ceremony of the receivership of the apprentices, both Amella and Professor Valentino had seen *the sign*. Bridgemear shook these dark thoughts from his mind and returned to the matter at hand, keeping his brain focused on the future of his daughter and his wife's kingdom.

'As you are aware,' he began, 'the Queen and I wish for you to learn your trade as a mage with our daughter, Crystal.' Bridgemear heard the sharp whoosh as Niculmus exhaled and the look on his face told him he may as well have given him a fatal blow. The boy looked stricken and Bridgemear couldn't help but to burst out laughing.

'Come now, what is this nonsense?' he bellowed in a cheerful tone, gesturing for them both to sit. 'Princess Crystal may not be in the same league as you at the moment, but she is quick to learn and I bet within a few weeks you're going to wish you really were with the other apprentices when she whips your arse,' Bridgemear chuckled and Niculmus couldn't help but let an unwanted grin press his lips.

Bridgemear guided his charge to a chair.

'Sire, may I speak frankly?'

'Yes, of course let's talk,' said Bridgemear, gesturing for him to take his place at his side. 'It's time you got whatever's bothering you off your chest.'

Niculmus stared awkwardly at Bridgemear; understanding the implications of the Prince Regent's last sentence. He wanted to be an apprentice so badly he could taste it, yet here he was, certain if he declined the royal offer he was as good as gone from the Royal Circle of Mages.

He felt his resolve slip away and with it any chance to escape his fate.

'Why me?' he asked, his eyes filling with regret. Bridgemear regarded the apprentice with a look of sympathy.

'The reason why you have been chosen is because you are the head apprentice and the most intelligent student we have. Crystal needs to be with someone who is both confident and bright and also someone who will be able to continually keep her up to speed, surely that's enough?'

Niculmus nodded, but his head was hung low. 'I see,' he said, not really seeing at all, 'I should have known it would be all of my own doing.' Bridgemear reached out and slapped him encouragingly on the back, sending him almost reeling off his chair.

'You'll be fine,' said Bridgemear, clicking his fingers and drawing the silver cloud to where it hovered just under his nose before placing the goblet upon it.

'I think we should get you and Crystal into the classroom with Professor Valentino and Sawbones this very afternoon; there, I am sure, we will see just what the two of you are made of.'

Niculmus nodded and forced a weak smile. He was certain his glowing career had been snatched away from under his nose by the princess and the pain of it felt inhumanly real. With their conversation running dry, Bridgemear guided him out of the chamber and towards the Academie, but Niculmus couldn't shift the feeling that his life was over before it even had time to begin.

*

When Crystal entered the Great Hall, heading towards the wing which housed the Academie, the first person she spots is Tremlon. She hasn't seen him since leaving Nine Winters and she shouts out his name in a burst of excitement. Two soldiers standing on guard give her a grim expression which suggests she isn't supposed to raise her voice as a dutiful princess but she ignores their scolding stares and runs towards the shape-changer, grinning widely when he turns and smiles at her. He opens his arms and she flies into them, wrapping her own arms around him and hugging him tight.

'Tremlon, where have you been?' she scolds, giving him another hug. Tremlon chuckles heartily before holding her at arm's length and looking at her with his strange, blood-red eyes.

'I've been here all the time,' he says, giving her a huge grin. 'Why, you're the one who went away, remember?'

She sighs, realising his statement is true.

'Okay, I'll give you that, so what are you doing here?' she asks, pulling him towards the great doors which lead away from the hall.

'I'm here on royal business,' he explains, pushing out his pigeon chest to show self-importance. 'But what about you? Are you here on a fleeting visit?'

Crystal stands debating his question.

'Well, I did come intentionally for a short stay, but now I am to become an apprentice and learn the art of magic,' she tells him, her eyes bright.

Tremlon merely chuckles.

'Yes, I heard,' he acknowledges, becoming distracted when one of the Queen's lovely handmaidens emerges from a side door. He watches her hurry by, his concentration momentarily elsewhere.

'Running late are we?' he teases when she turns to give him a quick wave. 'You should get yourself a time stopper,' he adds, pointing to his chest pocket.

'What's one of those?' Crystal interrupts, sounding curious.

'I'm not telling,' Tremlon says, turning towards her and trying to look serious. 'After all, you always end up getting me into trouble when I show you something I shouldn't.' They both burst into a fit of giggles, grinning like naughty schoolchildren until Tremlon reaches out and pats her arm affectionately.

'I must be on my way before I'm late, perhaps we can meet tonight for dinner?' he suggests.

'Yes, that would be great,' Crystal replies, brushing her hair away from her face. 'Dinner's normally at eight.'

'I will be there on the dot,' Tremlon tells her, bowing low and heading in the opposite direction.

'I look forward to your company and all your stories!' Crystal cries after him, her eyes sparkling, 'but if you keep me waiting, I will think up something horrible for your punishment.'

Tremlon can be heard laughing, but once his laughter dies away, she sees him transmute into his favourite likeness, a dove. His long, feathery wings whoosh past her head when he dive-bombs her and she exaggerates a crouching position so as not to collide with the kamikaze bird. His gentle coo of goodbye echoes along the corridor before he swiftly disappears around a rather tight bend.

'Is he a friend of yours?'

Crystal spins around and is surprised to see Niculmus standing next to her. Her face glows red as she remembers his stolen kiss and then the memory of him creeping from out of the shadows comes to the forefront of her mind and she automatically turns defensive.

'Yes, he is actually,' she snaps, lowering her lashes and breaking eye contact. She had seen a glint of amusement explode deep within his dark brown eyes and for some strange reason his manner really irritates her.

Niculmus snorts loudly.

'Hope I didn't make you jump again?' he says, sliding a sliver of sarcasm through his voice. He tries to brush past her and Crystal feels a thrill run down her spine when he accidentally touches her hand and her cheeks flood once again. Her fingertips start to tingle and then, like all the other times before, everything falls away and an extra-sensory vision explodes in front of her wide eyes. She is no longer within the safe confines of the palace walls but instead finds herself to be somewhere outside. A bitter wind is blowing through her wild red hair, causing her long tresses to whip around her face, and she starts to tremble when she finds herself to be in the confines of a dark forest. It is barely daylight, and the few birds that are visiting the forest floor are singing their tell-tale trills of evensong. It was then, whilst growing accustomed to her wintry surroundings and looking through the leafy gaps of the thinning trees, that she espied a lone rider, riding a shiny black horse. The hooves of his mount were silent as they press the fallen pine needles and bracken deeper into the earth, the ghostly rider venturing further into the darkening forest, unaware of her watchful eyes.

Crystal realises she can't quite make out his facial features because part of his face is covered by a small, black hood but she can make out the shape of a pointed ear and she senses he could be deemed as dangerous. The rider dismounts, pulling his hood closer as he walks, his eyes alert to where the shadows of the forest are beginning to lengthen as the day shifts ever closer to dusk. She watches him prepare for his evening alone, searching for small branches and a few flimsy twigs to help build a fire. Once the flames are alight, he dampens them down, so as not to attract unwanted attention and he makes himself something to eat. His horse snorts with his unsatisfactory accommodation and the rider snatches hold of the reins, pulling them tighter and drawing the horse closer to the fire. The horse drops its head and begins to nuzzle the hard earth for a few meagre shoots of green and snorts once again when there are none to be found.

Crystal tries to move a little closer, but she is not in control of her vision and therefore cannot manipulate her proximity to the rider. She watches the elf fumble in a small bag hanging over his shoulder and take something from it. It looks like a tattered piece of vellum, similar to that of the poster which had not long since proclaimed the Four Quarters Festival. The print isn't clear but she concentrates on becoming focused, determined to read the bold headline and when her brain digests what her eyes can finally explain, the blood around her heart seems to stop pumping and a sickening sob leaves her stricken lips. She rereads the significant words once again, hoping she has somehow misread the damning statement, praying her eyes are clouded and they have somehow made a terrible mistake, but the written words are burning inside her brain, branded there for all eternity.

The parchment read: *The Queen of Nine Winters is put to Death ...*

She can't help taking an involuntary breath when Niculmus shakes her back to reality. The image of the forest shoots from her mind, as though someone has just pulled the plug on her sanity and allowed the scene to swirl rapidly away from her grasp. She looks up at his face to see his eyes wide with alarm as he, in turn, digests the look of horror on her frightened face.

'Are you alright?' he asks, pulling her close and rubbing her back as though she needed winding. Crystal automatically pushes him away. Hot tears are brimming close to the surface as she tries to absorb what she has just witnessed and she finds herself to be burbling.

'I'm fine, really, I just need a minute,' she mumbles, trying not to fall apart in front of him. She wants to run to her mother's side, throw her arms around her and tell her what she has just seen, but her senses tell her otherwise. She knows she has no choice, if she informs anyone within the royal circle what she's just witnessed she realises she could be putting her mother in grave danger and perhaps make the prediction happen much faster than first intended. No, she must do what she's always done in the past; she must work it out alone. However, Niculmus is now looking furious.

'You're anything but fine,' he snaps, trying to wrap his arm around her shoulders once again so he can guide her to Sawbones and seek medical advice.

'No, really, I'm okay!' she insists, wiping her eyes with the back of her hand and flicking his hand from her shoulder. 'Just give me a minute to sort myself out; it's just a really bad migraine, that's all.'

'Do you really expect me to believe that,' Niculmus almost spits, sounding flabbergasted. Crystal nods, unable to look him in the eye and so she looks down at her feet instead.

'Well, I must say it's the weirdest migraine I've ever witnessed and I'm guessing you must be a medical wonder seeing as people don't normally go into a trance when they're suffering a severe headache. Still, I'm told you're unique, so I guess anything can happen to you.'

She looks up to see the anger in his eyes is fighting with an emotion she can't quite simplify, causing her to feel a pang of guilt, but she remains steadfast in her theory and both arrived moments later at Professor Valentino's classroom with faces as long as a giraffe's neck.

'Come in, come in,' encourages Valentino, pulling his spectacles down over the bump on his nose so he can inspect his new students more closely. Both Crystal and Niculmus hesitate until Niculmus, remembering his manners, stands aside to allow the princess to enter first. Crystal pushes what had just happened to the furthest corner of her mind, accepting Niculmus's gentlemanly gesture. She realises she has to concentrate fully on her ability to learn magic if she has any chance of changing the future and what she has just seen and she prays for the gift of time, not knowing when that terrible event could unfold.

Crystal takes a step and enters the chamber. It isn't really a classroom at all, but more like an old cavern. It's quite bright inside, with dozens of jagged, open pores peppering the main elevation, allowing daylight to enter in a haphazard, jumbled sequence. The cavern appears to be layered with rock formations which have grown into the shapes of shrunken bat wings, hanging in dark clusters along the roofline, the tips of the wings precariously low.

Crystal looks down to see there are only three steps visible to the naked eye and then a vast hole where more steps should have been. She starts to descend, unsure how she will get to the bottom and she looks towards the magician, expecting him to shed some light on how she is suppose to reach him. The steps are well worn where countless feet have trodden them over the centuries and her footsteps make a hollow sound when they make contact with the stone. Suddenly, when both of her feet land on the last step, the stone springs to life, growing a long thick trunk from its centre and it slides off, taking her with it. She cries out in surprise and almost slips when the step transforms into a large snake's head but she somehow managed to keep her balance and the enchanted stone twists and slithers down towards the cavern floor to where the magician stands waiting. Crystal immediately jumps down, seemingly repulsed at the strange set of stairs and she turns to watch the snake recoil to where Niculmus is patiently waiting.

'Welcome, welcome, Princess Crystal,' Professor Valentino says, moving towards her and he takes her hand in greeting. She manages a weak smile, her face showing clear signs of distress but this only causes the magician to chortle and hold her hand tighter.

'There's nothing to fear here, my dear,' he announces, waving for Niculmus to hurry up. 'It's just a little magic to get you in the mood.'

Crystal clearly isn't so sure but once Niculmus joins them, Valentino gestures for them to follow him deeper into the cavern. He leads them to where a cluster of limestone deposits have grown to create a misshapen arc and where a small, shimmering pool lies almost hidden away. Valentino waves his hand across its surface and the water evaporates to expose a mass of dry, dusty old tomes and newly appointed spell books.

He then turns towards his students his eyes sparkling with knowledge. 'Right, now let me clarify what is going to happen. Over the next few months, this classroom is where you will learn your art of magic,' he explains, bending towards two tattered volumes and then passing each one to his new pupils. 'I have been a teacher here in Nine Winters for many, many years and I have been given the added task of being your mentor during this new period in your lives. I sincerely hope that you will use this time wisely and come to me if you are having any problems with your wizardry.'

From somewhere way up high there came a delicate, light cough and everyone turned to see Amella standing at the top of the enchanted stairs. Crystal was surprised by the unexpected visit from her mother and she smiled, but her smile did not reach her eyes. She turned her attention back towards Valentino, asking for his permission to go and speak with her mother.

'Yes, of course, off you go,' he nodded, reading the pleading look in her eyes. 'I'm sure you won't be long and then we must get down to serious business,' he added, looking past her for his own copy of spells.

Crystal didn't wait a moment longer and ran to where the snake had been moments earlier and before she could say anything to Professor Valentino about them not being there, the head and body of a snake slid down to her feet. She jumped onboard and rose into the air and seconds later she was hugging her mother fiercely. Amella smiled warmly, returning the embrace, totally unaware of her daughter's hidden turmoil, her own face merely glowing with happiness at having her daughter by her side.

'Dear Crystal,' she began. 'I'm sorry to interrupt your first lesson, but I needed to bring you this ...' Crystal dropped her gaze and saw her mother was holding the Spirit of Eternity, the necklace which gave her immense power. She couldn't help shuddering because she automatically remembered the last time she'd worn it and felt a moment of revulsion run down her spine.

'You need it,' Amella pressed. 'Without the amulet, your magic will be very weak. Niculmus needs a wand and you need this amulet, be brave, young one, for this necklace will be your saving grace one day.'

Crystal felt bile rise in her throat. The face of Forusian flooded her mind like ink running over paper and the agony she had suffered at his violent hands felt real again. She brushed her fingers lightly over the centre stone and the jewel shone like fire. She pulled her fingers away, still torn by the thought of having to wear it again and how Forusian had been willing to kill her all because of the power held inside the necklace.

'Be brave,' her mother urged again. 'I now wear a pendant, created within the Stannary Mines of The Lost Trinity. This ancient necklace can only be worn by someone who is pure of heart and it is said it will therefore keep hidden demons from my door.' She stroked the chest-length pendant which was made in the shape of a large cartwheel, encrusted with a circle of pink diamonds. Inside the circle sat twenty-four spokes, each silver spine displaying an elusive coloured stone representing the extraordinary powers it possessed such as wisdom, inner peace and the ability to conjure physical well-being.

Amella pulled her daughter close and whispered softly in her ear, 'The Spirit of Eternity is rightfully yours, as princess. You must learn how to use it properly so that, in time, you will never again be used as you once were by that wicked sorcerer.'

Crystal noted her mother didn't say Forusian's name and she was glad. Against her own better judgement she took the necklace from her mother's grasp, her fingers trembling as she watched the large stone in its centre change from fiery red to a deep, sapphire blue.

'The necklace senses your magic,' Amella told her, helping her daughter to fasten the string of orbs around her throat. 'You will learn quickly that this necklace is part of who you are, dear child.' Crystal nodded, but she felt a little uncomfortable when the silver clasp was fastened onto her bare skin.

'Just a little time,' Amella encouraged, 'and you will see what I'm talking about. Now off with you, for I am keeping Professor Valentino waiting.'

Crystal remained silent, but then she remembered seeing the shape-changer earlier. 'Oh, I've invited Tremlon to dinner,' she suddenly burst out, 'I hope that's alright?'

Amella laughed. 'I had already invited him,' she said, shaking her head at Tremlon's ease at manipulation.

'Humph, I should've guessed,' said Crystal, seeing the funny side, 'but you know, he really is devious at times!' Amella nodded in agreement and left her daughter soon after.

Crystal returned to her lessons. Firstly, Professor Valentino refilled the arc with water and prepared his students for their very first tutorial. He needed to see at what level his two new apprentices should begin, so he did a simple test and found that although Crystal's magic was indeed supreme within her aura as expected, Niculmus was far more advanced in knowledge and skill.

Niculmus read the beginner's spell book as instructed by his mentor until the first niggles of boredom aggravated his power-hungry mind.

'We must all start at the very beginning,' instructed Valentino when he spotted the look of tedium sweeping over the young apprentice's face. 'Princess Crystal will soon be up to speed if you will just show a little patience and understanding,' he insisted dryly, pulling out his teaching wand unexpectedly from his tight-fitting sleeve. Niculmus's eyes shot to the ground, realising the professor had read his expression as easily as he could read the stupid spell book.

'Now, both of you please read aloud the first spell,' commanded Valentino, giving Niculmus a warning glare. 'Princess Crystal, I wish for you to touch your necklace and at the same time push your hand outwards like so.' Professor Valentino motioned for her to concentrate, demonstrating the particular hand movement he wished her to learn; she immediately obliged, pushing her hand out in a rather dramatic display.

'Yes, that's about right,' he said, coming over and lowering her fingers a little. 'Niculmus, you must simply point your wand to the area you wish the spell to reach. I want you both to focus on this area of water over here and let's see if you can cast your spell simultaneously.'

'Are you ready? Now together, say after me, *Spridiúil fear tom tobacadóir.*'

A shot from Niculmus's wand hit the water a fifth of a second faster than the spear of light which left Crystal's fingertips. The water exploded into a fountain of colours, vivid greens, purples and violent reds bubbled like volcanic lava high above the surface.

'Excellent, excellent,' smiled Valentino, showing encouragement and waving his wand to force the spectacular gamut of colours to cease.

'That's not bad for a first attempt and is just what I wanted to see. Right, Niculmus, I think you've got the hang of that. Princess Crystal, however, I feel we should let you try the next spell alone.'

'Please, just call me Crystal,' she blurted, wincing slightly. 'It's such a big mouthful calling me Princess Crystal every time you address me.'

85

'As you wish,' Professor Valentino said, bowing low. 'However, it is your royal title and I must therefore insist on calling you by this, whenever we are not in the classroom.'

'Agreed,' said Crystal, nodding her head several times with enthusiasm.

'Very well,' said Valentino, giving her a light smile. 'Now, let's get back to work.'

Crystal dropped her gaze onto the ancient text and read the words which seemingly moved over the page of their own accord, explaining to her the procedure of casting the next spell. The illustrations blazed with intricate designs and colours until she felt each enchantment appeared to *talk* to her, inside her head.

'Err, shall I begin?'

'When you're ready,' Valentino concluded. 'Think of the fire, think of what you are asking yourself to produce, concentrate and then focus on the flow of your words.'

Crystal took a deep breath.

'Dragart ina mangaee tobacadòir.'

Instantly a dwarfed dragon materialised high in the air, lying in a manger, dressed in a long, lacy nightshirt. A huge, white frilly nightcap fell between its scaled ears, the lace on the bonnet covering a large part of its long face. Crystal couldn't help but burst out laughing and Niculmus failed to contain his own amusement. He put his hand to his mouth to try and stifle the laughter that bubbled in his throat, but couldn't quite manage to stop it coming out.

The dragon, somewhat confused, looked up with startled surprise. Then his image became translucent and the small dragon looked about and grabbed hold of the sides of the crib, his face turning anxious when the crib began spinning like a flicked coin; over and over, faster and faster it flew until the whole illusion spun so fast it shattered into smithereens, sending thousands of red, glittering particles straight into the atmosphere. The professor's hand shot out and he immediately pointed his wand towards the oncoming red fragments. Using his wand like a vacuum cleaner, he suctioned the broken remains of magic out of the air, drawing them straight towards the tip of his wand. The long, red trail disappeared when it reached the stem of his wand. Loud crackles spat and hissed when the wand acknowledged receipt of the defective spell and once all evidence was removed, Professor Valentino looked rather relieved.

'That wasn't, err, quite what I expected!' he stated, trying to stay professional.

'Err, no, not really,' said Crystal, grinning and unable to look apologetic. She looked down at the neatly written set of instructions in her spell book once again and soon realised she had somehow managed to say the words the wrong way round.

'Shall I try again?' she asked, looking a tad sheepish. Valentino nodded.

'Yes, indeed, I think that would be a good idea,' he said, stroking his beard absentmindedly, 'but I think it would be best if you didn't use quite so much enthusiasm this time.'

Crystal caught Niculmus's eye and saw the look of amusement dancing in his dark eyes. She huffed aloud, determined to prove to him she would succeed. She closed her eyes, focusing her mind on the spell.

'Dragart mangaee ina tobacadòir.'

This time only the face of a red dragon materialised high above the water. There was no body, just an enormous scaly head and its firm jaws breathed a long blaze of golden fire. The flames shot from its mouth down towards the water, vaporising the pool in seconds. A loud roar filled the air followed by a stream of intense fire which ravaged the rocks below, causing a billow of black smoke to rise from the cavern floor. Valentino moved with haste towards the dragon; with a flick of his wrist he signalled his wand to put out the fire and the dragon instantly vanished.

'Mmm, you almost had it,' Valentino said, inspecting inside the arc for superficial burns. He circled his wand in the air with the technique of an orchestral conductor and then the pool reappeared before their eyes as if the spell had never been cast.

'Try not to hold the spell for too long next time,' he explained, turning to face the princess with a light smile, 'other than that, you did very well, my dear.'

The rest of the day passed without incident and then the afternoon drifted into their late session with the healer Sawbones, learning the art of creating basic potions and elixirs. They started their first lesson by dissecting a frog, a dead bird and the stems of a few wild flowers. The healer wished for them to understand the serious implications and importance of remembering the powers held inside each revealed ingredient and also the perils of making thoughtless mistakes.

Crystal and Niculmus were then asked to move from the large dissecting table to where a carved pestle sat inside a metre high stone mortar bowl. The bowl had been made from a chunk of grey rock, believed to have been formed by the petrifying tears of an ice dragon many centuries ago. On the rim of the bowl, circlets of facial images of the long-forgotten healers were carved, depicting those who had become legends amongst their own kind. The carvings were exquisite, showing that the ancient stonemasons had been natural, gifted artists.

Niculmus and Crystal tried to keep their distance from one another as they approached the mortar bowl, both acting as though some kind of barrier had been erected between them, their negative energy oozing from their bodies like pus, ensuring they each kept well away from one another. Sawbones seemed oblivious to their rather childish behaviour and was too busy babbling on about how to make the best of limited ingredients, never once noticing how the atmosphere inside his classroom crackled with negativity.

'Of all the potions I will teach you,' he mumbled, breaking berries from a recently acquired stem, 'I have to say that this is one of the most important, you will ever learn.'

Crystal watched him throw the wolfberries together with a handful of cedar shavings and the blood of a sparrowhawk inside the mortar. The pestle mashed the strange ingredients unaided, driven by a simple mixing spell Sawbones used to allow him free rein. The heavy baton crushed what lay inside with purpose, until the herbal concoction became a vibrant, muddy paste.

Sawbones moved closer to his students, his black robe rustling like a gentle breeze when he pulled the dark fabric away from his feet.

'You must always remember, young ones, no matter how badly hurt someone may be, you must never give more than one thumbnail of this paste at any given time, too much is as good as too little and could kill your patient outright.'

Crystal shuddered. She hadn't expected to learn such complex knowledge so early in her apprenticeship. Niculmus, however, soon snapped her out of her train of thought with yet another of his spiteful comments.

'Did you take all that in?' he asked, giving her a scornful smile. 'After all, what I would really like to know is when would a princess who lives in a grand palace ever get the opportunity to use a potion such as this?' Crystal eyed him with a growing distaste and saw the mockery ablaze within his eyes. She knew he resented being with her and she jutted her chin with disdain.

'You don't know anything about me,' she hissed, feeling mounting pressure build behind her eyes. 'You think you're so smart and that you have the advantage over me, well, let me tell you Niculmus DeGrunt, you could not be further from the truth. I realise we have no choice but to study together for the time being, but let's just get something straight, I am not a pushover and I am not afraid of your level of magic, but I am fed up to the back teeth of listening to your nasty innuendoes.'

Niculmus clearly looked stunned at her unexpected outburst but Crystal didn't wait for a reaction, instead she grabbed her spell books and ran from the classroom with Sawbones looking on in bemusement. Crystal lost no time scurrying along the corridor, hitting the main hallway as all the other apprentices spewed from their own lecture halls, heading for the maze of allocated dormitories. Niculmus tried to call after her, his face aghast at his dressing down but the incessant noise of the other pupils drowned his voice out completely. A sudden shout from his new friend, Guylin, caught his attention and brought him back to his senses. He ran over to meet his friend, a wide grin on his face where only a moment ago sat a dark frown.

'Let's get the horses and go for a ride,' Niculmus urged, putting his arm around Guylin's shoulders and giving his neck a sharp tug.

'Ease off,' laughed Guylin, pulling away and staring with suspicion at his friend. 'You're not the only one who's had enough of this place for one day why, there's a whole bloody Academie of us.'

Niculmus shook his head and his smile slipped from his lips.

'I'm not so sure,' he said, heading for the stables, 'I'm beginning to believe things aren't quite what they seem here, and what makes matters worse is that I'm becoming intrigued to the point where I'm going to have to find out the reasons why.'

Chapter 9

Weeks drifted by and Crystal's magic ability and knowledge strengthened with each passing day, but still she couldn't surpass Niculmus's highest level, much to her dismay. They'd finally called an unmentionable truce, both tired of their constant bickering and childish fights, so together they learned the ability of performing enchantments, creating life-saving potions and, most importantly, the art of self-preservation.

Needless to say they still detested one another and Niculmus had never managed to get to the bottom of what had occurred on the night of the festival or the incident in the Great Hall, but like the calm after the storm, peace finally came.

Then something terrible occurred. It happened the day they were sent to the lake of Minerva, a lake renowned for its alluring scenery and its incessant beauty. Magician Phin decided to take them there on a kind of field trip. The weather, although still cold, had changed to calm and so three amiable horses were saddled and Magician Phin and his two students set out on what was expected to be a bit of a treat. The lake was at least a half day's swift ride away and the riders were eager to reach their destination as soon as possible. Magician Phin had changed into a less elaborate robe, poorly fashioned and totally inappropriate for riding, however, both Crystal and Niculmus wore thick leathery trousers and substantial pelts made of fur to help keep the cold at bay. They rode to the west, as a wintry sun tried in vain to warm the hardened earth. The galloping horses grounded their hooves into the dirt and their nostrils flared with exertion and it soon became clear that Magician Phin was no horseman and several times was seen to be lagging behind his students. Crystal, however, couldn't help laughing at his desperate antics, for she had never known anyone look so uncomfortable on the back of a horse before.

Finally, they reached the lake and Niculmus jumped down and grabbed Crystal's horse to steady her. A second later he was holding out his hand to help the princess dismount and she eyed him warily, half expecting him to pull his hand away when she reached out to accept it and was surprised when he held her firm. She followed his gaze when he became distracted by a flock of white swans flying overhead, both lost for a moment by the birds' grace and beauty until he dropped her hand.

Magician Phin arrived at the lake seconds later sounding extremely out of breath, as though he had just galloped all the way from the palace instead of his horse and when he tried to dismount he showed his inability to descend gracefully, almost falling on his face when he got his foot accidentally caught in his stirrup.

'Are you alright?' both Crystal and Niculmus cried out, rushing with sudden urgency to his side. Magician Phin turned bright red and immediately tried to compose himself, shifting his cloak from off his shoulders to allow fresh air to circulate around his neck and throat in the hope it would ease the burning sensation to his skin.

'Oh, please, don't fuss,' he stressed, waving a dismissive hand in the air. 'I have never been one with a horse and I don't think that's ever going to change no matter how much I try.'

Niculmus backed away, moving instead to where a small, green bush sprouted from the ground. He threw his horse's reins over it and watched them sink into its branches before turning and heading towards the water. A moment later both Crystal and Magician Phin stood alongside him. Their eyes drank in the magnificent scenery stretching before them like a lush carpet of green. The lake was nothing less than exquisite. The water shimmered silver and the reflection of the hills and blue sky was mirrored in the perfectly still surface. The lake looked tranquil and at peace with its surroundings, with wild birds filling the air with their beautiful songs.

Magician Phin eventually cleared his throat and said, 'Right, now we have made it here in one piece it's time to learn something new.' He bent down and tried to look under the cold surface of the lake and signalled for his students to do the same.

'You know, Minerva Lake is a very special place and I don't just mean because it's surrounded by natural beauty, although I have to say it is quite breathtaking out here, but because there are rare, magical creatures that live deep beneath its surface.' He gestured for them to take a closer look and both Crystal and Niculmus obeyed; kneeling down beside him, they each strained their necks to stare beneath the lake's glistening exterior.

'What exactly are we looking for?' Crystal asked, unable to find anything of interest. 'I can see a few fat fish swimming about but that's about all.'

'Kelpies!' roared Phin unexpectedly, flashing an excited smile and bending so close to the water she thought he might fall in. 'We're looking for water kelpies.'

Crystal screwed up her nose, obviously none the wiser.

'What on earth are water kelpies?' she asked, sitting on the backs of her legs. She moved her arms behind her, feeling the soft green grass slip between her fingers, enjoying the tickling sensation she felt in the palm of her hand.

Niculmus intercepted Magician Phin's reply.

'Kelpies are a type of faerie horse which live in deep water,' he explained, with a lean smile. 'They are native to the Kingdom of Nine Winters and can be found in only a few other places such as the ice lakes near the Valley of the Green Witch.'

'Oh, they have dragons there!' Crystal beamed, remembering the tournament and what Mordorma had told her about the fire-breathing dragons.

'That's right,' said Phin, looking impressed with her knowledge. 'However, kelpies aren't quite as vicious as those dragons,' he added, encouragingly. He dropped his hand beneath the surface of the water, swishing his podgy fingers through the sweeping grasses as though this gesture would somehow attract the elusive and somewhat shy creatures.

Crystal's eyes shone with expectation.

'How big are these kelpies anyway?' she asked, wondering if they were as large as regular horses. She began shuffling forward, trying to see if she could spot anything remotely resembling anything equestrian floating by.

'They're only about an inch long,' said Magician Phin, lifting his hand out of the water and measuring what he thought was roughly an inch between his thumb and forefinger.

'They're very small creatures and can be hard to spot, but I've brought with me something that may help us to catch one or two. He rummaged through the inside of his cloak until he pulled out something small, wizened and covered in fluff.

'Ha-ha, yes, here it is, a nibble of sweetcorn.'

Crystal burst out laughing.

'I thought I'd seen it all,' she said, light-heartedly, 'but I didn't expect to be catching faeries with a dried-up piece of veg!' Niculmus let out a snigger, unable to suppress his own amusement at finding her comment humorous. Magician Phin eyed them with his own glint of amusement shining like stars in his eyes.

'Oh, ye of little faith,' he mocked, placing the niblet straight under the water. 'You must both understand that you don't always need to use magic to get what you want out of life.' He pulled his concentration towards the job at hand, grinning with unexpected surprise when he found two kelpies already nibbling at the corn.

'Quick!' he coaxed his apprentices, who were spellbound by the little creatures. 'Go and get something I can put them in before these critters escape.'

Niculmus was the first to jump up and, with his wand pointing towards his horse, he mumbled a spell which unfastened the leather strap on his saddle. His water bottle flew to his side and with a quick flick of his wrist he unscrewed the cap which he used as a cup and handed it to the magician.

'Excellent work,' said Phin, pulling his hand from the water and dropping the cube with its newly gained attachments straight into the cup.

'There, what do you think?' he asked, filling the small container with water and then passing his treasures towards the princess. Crystal was transfixed by the miniature creatures floating inside and at first glance thought they were simply tiny seahorses, but then as she studied them further she realised they had small wings where you would normally find fins and she gasped in surprise. Their tails were longer too, reminding her of an electric eel when a spark of light exploded at the end of their silky tails. Their skin was paper thin, showing most of their internal organs and she thought about the giant shrimps she had seen at the local fish market when

94

out shopping with Beatrice, and felt a flicker of homesickness ignite inside her stomach.

'So these are kelpies,' she said, handing the cup back to Phin with a smile. 'So tell me, what's so good about these little creatures?'

Magician Phin looked stunned.

'Why these creatures are the fastest things without legs,' he boasted, looking rather dumbfounded by his student's nonchalant reaction. He had expected the princess to be captivated by their magical abilities but instead, by the look on her face, she was anything but.

'I'm going to show you how to cast a spell which will enable you to ride them like real horses,' he huffed. Straightening his cloak, he puffed out his chest in a manner that reminded Crystal of an overstuffed pig and she managed to stifle a giggle when he walked with a theatrical stride towards the lake, placing the cup and its precious cargo on the very edge. Magician Phin turned and eyed her with a sour expression.

'Niculmus,' he called. 'Hold up your wand for me and Crystal; well, you both know the drill by now,' he said, allowing a hint of complacency to slip from his tongue. He watched his students prepare themselves for the new task and Crystal held her amulet with one hand whilst pointing the other towards the cup.

'Right, now say after me: *Ribin arua puscan uspog!*'

As soon as the words left the apprentices' moving lips the kelpies began to grow at a rapid rate. In seconds they burst out of the cup, snorting and shrieking to one another in their underwater tongue.

'Hurry,' urged Phin when the kelpies reached over six feet tall and looked ready to speed off without a rider, 'jump on their backs before it's too late!'

Crystal and Niculmus eyed one another before they both shot like arrows from a bow, straight onto the faerie horses' grey-black backs. As soon as their backsides made contact with the kelpies' skin, an electrical charge pulsated straight through their excited bodies, causing the hair on the top of their heads to stand, poker straight. As quickly as it came, the current abated and their hair dropped back into place, like a puppet severed from its strings. Niculmus pushed his fingers through his blonde locks, patting his crown as though he expected some of it to be missing, but Crystal didn't care about her hair. She was in awe of the kelpies, watching them grow and grow until they were at least ten feet tall. Having slipped from the lakeside into the water, the huge horses sat afloat its surface like a couple of over-inflated dinghies. Their necks shook with excitement and their long green manes of scaly hair and plankton blew gently in the afternoon breeze.

Then the kelpies whinnied like real horses, their tails spinning with adrenalin and, seconds later, they were racing along the surface of the lake at an astonishing pace. Crystal clung onto her horse's mane as though her life depended on it. Both of the seahorses were using their tails as waterwheels, spinning the external organ at an astounding rate and their tiny wings buzzed like a hummingbird's, helping to keep them well balanced.

Crystal had never experienced anything like this in her entire life, it was the most exhilarating moment she had ever known. Then, out of the corner of her eye, she espied Niculmus coming up on the rear and she cried out for her horse to go faster. She saw his clothes were soaking wet and a continual spray of icy water washed over his face but, just like herself, she could see he didn't care. Rapturous laughter filled the air as both apprentices enjoyed their newfound delights, enjoying the thrill of the chase on the backs of these wonderful beasts.

A long, dark shadow crept over the bright wintry sun, causing a cold chill to fill the air. The darkness spread swiftly, looming over the lake like a thickening blanket but Crystal was having far too much fun to notice. Niculmus was the first to sense that the darkness could perhaps be holding something more sinister and when he realised he was right, he produced a blood-curdling cry. Crystal couldn't hear his stricken shout over the loud noise of her excited horse that was still busily swishing its tail and enjoying watching the waves break over dry land.

Niculmus was dumbstruck, his eyes filled with concern when two gigantic claws shot from out of the heavens, breaking the serenity of the once perfect day. He soon found his voice, screaming a warning to the princess yet again but much to his dismay he saw something swoop low, heading straight towards Crystal. Two hooked claws swung with direct precision and punctured the outer skin of her jacket to take hold of the pelt of fur she was wearing. The powerful sound of a 'swoosh' filled the air and Niculmus watched in horror as Crystal was ripped off the unsuspecting kelpie's back by an enormous bird.

Crystal screamed out in blind panic when she felt herself rising up into the air, her arms and legs flaying in a frantic dance as she rose higher and higher. She flashed her terrified eyes up towards the looming sky and saw two beady black eyes stare intently back at her. The bird flashed its underbelly and chest, exposing a large oval-shaped crest of succulent sulphur, its enormous wings blazing fiery red. Short tufts of brilliant orange lay in its long, tapered tail feathers of gold, causing the bird to look extraordinarily exotic as it soared upwards, towards the mountains.

Crystal tried to judge the size of the bird and calculated it to be at least twelve feet long with a wingspan which covered at least twenty. She thought she recognised the bird from a picture she had seen in one of Magician Phin's antiquated books and believed she was being snatched by what she thought to be a mythical firebird. She forced her tearful gaze down towards the ground and saw Niculmus sitting on his kelpie with his wand outstretched, and Magician Phin looked as though he was frozen to the spot.

Without a moment to lose, she reached up towards the firebird's curved talons in a desperate attempt to free herself but as soon as she tugged at her jacket she heard something rip at the back of her neck. At the same time a bright shimmer exploded high above her head, followed by a kind of wispy noise which seemed to echo forever in her ears and then she was falling, her clothing having finally ripped from the firebird's claws. She screamed with absolute terror when she realised what was happening and she fought with gravity, grabbing in desperation at nothing but air when the whoosh in her ears grew louder and louder until she thought she was going to pass out.

The earth was flying so quickly towards her stricken face she decided it inevitable that she was about to fall to her death. She closed her eyes, unable to summon any powers through fear and she waited for the ground to swallow her whole. A desperate screech somewhere overhead filled her ears, causing her blood to run cold and then there was a heavy thud and pain rippled down her spine and her fingers reached out to find she had landed on the back of something soft and fluffy. Frozen with fear, she only allowed her eyes to open when the smooth rhythm of the firebird's wings flapped in firm, even strokes. She associated the soothing sound they made with riding on her father's back and logic tried to clear her fuzzy brain to enable her to acknowledge that she had miraculously landed in one piece.

Crystal rolled onto her side and looked down to where Niculmus and Magician Phin were now two tiny specks. She thought she could see Niculmus standing on the side of the lake, but she couldn't be sure for she could no longer see his face as he was now a distant blur. Crystal sighed. Opening her mind portal she tried to send a message to him, but the fuzziness in her head was lingering and she fell back into the warm feathers, defeated. Feeling upset and all alone she watched the firebird fly towards the horizon and she cried over perhaps never seeing her friends or family again. Hot tears rushed down her frozen cheeks and Matt's bitter words of warning ran too late inside her frightened mind. She prayed she was not to meet her maker just yet, deeply concerned she would be classed as rich pickings and end up in a nest to be fed to some hungry chicks for dinner, thinking there could be no other reason why this beautiful creature would take her and so she began visualising her flesh being stripped from her bones. After causing herself immense distress, she turned her attention to casting a simple spell which mended her clothing and kept the cold chill at bay. She then dithered for far too long on choosing an incantation which she could use to free herself from the firebird's grasp. Her confidence had been severely knocked and she worried herself silly on which she should use. She was conscious that she must be careful what spell she used because she couldn't just simply make the bird disappear otherwise she would fall to her death and her own demise would be her own doing.

She closed her eyes and whispered words against the cold breeze, her mouth churning out a newly acquired spell which she hoped would change the bird into some kind of giant balloon. She grasped her amulet and prayed she would live to tell the tale and when she finally opened her eyes she was extremely disappointed to find her spell hadn't worked one iota.

Chapter 10

Niculmus and Magician Phin stood in the Queen's private chamber with long, dismal faces and rather bleak expressions. On their arrival back to the palace, Bridgemear had been summoned by the Lord High Chamberlain to speak with sudden urgency to his two despondent subjects.

Niculmus, however, was suffering from delayed shock and Magician Phin, who was of little help or support to him, stood gravely by his side. Since returning from the lake, Phin had seemingly been in a world of his own and had not thought to seek any relevant medical treatment for his pupil or advise him to find any help for himself, his thoughts clearly only of the princess.

In the chamber, Bridgemear soon arrived and the moment he saw the look on Niculmus's face, he felt the blood drain from his own. Magician Phin looked equally grim and bowed low, trying to hide the look of anguish burning deep within his eyes and for a moment Bridgemear felt a stab of pity towards the lowly mage.

The Prince Regent shook his head, looking openly worried at the two men who stood before him like submissive children. Their stature and nervous disposition screamed panic at him and he opened his pursed lips, his mouth ready to fire mild obscenities at the pair as he demanded to know what had happened to his daughter, but then the oak doors were pushed inward and Amella stood blocking the arched doorway.

They each bowed when she entered and Bridgemear walked over to greet her, kissing her quivering fingertips. She forced a smile, her eyes looking lost and wild and her ruby-red lips were seen to tremble. She turned her attention from her husband and rested her gaze on her two loyal subjects before gesturing for them to sit.

'Where's my daughter?' she asked, in an anxious tone when they politely declined her offer. Magician Phin's taunt expression gave her no answers and it was Niculmus who tried to force a reply, however, it was obvious he was unable to form any words in his frozen mouth, forcing Magician Phin to find his voice instead.

'The princess is not here,' he began, allowing a trickle of sweat to run down his troubled brow.

'I can see that, you fool!' Amella snapped, flying to the small sash window and looking out towards the distant mountains. 'What the hell happened out there? You only went out this morning to teach her to ride the kelpies for goodness' sake. So what went so terribly wrong?'

'Princess Crystal was taken from right under our noses,' blurted Niculmus, forcing a step towards the Queen. 'And I think she's been kidnapped by what I believe to be a gigantic firebird.'

Amella spun round so fast she caused a tall, ornate vase of jewel-encrusted water lilies to fall to the ground. The vase smashed by her feet, the water soaking her gown and surrounding her in a rush of sparkling debris. Magician Phin sprang to her side and dropped to his knees, picking up the large broken pieces of crystal which lay dangerously close to her majestic feet. A jagged piece of glass slipped in his trembling hand, slicing open his thumb. He cried out at being so clumsy, cursing his own stupidity when his blood oozed onto the cold, stone floor, allowing the jarred fragments to shine as red as rubies.

'Leave it!' Bridgemear insisted, his face turning ashen and he pulled Amella away, wrapping her protectively in his arms as though to keep her safe. His eyes suddenly searched out Phin's.

'You were supposed to be looking after our daughter,' he flared, 'we trusted you with her safety and this is how you repay us.' Phin blanched and Bridgemear saw the look of raw pain swell in his round eyes.

'My lord, it all happened so fast,' Phin rushed, his voice sounding high pitched as he forced his throat clear.

'It's true,' Niculmus conceded, unable to stop himself from interrupting. 'One minute we were riding the kelpies as part of our training and the next, this enormous firebird appears from nowhere, swoops down as fast as lightning and takes off with the princess.'

'Why didn't you try and stop her?' Amella suddenly screeched, pulling away from Bridgemear's grasp and moving closer to magician Phin, trying to lay the blame at his feet. Her eyes bore into his while she searched his grim expression in the hope of finding an explanation there.

'We did try!' said Magician Phin, sounding desperate. 'We managed to cast a spell which tore her bonds from the firebird's talons, causing her to fall from its grasp, but the firebird was too quick and immediately dive-bombed the sky, recapturing Princess Crystal by catching her on its back. Before we had time to cast another, they were both so high in the heavens only the gods could save her.'

Amella stared at him in disbelief. The anguish shown on her beautiful face was unbearable to see and Phin couldn't stand to see her pain a moment longer and immediately pulled back towards the shadows.

'We must send out a search party,' said Bridgemear, taking charge. 'I will go with them and we will not rest until our daughter is found,' he added, shouting for one of the soldiers to take word to his Captain of the Guard.

'Who will you take with you?' Amella rasped, returning to his side and clutching his arm for support. She began to cry, immediately hiding her face with the back of her hand and on seeing her tears Bridgemear reached out and touched her face, his fingers brushing them away.

'Do not weep, my love. I promise you we will find her. Unfortunately my blood brothers have gone in search of Elveria so I need to take two of our best men instead,' he said, producing a cloth and drying her eyes. 'I will take Arhdel and Amadeus. They know Crystal better than anyone and they are the best trackers we have. I will send a messenger forthwith telling them I will meet them at their base camp,' he added, breaking his gaze from his beloved and studying Niculmus's face instead.

'You will come too,' he said, reading the look of anguish on the young apprentice's face, 'but understand this: you are not to blame for what happened today, it's clear you did your best, I could ask no more of you. I feel my daughter's kidnap has been caused by another's hand and there was nothing either of you could have done to stop this terrible event from occurring.'

'Elveria!' gasped Amella when his words sank like quicksand into her brain.

'No, Amella, we don't know that for sure,' said Bridgemear, putting a gentle finger to her lips to make her fall quiet, but his eyes told her something different.

'Of course it's Elveria, who else could it possibly be!' she insisted, pulling away from his touch. 'We all know firebirds don't just swoop down willy-nilly and fly off with real live people. They are mythical creations; therefore, I want to know how was something that isn't real able to take her from us?'

Bridgemear suddenly leant back, supporting himself on the oaken door frame. He looked into his wife's face and knew the words she spoke held more than a spark of truth. Niculmus and Phin exchanged wary glances, but none dared speak. It was as though the prince and their Queen had forgotten they were in the room.

The next thing, Bridgemear stormed out of the chamber and the Queen dismissed Niculmus and Magician Phin with a wave of her weary hand, ordering Niculmus to wait in his quarters until a message was sent to him that the horses were ready to ride. Niculmus rushed to his dorm, ripping his smelly clothes from his body as soon as he had the chance. He washed away all the stubborn traces of ground-in dirt and dried algae which had stained his flesh. He scrubbed so hard he turned his skin raw but he didn't care, the burning pain made him feel he was suffering a well-deserved penance as he tried to obliterate the condemning evidence which lay so obvious on his skin, telling of his inadvertent involvement with the now missing princess.

Eventually he dressed in fresh, clean clothes and then moved to the sanctuary of his bed where he sat quietly, waiting to be summoned by the Captain of the Guard and when Guylin came in some time later, he found Niculmus to be hunched over and fast asleep.

Guylin was surprised to see his friend sleeping at such an odd time of day. He sat on his own bunk and pulled off his heavy boots. The smell of sweaty feet made him wrinkle his nose and he tossed the boots to the other side of the room to get rid of the offensive odour. Niculmus stirred, causing Guylin to jump up and bounce over to his bed.

'Hey, what are you doing?' he asked, slapping Niculmus playfully on both cheeks. Niculmus awoke, startled by the blows, blinking back into consciousness as he wondered who was stupid enough to have dared to hit him.

'Oh, it's you,' he said, letting his head fall back onto the pillow, 'I almost forgot for a moment where I was.' The morning's events flooded his brain and painful memories of Crystal's abduction swamped his thoughts.

'What's wrong with you?' Guylin persisted, when Niculmus refused to take the bait and retaliate. He continued to slap his friend's face and upper body, trying his best to goad him into a fight but eventually he gave up, sliding back to his bunk when Niculmus continued to push him away. He eyed Niculmus sulkily before grabbing a clean pair of socks from a small cloth bag he kept at the foot of his bed and putting them on.

'I wouldn't have expected you back from the lake until at least dusk,' he said, stretching a woollen sock over his toes. 'So, are you going to tell me why you're back so soon?'

Niculmus noticed a bitter flavour forming in his mouth and he brushed his tongue over his teeth as though this would wash the vile taste away. His hand shot behind him and he reached for his pillow, his fingers clasping the soft, cotton case and he drew it over his face. The sudden lack of oxygen made him feel like he could escape from what was certainly the worst day of his life. For all that he didn't care much for the princess he had never wanted anything bad to happen to her, yet here he was, caught up in an unexpected tangle of suspicious circumstances.

Then Guylin was standing over him, having snatched the pillow away and he stood staring down at his friend with obvious concern. Guylin reached down, pulling at Niculmus with his strong arms, forcing him to sit up.

'Tell me, what did you do?' he pleaded. Niculmus jumped to his feet and smacked his hands away, his face contorted with guilt. He started to search for the right words, something that would resemble an explanation but instead he heard the Captain of the

Guard shout his arrival. The soldier's leathery face, tanned from many years of exposure to the sun, eyed him with open distaste when he entered.

'It's time,' he bellowed towards the apprentice, his voice sounding harsh and impatient. 'Come on, let's go.' The soldier stood tall and erect, blocking the small doorway with his solid frame, his calloused hand holding on to the hilt of his sword as though he would draw it and stab Niculmus if he didn't do as he was told there and then. The Captain of the Guard cleared his throat before he continued.

'You are to go to the armoury and collect a sword. Once you have one in your sweaty little grasp you are to meet the Prince Regent in the courtyard.'

'W-w-what have you done?' stammered Guylin, as his grey eyes grew wide. 'Niculmus, tell me, are you in some kind of trouble?' Niculmus's tongue lay quite still and Guylin continued to stare from one face to the other, hoping that someone would give him a clear and simple answer, but neither would yield to his plea.

'I'm ready,' stated Niculmus, ignoring his friend and grabbing his cloak and small hunting knife. He found he was unable to look Guylin in the eye so he marched off after the Captain, his footsteps echoing along the cold stone floor but as he walked he was unable to shake Guylin's intense stare, burning like fire against his back. He felt a mind link tap inside his head and he immediately blocked it like a dam halts a moving river. He understood that Guylin wanted to know what he had seen, but he couldn't face telling anyone, not even Guylin, not until he helped unravel the mystery concerning the missing princess. He heard Guylin call to him once last time and then he was turning down a familiar corridor and onwards to where his friend could no longer reach him. He relaxed his shoulders, moving his neck from side to side to ease the tension which was building. He headed for the armoury and once he accepted his sword he moved on and entered the courtyard and mounted his horse. Bridgemear was already there, waiting for him at the large main gates and Niculmus was surprised to find they would not be riding with an escort.

There were no pleasantries said when he approached the Prince Regent, instead the gates were forced open and the elite magician cried for his horse to make haste and ride like the wind. A silver-grey moon hid behind a constant stream of thinning cloud, Niculmus rode next to his master, his mind in turmoil as he worried about meeting the two most infamous warriors, Arhdel and Amadeus, for the very first time.

Chapter 11

The cave was scarily dark when the Windigo finally entered it. As he climbed into its long, sneering mouth, he cautiously moved his hands over the cold, damp surface of the ragged walls and felt a bleak and uninviting coolness penetrate through his calloused fingers. Unexpectedly, he stumbled. Bone weary from such a long and dangerous climb, he sat on a little shelf of stone, thankful there was at least somewhere for him to rest his tired bones for a moment and so he plonked himself down, relieved to find a place in which to gather his somewhat jangled senses.

It had been a very hard climb, even for someone with his many years of experience, for as soon as he ascended the rock face, the dark, orange stone crumbled under his heavy, cumbersome feet. The sheer weight from his body had caused the rocks to break away at every given opportunity, falling straight into the river which ran below him in a swell of pale chocolate. Unperturbed, the Windigo carried on, his strong fingertips gripping yet another precarious ledge and he forced himself on, pulling his huge body further away from the sanctuary of the canyon floor and closer to his final destination.

His journey had been fraught with hidden dangers from the very beginning, the climb not only treacherous, but renowned to conceal vicious mountain trolls and malicious magic folk who were more than happy to make his already miserable life less bearable should they manage to capture him. He was aware of the consequences awaiting him if he was spotted in their territory, but he cast these frightening thoughts aside, focusing only on what he had been asked to do.

He had found the cave many moons ago when forced to hide from his father and recently decided that this place could perhaps serve a more useful purpose. A large, ghastly insect with two flat heads and rounded eyes buzzed past the entranceway and took the Windigo completely by surprise. He sucked in his breath, afraid he had been seen and he gulped in air like a stricken goldfish until his lungs were almost bursting, then he exhaled sharply, causing snot to run down his chin. He sniffed and then wiped the river of slimy mucus from his face with the back of his hand. Eventually his courage returned and he was able to scoff away any trepidation which lingered in his mind and so he shuffled uncomfortably on his cushion of broken rocks to head for the back of the cave instead.

His large frame, thick and solidly built, had made the stone shelf collapse under his weight. His upper torso was as broad as a small oak tree and his hands were as huge as metal coal shovels. He pulled himself to his feet, the exertion causing his chest to expand like a huge balloon and his large bare feet crushed the dried leaves trapped beneath his toes into nothing more than minute particles of dust.

He was dressed in clothes familiar to the mountain folk, a light brown tunic worn like a dress with a little coarse beading sewn sparsely around the slit of fabric, which allowed his fat neck to protrude. He wore no trousers at all and he placed a small bag made of animal fur which had been slung over his shoulder to the floor whilst his strong arms searched for anything he could use to build a fire. He collected dried branches and wispy leaves which he found huddled together in small dirty piles, brought in from the heavy winds of time.

His naked arms were covered in thick black hair, almost on the verge of an animal's coat and the hair on his head was severely matted and long. His ears were long too, almost like a hound's, and he stopped abruptly to listen to the unfamiliar echoes bouncing along the hollows of the empty cave as he snapped each branch into manageable pieces.

The Windigo set about lighting a small but adequate campfire, making himself warm and chasing the chill from the night air. Night was fast approaching, but his eyes didn't struggle with the darkness. He stared out towards the mountains and watched the birds which flew by day abandon the darkening skies. As the fire crackled and shrivelled the thin pieces of tinder to nothing more than charred remains, he felt a ripple of expectancy grow in the pit of his stomach. Becoming restless, he moved away from the flames and out towards the mouth of the cave, looking towards the invisible horizon and across the night sky, watching the stars which had broken out in to a light dusting of sparkling glitter twinkle as they permitted the half-moon to surface amongst them like a phoenix rising from the ashes.

A few hours later, the Windigo felt a shiver run down his spine when he spotted the silhouette of a large bird cross the surface of the moon and he immediately fell back into the safety of the shadows. For a moment he felt anxious, his heart thumping like a beating drum in his chest and his eyes twitched as he unconsciously brought his large fingers to his mouth like a child who was about to be chastised for doing something wrong. He wasn't the brightest of creatures and could at times become fierce through ignorance or through feelings of inadequacy, but at this moment in time only the fear of the unknown lingered.

*

Up in the sky, the firebird began to lose momentum and circled the air like a feathery predator. Its beady eyes searched for the entrance to the cave and the bitter mountain air brought with it a fine drizzle which helped to dampen Crystal's already flagging spirits. The huge bird started to descend from the sky, the moon illuminating its path and then a sharp cry pierced through the canyon and the bird swooped closer to the cave's awaiting mouth.

Startled, Crystal gripped the bird's neck feathers tightly within her fingers when it suddenly turned a swift thirty degrees. A strong undercurrent rose from the canyon floor and the firebird lunged forward, pinning its wings back and nose-diving straight into the cave's entranceway. Uncertainty filled Crystal's heart when the bird flapped and fluttered in the air, causing her mouth to turn instantly dry. Then came a shrill cry of warning as the bird landed and Crystal found she was genuinely frightened when the dark walls enfolded her like a ready-made coffin and she squeezed her eyes tightly closed, petrified.

Eventually, after several minutes, she was brave enough to open her eyes and peek. She blinked, trying to clear the dazzling stars that exploded in front of her eyes and once they became accustomed to the gloom she spotted light shadows dancing along the ragged walls and the smell of an open fire made her nostrils flare. She instantly felt confused, undecided whether she should feel relieved or frightened at the thought that someone else was also in the cave and, with mounting trepidation, she guardedly climbed down from the firebird's back. Its soft plumage yielded to her as she swung her legs from off its body and she held the feathers tight before dropping onto the ground, thankful to feel the earth beneath her feet once more.

The bird gave an unexpected sweet trill, as though in way of an apology for bringing her to this godforsaken place and Crystal reached out and stroked the spiky golden feathers that sat like a glorified crown on the top of its head. She eyed the bird thoughtfully, both curious and concerned as to why it had brought her here and when the bird looked as though it was about to drift off to sleep, Crystal dropped her arm and slid her attention to the glow from the flickering flames instead.

With small, calculated steps, Crystal drew closer to the beckoning warmth, her footsteps silent as she approached and she was unable to stop herself from shivering when the heat finally touched her damp skin. She reached out her frozen fingers, desperate to feel the warmth from the golden flames but suddenly a large, black shadow loomed over the surface of the cave and covered her face in darkness.

Crystal screamed in terror and immediately turned tail and fled back to the firebird. A dark silhouette hurried after her, its long, flaying arms waving in the air like a giant ogre's and in seconds she was climbing up onto the firebird's back, desperate to flee from the terrifying monster, but the firebird refused to budge an inch.

In desperation, Crystal grabbed hold of her amulet, gripping it with both hands and she pressed her tongue to say an enchantment but before she could utter a single word, two strong arms enfolded her, gripping her waist as easily as a boa constrictor coils itself around its prey. The clench was so tight she felt her lungs deflate, and then her mind went dizzy through lack of oxygen and darkness lurked in every corner of her subconscious.

'Don't be afraid!' boomed a panicky, male voice in her ear, 'I promise, I won't hurt you!'

Unable to reply, Crystal felt a whoosh of sweet air pour back into her lungs and she coughed and spluttered involuntarily when the two great arms which had been wrapped around her cautiously loosened their grip. She pushed them away feeling fur under her fingertips and she raised her arms to protect herself, waiting for a succession of fatal blows to rain down on her head and kill her. Seconds ticked by and when nothing happened she eventually lowered her arms to see the face of a monster staring intently at her. The terrifying face which was dominating most of her air space was the hairiest thing she had ever seen and she couldn't stop the blood-curdling scream falling from her stricken lips.

'Please, I beg you, calm down, I'm really not as scary as I look,' said the monster, shoving his enormous face even closer to her own as though this would pacify her. He shook his head and scratched his temple with frustration.

'I knew you would scream to the high heavens when you first met me,' he said, sounding irritated that he had been right. 'That's why I had the firebird bring you way up here, where no one can hear you.'

'Who are you?' she finally rasped, unable to turn her face away. 'You're not like anything I've ever seen before.'

'I'm a Windigo,' said the monster, hanging his head low.

'A what?' Crystal exclaimed, unconsciously raising an eyebrow.

'A Windigo. A type of changeling.'

Unexpectedly he reached out and picked her up in his arms like she was nothing more than a rag doll. Crystal kicked and screamed for him to put her down, but he ignored her rantings and took her to where the fire still crackled with life. He then placed her feet on the ground as though they were made from fine bone china.

Crystal's mind raced ahead as she tried to remember what Magician Phin had taught her about changelings. Her brain searched the dark crevices of her stored memories, her eyes suddenly widening when she remembered that a changeling could only morph into one other being.

'If you're a Windigo, would you mind if I ask what you actually change into?' she asked, trying to keep a safe distance.

'Why, all Windigos change into timber wolves,' he replied, sounding somewhat surprised that she had to ask. 'I thought everyone knew how there are only two types of wolf in this world, Windigos and Werewolves.'

'What! Are there werewolves here too?' Crystal gasped, when the light from the flames bounced wickedly in his eyes and she felt a moment of panic return.

'Of course not, silly,' he chuckled, giving her an unexpected grin. 'Why, they've been extinct for over a thousand years.'

'Phew, that's a relief,' Crystal said, genuinely thankful. 'So tell me, Windigo, will you be changing any time soon?'

'The usual time, midnight,' he answered, looking at her from out of the corner of his eye.

'Oh, I see,' said Crystal, nodding her head thoughtfully. 'May I ask how long you stay like that?'

'Till dawn,' the monster told her, his tone matter of fact. 'And may I take a moment to ask you if you have finished your interrogation?'

Crystal pulled a face and smiled sheepishly, realising she was being rude. She thought he somehow reminded her of a character from a fairy tale and 'Jack and the Beanstalk' flashed into her mind. He was so huge that she thought he looked like an ogre, only hairier, yet somehow this made her fear of him abate.

'Can I ask if you have a name?' she probed, dropping to the floor and pushing her hands towards the tiny blaze, enjoying the welcoming tingle it brought to her numb fingers and she looked up at him with expectation dancing in her eyes.

'Of course,' he said, taking her cue and forced his large frame to sit crossed-legged on the floor. 'Those who know me call me Clump.'

Crystal threw a quizzical look straight at him.

'Is that your real name?' she asked, in wide-eyed surprise.

'Yes it is,' Clump huffed, unable to hide his annoyance. 'Why, what's wrong with it?'

'Why, nothing at all,' she answered, sounding apologetic. 'It's just that I've never met anyone called Clump before.'

Clump sniffed dismissively and Crystal moved a little closer to the fire.

'My name's Crystal,' she explained, feeling she should somehow introduce herself and show she hadn't meant to hurt his feelings.

'Indeed, I know who you are,' Clump said, turning his head and staring into the flames and its golden glow appeared to make his dark eyes turn to liquid.

'Oh, so how come you know my name?' she asked, feeling the heat from the flames begin to penetrate her skin.

'Oh, I know lots about you,' Clump said, turning a beady eye to look at her, but before she could question him further, he was reaching for his bag which was resting against a rock. He delved inside, his large hands searching deep within until he brought out three shiny fishes. The firebird suddenly squawked quite noisily from her resting place when she spotted the tasty supper and Clump immediately jumped up and took the largest fish over to her.

'You deserve it, my girl,' he told her, patting her lightly on the head. 'You have done well to bring Crystal here, safe and sound.'

'Mmm, does that mean there is something you should be telling me?' Crystal asked, watching the firebird swallow the fish in one huge gulp. 'Like, for instance, the reason why I've been kidnapped and brought to this place?'

The Windigo turned stealthily, gesturing for Crystal to come over and stand by his side.

'Much as you may not believe me, I'm truly not here to harm you,' he said, stroking the firebird with such gentleness Crystal found herself drawing closer.

'You see, she will only live for a short time longer before the spell which created her diminishes and she disappears forever,' he continued, sadly.

Crystal watched the firebird preen herself like some kind of overgrown cockatiel. The bird pulled at her beautiful feathers with her large black beak, straightening her sulphur-coloured crest before moving down the length of her body until she was pulling at her smaller tail feathers, nipping them repeatedly until a feather was dislodged and fell to the ground. The Windigo patted the bird's neck and then he bent down to retrieve the orange-coloured feather. He offered it to Crystal.

'She wants you to have this,' he said, holding it up to the light. Crystal shook her head, realising that the feather would most probably remain long after the firebird was gone.

'Just take it,' the Windigo insisted, stretching out his hand. 'The tail feather of a firebird is very special, for it will light up like a thousand candles if you rub it between your thumb and forefinger.'

With some reluctance, Crystal accepted the gift and when she looked down she saw a shimmer of magic shoot along the quill.

'Thank you,' she whispered towards the firebird, stroking the soft plume and playing with the fringe of barbules. 'It's very kind of you to give me such a wonderful present and I promise I will use it wisely.'

The magnificent bird cooed in acknowledgement and then both Clump and Crystal left her side and headed back towards the sanctuary of the fire. Clump placed more wood on the flames and then roasted the remaining two fish deep inside the red hot embers and by the time they were ready, Crystal had to admit she was starving.

It wasn't long before they had finished eating and Clump somehow produced fresh water. Whilst he was pouring her a drink, Crystal asked Clump why she had been taken.

Clump stopped what he was doing and his face turned serious.

'I don't know if you are aware but there are people who wish to see your family dead because of what they have done and I have been ordered by those who wish only to protect you to take you to the Stannary Mines of the Lost Trinity where we must try and locate the Book of Souls. You see, if we manage to obtain the ancient tome we may be able to stop a terrible injustice occurring.'

'I've heard of the Stannary Mines,' Crystal blurted, visualising her mother's pretty necklace. 'But tell me, Clump, why is this book so important?'

The Windigo's demeanour appeared to sag and he started playing in the dirt, clearly delaying the moment he would have to tell her.

'It's a very long story,' he said, when he caught her staring at him from the corner of his eye. 'Do you really want to hear it?'

'Of course I do!' Crystal cried, in exasperation. 'If this book is so important that someone is willing to have me taken from my family, then I need to know why.'

Clump nodded and his eyes glazed over.

'Many centuries ago, when the world had fallen into desperate times, there were four newly appointed magicians who became frustrated by their leader's weaknesses and inability to help those who were less fortunate than themselves. They each decided to search for the infamous sorcerer, Merguld, a very powerful magician who lived alone in the forbidden mountains for all of his three hundred years.

'The four magicians travelled together, enduring many dangers along the away and fighting to stay alive, each convinced that he alone would be the one to have his wish granted by the powerful mage. On arrival the first mage found Merguld to be in good spirits. The young magician declared his wish to live forever so that he could oversee his people for all time, explaining he wished to take those who supported him from the darkness into the light.

'The second mage standing by his side and who was already a revered warrior explained to the sorcerer how he wished to stand taller, demanding immense power far beyond his young years so he could win any battle he should ever have to face and therefore protect his people until he had created a better life for everyone.

'The third magician pushed the second mage aside, stating how he should have wealth beyond reality, believing money and jewels would change the world he had seen grow poor, explaining how his fortune would influence his people and eventually see him become the greatest leader of all.

'The fourth mage shook his head with despair for he had a good heart and cared about all walks of life. His only wish was to provide any deserving creature with enough food and shelter to help wipe away what had become a miserable existence in his realm and wanted a place where he could build more dwellings for those who feared destitution.

'The sorcerer, amused by the misconceptions of youth, agreed to strike an unlikely bargain and told each mage he would indeed grant each of them their wish. In return they must repay the mage by giving him their soul on their death. Each magician, desperate to fulfil his destiny, agreed to the sorcerer's outrageous demands including the magician who believed he would live forever and Merguld gave them each a small leather pouch, telling them not to open it until they reached their homeland …

114

'The first mage became impatient almost as soon as he mounted his horse and left the others as they travelled on home. He desperately wanted to see what was inside the pouch, unable to wait until he reached his own realm. The magician opened the leather purse as soon as he was alone. The moment he untied the strings he immediately turned to stone, becoming a large grey boulder perched on the slope of a mountain and there he sat for thousands of years, longer than the life of anyone born before him.

'The second mage also became impatient and rode off on his horse to hide within the seclusion of the trees. As soon as he opened the leather pouch he turned into a pine tree. The pine tree is the tallest tree of all, taller than any other and very strong and to this day the lonely mage can be found somewhere between the high ridges and if you listen hard enough you may hear him whispering on the wind, bragging about how tall and fierce and strong he is compared to all the others.

'The third magician had grown greedy for what lay inside his pouch and he too pulled on the strings and placed his hand inside. Immediately gold and jewels poured like a fountain from his pouch and he laughed loudly when his hands grasped a multitude of gold coins. He pressed them to his chest in a considerate embrace until he was forced off his horse when they grew too heavy for him to carry. The gold continued to spew over his feet and he fell to the ground when they became crushed from the sheer weight and he found his trembling fingers were unable to close the pouch to stem the flow. The constant stream of gold and jewels continued until he was finally buried alive, unable to move until he suffocated, entombed in a mountain of his own greed.

'The fourth mage did as he was told and went straight home and only then did he open the leather bag. He found it to be empty and was extremely disappointed but then he heard voices and the voices whispered many words of wisdom inside his head. He realised the best way to succeed as a leader was to listen to others and he became perceptive and astute. He learned how to care for those in dire need due to his immense commitment to his people and in time he became known to be the greatest ruler that ever lived. Many years later Merguld paid the fourth mage a visit and told him he had come to claim his prize by taking his soul. The magician was now much wiser and pointed out that when they struck the bargain Merguld had never stated that he wanted his soul for all eternity and therefore he would keep his promise as long as he could return should storm clouds gather over his people in the future. Merguld was overwhelmed by his wisdom and eventually agreed, impressed by the mage's loyalty and dedication even when facing mortality. Then, time and tide passed by and Merguld's magic book, which held the four souls, was eventually lost when the Green Witch destroyed the powerful magician and took the mountain for herself.'

'Wow! That's such an amazing story,' Crystal said, trying to digest it all and understand its meaning. 'So, what do we actually have to do?'

'It's simple, we have to find the book and then *you* have to awaken the fourth mage.'

'Me!' Crystal declared, her eyes rounding in surprise. 'How the hell am I going to do that?'

'How should I know?' Clump shot back, shrugging his shoulders and pulling a sour face. 'The only thing I can tell you is that it is imperative that we find it sooner rather than later.'

'How come you know so much about all this?' Crystal asked, turning suspicious. She reached out and grabbed a handful of tinder, trying to mask her mistrust. She sprinkled the few dried twigs over the flames and the heat soared, casting a golden glow over Clump's face.

'Everyone knows about the Book of Souls,' Clump said, turning doleful. 'The difference is, not everyone knows where the book's been hidden.'

'I thought you said the book was lost,' Crystal insisted, feeling pressure build between her eyes, 'something to do with a green witch and the taking of a mountain?'

Clump instantly grew defensive.

'Now look here, Princess. I don't pretend to have all the answers, those who are much wiser than I have watched your family over the past few months with growing concern. All I know is that I have been given the task of helping you travel to the Stannary Mines in order to seek out what is surely to be your family's salvation.'

Crystal fell silent, realising she had been given a quest which was bordering on impossible. She didn't believe for one moment that they would ever be able to find the Book of Souls even if Clump believed otherwise. Her mind travelled back to Matt and the warning he had given her before she had so thoughtlessly abandoned him and guilt flooded her mind as she admitted to herself that if she'd stayed away like Matt advised, none of this would be happening right now.

With startling clarity Crystal saw that everything which had come to pass over the last couple of days was all of her own doing. She felt the tears of comprehension fill her tired eyes and the Windigo looked startled when she started to cry.

'Tell me, Clump,' she sobbed, 'who is it who wants to see us dead?'

The Windigo shifted uncomfortably on the floor, clearly rattled by her tears.

'I'm afraid to say that there are many who wish to see your kind gone, but there are more who wish to see you stay. However, it is unclear as to who the actual ringleader could be.'

'Is it Elveria?' she finally blurted, wiping her tears away with the back of her hand, 'is he behind all this?'

'The great wizard?' asked Clump, raising a hairy eyebrow in surprise. 'I truly don't know,' he told her, shaking his head in bewilderment. It was his turn to reach out and throw a little tinder onto the fire and it hissed when it made contact with the flames, sounding like mockery against his soulful expression.

'We must concentrate only on finding the Book of Souls,' Clump insisted when the noise finally died away. 'Without the book, we will not see a new dawn of time.'

Crystal gasped out loud.

'I think I understand why you're asking me to come with you, but if we are lucky enough to find the Book of Souls, I fear I will not know how to awaken the fourth mage. However, one thing is for certain, if I make it out of this mess alive I will leave this world and never return.'

The Windigo looked horrified.

'No!' Clump declared, startling her. 'This isn't the reason why we need the fourth mage, we need you here and you must stay with us for all time.'

Crystal shook her head repeatedly.

'No, I won't,' she said, showing him she wielded a stubborn streak, 'I should never have returned here in the first place.'

The Windigo dropped his head and then, as if to change the subject, he said, 'Crystal, you must try and get some rest. You have suffered a very traumatic day and I have no choice but to leave you 'til dawn.' He reached into his bag and pulled out a rather tatty looking blanket.

'Here, take this,' he said, throwing it to her, 'go and make yourself comfortable close to the fire and I will see you in the morning.'

Crystal screwed up her nose when the smell of oily fish reached her nostrils and the sight of what looked like dandruff turned out to be a gathering of tiny, white fish scales embedded between the woven fibres.

She grasped her amulet and pushed out her hand in the direction of the floor, mumbling a common spell which produced a small hammock covered with a very clean looking blanket. She smiled with satisfaction before handing back the blanket.

Clump looked very impressed with the hammock.

'That's a great idea,' he said, walking over and giving it a nudge. He drew back when the hammock swung towards him and he giggled like an excited child. 'I would like one of those,' he said, his eyes igniting with longing, 'but not now, because I have to be on my way,' he added, his smile disappearing as quickly as it had come.

Crystal watched him leave with a slight feeling of apprehension, yet she knew she had the firebird for protection for a little while longer at least.

'I'll be back to make you breakfast,' Clump promised, heading towards the awaiting night. 'Sleep tight, Princess,' he chuckled lightly, 'and don't let the bed bugs bite!'

Crystal rolled her eyes at his attempt at humour, listening instead to his heavy footsteps as they faded away when he began to make his descent. Silence soon engulfed her and so she snuggled down into her bed and allowed her mind to trace over the last few hours and what was turning out to be a very eventful day. She thought of her parents and how upset they would be when they finally learnt of her kidnap and she unconsciously played with the bangle her father had given her. Stroking the smooth metal gave her a rush of comfort and she wished she had locked a memory inside the butterfly's abdomen so that she could use it to console herself. Her eyes grew heavy, but sleep wouldn't come to her. She tossed and turned for most of the night, causing her to wrestle with her blanket when she couldn't get comfortable, until the firebird squawked a warning of the Windigo's return and she realised she hadn't slept a wink all night.

Chapter 12

The weather was turning cooler as the day progressed and Arhdel and Amadeus sat waiting on their horses as a strong wind licked with malice against their hardened skin. The news of the princess's abduction had already reached their ears and both were upset by the knowledge that this incident could not have been foreseen. Arhdel, although known at times to be fierce, suffered Crystal's abduction in stony silence, however, Amadeus appeared unable to hide the fear that was growing inside him with each passing hour.

A bloodied sun was setting on the horizon and a beacon was lit in camp to destroy the darkness which came to wash away what was left of the daylight. Arhdel kicked at his horse and urged her to gallop away from the continual drone of uneasy soldiers and Amadeus rode by his side, his horse just as fast, both heading towards two approaching riders with haste and equal speed.

Bridgemear gave a wave when he recognised the two warriors and he stole a look at Niculmus, who was now predictably silent. The mage let out an unexpected cry when the Queen's two most devoted elves pulled their horses to a halt.

'I'm sorry we have to meet through such incomprehensible circumstances so soon,' Bridgemear stated, allowing his horse to drop its head and munch the rich grassland by its feet. Arhdel appeared to flinch at his words and Amadeus grasped the hilt of his sword and a nerve was seen to twitch at the side of his temple. A horse snorted and Arhdel pushed forward, pulling off his leather glove to offer his hand to the Prince Regent; the mage accepted his gesture by grabbing hold of his opened fist and he welcomed the warrior like a brother.

'Who is this who rides with you?' asked Amadeus, throwing Niculmus a suspicious glare. The magician turned in his saddle and saw his apprentice squirm under their watchful gaze.

'Why, this is Niculmus DeGrunt, our most promising apprentice and one of two people who witnessed Crystal's abduction,' Bridgemear explained, flicking his hand in the boy's direction. The two warriors nodded looking thoughtful, greeting the apprentice with the patience of those who found it hard to tolerate the young.

'Welcome, young pup,' said Arhdel eventually, remembering his manners but unable to show any enthusiasm. 'Sire, let us get back to camp where we can feed your horse and perhaps sit and mull over what might have happened to our princess.'

Niculmus betrayed no emotion as he watched Bridgemear nod his agreement, but uncertainty showed in his eyes. Amadeus kept staring at him for the longest time, a hard smile playing along the corners of his mouth. Suddenly a loud cry left his lips and a sharp kick from his boot spurred his horse into a gallop as he headed back to camp.

The others followed him, each riding with the stature of those carrying a heavy burden and much later, when the horses were stabled, they were shown to a large stone hut set against a clearing and as soon as they entered, Niculmus was asked to tell the warriors what he had seen happen to Crystal.

The two warriors sat pale faced around a hardy table. The stone wall situated behind them was covered with a giant banner and a large ceremonial tapestry of the Royal Emblem of Nine Winters adorned its centre. The realm's strength was depicted by a magnificent image of a huge golden dragon and it was covered with a thick dusting of pure, white snow along its back, head and tail. The dragon was holding a mighty sword in one large claw and a cluster of nine giant icicles in the other. The colours held within the ice were rich and luscious, a fruitful and significant gesture made to show the wealth and prosperity believed to be held within the realm of Nine Winters.

The noise of low-ranking soldiers who were bustling in and out of the hut carrying large platters of food and heavy jugs of wine broke the tense atmosphere and Bridgemear grew impatient, signalling for them to leave and only the wine was encouraged to stay.

Niculmus watched Bridgemear cast a spell which prevented those loitering outside to be able to eavesdrop on their conversation. The apprentice grew nervous when three sets of eyes turned their attention towards him, their intensity already boring deep into his skull. He felt like each pair of eyeballs was trying to burrow into his confused brain in a bid to find vital fragments of information which he may have unconsciously omitted.

Eventually Arhdel took out a pipe from his pocket and began to chew on the slender mouthpiece as though he had a piece of nut in his mouth that he just couldn't seem to get rid of. He listened to what Niculmus had to say and once the apprentice finished his tale he shook his head in dismay.

'Unfortunately your version of events doesn't really tell us anything we don't already know,' he said, puffing on his pipe. His voice sounded troubled, held an edge, but then he was coughing repeatedly when the smoke suddenly went down the wrong hole and started to choke him. The warrior turned a strange shade of purple when the coughing fit refused to ease and he grabbed his wine, gulping the rich, dark liquid a little too quickly.

The air brushed Niculmus's cheek and his startled eyes saw Bridgemear rush to Arhdel's side and he was slapping him hard on his back. There came a splutter of objection before Arhdel finally managed to control his breathing and soon after became recomposed. Throwing his pipe to the ground, he moaned about the harmful effects of smoking, refusing to relight his pipe when Bridgemear bent down to pick it up from the floor, thus causing the mage to chuckle.

Wiping his streaming eyes, Arhdel then said, 'Right, let's get back to the matter at hand. The only thing we have to go on is the direction in which the firebird flew off. No one has used such profound magic in centuries, yet why a firebird when they could have so easily used a dragon? None of this makes any sense to me yet the firebird must be a clue in itself.'

Bridgemear touched Niculmus on the shoulder and he turned like a startled deer towards the towering mage. Bridgemear smiled down at him, pointing to his empty cup and gestured for him to have it refilled. Niculmus's cheeks burned with embarrassment and he immediately declined, causing Bridgemear to shake his head and turn his attention towards Amadeus instead.

Amadeus was busy running a distracted hand through his thinning locks. He pulled his hand away from what was left of his greying hair to accept Bridgemear's offer of a refill and once his cup was almost brimming over, he took three large gulps to empty the chalice and then replaced it back onto the table.

'It's clear to me why the kidnappers used a firebird,' said Amadeus, wiping the corners of his mouth with the tip of his finger. 'I believe the reason why a mystical being was chosen was because it cannot be traced.' Bridgemear's eyes fill with doubt, but before the mage had time to contradict his suspicions, Amadeus added, 'As far as I can see, it stands to reason that if the kidnappers had used any other creature, let's say for arguments sake a dragon, then we would have known by its species where it had come from or at best we would have been able to track down its master. All that aside, I think we should concentrate less on the mode of transportation and instead find the firebird's destination. All we know for sure is that it was heading north and up towards the mountains. The questions we should be asking now are, why and who could possibly want Crystal who lives in the north?'

He turned and faced Bridgemear and was relieved to see the mage appeared to be pondering over his suggestions. Amadeus didn't waver having grabbed the magician's attention so he continued to explain his theory.

'Right, let's look at the facts. Bridgemear, didn't I hear you say earlier that both Amella and your band of mages have been unable to locate Crystal through any magical abilities?'

The mage nodded, the light in his eyes diminishing and only the look of raw pain appeared to linger there. Bridgemear let out a groan and he threw a punch. The crunch of stone filled the room when his knuckles penetrated through the wall and small pieces of rubble rained down towards the mage's feet when he reclaimed his fist, the debris pouring to the floor like a roughly-made crumble topping.

Amadeus gasped in surprise.

'Your Highness, calm yourself! I know nothing is making any sense for there has been no ransom note or outrageous demands set against the realm for Crystal's safe return, therefore we can only presume that whoever has captured the princess must want her for her powers, just like last time.'

Niculmus's ears pricked up as he digested the last sentence, unable to find the courage to ask Amadeus what he meant by, *'just like last time'* and his curiosity ignited.

Bridgemear was seen to bristle at the warrior's startling words.

'That is not the truth of it,' the mage declared, slamming the jug down so hard on the table Niculmus suspected it would leave a permanent imprint in the wood. 'However, there's something I need to tell you all. I have recently learnt that the Elders have decided to contest Amella's new constitution accepting Crystal as our daughter and therefore stopping her becoming the rightful heir to the throne. They are afraid that we have now set a precedent which will allow other, shall we say, less popular species to spawn what the Elders believe to be monsters and therefore in time create an abomination which will bring utter chaos within our realms.'

Amadeus's eyes flared with fury.

'This is nothing more than propaganda!' he roared, kicking at the table in frustration. 'Why must the Elders always go to the extreme?' he demanded, unable to contain his anger any longer.

'This is one can of worms I had hoped would never be opened,' Bridgemear sighed, trying to keep a grip on his sanity. 'We simply have to look at the few threads of evidence we have managed to gather and try and find a solution to all this mess.'

Arhdel sank back wearily into his chair, the expression of unease sat thickly on his rugged face.

'I have never been known to be a clever elf,' he stated in what could only be described as a gritty whisper, 'but I can always tell when I smell a rat!'

'Whatever do you mean by that?' asked Niculmus, suddenly finding enough courage to speak. His words tumbled out from his mouth before he had time to think what he was saying and then looked a little sheepish when Arhdel stared at him as though seeing him for the first time.

'What I mean, my boy, is that there's more to this plot than first meets the eye. This revolt within the Order of the Guild and the disappearance of both Crystal and Elveria makes all this a little too hard to swallow for my liking.'

Bridgemear winced at the sound of Elveria's name, causing all but Niculmus to think back to a time when the elder mage had tried to take both Bridgemear's daughter and his lover away, all in the name of justice.

'I think we should call it a night,' said Amadeus suddenly, when he heard a stifled yawn escape from Niculmus's languid mouth. 'At least let us get some rest and then we can make haste first thing in the morning,' he declared, pulling on his cloak and then throwing Niculmus his own.

Bridgemear nodded, pouring the last of his wine down his throat.

'You're right, it's late and the mountains are not too far from here. I have already sent Mordorma, Amafar and Voleton in search of Elveria in the south and they are willing to travel into unknown territories if the need arises. I have given them seven days to find him or abandon the quest. Come, let us go to our beds, for I wish for us to make an early start in the morning. The sooner we pick up my daughter's trail the better.'

'Very well,' said Arhdel, pulling himself from his chair, 'we have at least formed some kind of plan, if not a conclusion this night.'

They each nodded their farewells and made for their beds, the spell protecting them from any earwigging was lifted and they walked into the darkness, simultaneously stretching their necks and shoulders to allow the weariness and tension knotted within their muscles to unravel like thick rope.

Niculmus followed Bridgemear to his tent, noting his master's mood was dark and his eyes unreadable.

'Sire, I was wondering,' said Niculmus, when Bridgemear was about to bid him goodnight, 'if you wouldn't mind shedding some light and telling me what all this secrecy is about surrounding Crystal's past?'

Bridgemear stopped dead in his tracks and his shoulders were seen to stiffen. His stature changed to one of authority and a look of caution swept over his face as easily as minute particles of sand sweep over the silent dunes.

'The princess has suffered in ways far beyond your imagination,' the mage said, his eyes turning defensive. 'Those terrifying events of which I cannot bring myself to speak of must stay buried because I never want Crystal to be haunted by such horrific memories ever again.'

'Err, why yes, of course, Your Majesty,' Niculmus acknowledged with obvious confusion. 'Please forgive my impertinence for I truly did not wish to interfere in matters that are clearly not of my concern. It is just that I wish to understand the princess a little more and perhaps find a connection with what has happened to her now with past events. Again I apologise, sire, for being so bold and bid you goodnight.'

Bridgemear watched his apprentice rush from his side like a scalded cat and for the first time acknowledged the boy's sensitivity. The boy was clever too but Bridgemear's main priority was to protect Amella and Crystal and if possible lay the past to rest in the deepest grave imaginable. Yet hadn't Niculmus been unwillingly drawn into events which may well have been created through these lingering threads and which stopped the past from being severed altogether? Furthermore, perhaps Niculmus was right, perhaps he should be told of what happened to the princess previously.

The mage mulled over these thoughts and once inside his tent washed his hands and face in a large stone bowl, pulling at a fresh, clean towel from a carved, wooden perch. He scrubbed his face hard, hoping he would somehow erase the painful thoughts which bounced inside his head and tormented him so, but instead all he did was rub his skin too hard and turn it rather red.

Three memories came to him when he lay in his bed. The first was of Crystal when she entered the tournament, her head held high and her emerald green gown blowing gently in the wind, her smile radiant, her happiness so clearly obvious.

The second was of Amella pleading to him to return with their daughter, her face glistening, wet with tears as she refused to come to terms with losing her daughter yet again.

He felt a sob escape from his throat when Elveria somehow barged his way into his mind, a distinct memory of the elder wizard rising to the surface of his subconscious, demanding a brutal punishment and forcing the Guild to make a terrible decision concerning his child. He had hated Elveria ever since that very moment and in time come to realise he'd made a powerful enemy. He lay there unable to sleep, the last few days playing on his mind like a continual un-erasable tune.

He shifted onto his side, tossing and turning on his makeshift bed, realising the dawn would soon be breaking and then he would ride with purpose into the open arms of uncertainty. He was not afraid, but conscious that they were each going into unknown territory. A small bird started singing somewhere in the distance but its continual chirping and happy trill grated on his nerves until he pulled his covers over his head to drown out the noise. Without success, he closed his eyes and tried to force sleep upon himself and when dawn broke, he fell into a fitful slumber, only to be woken by the loud cry of the soldiers as they made their way to breakfast, eager to discuss the reasons why their Prince Regent had seen fit to intercept their camp.

Chapter 13

Elveria stood over his moonwater font waving his long, bony fingers in the air as though he was conducting his own private orchestra. He swayed to and fro, his eyes closed, and he performed a ritual which made the silver liquid inside the bowl pool beneath his fingertips.

He took a deep breath, the cold air infiltrating his ancient lungs and a bone-rattling shiver shot unexpectedly down his spine. He felt the menace of old age knocking at his door, but he pushed his unwelcomed guest aside, concentrating only on the spell he wished to perform. Magic rose like thunder clouds inside his mind and he clicked his fingers and produced a single white feather which he dropped inside the font with a flick of his wrist. He watched in fascination when the silver liquid broke over the snowy plume, drowning the quill and eliminating it immediately from his sight.

He suddenly glanced up and gave a soft whistle, low and tuneless, and a fluttering noise filled the air. Out of the gloom a barn owl flew and headed towards the magician. The mage lifted his arm and the owl's wings were seen to dip in the air and the bird hooted softly as it landed in a flurry of feathers onto his master's shoulder. Its white, heart-shaped face with its brownish edging looked superior against the magician's dull blue robes and for a moment Elveria was disgruntled.

The magician cast his gaze downwards. Dipping his hand inside the moonwater he caught two drops of silver on the tips of his fingers and with a flourish of his hand, he dabbed them straight onto the owl's eyelids. The bird ruffled its feathers and spun its head twice in surprise but once it stilled, its wide, rimless eyes clicked open like a camera lens to reveal to his master a vision.

The wizard gazed into the bird's large retinas, watching the darkness lift and show, instead, bright, colourful images which were somehow less pictorial than reality. He drew closer, captivated by what he could see and he was surprised to learn that Bridgemear and his entourage were leaving the comforts of camp and heading towards the distant mountains of the Green Witch. This revelation sent him awash with ecstasy and he laughed so much he was soon bordering on hysteria. Spittle left the corners of his mouth and his eyes shone with euphoria borne from the owl's unexpected reveal. He'd already heard the darkened whispers regarding Crystal's kidnapping and secretly thanked those with unknown faces who were unwittingly helping him. A moment later, the picture was washed away and the owl's retinas returned to black and so the mage shook the bird free, watching it fly back into the darkness from which it came.

The magician threw his hands up in the air and beacons of light flooded his refuge. Forged under the earth at least a hundred years ago when he had been foolish to believe he could one day be the ruler of Raven's Rainbow, he saw a domain fit for a king. He clucked his tongue in the roof of his mouth, his mind drifting to another time where his dreams had seemed a reality and although they appeared to have diminished somewhat, he still believed he held the key to unlocking his own future. However, now that it was no longer a secret as to how he felt about the Queen and her offspring, he decided he would stay underground for a little while longer. This had been a decision he readily accepted knowing what would be in store for him should he have the misfortune of being found by those who wished to see him punished. Yes, some would say he had turned against his own too, but it was all for the greater good, of that he truly believed.

He called out for a servant to attend to him and a small, wizened dwarf appeared in a flash by the doorway.

'Send a hawk with a message to the Wanderer,' said Elveria, his face set as hard as flint. 'Tell him the time has come for him to put my plans into action.' The old dwarf acknowledged his command with a nod of his greying head and immediately left the chamber, heading as instructed straight to where the magician kept less practical familiars and his everyday beasts. He soon reached the chamber, which was a warren of dark alcoves and small burrows and in each one sat something magical.

The dwarf moved to a small wooden table and grabbed the tinniest of parchments. His gnarled fingers snatched a feather from the solitary inkpot and he wrote the note with an indiscernible scribble before placing a metal ring around an awaiting hawk's leg. He quickly took the bird down a passageway which had a multitude of long, dark pipes running horizontally. The pipes had cast iron flaps moulded onto their outer casing; these were the portals which allowed those underground to materialise into the upper world.

The dwarf stopped at a particularly well-worn flap and his spare hand searched for a key which was lost somewhere within the ripped lining of his pocket. He hunted high and low until he was fortunate to locate it in the hem of his clothing. He quickly unlocked the flap, letting it fall from its resting place and the hawk shrieked loudly when it fell with a mighty clang.

'No need to be frightened,' the dwarf assured her, stroking a mass of light-brown chest feathers. The bird looked back at him with small, anxious eyes and the dwarf continued to pet her when he shifted her carefully inside the portal.

'Off you go and deliver your master's message,' he instructed. 'The sooner you get going the sooner you'll be back,' he added, closing the little door with a flick of his hand. A green and orange flame burst inside the pipe and then the bird was gone.

*

Moments later in nearby woods, the hawk stretched her tawny feathers, having settled on a nice, thick branch. Her beady eyes scoured the open countryside, wary of possible predators, before flying into the direction of the distant city walls.

The Wanderer was just leaving the warm confines of the Stumble Inn when the bird of prey cried out for his attention. He immediately went on high alert and his eyes blazed with concern, searching for any tell-tale signs which signified that someone else had also witnessed the hawk's cry. His sharp eyes watched the bird circle overhead and he unconsciously pulled at his recently acquired cloak as though to make himself less visible. Even though his clothes were well worn and twice owned, there were enough bare threads left to help him keep warm and not look as though he was suffering destitution.

He was a noticeably thin elf, scrawny and pale skinned and his face always looked undernourished. His eyes were colourless like his soul and he licked his lips nervously when the hawk continued to circle over his head. Eventually he held out his stick of an arm and whistled. In a second the bird was there, resting its claws in his hand and he wasted no time untying the strings fastened around its leg and with some difficulty pulled out the parchment from inside the protective cover. Once the message was retrieved, he shook the bird free from his grasp as though she was carrying some infectious disease and he ran like the common thief he was into the darkest confines of a corner.

His heart was thumping when he opened the parchment, his hands refusing to keep still. He read the note twice over before stuffing it deep into an inner pocket and checking to see he wasn't being watched. He dropped his head, his mind suddenly full of scheming plans and devious tricks against the powerful wizard who was ordering him to do his bidding. He could feel nervous energy mixing with his adrenalin and treachery simmered in the pit of his stomach. He admitted to himself that he feared Elveria, forged from the wisdom of his own life experiences of dealing with those who lived only for their own gain. He sniggered inwardly, readily accepting he was just the same, but there was one thing that made him far greater than his peers and that was his own pyramid of vile greed. He felt a strange sensation quiver over his body, like someone was walking over his grave and he gave an immediate shudder. He slunk away; a black cloud of cunning shifting somewhere behind his eyes.

Suddenly he felt unwell and a dull ache filled his chest as though something was gripping his heart and trying to stop it from beating. The pain was so excruciating that beads of sweat poured down his face and the Wanderer fell to his knees, unable to breathe. As quickly as it came, the pressure around his heart retracted, causing the Wanderer to heave a river of vomit all over the ground. He lay there for several minutes trying to clear his head and get to grips with what had just happened and then it dawned on him that he had just suffered a warning left by Elveria. Anger ignited inside his dark eyes and when the pain finally ebbed away, it was replaced by nothing more than cold resentment.

He became furious. There had been no reason for Elveria to show him his superiority in such a way and the Wanderer suddenly sprang to his feet, wiping his mouth and chin clean with the back of his sleeve. He looked down to see a sickly stain forming on the front of his shirt and his eyes blazed with hatred. Reluctantly, he made for the edge of the city instead of his den as instructed, the warning from Elveria still burning in his chest like a sizzling branding iron. He had no illusion who was the master and who was the unwilling servant here, acknowledging that he would never be able to shed the magician's grasp until his wishes were totally fulfilled. He realised how stupid he had been to agree to the magician's terms and that he had bitten off more than he could chew. He rubbed his sweaty palms over his chest and thought of his master's persuasive techniques.

Without another thought, the Wanderer made his way to a common blacksmith's stables. There a horse was saddled and awaiting his arrival and the Wanderer clutched the sword, the hemp bag and the lantern which had been left by the stable door. He had been given everything he would need for his journey, without reason or explanation, but he was well aware he would find out soon enough. When the darkness of the trees enfolded them both, he rode away from the city and never looked back.

Chapter 14

The new morning brought with it a warm but clouded sun. Crystal kept the fire alight all night and when the darkness drew to a close, she waited patiently for the golden embers to mellow and the Windigo to return.

When Clump finally reappeared, his bag was filled with fresh supplies and he busied himself preparing breakfast as promised, giving Crystal a hot brew which he made using specially prepared herbs. Crystal took the small, wooden cup from his large hands and sipped the hot liquid, feeling the benefit of its warmth seep through her fingers. Its flavour reminded her of mid-summer and the mild aroma of blackberries mixed with orange blossom coaxed her senses to remember a far sweeter time than this.

Clump sat passively whilst he prepared his meagre offerings of wild berries and a flowery cactus. Crystal watched with open curiosity when the Windigo delved inside his bag and pulled out an array of primitive tools. His large hands curled around a spindly looking object and he drew it out of the bag like he had found something precious.

Crystal pulled a surprised face and the light in her eyes danced with amusement.

'I wouldn't have thought now was a good time to start combing your hair,' she declared, screwing up her nose and pulling her lips into a grin. Clump looked down at the comb he was holding and then glanced at her as though she had gone quite mad.

'Oh, is that what you think it's for?' he asked, flicking what was left of its teeth. He tried to rake his fat fingers through his matted locks, wincing when he got them caught in a spiral of knots.

'Think I'm well past a bit of light grooming,' he said, with a hearty chuckle. 'No, I have a much better purpose for this utensil today.'

Crystal looked at his dishevelled appearance and decided he had probably never swept a brush through his hair in his entire life. She made an instant decision that when they had more time, she would work hard on untangling his coat.

Clump continued his work by washing both his hands and the comb in a little water. He picked up the cactus, careful to keep his fat cumbersome fingers well away from the long, prickly spines and, grasping the comb, raked the cactus in a downward motion along the main shaft of the plant. Some of the spikes broke off but the fruit hidden behind them popped off the stem and become trapped between the teeth. He made a simple skewer from a small branch and placed the fruit over the fire to cook until the rest of the spines hanging on the fruit turned black and charred and eventually broke away. He wiped the last remaining remnants with the flat of his hand before peeling off the scorched skin and roasting them over the fire a little longer. Crystal watched with widening eyes, fascinated by how easily Clump prepared the alien dish.

'Here you go,' said the Windigo, once the fruit had cooled. Crystal hesitated, staring down at the burnt orange pieces and unconsciously screwed up her nose. Clump made a sound that could have been a whimper and when she looked up, she saw hurt welling in his eyes and so she held out her hands and received the small bounty with a gracious smile.

'I've something else for you to try too,' Clump mumbled, producing a rich cluster of red winter berries. Their colour was vibrant against the dull shade of his clothing and she found herself reaching out and brushing the plump, fat berries with her inquisitive fingers.

'Wow! They're a really good size,' she announced, sounding rather impressed. 'Why, I've never seen berries that big before!'

She saw Clump's chest swell with pride.

'You have to know where to look,' he told her, tapping the side of his nose. He started to count the small heap of fruit to ensure his guest received enough to satisfy her hunger. Once he was happy with his two piles of red, he stuffed the rest of his cactus into his mouth followed immediately by the juicy red berries, slurping noisily when a burst of sweetness poured down his throat.

134

Unlike Clump, Crystal ate her cactus like a timid mouse, nibbling the cooked fruit with extreme caution. She resisted swallowing for as long as possible, her taste buds trying to decipher the unusual flavour. Eventually the signal sent to her brain told her the cactus had a similar taste to the humble artichoke which made her feel that this strange dish was not one she would have chosen for breakfast herself. She finished her meal off with the sweet tasting berries and noticed how they helped to quash the odd tanginess which was lingering in her mouth.

'What type of cactus have we just eaten?' Crystal asked Clump when a trickle of berry juice slipped from the corners of his lips and down onto his chin.

'It's a type of Cholla cactus,' he said, wiping his mouth with the back of his hand and them smacking his lips together to emphasise his enjoyment. 'There are many types of cactus growing wild around these parts but the one we have eaten today is definitely the most nourishing.' Crystal was impressed at how much knowledge he had about the wilderness, grateful to have eaten something seemingly nutritious even though it was playing havoc with her digestion.

'It's time for us to be on our way,' Clump said, suddenly kicking at the last of the embers with his bare feet and choking them with dirt. He gathered the few items which had been left about the cave, refilling his bag and then he headed straight towards the firebird.

The bird was seemingly still sleeping and Clump commented to Crystal that the bird's feathers were starting to fade, their colour no longer rich and vibrant, but pale like pastel shades of summer. Crystal agreed, stroking the soft plumes with tenderness.

'We must hurry if we wish to ride her,' Clump said, producing a handful of dried seed and sticking it unceremoniously under the firebird's beak.

'I'm ready when you are,' Crystal acknowledged, clicking her fingers to disperse the hammock. 'I think you're right, we shouldn't linger any longer than we need to.'

The Windigo shook the few bits of seed about in his hand and nudged the firebird awake. Once she had eaten and became more alert, Clump held out his hands for Crystal to use as a step. The princess didn't waste any time climbing aboard, settling on the bird's back with the Windigo soon at her side.

'To the Valley of the Green Witch!' shouted the Windigo and within a blink of an eye the firebird was dropping like a stone from the cave's mouth and heading straight for the canyon floor. She stretched out her huge wings and soared through the air like a majestic token of the sky, causing the wind to trill through her silken feathers. They flew towards the horizon, the morning sun slowly rising in the sky but after only a few miles the firebird started to shriek in distress.

Crystal felt a violent shudder vibrate beneath her and to her horror the bird started falling from the sky at a tremendous rate. Within seconds parts of the firebird's abdomen and one of her wings broke away from her body and Crystal screamed in terror.

'She's breaking up!' the Windigo exclaimed and Crystal turned to see his face was deathly pale. 'We just have to hold on as best we can and if we're lucky we'll make it to the canyon floor before she disintegrates altogether!' he bellowed.

Sure enough, seconds later they crash landed and the firebird gave a shriek of what was to be her final cry before she shattered like glass right before their eyes.

For a moment Crystal just lay there, stunned. Eventually she sat up, feeling shaken and concussed amidst an array of sharp rocks and huge clumps of brushwood. She looked about her, rubbing her eyes fiercely when she suffered a bout of double vision. She gave herself a moment or two until her eyesight was back to normal and then pulled herself to her feet. Moving stiffly over the monotonous, stony ground, she scanned the rocky area and noticed the terrain was arid and very dry compared to the Kingdom of Nine Winters.

Crystal brushed herself down with the palm of her hand and was relieved to see she had landed without breaking any bones. She was sad that the firebird was gone but her attention turned to Clump who was crying like a baby and so she rushed over to his side, thinking he was hurt.

'No, I'm alright,' he bleated when she lifted his tear-stained face to see what was the matter. He wiped his snotty nose with a rather dirty looking finger and then proceeded to clean it down the front of his tunic.

'It's just that I never got to say goodbye,' he sniffed and Crystal felt a stab of sympathy for the soft-hearted Windigo. She put her arms around his slumping shoulders and hugged him tight in the hope it would help soothe him.

'I understand how you feel,' she said kindly, 'but at least you got to meet a firebird, which is more than most can say.'

Clump nodded and his tears began to subside.

'You're right,' he said, pulling up his legs and hitching himself from the ground. 'She's the only one who has visited these lands in over five hundred years and another may not come again in our lifetime.'

Crystal pulled her lips into a sad smile, throwing her head and forcing her red locks to dance away from her face. From the corner of her eyes she spotted Clump's bag lying behind a large, discoloured stone and she left his side, heading over to collect it.

'Where are we?' she called out, grabbing the thick strap and shaking the dust and grains of dirt from it. Clump stumbled forward, taking the bag from her when she thrust it into his large, hairy hands. His attention turned towards the horizon and then it looked by his expression that he was debating which direction they should travel. He lifted his strong arms and shielded his eyes from the blinding sun, screwing up his lids when the sun tried to penetrate too deeply.

'Thankfully we are only just outside the Valley of the Green Witch,' he said, throwing the bag over his shoulder and holding onto the strap. 'I'd hoped we would have been able to travel much further afield but alas, I didn't realise the firebird would vanish quite so soon.' He pointed way beyond the distant mountain range to where swirling clouds of blue-white mist covered the skyline.

'We must keep travelling north until we reach the other side of those mountains,' he explained, starting to walk as the crow flies. He turned to see if Crystal was close on his heels and he called for her to follow when he realised she was messing about in the dirt and loitering.

'Once we have made it over the mountains, we should find the opening shaft which will take us into the Stannary Mines,' he said, looking down at her and Crystal placed her hand in his.

'We'll make it,' she said, trying to entwine her slim fingers between his extremely fat ones. 'You know we have no option but to succeed.'

All of a sudden Clump leapt several inches into the air.

'Ouch! That hurt!' he cried, bringing his fingers quickly to his lips. A powerful charge had shot through his fingertips when she touched him, causing him to blow on each of his fingers until the pain subsided.

Crystal looked down at her hands and started to mumble an apology, unable to understand what had just happened.

'Wow! That was a very powerful surge of energy that just ran through my hands,' Clump puffed, clearly shaken. 'However, we are easy game in these open spaces and the fact that your magic is uncontrollable at times will only bring us unwanted attention.'

The Windigo turned tail and headed for a cluster of tall, spindly pine trees. The dusty, dry soil ran like a river between their skinny trunks, stopped only by a spiky growth of brushwood. The wind carried the scent of dry earth and sagebrush in the air and Crystal's gaze wandered over towards the horizon and a shiver ran down her spine when she saw only miles and miles of desolate landscape.

They walked on with little conversation because the wind kept snatching their words away like a spiteful ghoul, but it wasn't long before Clump sensed they were not alone and his demeanour changed and a low-throated growl left his shuddering lips.

'Stay here!' he commanded. His wet nose twitched and he sniffed the air when he caught a faint whiff of scent. He raced off at considerable speed considering his size, slipping through the trees and was soon out of sight. Crystal watched him leave her with a stab of unease. Grabbing hold of the amulet for protection, she waited for the Windigo to return whilst anxiety churned her stomach into knots. She understood the laws of these lands which forbade anyone using powerful magic but she knew without question that she would not hesitate to use it should the situation arise. The day was beginning to turn into night and with it the sound of the wild became more prominent. She sat under a tree with her legs drawn up to her chest, resting her chin on her knees, hoping Clump wouldn't leave her alone for too long. The temperature was dropping and for the first time Crystal was grateful she was still wearing her winter pelts.

In the distance, a branch snapped underfoot, grabbing her attention and Crystal quickly scrambled to her feet. She felt a wave of relief wash over her when she saw Clump appear through the trees heading towards her, but soon realised he was not alone.

'There's nothing to fear,' Clump reassured her, when he eventually arrived at her side. 'Please, let me introduce you to Bruis who is a plainwalker,' he said, giving her an encouraging smile which made his eyes crease up at the corners.

Crystal tried not to stare at the stranger who had the weirdest eyes ever.

Bruis was a thin, willowy man with black wavy hair that covered most of his equally dark face. His skin was chocolate brown and his eyes were the shape of almonds, their colour almost milky white, as though they had been carved from two chunks of cream ivory, his chromosomes somehow forgetting to create black pupils to break up their startling milkiness. On his chin sat a thin, ropy beard, the colour of dulled snow and it somehow looked odd set against his dark skin. His clothes were made from a simple weave, the cloth having been roughly cut and the hem of his garment was raw with a multitude of dangling threads which looked like a thick fringe against his bare legs. In his hand he held a dark rod made from the finest acacia and Crystal thought it looked very majestic.

'Why, I didn't know it but Bruis has been following us ever since we *landed*,' Clump chuckled, patting the plainwalker on the back and Crystal decided they were most probably old acquaintances.

Crystal held out her hand in greeting.

'It's a pleasure to meet you,' she said, shaking his hand and giving him a weak smile. However, Bruis didn't smile back.

'I'm afraid to say that you shouldn't linger here for it is far too dangerous,' he replied, looking sombre.

Crystal shot an uncomfortable expression at Clump and swiftly let go of the stranger's hand.

Clump cleared his throat and his own expression turned serious.

'Bruis is a very good friend of mine and has offered to give you shelter for the night,' he told her, putting his arm around her shoulder and ushering her further into the trees.

'Bruis has a hidden camp just over a quarter mile from here where I know you will be safe and well protected.'

'But what about you?' asked Crystal suddenly, unable to hide her concern. 'Aren't you going to come with us?'

Clump looked a tad doleful.

'Have you forgotten that I'm a changeling and have no need of a bed?' he asked, and his eyebrows appeared to knit together. 'I will go with you as far as the camp, but then I must leave you until dawn. I will go and find myself some food, for to stay close to the camp once I have changed into a wolf would be foolish for everyone. You have to understand I will not remember who you are and therefore I could attack you on sight.'

Crystal's eyes gleamed with perplexity. Although she understood Clump's shocking dilemma, she also realised she hadn't digested the true fact of Clump's transformation into a timber wolf. She'd only known him for such a short time yet she had never thought about him being capable of actually harming her. Clump saw the bewilderment in her beautiful blue eyes and he outwardly cringed.

'It can't be helped,' he shrugged, grabbing hold of her arms and gently pulling her to his huge chest. He hugged her affectionately, which was something which didn't come easily to the Windigo, and Crystal began to giggle when the thick, dark hairs which protruded from his tunic tickled her nose.

'I am trying to understand all this,' she whispered, eventually pulling away from his strong embrace and taking a step back. She stared at the awaiting plainwalker.

'Alright, let's go, before I change my mind,' she said, and Bruis pointed towards a copse of trees. They all moved as quickly as the terrain and Crystal's legs would allow. The plainwalker was seemingly concerned that they would not reach his camp before nightfall but with much persuasion to the princess to hurry, they eventually reached the edge of the canyon. The ground had become far less baron and tiny green shoots with clusters of common wild flowers were sprouting over the once bare terrain in little tufts.

Bruis walked towards a large, grey boulder and struck it several times with his acacia rod. He took a step backwards and then the stone began to shudder and the earth beneath their feet trembled with agitation. As Crystal watched, a revolving circular matter formed where the boulder had stood firm. It made a strange gritty sound as it gyrated to form two thick layers of ghostly mist, the pale mixture moving in a gentle circular motion as it expanded until a tunnel of silvery white appeared.

'You will be safe in here,' said Bruis, gesturing for Crystal to enter the tunnel. She felt her throat go dry and she looked back at Clump for reassurance.

'It's just until tomorrow,' he mouthed, shooing her inside the tunnel like a disobedient cat. She tried to protest, feeling the pressure of his huge hands on her back and then her feet were sliding in the dirt as she continued to resist. He gave her a little push and she shrugged his hands away from her back and stomped inside. The mist enveloped her like a soft, fluffy cloud and she brushed the soft consistency with her fingertips, smiling when a wet sensation ran down her hand like rain. She turned to face Bruis when she found Clump to have scurried away and whilst her stomach danced with the fear of the unknown, she crossed into another's domain, aware that there were yet still more magical experiences for her to explore.

Chapter 15

Amella waved an acknowledgement to Professor Valentino who was just leaving the dining hall of the Academie. It was noisy inside the hall with many of the apprentices enjoying a hearty meal with their newly acquired comrades.

'Your Majesty!' Valentino called after her, rushing to her side. 'Have you heard any news?'

She turned her gaze towards the magician, noticing how his steps were not so quick as they once had been. She had always seen him as a tower of strength and a loyal confidante, but now all she saw was a very old magician with worry growing in his eyes.

'No, I'm afraid to say, I've heard nothing,' she sighed, smiling weakly when the Professor squeezed her hand. A hungry student, late for his supper, hurried on by, taking them both by surprise and the magician immediately dropped his hand from hers, hiding it somewhere inside his sleeve. Once the apprentice passed by and was well out of earshot, Professor Valentino tried to reassure the Queen of her daughter's imminent return.

'Just give them a little more time to find her,' he said encouragingly. 'You know they won't give up until they do.'

Amella nodded, but this time she broke his gaze, settling her eyes on the many young elves who seemed content to be living within the confines of the palace walls, oblivious to her own painful dilemma.

'It appears our apprentices have settled in well,' she mused, changing the subject and watching the late apprentice place himself alongside his pals. The tables were laid with succulent meats and an assortment of delicious cheeses and shelled nuts. Stewed apples and pears sat in deep serving vessels and wild cherries, gooseberries and plums were immersed in their own syrupy juices with voluptuous moulds of jellies lying in abundance for the apprentices to eat at will.

'Yes, indeed, Your Majesty,' Valentino interjected, enjoying the delicious aromas that hung heavily in the air and his nostrils inhaled deeply. He shifted his gaze towards the mountain of goodies and stroked his beard wistfully. 'I have to say it looks as if we have many good students this year and I hope to see quite a few do well in the ways of magic by the end of term.'

Amella looked pleased, nodding her approval and then a loud noise caught her attention and she turned quickly to see Mordorma, Voleton and Amafar making their way through the hall. A hush swept over the students when the magicians moved towards the Queen and Amella felt her heart skip a beat. The three mages rushed down the marble corridor, their powerful bodies charged with hidden urgency and their faces were set like stone.

Mordorma was the first to cross the hall and address both the Queen and the professor.

'Your Majesty,' he began, 'Professor Valentino. I'm sorry for the unexpected intrusion but I'm afraid we must talk in private and I think that Professor Valentino, who is your closest advisor, should be privy to what we have to say.'

Amella instantly paled.

'Very well,' she said, heading away from the dining hall. 'I think you had better follow me.'

The band of mages stayed tight-lipped as they walked close behind her. The two soldiers on sentry duty bowed as they opened the library doors to their Queen and she signalled she did not wish to be disturbed when the doors were closing behind her.

'What is it that is so urgent? Have you found Elveria?' she asked, moving towards a table and arranging four drinking vessels. She poured a golden liquid into each vessel before offering one to each mage in turn. 'Please, all of you, be seated,' she commanded, waving her hand rather insistently.

Mordorma obliged and sat close to the fire. The chill wrapping around his body would not leave him and the heat of the flames seemed unable to penetrate through to his skin. Amafar and Voleton were just as dismal, looking as though a cold blade of steel had sliced through their guts and both refused her kind invitation with a respectful shake of the head.

Mordorma took a breath.

'No, unfortunately we haven't found Elveria, but on our journey we met one of the members of the Guild, a sympathiser to the crown, someone it seems who fears you are about to be unjustly treated. We met Lord Kane and he told us some very grave news. The news is this, the Inquisitor's spies have learned that a common elf woman has conjured a relationship with a lonely land dwarf and rumours are rife that she is now with child. It appears the blame for all this has fallen at your feet because of what you did in the past and it has therefore been ordered by the Guild that you should be taken into custody as you yourself have broken ancient laws by marrying a magician.'

Amella looked back at him as though she had been physically slapped. Her lips were drawn back and her eyes flashed with indignity.

'These accusations are totally preposterous,' she cried in her defence. 'I am the Queen of Nine Winters and therefore it is within my rights to change the laws of this land as I see fit. It is the Guild that has overstepped their mark and they should be thrown into gaol due to their disloyalty to the crown, not me,' she hissed dangerously.

Amafar shook his head at her words and Voleton placed his goblet on the ornate mantle, placing himself directly in full view of the Queen.

'Amella, it's not that simple. The Guild is baying for your blood and sees you as an enemy of the state. They feel certain you have become a Queen who is willing to risk peace for what they believe to be our once perfectly balanced civilisation to merely hide your own sins of the flesh. Now they have found others who are following your precedent, giving them the long-awaited excuse to wage this war against you.'

Amella was stricken and she fell like a rag doll into the awaiting arms of a chair, her eyes glistening with sorrow.

'I can't believe what you're telling me,' she whispered, staring at Mordorma as though she was seeing a phantom. 'What is it we must do?'

Mordorma moved to her side and took her trembling hand in his.

'We have no choice, Amella, but to take you into hiding. Very soon the Guild will be sending members of the assembly to formally accuse you of both treason and unlawful fornication.'

'But both myself and Bridgemear were tried for the latter crime already,' Amella cried, as a river of tears started streaming down her face unchecked. 'They ripped my baby daughter from my very arms whilst she was still stained with my blood and then years later *they* brought her back to try and use her as a tool of power to help them win their battle with Forusian.'

'I remember,' said Mordorma sadly, glancing at the other magicians and seeing how ashen their faces had become. 'However, there are those who want you punished for allowing her to stay here with us, therefore changing the way we live our lives forever. According to the ancient scriptures, you're seen as nothing more than a Jezebel, a sickening disgrace to the nation whose disloyalty has been seen as a breach of faith.'

'I think we've heard quite enough!' roared Valentino, watching his dear Queen crumple before his very eyes. 'Mordorma, I think you can safely say – we get the bigger picture!'

The other mage turned to stare angrily at the professor, his eyes flashing with fury and his body language told the elder mage he was unwilling to be put in his place.

'We are not here to hurt the Queen,' Mordorma hissed, spinning on his heels so fast his cloak caught the air and billowed around him. 'We merely wish Amella to understand the seriousness of this matter and therefore comprehend how imperative it is that she leaves this palace tonight.'

Amella gave a heavy sigh and patted his hand.

'I'm afraid I cannot just run away from here for I have too many people relying on me and then there is the Academie to think about.'

'You simply have no choice,' interrupted Voleton, his eyes narrowing. 'If you stay here you will be arrested and we all worry what the outcome will be. However, if you leave now, you can at least escape the hands of the persecutors for a little while longer until we discover a way to get you out of this terrible situation.'

Professor Valentino pursed his lips and then cleared his throat.

'For once I agree with the Oakwood wizards. If you stay here you will be arrested and good to no one. Amella, you know you don't have to worry about the Academie or the running of the palace for I have been here long enough to know what to do. Everything will be safe in my hands and I promise I will not make any hasty decisions until you return.'

The Queen's eyes shone with uncertainty, accepting a crisp, white handkerchief which Amafar produced with an artistic flurry of his hand and she wiped the last of her tears away.

'I know, Valentino,' she said thickly and her expression turned thoughtful. 'However, I feel as though I am abandoning my people just to save my own skin. Why should I run? I am the Queen of Nine Winters and therefore it is my duty to stay.'

Mordorma broke her ranting.

'No, Amella, that is not the answer and we need to leave now.'

'If I should agree, where will we go?' she sniffed, her eyes red and puffy. She absentmindedly stroked her necklace and the redness instantly faded.

Mordorma dropped his gaze and Amafar looked a little hesitant and so it was Voleton who broke the silence, his voice crackling with anticipation.

'It took us some time to decide,' he began. 'We realised we could not take you to Raven's Rainbow and that it isn't safe anywhere in the surrounding realms let alone here, so we thought it best to conceal you within the boundaries of Fortune's End, at least there if someone should come across you they will be unable to harm you.'

Valentino shot from out of his chair and he came and sat beside Amella, gazing into her eyes.

Remember the prophecy my Queen, for all is not lost yet.

Amella looked back at him and heard his message infiltrate her mind. His words gave her a thread of hope until Mordorma's voice brought her back to reality.

'We must not be seen leaving together,' he stated, unaware of Amella's link to the professor. 'The slightest hint we are involved will have us all in chains, therefore we will leave on horseback and meet you there.'

Amella rose from her chair, her composure suddenly returning.

'Very well,' she sighed, smoothing down her robes. 'It appears I have no choice, therefore I will do as you ask.'

The Queen saw the three mages' faces soften; however, the dark shadows of worry never left their eyes. She sighed again and gratefully received the wine Professor Valentino offered her whilst she, in turn, stared into the fire to watch the red and gold flames lick the air. She found the drink to be bitter and she threw the wine onto the fire; in retaliation the flames flared viciously towards her, the sudden heat almost burning her skin but she didn't move away.

'Against my better judgement, I will leave for Fortune's End,' she declared, hunching her shoulders and grabbing the ornate mantle. 'However, I do agree that we must not be seen together and whatever you do, act as natural as possible. Do not use any magic other than for essentiality or the Elders and their crones will soon grow suspicious.'

'We will leave at once,' Mordorma said, jumping to his feet and looking at the others in relief. He shuddered as the cold returned to his bones and unconsciously pulled his cloak closer. He gestured for the others to follow and Amella saw the sadness in his eyes and her heart filled with sorrow, but then she heard raised voices and the angry cry of the guards.

'They're here already!' she gasped, throwing her hands in the air in despair. Her eyes reached all three mages, her face turning as white as snow.

'Quick, go, they must not find you here!' she insisted, shooing them like flies towards a secret passageway.

Amafar and Voleton fastened their cloaks and swiftly made their departure. Mordorma dragged behind, a little less enthusiastic to leave Bridgemear's wife with just the elderly mage for protection and he hesitated, forcing the Queen to rush to his side and place a caring hand onto his sleeve.

'You are no use to me if you get yourself arrested,' she pressed, seeing his lip tremble as he fought the need to stay. 'You know we have no choice but to go with this mad chain of events and to wait until Bridgemear returns, for I'm sure he will know what to do.'

Mordorma grabbed her hand and squeezed it tight.

'We will not be far away,' he told her, allowing her hand to fall from his grasp, 'and I promise you, we will do everything in our power to try and find a solution to all this mess.'

She tried to press a smile, but the corners of her mouth didn't quite make it. 'I don't think that is likely to happen any time soon,' she said wisely, 'now hurry and be gone before you are caught.'

Only a few moments later, the doors to the library were flung open and two of the Inquisitor's men were standing before her, their eyes flashing with obvious malice.

'You have no right to enter here without invitation!' she cried, pulling herself to her full height. 'Tell me, on whose authority do you warrant this visit?'

'Good evening, Your Majesty,' they sneered, taking a few steps closer. 'Please, allow us to introduce ourselves, we are Lord Taurion and Master Fangfoss and we have been sent here by request of the Order of the Guild.'

The Queen eyed them suspiciously. She didn't recognise either of the Guild members but both were wearing the dark robes of the High Council. The one claiming to be Lord Taurion held her gaze a moment too long, scorn dripping from his mouth like acid. He was a broad elf with dark hair and angry-looking eyes and from his physical stature it was obvious he had long since passed his prime. His mouth held a continual sneer, making him look ghoulish and she noticed his hands were shaking as though he was suffering from delirium. As she was sizing him up, he pulled out a rolled piece of parchment from under his cloak and started to read it aloud.

'It is by command and the duty of the Order of the Guild that her Royal Highness, Amella, Queen to the Kingdom of Nine Winters, be hereby taken upon this day and held by the Elite Council until such a time when a trial will be held against the accused and the alleged charges will be proceeded by the prosecution in a court of the Elders' choosing.'

'And of what am I accused?' she asked, already aware of the answer. Her eyes flashed with indignation and her mouth pulled into a bitter, hard line.

'My lady, I am afraid to say you are hereby arrested on the grounds of high treason and unlawful fornication.'

'This is an outrage!' she shouted, turning to Professor Valentino for support. 'Why, you have no power of jurisdiction here, be gone before I have *you* arrested and sent to my own gaol.'

Valentino flew to her side, sensing the hostility building up inside her and he placed a careful hand upon her shoulder in the hope it would somehow calm her.

The two council members watched him with mockery dancing in their eyes.

'You are very keen to comfort the Queen,' Master Fangfoss hissed with an underlying viciousness to his voice. 'Perhaps, Professor, you are just as guilty as the Queen?'

Professor Valentino's eyes almost shot out of their watery sockets as he digested the preposterous accusation and he raised his arm and pointed a bony finger towards the offender, his fury blinding him with rage.

'How dare you!' he bellowed in a deep, dangerous tone.

'Enough!' cried Amella, realising she had to stop the elderly mage before he did something foolish. She reached out and grabbed Professor Valentino's arm, pulling it to her side so that his finger pointed to the floor, where it could do no harm.

She immediately cast a link.

I need you here and not in prison, be calm wizard and bide your time.

'So,' she said aloud, 'where exactly will you be taking me?' she asked, staring at her accusers and severing the link. Her mouth filled with bile when Lord Taurion undressed her with his ghastly pale eyes and she thought for a moment she was going to be physically sick.

'We will take you to the White Tower, Your Highness,' Lord Taurion answered, constantly licking his dry lips. 'Where else would a lady of your exquisite breeding be held?' Each of the two elves looked at her with an arrogance born from the belief of their own self-importance and Amella jutted out her chin in disgust.

However, it was Professor Valentino who broke into their darkening thoughts.

'Be warned both of you,' he said, when the Queen put on her outer coat and pulled it close. 'Should you harm a single hair on her royal head you will have me to answer to.'

The two men turned to stare at him in astonishment and it was Master Fangfoss who appeared to look as though he had misheard the wizard. He stared a moment too long, his face set in a dark, arrogant scowl.

'What is that I hear you say?' he said, turning to Lord Taurion, pretending the professor had made some kind of a joke. 'Are you actually threatening us?'

'Oh yes, and if you are wise enough I would take heed, my lord, of what I say, for I do not make idle threats,' said Professor Valentino, his eyes turning hard. 'And believe me when I tell you that I never forget a miserable face no matter how many years may pass.'

Lord Taurion looked slightly uneasy when the professor's stare lingered and Amella squeezed his hand, clearly grateful to the mage for cutting them down to size.

Amella then let go of him and stepped towards the two council members.

'So, it would appear by the laws of the Guild that I must go with you,' she said, holding tight to what remained of her dignity. 'However, be warned men of the so-called 'Great Council', in time you will learn to regret the day you ever laid eyes on the Queen of Nine Winters and for your costly mistake you *will* pay the ultimate price for what you have just done to me.'

Chapter 16

Bridgemear and his entourage followed a sun that, although bright, was already turning lazy and weak. The morning brought with it a numbness that enfolded the four riders with an invisible shroud of gloom and the two magicians were unable to shake off the feeling of foreboding.

They rode in silence for what seemed like hours, the four men having nothing in their heads which could be of comfort to those who rode by their side.

They soon entered a huge forest which was thick and overgrown. The ground was littered with bright, colourful woodland flowers, their perfume powerful and heady and the sun twinkled between the bowing branches, adding the illusion of late summer. All around them the cold air stirred, sending a chill to brush against their skin until they had no choice but to shield their faces with their gloved hands to alleviate the sharpest stabs of bitter cold.

As they continued on their journey, wandering vines were seen to have wrapped themselves around the tree trunks and their dark green leaves twisted like rope in-between their long branches. Their tendrils ran along the forest floor like probing fingers, spreading over the rich earth in search of yet another tree to claim as its own. The dense mishmash of ground-hugging scrub and creeping vines caused the horses to trip when their hooves became entangled by the spidery undergrowth, hindering their journey and causing them to whinny in distress.

Arhdel shook his head, feeling cantankerous and impatient when his horse stumbled, jolting his spine.

'These woods are much denser than what I'm used to,' he snapped, pulling on his horse when it stumbled yet again. 'I have never seen such a vast blanket of undergrowth before.'

Bridgemear turned in his saddle to face him.

'Then you have never entered the Great Forest before I wager,' he said, bending over his horse and sliding onto one side of his saddle. He patted the horse's neck when his reflection appeared in its golden brown eye, not wishing to unnerve the beast. He gripped the reins tightly whilst he searched for his sword and then his silvery blade sliced through the ropy vegetation as slick as butter. A pathway was soon cleared so the others could pass without further incident and the forest creepers were seen to shrink away from his sword. Their long, green tendrils curled inwards like retracting coils, sending a high-pitched squeal to ring throughout the forest, disturbing the small, orange-blue lizards which hid beneath their dark, shady leaves.

The noise within the forest intensified and several startled oozlefinches took flight, flying backwards and away from the four riders. The birds whistled their protest and fluttered near to their roosts, adding an unexpected trill to the forest. The strange birds flew closer, their large blood-shot eyes looking like large bowls of tomato soup and they hovered tail first over the riders' heads, flapping their featherless wings aggressively until the group passed by without further ado and they returned somewhat ruffled and upset to the sanctuary of their nests.

Niculmus turned to Bridgemear and eyed him with open curiosity.

'This forest is enchanted!' he stated when a loud-pitched squeal reached his ears and a two-headed boar split through the trees and followed them with its four piggy eyes. Its snouts sniffed the air with discontent and the magician studied the creature until it finally turned tail and ran back into the undergrowth.

Bridgemear focused his attention on to his apprentice.

'Tell me, Niculmus, why would you think any differently?' Bridgemear asked, sounding a little bemused. 'Have you not learned that no matter where you go there are always places filled with enchantments and hidden dangers. It's whether these places are filled with good magic or bad that really matters in the end.'

Niculmus nodded, pulling his reins tight so he could move his horse a little closer to Bridgemear's side and they rode at a quiet pace. By mid-morning they stopped to rest the animals and eat a little cold meat. They each checked their horses for signs of injury and Arhdel was particularly relieved to see his horse had not turned lame. Once they had eaten, they remounted and rode for several hours until they reached a dissected plateau. This place was highly eroded and the ground was covered in a river of rocks and broken stones, strewn over the terrain as though anything green would never be allowed to live. At a time when the first dragons were born, magma had risen from the mantle, causing the ground to swell upward and creating a large, flat area of rock which had been uplifted from deep within the earth's core. Now, only dragons wishing to mate came here and it was not a place to linger.

In the distance the canyon loomed before them like a menacing god and Bridgemear felt the first threads of apprehension tighten his inner senses. The imminence of dark magic gnarled like teeth inside his gut and he rubbed at his stomach to awaken his power of light. He signalled for the others to be wary, his instincts telling him to stay alert and so they made their way through the plateau and towards the canyon, a dark cloud of misery wrapping itself around the magician like an unwanted cloak of doom.

*

The Wanderer travelled a night and a day on the horse of Elveria's choosing. The Friesian had been bewitched and the stallion whinnied nervously when he glanced down and saw each of his hooves swirling in a light grey mist, empowering him with speed. He could run as fast as sixteen horses and he flared his nostrils and reared his front legs, kicking his hooves as though it would loosen the clinging fog which fell about his dancing feet.

Rushing out into the darkness, the Wanderer had been grateful for the magician's spell when he accidentally charged into the path of forest scavengers. The thieves saw only a sharp, bright flash, for the horse moved so fast like a ghost in the night that they screamed in the darkness like frightened children. The stolen ale they'd been engorging upon was hastily thrown to the ground, creating a stream of dirty, brown froth and the scavengers whimpered, terrified that the ghostly apparition would return and devour them whole. The Wanderer couldn't help but laugh at their fearful antics, repeatedly turning his horse towards them, enjoying taunting his victims, his cruel nature seeping to the surface like a festering scab. Finally, when he grew tired of their frightened screams, he headed north.

As darkness descended, the Wanderer came across Bridgemear's night camp and he espied the group whilst keeping downwind. He saw the flames and whirls of smoke rising from the fire and from the safety of the shadows he saw a roasting pig glow golden, causing him to drool like a simpleton.

He stared with envious eyes until his own hunger threatened to make him sick and then he stole away to sit alone and eat his daily quantity of tough meats and a little grain bread. Like so many of his kind he had limited magical powers. Born the lowly son of a common criminal he could only use the simplest of spells and his survival had been through using his own wits. His life had been harder than most, his parents nothing more than worthless scroungers, two cruel elves who used their only son for their own selfish means to deprive others of what was rightfully theirs. From an early age he had been taught the art of having 'light fingers', turning into an experienced thief and pickpocket after only seven birth moons and as he grew, so did his larcenous connections and scheming ideas. His crafty nature was moulded by those in power until there was no one he couldn't seduce with his cunning ways.

He felt the cold begin to nudge his bones and he cursed through clenched teeth, knowing he would not be able to light a fire with Elveria's enemies being so close. So he settled himself in a large enough hollow and carefully opened the bag which Elveria had given to him. His fingers probed the inner pockets with care, cautious of what lay hidden in its depths. There appeared to be a few items stored inside and he pulled out each object in turn, laying them gently onto the ground to inspect his newfound wares.

He grasped a cluster of potion bottles and long, colourful vials, enjoying the smooth sensation they left on his cold fingertips. His eagle eyes searched for a clue to tell him what he should do with these bottles and he held them up one at a time in front of his eyes to try and catch the light of the moon. Unable to see what was inside, he was starting to lose interest when he spotted a large, circular vial. The dark-blue bottle had a thick cork pushed deep inside its bottle neck and he rubbed the glass with his thumb and forefinger when condensation began to cover it from the cold. He pulled the stopper from the bottle and took a peek inside. Before he had time to comprehend what was happening, a ghostly yellow smoke oozed from out of the bottle's neck and hung in the air like thinning fog. The tendrils of fog clung together to create floating letters and then they rearranged themselves to form words and then sentences ...

This is the first draft you must use – the letters spelt in a wispy trail. They floated away on the breeze, only to be replaced by more.

At dawn make haste to the nearest river. When you see the magician Bridgemear close to the water's edge, drop seven droplets from this bottle into the babbling water ...

The Wanderer felt a knot of apprehension drop into his gut and he gave a sharp curse when rain began to fall, dispersing the ghostly writing he was trying so hard to understand. He replaced the cork and stuffed the bottle inside his cloak for safe keeping. The cold and wet were seeping into his hair and running down the back of his neck and his clothes were soon soaked through. His skin turned clammy, the heavy thrum of the raindrops assaulting his body and he shivered uncontrollably. He shoved the rest of Elveria's magical paraphernalia back inside the hemp bag before trying to retract deeper into the hollow, his horse thankfully silent as the rain continued to fall.

He prayed for the dawn to hurry, his mind playing out the imaginary scene of what was yet to come and then he prayed again in the hope that his quest would soon be over and he would no longer be at the mercy of Elveria. He took a little comfort in this thought and when the rain finally petered away, he drifted off to sleep dreaming of better times ahead and the promised fortune yet to come.

He awoke with a start when the morning was about to awaken and he jolted upright, fearing he had overslept. The Wanderer looked about and found to his relief that his mount had not wandered off and he swiftly made ready to leave. Once in the saddle, he spurred his horse onward and rode over the ridge which loomed before him. His laugh was heavy with malice when the river came into view and he dismounted, tethering his horse further downstream behind the cover of rocks and a cluster of thick pine trees.

The Wanderer waited as the morning grew old and watched with hawk eyes when Bridgemear and the other riders splashed noisily when their horses entered the river. He didn't dally on executing his orders from Elveria and pulled the small stopper from the favoured blue vial with his teeth, spitting the cork down on the ground, close to his feet. He nervously tipped the vial, dropping seven deadly droplets into the continual steam and felt a sudden twitch above his right eye, realising there was no turning back now. The water was turning a vivid red, the droplets spreading like diluted blood deep under its cold surface before splitting into tendrils of spindly veins, the deadly substance moving rapidly towards the unsuspecting riders like a stream of slithering red snakes.

A sudden explosion of noise sounding like thunder broke from under the depths of the river. Bridgemear pulled on his horse's reins, forcing his steed to stand still in the strong, rippling current whilst it whinnied hysterically in protest and he signalled for the others to do the same. Niculmus threw a questioning look towards the mage and both Amadeus and Arhdel drew their swords, spinning their horses, already assuming they were under attack.

'What the hell's happening here?' shouted Niculmus when his horse reared and the water started to bubble as though a volcanic geyser was about to erupt. The vibrations grew stronger in intensity and the river appeared to shudder. All of a sudden the whole river leapt into the air like a giant water fountain and formed a rolling tidal wave, standing at least sixty feet high. The noise was almost deafening, the power of the blue-green wave majestic, but the riverbed had run dry and the many fishes and river creatures that had been left behind flapped their fins and tossed their bodies in a desperate bid to try and survive.

'What are we to do?' shouted Niculmus, drawing his sword and pushing it out as a warning to those he could not see.

Arhdel looked grim.

'You must fight, lad,' the warrior shouted, waving his sword menacingly in the air. 'Or at least show us all that you have some capabilities of defending those who may need you.'

For the first time in his memory Niculmus felt angry at the slight, but before he could retaliate there came a piecing cry that made his blood run cold and one of the horses appeared to almost scream.

The whole of the river was being pushed towards the sky and the powerful surge shimmered like glass until several images of gigantic watery ghouls loomed from its centre. Now standing in front of Bridgemear were seven monstrous water kelpies. These were nothing like the gentle creatures Niculmus had seen at the lake with Crystal and Magician Phin, indeed these were several feet taller and their once pleasant faces were distorted with jaws that snapped and snarled like vicious, wild dogs. On their backs rode the most terrifying creatures Niculmus had ever seen and he almost shook with fear when he heard Bridgemear shout out they were being barred access by a group of Challicums.

Involuntarily he found his gaze to rest on the evil water spirits who were sitting on the kelpies' backs. Their features were not very clear because the water spilled down over their faces and poured from every orifice imaginable but it was obvious their heads were shaped liked viperfish. Four long, thin-needled fangs fell from their gaping mouths, giving them an unapproachable visage and they could be heard hissing their displeasure when the water continued to pour over them. Their bodies were green and slimy, their huge hind legs were remarkably thick and they appeared to have the added bonus of two stronger forelegs which were furnished with long, sickening claws.

'Prepare yourselves!' shouted Bridgemear over the constant din. 'This is a spell from the dark side and I'm not sure if my powers alone are enough to save us from these creatures. I have enough energy to force the Challicums to stay still for a few seconds, perhaps a minute if we are lucky, but if you don't manage to kill most of them within that time we will not make it out of here alive.' Raising his arm, Bridgemear held out the Sword of Truth towards Amadeus.

'Use it well,' he urged, when the warrior reached out and took it from his grasp. Amadeus nodded, kicking his horse so that he could fight as front runner and Arhdel stayed firmly at his right flank. Bridgemear grabbed his sceptre and closed his eyes in silent prayer when the water spirits screamed their advance.

Niculmus felt the pulse in his temple grow strong. He too closed his eyes but now he was reaching for his wand, his memory pulling at magic threads which were pushing and squirming their way to the surface in a bid to help him stay alive. Whilst all around him was chaos, Niculmus whispered an incantation which he had learned not from the Circle of Mages but from the village witch. He pointed his wand towards the assaulting riders and the words she had taught him spilled from his mouth and a twisted line of silvery magic connected with the ghouls who were hurtling towards him.

Just as Bridgemear predicted, his own spell stopped the Challicums dead in their tracks.

All seven water kelpies froze in their advance and it was Arhdel and Amadeus who rode towards them as though the devil himself was in pursuit. The Sword of Truth sliced through the first water spirit with little effort. Watery black blood tarnished with green gushed dramatically from the open wound and oozed into the rush of water. Amadeus was shocked to see the colour of their blood but he didn't falter and his blade returned to direct a fatal blow. A piercing scream left the deathly ghoul's mouth, but Amadeus didn't wait to see it fall, instead he forced his horse inside the rolling wave and thrust the sword through the streaming torrent, attacking yet another Challicum, his sword piercing straight through its chest cavity. He retracted his blade having stabbed it clean through the heart and its death was instantaneous. He continued on, swirling the sword high above his head and thrusting the weapon into every evil creature he reached.

Arhdel, meanwhile, had rained a stream of deadly blows against a ghoul's head and thought the skull must be made of stone when his sword had trouble breaking through it. It took much longer to kill the water spirit with his ordinary blade, but he was not an elf born to take defeat and he used all of his strength, his breath becoming ragged, until he battered the creature senseless, stopping only when the Challicum's skull finally caved in. It had taken quite a considerable amount of time to kill the evil spirits, but only Bridgemear had noticed this fact.

When the last Challicum took its final breath, Elveria's spell broke and the tidal wave dropped like a heavy stone back towards the riverbed, drenching the two magicians and their horses in a torrent of freezing water. The river flowed gently downstream, washing away the deathly remnants of what had just occurred and the kelpies vanished like mist beneath its surface.

158

A sad sound, a neighing cry, left the quivering muzzles of Arhdel and Amadeus's horses and both of the exhausted warriors slapped their necks in silent gratitude.

Niculmus replaced his wand back inside its protective sheath. Bridgemear cocked an inquisitive brow and nodded his acknowledgement as to what the young apprentice had just achieved by assisting him, but he stayed tight-lipped and returned his attention to the two warriors instead.

'Where did they come from?' gasped Amadeus, sounding both exhausted and drained. He approached the mage and offered him the Sword of Truth and noticed that he was also drenched from head to foot and the aide shuddered with cold. Bridgemear seemed distant as he grasped the hilt, placing the sword swiftly into its scabbard and he eyed his comrade with deep concern.

'This was not what I expected,' he said at last, gazing down into the depths of the river which looked innocent enough now.

Amadeus shrugged his shoulders at his words.

'What exactly did you expect?' he asked, raising an eyebrow.

Bridgemear looked troubled and his ice-blue eyes clouded.

'That was not a spell of the forest or from some old crone protecting her land. Having stayed alive longer than most and learning intensive wizardry I can assure you whoever cast that spell over these waters had years of experience in the art of black magic.'

Arhdel said sharply, 'Then let us be on our way, sire, there is no reason to stay here. The canyon is over the very next ridge and the sooner we reach it the better for all of us.'

Bridgemear nodded and signalled for Niculmus to follow by the rear.

'You're right,' he said, as his lips curled with frustration. 'Only my senses tell me there is far more danger yet to come.'

Amadeus pursed his own lips, understanding the mage's concern.

'We did not expect anything less,' he drawled, raking his fingers through his wet hair and shuddering when the water ran down the back of his neck.

Bridgemear's eyes grew grim and there was tension mixed with worry in his voice when he said, 'I know, but I sense we are going to have to face a greater ordeal than even I expected before this episode with my daughter is put to rest and I'm afraid things may get far worse.'

'How much worse?' Niculmus piped up when his horse lunged forward, desperate to reach dry land.

'By dying, you idiot!' snapped Arhdel, making his way up the bank and then shooting him a look which told him to keep his mouth shut in future. Niculmus looked away, smarting from his comment and although he wanted to retaliate by giving Arhdel a severe lashing with his tongue, he was somehow able to remain silent through a born respect of his elders. However, he wasn't going to end up dead no matter what the crotchety old warrior said. He spurred his horse on until they all reached the entrance to the canyon. Numb with fatigue he was grateful when they stopped to rest and unsaddled their horses for the night. Niculmus thought about his quest whilst he rubbed down his horse with handfuls of grass and vowed to himself that if anyone was to die by the end of all this, it most certainly would not be him.

Chapter 17

Crystal and Bruis sat hidden together inside his secret camp whilst the world outside carried on as though they never existed. His camp was sealed within a fuzzy, white cloud as if they were hiding somewhere close to heaven and Crystal would not have been more surprised to see an angel materialise wearing a long, flowing gown, a pair of fluttering wings and singing 'hallelujah'.

She thought this place looked 'godly' and saw how his dwelling consisted of a simple hut, a well maintained granary, which housed his few sacks of wheat, grain and flour, and a strange circular piece of land, which enclosed a goat and a few well-fed chickens. However, everything she saw was cocooned within this white, fluffy cloud and the fresh aroma of summer rain lingered in the air.

Bruis gestured for her make her way inside his hut and the wooden door groaned when he pushed it wide, causing him to grimace when it continued to creak. She smiled lightly, her eyes sparkling with amusement when he pulled a long face and she stepped over the threshold with him close on her heels.

'I've been meaning to get that fixed for ages,' he said, striding towards a hook embedded in the wall and placing his staff there, 'only I never seem to have the time,' he added, looking sheepish.

Crystal gave him a warm smile, her eyes taking in her surroundings and she wasn't surprised at all to see his house was just as basic on the inside as on the outside, yet there was something rather soothing and natural within the cool, whitewashed walls. Bruis touched her elbow and she followed him through an open archway. As she walked with him, it became obvious the plainwalker led a very simple and humble life for there was a great lack of material possessions set against the bare walls, yet his home seemed to ripple with a warm, welcoming sensation.

She thought it strange though, that Bruis had a small circular window inside his hut which looked out over a beautiful garden. It was sunny in the garden and she could see an abundance of green and red apple trees mixed with rich vibrant plums blowing gently in the breeze, yet she knew this could not be real and to surely be an illusion.

'Crystal,' said Bruis, interrupting her thoughts, 'shall we walk in my garden this good evening?'

She nodded keen to go back outside whilst the sun was still shining. She followed him at a distance and noted how his spiritual prowess calmed her trembling nerves. He led her through a wooden doorway, entangled with thick vines and studded with dozens of wild, pink roses and the smell of the Grand Meadow flooded her mind. She looked around her and was surprised to see that she could see for miles and miles and that the scenery reminded her very much of Nine Winters. The rich aroma of freshly dug earth and delicious tangy fruits filled her nostrils and she turned to Bruis when an overwhelming feeling of inner peace washed over her.

'Who *are* you?' she breathed, puzzled by his spiritual enigma. Bruis, who was busy pruning back a rose bush, looked up at her and she sensed by the vacant expression on his face that his mind had been wandering far away.

'I had thought all that would become obvious to you,' he said, giving her a light smile. 'I am a plainwalker, a person who tends the lands, lakes and skies of this earth.'

Crystal burst out laughing.

'You're teasing me!' she gushed, unable to take him seriously and she bent down to smell one of the dark, red roses growing close to her feet, 'why, everyone knows that Mother Nature does all that,' she added when Bruis broke the flower from off its stem and offered it to her.

Bruis looked a little taken aback and absentmindedly stroked his beard.

'I believe you are talking of the good work of my dear sister,' he said, looking up towards the darkening sky.

162

'Oh, really?' she gasped, feeling her jaw drop in astonishment and he nodded and Crystal then looked into his eyes and read the truth deep inside them.

'This garden is the secret to your realm's prosperity,' he explained, pulling yet another rose from its stem and placing it in her hair. 'You see, as long as I tend to this garden and ensure it is well maintained your kingdom will stay prosperous and wealthy. My dear sister has a terrible habit of destroying more than she creates, a minor defect within her creative make-up which has been known to have devastating results. However, we have managed to reach a compromise and she tends to leave me well alone to tend my many gardens in peace.'

'What, you have more than one garden?'

'Oh, several!' Bruis chuckled softly. 'But there isn't enough light left to show you them all now.'

They wandered through the garden until it grew dark and the stars dazzled the night sky.

Later, when they were both inside and seated around a small fire set within a backdrop of stone, Crystal asked Bruis how he met Clump.

'I have known Clump for many years,' Bruis told her, allowing a gentle smile to twitch at the corners of his mouth. 'I came across him when he was just a small Windigo, when he had become an outcast amongst his people because he wouldn't eat meat.'

'What!' she cried, her mouth dropping. 'Since when has not eating meat become a crime?' she flounced, flabbergasted at his revelation. Her eyes widened at the thought of the terrible injustice he must have endured just because he was born a vegetarian.

'Why, I have loads of friends who are vegetarians and even vegans,' she huffed, shaking her head in disgust.

Bruis gave her a strange look and then moved to the hearth and began to build up the fire. His long arms had no trouble placing the logs into a tall heap and soon they were alight with a barrage of flickering flames.

'I don't think you quite understand the implications,' he said, wiping the soot off his hands onto a ragged piece of cloth. 'You see, Windigos are normally a cruel and vicious race. Their sole diet is raw meat and they live on eating the flesh of humans and

163

sucking their bones dry until they turn to powder, but for some strange reason Clump wasn't born with the same palette as his ancestors and because of this he was eventually ostracised by his family.'

Crystal simply stared at him, clearly unable to comprehend Bruis's shocking secret.

'Are you making this up?' she asked suspiciously and his downcast expression told her he was speaking the truth.

'No, I'm afraid I'm not,' Bruis said, moving towards a small stove and taking out bread which he'd had the sense to prepare earlier in the day. He placed the small golden rolls into a simple weaved dish, the smell of newly baked bread filling the air, and he came over to offer them to Crystal.

'I'm guessing you still have some kind of appetite?' he probed, trying to keep the atmosphere between them light. Crystal glared at him with open hostility, angry that he had decided to burden her with such a terrible revelation. She began to worry at her newfound knowledge and she chewed the inside of her mouth, unsure how she would react when Clump came to collect her the following morning. Yet again it was as though Bruis read her mind for he said, 'Clump would never hurt you intentionally.'

Crystal sighed deeply.

'If what you're telling me is the truth then how can you be so sure?' she argued, accepting one of the bread rolls.

'Please, listen to me. You have to understand, I've known Clump for a very long time and in all that time not one morsel of flesh has ever passed his lips,' he insisted.

Crystal broke the bread into two chunks and was about to take a bite when a sudden flash came before her eyes and she saw Clump snarling and ripping at bare flesh, his eyes wild with savagery. She blinked rapidly, overcome with despair but thankful that her mind was simply working overtime and not showing her a true vision of what Clump was up to. She immediately lost what little appetite she had and she placed the pieces of bread on a small table by her side.

'I understand your concern and quite rightly so but I promise you he doesn't eat meat of any kind, even when he's a wolf,' Bruis said, retrieving the bread and putting it on his own plate. She stared at him clearly flummoxed and she noticed how the flames of the fire were dancing against his dark skin, giving his face a bright, golden glow.

How does he manage to always read my mind! she thought to herself, totally mystified. Bruis came and sat by her side on a crudely made stool and quietly ate his supper. He looked thoughtful as he chewed and Crystal sensed that he was still troubled and so she pressed him to tell her why.

'Well, it's just that Clump told me that you are heading for the Stannary Mines,' he said, taking another mouthful of food. Crystal nodded, transfixed on watching him chew. She was unable to drop her gaze, finding him fascinating although her thoughts flew to what she thought the mine held deep inside, hidden away from the rest of the world and she caught the look of concern growing dark behind his milky eyes.

'The mine is a very dangerous place and it's filled with evil magic and I wonder if you and Clump are really prepared to take on such a feat all by yourselves?' he explained, between mouthfuls.

She couldn't answer him. Her fear of what the future held combined with the heat of the fire made her increasingly restless and when Crystal started to cry, Bruis moved closer and gently put his arms around her shoulders.

'There child, why do you weep?' he asked, gently stroking her hair with the palm of his hand.

'Because you're right. I have no idea what I'm doing here and I'm frightened I'm going to get either Clump or myself killed,' she told him in choked tones. 'And, on top of all that, how am I supposed to save my family when nothing is as it seems? I feel I will always be at another's mercy and my magic is still not as strong as everyone believes.'

The plainwalker's eyes filled with understanding and he patted her hand in reassurance.

'Hush, hush little one, you may be young at heart but you have such strength of character. Yes, I agree, you do have much to learn and yet you cannot expect to know everything there is to know in a blink of an eye. Life is an experience and to experience life you have to live it. All you can do is trust your instincts and tell me,

165

would it be fair to say that you haven't fallen foul by another's hand, so far?'

Crystal sniffed loudly and as quickly as they had come her tears vanished and she looked up into his kind face and was relieved to see it was soft and comforting.

'Well, no, not exactly,' she said gruffly, her eyes still sparkling with unshed tears and it was clear her heart was filled with doubt. 'But I was unable to stop the firebird from taking me,' she added, sounding rather dejected.

'Yes, that's true, but from what Clump tells me, you were taken from the white side of magic and not the dark so would it be also fair to say you were not actually harmed in any way?'

'Well, yes, I guess that's true,' Crystal sniffed, pulling from his light embrace and staring towards the flames instead. The golden embers gave her face an angelic glow and Bruis thought she looked beautiful.

'Come, my child, I think it's time we settled for the night,' he said, smiling paternally.

He took Crystal to a small room which housed a simple carpet and a small rickety table. On top of the table sat a candle which was flickering invitingly towards her; Bruis raised his hand and the carpet rose roughly three feet into the air.

'I'm afraid this will have to be your bed for the night,' he told her apologetically, but Crystal didn't care for she was suddenly bone weary. Bruis wished her goodnight and she soon climbed aboard the soft carpet, finding it to be very comfortable, and once settled she blew out the flame to let the darkness enfold her. In the shadowed light she could see images of the clouds scudding by through the tiny oblong window, built almost in the roofline. The night seemed hot and the air thick and it took a long time for her to finally fall asleep. Her thoughts drifted to Clump hunting alone in the nearby wilderness with blood dripping from his fur-covered lips and his eyes narrow with intent. In her sleep she tossed and turned, unable to accept he had been born a monster and she grew restless as her bad dreams turned into nightmares. She awoke later drenched in sweat and sobbing for breath. She missed her parents so much and the loneliness of being parted from them tore at her heart to the point where she felt she was suffocating. She sat on the edge of the carpet and threw her hand to relight the candle. The walls instantly became covered in a warm, golden glow and Crystal felt her breathing calm.

She stared at the whitewashed walls and concentrated on opening her mind portal. The cold emptiness of nothing grasped her as she realised she was still unable to forge a connection with her family. Then, just when she was about to break her concentration, she felt a slight shake in her mind as though her thoughts had almost been able to penetrate upon another's, but like a rubber bullet, they came bouncing back unheard, unable to break through the solid wall of silence. Defeated, she lay back down, the carpet pliable against her skin but her loneliness soon reappeared like an unwanted rash and she turned to face the wall, deciding she would not try again. When she finally drifted off it was with the knowledge that she had never been more alone than she was at this moment in time.

*

The following morning Crystal awoke and heard Bruis busy at work in the kitchen, baking again. In her room, she washed in a bowl which had been placed in preparation for her and she conjured a spell which provided hot, soapy water and a clean towel, not wanting to bother Bruis. Then she proceeded to conjure another spell which Magician Phin had taught her which changed her rather smelly clothes into fresh, clean ones. The spell created identical clothing to what she was already wearing, only in different shades of blue and Crystal grinned at its simplicity.

Once she was ready Crystal hunted for Bruis, finding him toying with something small hanging on his belt. She saw him untie a brown leather pouch and, feeling curious, was about to ask him what was held inside, but before she could utter a word Bruis was telling her.

'It's prairie dust,' he explained, and he grinned when he saw a spark of interest ignite behind her dazzling, blue eyes. He rummaged within the pouch, and then held what looked to be a few grains of sand between his thumb and forefinger. Crystal thought the tiny fragments of gold looked rather ordinary and screwed up her nose in disappointment.

'I will be able to magic you a fine horse,' Bruis told her, placing the grains into the palm of his hand. 'I will enjoy making you the greatest beast you have seen, because the art of creation is part of my magical persona,' he added, looking rather smug.

Crystal gave him a doubtful smile, not having a clue what he was talking about and idly glanced around the room, looking for what was making her belly rumble with hunger. Bruis followed her gaze.

'I have prepared a small feast for you this morning,' he said, ushering her to a self-supporting table held against the wall by two small plinths of wood. He proceeded to roll down the sleeves of his long robe, the brightly coloured fabric sparkled unexpectedly when the morning sun filtered through the open doorway, making Bruis look like some kind of mythical Greek god. Crystal noticed his clothes were not as sparse as the previous days, indeed his fine clothes were made from beautifully woven fabrics which had a thick edging of pure gold interlaced between its knitted fibres and Crystal began to wonder if Bruis really was as poor as she'd been led to believe.

'Please, help yourself,' he exclaimed, reaching for a rather smelly homemade cheese. Crystal watched him take a bite and a look of pure ecstasy washed over his face and he let out a rapturous sigh which made Crystal giggle.

After a leisurely breakfast, Bruis took Crystal down the misty corridor which led back to reality and Clump. The Windigo was waiting for her outside the boulder, a look of sheer relief spreading across his hairy face when he saw her materialise, but then his eyes narrowed with suspicion when he saw a flash of uncertainty cross Crystal's face.

Bruis greeted the Windigo with a warm handshake and then said, 'I've told her about your family, there are no secrets between you now.' Clump looked stricken until Crystal walked towards him and placed a hand on his shoulder.

'I have trusted you ever since we first met,' she whispered in his ear. 'I believe you would never lay a finger on me, let alone think about eating me.'

Clump bowed his head in shame, but caught the look of forgiveness in Crystal's eyes and she reached out, tilting his chin towards her.

168

'We are in this together,' she told him firmly, 'and I want you to know that I trust you with my life.'

Clump gave a sharp sob. 'You will have no regrets, Princess,' he said, rubbing his eyes with the back of his hand. He raised a dark and hairy eyebrow and the last of his tears rolled down his cheek. 'Thank you for your kind words,' he rasped, his voice thick with genuine emotion. 'As you may have guessed, in this life I have not had many real friends, but in our short time of being together I have come to realise that you are indeed a very special person and I promise I will protect you, to the point where I would be willing to give up my life for you.'

Crystal felt both humbled and shocked by Clump's loyal declaration and she flushed scarlet with embarrassment.

'Come, come, enough of this emotional nonsense,' said Bruis, strolling towards the pair and waving his hand as though he was shooing a fly. He gestured for them to come to him and he drew their attention to the ground.

'I must find you a safe route to the Stannary Mines,' Bruis said, scratching his staff this way and that to create a crude looking map in the dirt. He continued by drawing a few basic symbols and a legend to explain a simple but effective route for them to travel.

'Speak to no one,' he insisted, looking with a stern expression at the Windigo. 'Try to keep within the sanctuary of the trees and whatever you do, keep to the trail.' They both nodded and once he was satisfied that they knew where they were headed, Bruis reached for his belt and opened the leather pouch which hung like a bag of gold at his side. He grabbed a small handful of prairie dust and threw it to the ground and then glanced at Crystal, tipping her a wink, when he spoke an enchantment. The words slipped easily from his mouth and Crystal had a sneaky suspicion that he was as much a magician as her father.

'Sibhse mo chairdese, durṅet homhaighṅese.'

As soon as the words left his lips, sand and dirt flew in the air and revolved in a spiral of white smoke. Within seconds the image of a ghost horse materialised and Crystal felt her heart flutter when its soft silhouette shimmered like glass. First to form was the animal's skeletal bones. The humerus and sternum hung inside the huge cavity and the cervical vertebra fell into place like a giant jigsaw puzzle. Then internal organs attached themselves with invisible threads onto the inner walls and millions of blood vessels ran in a mish-mash of red, spidery trails. Exquisite dips and arches flowed along its back followed by long fluid lines which became the animal's powerfully strong legs. Finally, the outer skin was fashioned from the dust like a fine, furry cloak, wrapping the core securely until the horse was seen to come alive. The last of the sand dissolved away to reveal a pure white stallion. The beast raised its head majestically towards the sky and the creature shook its silky mane and blinked two violet eyes.

Crystal was completely mesmerised. She saw his velvet nose, slightly tinged with grey, twitch sporadically when the light breeze teased his nostrils and his luxurious tail swished in response. The stallion's eyes were protected by a long, coarse fringe which fell between his ears and down towards his white-tipped lashes. He flicked his gaze towards the princess when she made a step towards him, but he kicked out his front legs and threw his head, causing her to step back in alarm.

'Hey! Calm yourself, you stupid creature!' Bruis demanded, reaching out and placing a firm hand on the horse's nose, patting his quivering neck. He stroked the stallion until he stopped snorting at his touch and Bruis whispered in his ear until he stood much calmer.

'That's more like it,' Bruis chastised, chuckling aloud when he caught Crystal's look of uncertainty. 'This beast only knows the voice of authority,' he warned her, placing a reassuring hand on the stallion's back. 'Do not treat him like a docile mare, otherwise you may find your backside smarting on the ground.'

When Crystal eventually found the courage to move closer, the horse raised its head, snorting a warning. She saw the fleeting shadow of stubbornness flicker behind its long lashes, but Bruis held him fast until she was able to touch his flanks with confidence. He flared his nostrils when she stroked his back, stomping his left hoof against the ground, raking at the dirt.

'I think he's beginning to like you,' Bruis said levelly.

'Well that's a start,' she grinned, throwing Clump a wary glance. 'But I cannot ride him without a saddle.'

Bruis chuckled until he became overwhelmed with laughter. 'You really are hilarious,' he said, pulling at the horse's mane with unexpected affection. 'Do you think because I live in the middle of nowhere, I'm not aware of how good a horsewoman you are?'

Crystal stared at the plainwalker as though he'd gone quite mad when he moved to her side, clasping his hands together and bending his ancient knees.

'It's time to go, Princess,' he huffed, and he was taken aback when she simply refused and ran to the sanctuary of Clump.

Bruis shook his head and cursed her under his breath.

'You have no time for dillydallying,' he insisted, his patience ebbing and he signalled for Clump to assist him.

Clump hesitated before grabbing her about the waist and she squealed like a baby piglet, causing him to giggle. He carried her in his arms and placed her, rather unladylike, on the back of the stallion, her cheeks flushed with humiliation.

Both Bruis and Clump took an immediate step back.

'You had no right to do that!' she said stroppily, feeling slightly silly when she realised they were both grinning like Cheshire cats. She felt her pride sting like a newfound graze until her embarrassment at being manhandled subsided. The horse whinnied and gave a loud neigh as if he too wasn't happy at the way she had been treated and she patted his neck in gratitude.

'What's his name?' Crystal asked, grabbing the horse's mane and noticing it felt like silk against her fingers.

'Kyte,' Bruis answered, smiling when the horse nudged him playfully. 'I have ridden him many times and I have never needed a saddle. However, because he is made of magic he will sense if you're in any danger of falling off.'

A sudden glance at the sun reminded him it was time for them to leave and he turned to face Clump, slapping the Windigo hard on his back before taking his enormous hand in his and shaking it fiercely.

'Remember what I told you,' Bruis said, his face turning grave. He hated saying farewell, the words making them both aware it might be the last goodbye they ever said. 'Beware of the dangers,' he whispered, once he was out of Crystal's earshot. 'You know as well as I do, no one has ever got out of that mine without being cursed one way or another.'

Clump nodded, trying to disperse the gloomy mood which threatened to settle upon him.

'Life's full of bitter disappointments, but defeat is not something I can easily swallow,' he declared pushing out his chest. 'However, we must all make sacrifices now and then and for me, these hidden traits of courage are what help to keep the monster in me at bay.'

Chapter 18

A line of soldiers stood by the dock in the half light of morning and watched the solitary sculling boat grow close. Steered by a lone figure dressed from head to toe in black, many of the soldiers decided the rower had an eeriness about him that made them thankful that they would not be travelling with him anytime soon. The still waters of the sea swirled mysteriously against the cold barrage of wooden stilts which protruded from its murky depths, and the continual lapping of the gentle waves created an illusion of calm and tranquillity.

The many guards belonging to the Order of the Guild stood with hard, stony faces along the quayside and several grunts and groans left their miserable lips when the boat appeared to linger upon the water for far too long. They were waiting for the Queen's arrival and both Lord Taurion and Master Fangfoss had been ordered to accompany Amella to the White Tower, much to her dismay. It appeared the Order was uneasy and, feeling rather fractious, had commanded their two most loyal servants to travel by her side, wishing for them to become the Guild's eyes and ears should anything untoward happen to her on the way.

Without further ado, the two Guild members had placed Amella inside a large, black carriage escorted by an assembly of swordmasters, elves who showed extraordinary skill and courage when using a blade. The small group rode on horseback at both the front and rear of the carriage. The procession, though sombre, held the swordmasters on high alert and when they finally left the sanctuary of Nine Winters, the commander ordered the elves to pull their swords from their sheaths and long, slender blades flashed silver in their hands.

The carriage bounced unsteadily as it made its way along several dirt tracks and only the heavy cry of the swordmasters spurring their horses on penetrated through Amella's frantic mind.

'It shouldn't be much further now, Your Highness,' Lord Taurion announced, breaking through her thoughts several hours later. He flicked his gaze outside the small window, pushing the blind to one side so he could catch a glimpse of the white-crested waves breaking against the myriad of black rocks. He turned and looked at the Queen, a slight smirk twitching at the corners of his mouth and he stretched out his legs to make himself more comfortable.

Amella shivered. She could see nothing outside the carriage but darkness and desolation and she caught the changing scents and sounds and felt a bitterness rise within her as she drew nearer to the coast. She heard the raucous cry of seabirds and the smell of sweet, damp grass was replaced by the sharp tang of salt which found its way inside her nostrils.

'You are making a very grave mistake,' Amella told Lord Taurion when she caught him staring at her. 'I was not the one who brought my daughter back to this world originally; indeed, the Elders ordered her return to the extraordinary world when they felt it was beneficial to them. Since that time, it has been proven by the ancient scriptures that she should not have been banished in the first place so why then do you now believe I am the one who has been treasonous and all this is not some revengeful plot by another to get themselves onto my throne?'

Lord Taurion shifted awkwardly when he was almost jerked out of his seat, his smirk having slipped from his face and he remained tight-lipped when her eyes bore directly into his, challenging him to respond. He pulled his dark cloak closer, refusing to be drawn into a battle of wills with the Queen, believing her to be guilty of her crimes and he eventually broke her stare, turning his concentration once again to what lay outside the window, watching the bleak and dreary scenery pass by.

The Queen was being accompanied by Rudessa, her faithful lady-in-waiting, and Amella turned to her, reaching out and clutching her hand for comfort. The older woman's smile was weak when her fingers entwined with the Queen's but Amella thought she appeared to sit a little straighter, her cheeks slightly flushed.

Eventually Lord Taurion and Master Fangfoss started chatting idly amongst themselves until a sudden cry from the commander broke their tiresome conversation and the carriage rolled to a halt. Lord Taurion reached out to grasp the handle of the carriage door but before he could do so, Rudessa rose and flung the door aside. The step let down, she allowed the Queen to leave the carriage and descend onto the quayside without his interference.

A light, wet drizzle was falling and Amella climbed down onto the bleak and lonely jetty, her knees shaking under her great cloak. The first thing she clapped eyes on was the dark shadow of the White Tower rising a few miles out to sea, looking like something huge and malignant in the water and a shiver ran down her spine.

She turned away and was greeted by the commander who spoke to her in a respectful but sharp tone of voice, directing both herself and Rudessa to a place where they could wait out of the rain until the boat was ready to take them to the tower. Amella bit her lower lip and felt tears well up in her eyes when the swordmaster left her side, but she refused to let them fall, calling to Rudessa to stay close, and she concentrated on her lack of belongings instead.

'Did you have time to pack my trunk?' Amella asked the dark-haired woman, whose eyes were as sorrowful as her own. The maid shrugged her shoulders, her thick lashes turning downcast.

'No, milady, they gave me no time,' the maid announced apologetically. 'However, Professor Valentino promised me he would send your things directly.'

Amella eyed Rudessa with kindness. She could not remember a time when she had not been awoken by this woman's warm smile and she saw the look of trepidation fill Rudessa's huge, liquid eyes. Reaching out, she squeezed her maid's hand once again for reassurance.

'We'll be alright,' she promised, patting her hand like you would a pet, 'we just need to ride the storm, that's all.'

Rudessa nodded, but she looked like she only half believed her.

Abruptly someone shouted, 'grab the rope!' and there was a commotion along the quayside until a small fishing boat was pulled close to shore by a pair of strapping arms and tethered firmly to the quay. Then came a loud, exaggerated cough and both the Queen and her maid turned, staring like startled rabbits into the pasty face

175

of Lord Taurion. He bowed, looking pleased to have grabbed their attention so quickly, but his eyes filled with indignation when he saw the strength in the Queen's own and he immediately stepped back.

'It's time for you to leave these shores, Your Highness,' he said, gesturing for Amella to take the lead. The rain had stopped falling but the Queen lingered, fastening the buttons of her gloved hand to give herself time to prepare, the fear of the unknown forcing her to take an involuntary breath, and then she was walking with an outer calm she did not really possess. Her legs were quivering when she made her way to the awaiting boat with her composure barely intact.

The boat was bobbing on the surface of the sea like an unwanted piece of cork and when Amella boarded the vessel, dread filled her heart over what was yet to come. Close on her heels, Rudessa followed behind her and when both women stepped cautiously inside, the boat tipped slightly and they grabbed hold of one another as though their survival depended upon it.

Morning mist was floating on the surface of the water and it lay voluptuously over the calm, gentle sea, thinning out as it spread over the quay and rolling sand, turning everything it touched into grey and white. Amella looked out across the water and felt the cold breeze blow the cobwebs from her eyes. Looking back at the White Tower she now thought it looked strangely beautiful and mysterious in the dim morning light, protruding from the centre of the ocean for everyone to bear witness to its invincible strength unlike when it had hugged the darkness. Amella was aware there was no point in trying to escape, not now. The Guild would eventually find her and bring her to trial no matter how long she kept running. No, her only way to survive was to be strong and wait until Bridgemear returned with their daughter in the hope he could find a way to end this madness which threatened to rip her life into emotional tatters yet again.

Eventually, after much delay, Lord Taurion and Master Fangfoss also boarded the fishing vessel and once his passengers were settled, the dark-hooded rower signalled for the soldiers to finally cast the rope. Amella watched him with growing unease. It was obvious to her that their hooded companion was a Satyr, a creature with the body of a man but the horns, ears and tail of a goat. These large creatures were born with powerful upper body strength and were known to be subversive and dangerous if challenged. Amella had known some to be cursed with the hideous facial features of a bull and these rare beasts could live in solitary places and suffer outrageously desolate conditions without being touched by insanity. The White Tower had become a predominant example of such bitter seclusion and had always been guarded by these terrifying creatures.

The Satyr pulled his hood closer and Amella was glad to see she could not see his face. She turned to see Rudessa's frown was grim and then she watched the Satyr take the oars into his strong, firm hands and start rowing towards the tall, penal column which loomed, in her opinion, like a solid monument of doom.

The last of the soldiers standing on the quayside watched the boat drift away, their eyes and ears alert for the command which would enable them to leave this dismal place and return to somewhere a little less bleak. Whilst they waited, they watched the surface of the water until the four passengers and the hooded Satyr finally vanished into thickening fog and each one was grateful that their task was over.

Once the group was out to sea and when the fog was at its thickest, to catch the Queen's attention, Lord Taurion reached out and lightly touched the tip of her elbow. Her immediate reaction was to pull away from his touch and she turned to face him, her eyes glowing red with contempt.

'Do not touch me!' she hissed, smoothing a sudden ruffle on her long, velvet sleeve. 'Being your prisoner does not give you the right to get over familiar.'

'Your Highness, I am not one for breaking the laws of protocol,' Lord Taurion insisted in a polite tone, 'however, I will beg your pardon if you think me so bold,' he added, sounding anything but apologetic. The mist suddenly thickened before his eyes, causing all his companions to abruptly disappear and his eyes narrowed whilst he searched for the Queen. He saw her silhouette reappear, his vision blurred from the cold, damp vapours but before he could open his mouth to speak she was gone again and he was cocooned in an abyss of white emptiness.

'I'm a little unnerved,' Amella admitted, when she suddenly reappeared and he almost jumped out of his skin. He yanked his cloak tighter around his shoulders and then took a deep breath.

'Come now,' he said, sounding contrite. 'There is nothing for you to worry about and should you need anything whilst staying in the White Tower, the Satyr will be at your total disposal.'

Amella simply scowled at him.

'I think that's highly unlikely, don't you? Especially since I have my lady-in-waiting to see to my every need,' she admonished. 'After all, I think it's safe to say that the Satyr will have enough to do, guarding the tower from the likes of you during my stay!'

As Amella continued to fume, there came a deep moan from the sea that sounded like something was in great pain and the Queen turned her head and cast her gaze over the water. The Satyr started rowing a little faster as though the noise prompted him to stop dawdling and the mist was seen to shift. Hazy patches wafted on by and the feeling of 'now you see me, now you don't' continued until the sun came out and dissolved what was left of the mist. When the vapours finally lifted, to their amazement they each saw that they were surrounded by a multitude of large blue-grey slimy humps.

'Oh, what are they?' Rudessa asked, brushing a stray curl from the side of her cheek and pushing it behind a pointed ear. She peered towards the surface of the sea and without a second thought reached out and tried to touch one of the humps.

'Stop!' the Satyr roared and she saw his hideous eyes glare dangerously at her from under his hood. 'Don't you know these are evil sea monsters and they will drag you under the water the first chance they get?' No sooner were the words out of his mouth than Rudessa was shrieking in terror.

'Look out! Something horrible is trying to jump inside the boat,' she cried, and sure enough, clinging to one of the sides, was a human hand. Its fat, blue fingers were gripping onto the outer rim whilst it tried to drag a sea creature's body to which it was attached on board. The rubbery creature suffered a long thick nose just above its mouth, hiding several rows of razor-sharp teeth which were placed on both sides of its fleshy gums, giving the hand free rein. The grotesque creature thrashed in the water as the hand

178

tried to pull itself on board and a flat fishy tail was helping to keep it afloat.

Rudessa turned to Amella and her face looked drained of blood. She grabbed hold of the princess, desperately trying to stay clear of the edge of the boat when the hand unexpectedly reached out and tried to grab her.

'Hit it with something!' the Satyr bellowed, his voice filling with fury and Amella spun in her seat, looking for something practical to use as a weapon. She called out to Lord Taurion and Master Fangfoss to help her but both shifted their gaze, unsure what they could do when her wide eyes urged them to use their wits. She felt blind panic rise and, in desperation, pulled off her gloves to grab hold of the powerful necklace. Her touch forced the wheel of encrusted pink diamonds and precious stones to rotate, generating a circle of magic. Amella pointed a trembling finger towards the monster. A blinding flash of white left her fingertips, hitting the hideous creature directly on its slippery back and a high pitched howl shot from its mouth and the hand instantly let go. The sea creature fell back into the sea with a loud splash, leaving behind a black, charred area of wood where its fingers had clung so tightly only moments ago.

Amella breathed a sigh of relief but it was short-lived. A second later the boat bobbed violently against the waves when something hit it full force at the bow and Amella and Rudessa screamed aloud, both petrified the boat was about to tip over and cast them into a watery grave.

The Satyr raised his monstrous head, the hood slipping and Amella felt her mouth go dry when she saw his facial features for the first time. He was indeed one of the rarer Satyrs who, unlike the Minotaur, had become extinct many centuries ago and she dropped her gaze, feeling a moment of repulsion when she saw the huge horns protruding from his ghastly head.

'We are surrounded by sea goblins!' the Satyr bellowed, his voice as deep as the ocean. 'Beware for these monsters are the most vicious predators known to live in the sea.'

Sea spray was salting the air when an enormous sea goblin leapt from the water and headed straight for the Satyr's throat. The hideous monster was seen to spread its huge jaws and a slimy hand flew out from its mouth, its fat, chubby fingers clearly ready to grab hold of the first thing it touched. However, the Satyr was one step ahead and he wrenched the oar from its iron clasp and whacked the huge, sea goblin straight in the jowls. A piercing wail left its bloodied lips and the hand instinctively retracted inside as its body fell back into the sea, drenching everyone on board. The Satyr gripped the oar even tighter whilst he shook the water from his eyes, his knuckles turning white in preparation for a second strike, and the elves watched him with panic growing in their frightened eyes.

'I don't understand, these monsters are never seen in daylight,' the Satyr muttered, keeping his eyes fixed firmly on the surface of the sea. 'I'm starting to wonder whether they are able to smell your fear and this is the true reason why they have clambered so eagerly to the surface or whether there is a darker motive to their unexpected arrival.'

Rudessa, unable to contain herself a moment longer, burst into tears. 'I've never seen anything so hideous,' she bleated, taking out her handkerchief from one of her long sleeves and dabbing her eyes daintily. 'Those creatures are not only grotesque but quite terrifying,' she continued, turning the handkerchief over and proceeding to blow her nose. 'No one warned us or said anything about the tower being guarded by evil creatures such as these.'

Lord Taurion nodded his agreement, staring open-mouthed towards the churning waves and when he spoke it was clear he was of the same conclusion.

'I too have never seen or heard of sea goblins before,' he said, looking baffled. 'And did you see the size of their huge black eyes? I thought that was harrowing enough, but no, to think there is a creature who spawns a human hand inside its mouth, why I feel nothing but loathing for these monsters.'

'You're right,' chimed up Master Fangfoss, who had been silent up to now. 'Why, I think it's very strange that no one warned us of the hidden dangers lurking beneath these murky waters,' he said, sounding bewildered.

Lord Taurion appeared to turn thoughtful, his left eyebrow twitching when he shot a suspicious glance directly at Master Fangfoss.

'There is no one I know who would wish me harm,' he said, hearing his own voice crackle with doubt. 'Yet, why do I get the feeling the goblins knew we were coming?'

'It's not just about you!' Amella declared, suddenly looking incredulous. 'Don't you see that whoever disturbed these demons and alerted them to our presence had more than our best interests at heart.'

'What absolute nonsense!' snapped Lord Taurion, waving his hand in the air and dismissing her comments. 'It's all a simple coincidence that's all. No one in their right mind would harm a hair of an influential member of the Guild let alone the Queen of Nine Winters.'

'Don't you be too sure,' Amella snapped back, clicking her tongue in frustration. 'It's obvious from your damning allegations against me that you have started a precedent which will enable plenty to benefit from my demise and as for yourself, well, there are always others who are ready and waiting to take your place.' Lord Taurion sniffed aloud and he folded his arms sulkily across his chest, turning his sour face out towards the sea.

The Queen gave a heavy sigh and looked away, but an odd noise soon caught her attention and she leaned forward, pushing her auburn hair behind her pointed ears. She listened for several seconds, unable to identify the strange sound but then recognition sparked inside her eyes and she felt her stomach knot when she heard what she thought to be the scraping of fingernails coming from underneath the boat. The noise was so awful it made her recoil and she looked up and saw Rudessa clap her hands over her ears to try and block out the sound that was making her teeth on edge, but it was to no avail, the noise was simply impossible to ignore.

'Here, take the oars!' roared the Satyr to Lord Taurion. 'I will do my best to keep these sharks at bay, but I need you to steer the boat towards the tower because I can't protect you and row at the same time.'

Lord Taurion scrambled to his feet, eager to please the Satyr. He reached out, grabbing the oars firmly in his hands, and his arms pulled stiffly at the poles, the paddle cutting through the water at only half the speed of the Satyr. The water rippled with each new stroke he produced and he was thankful they were moving at all until he saw a goblin shark swim over and attach itself to the lower part of one of his paddles, holding on by its teeth.

'Oh, no! They're attacking the oars!' he yelled, when a sharp tug almost tore the paddle from out of his hand. The Satyr swung round and grabbed the oar from Lord Taurion's sweaty clutches and he pulled the pole from the water. Catapulting the tip up towards the sky, the devil fish flew from the sanctuary of the sea, its huge body still connected with both rows of teeth. The Satyr rotated the long pole as though he was merely casting a fishing line. The speed alone made the goblin let go and it bounced on the surface of the sea like a fat, skimming pebble until it sank deep beneath the waves.

The Satyr bellowed in triumph, his voice sounding like a blustering horn and Amella felt an intense ripple of fear shudder down her soaking wet spine. The Satyr was about to pass the oar back to Lord Taurion when another sea goblin jumped from the icy depths. With its long nose quivering and its mouth open wide, the goblin revealed numerous rows of flesh ripping teeth. The Satyr saw it from out of the corner of his eye and before the hand had time to protrude, he spun his body, smashing his fist straight into the shark's gaping mouth. As soon as he retracted his hand, blood and broken teeth flew in the air like winter rain and the fish fell into the boat, momentarily stunned.

Rudessa and Amella began screaming in terror, pulling their feet under their skirts, petrified the sea monster was about to bite them with what was left of its splintered teeth. The Satyr didn't waste a second and he bent forward, grabbing the creature by its slippery head and with his huge hands opened its powerful jaws and ripped the fish clean in two. Blood and guts splattered all over Rudessa, only narrowly missing the Queen, and the lady-in-waiting screamed out in distress, squirming uncontrollably when she tried to wipe the entrails and pieces of slime from out of her plastered hair. The Satyr threw what was left of the goblin overboard and Master Fangfoss, who had turned as white as a ghost, pulled his damp cloak over his head as though this gesture would somehow make him invisible. Lord Taurion broke his illusion, shrieking for his immediate attention and pointing to where the White Tower was looming in the distance.

'We're almost there!' he bayed, gripping the oars and using the last of his strength in getting them to shore. 'Just keep yourself together you idiot for I haven't the time or inclination to watch you fall to pieces.'

The Satyr swiftly changed places with Lord Taurion, pushing him out of the way with the palm of one of his large, meaty hands and before they knew it, they were cutting through the waves at terrific speed.

Still terrified, the four passengers and the Satyr jumped ship the moment their feet were able to make it onto dry land. The dock was dark and forlorn, but it felt like a welcomed sanctuary compared to the demonic sea that was waiting behind them.

Lord Taurion's face twitched when he tried to calm himself.

'That's a journey I will not wish to repeat until I have found my nerve,' he gasped, tying the boat to the wooden ramp and checking it was secure. He stared out to sea and saw the goblins had already disappeared under the waves and he gasped with genuine relief.

'Can you believe it, the demons have already returned to the bottom of the sea,' he huffed, but he was thankful nonetheless that they had vanished so soon. He pulled his cloak about him and the damp chill of wet clothing made his blood almost freeze in his veins, and he immediately peeled off his cape and dropped it to the ground.

Amella glanced his way only briefly before sweeping her gaze over what was to be her new home and forced herself not to whimper when she felt terror break over her like a crushing wave. Leading from the dock and lower ridge was a long, winding stairway made from crystallised rocks. The rocks resembled colourless moonstones but they caught the light from the sun's weak morning rays and each step became illuminated. At the very top a huge doorway was moulded into the tower itself. The Satyr was known to be the only person who held the infamous 'chime key' which was used to unlock the entrance to the prison.

Amella's eyes strayed to the few acres of land that circled the tower and was unable to hold back the choking sob which escaped her. The earth was scattered with rugged rocks which smothered every blade of grass which had ever tried to take root and she realised she would not be able to feel the earth beneath her toes for a very long time to come.

A low sob caught her attention and she turned to see Rudessa sitting in a heap on the ground and so she walked over to her and knelt beside her. She put her arm around her maid's shoulders to shield her from the cold air and felt the dampness of her clothing.

'I know you're bone weary,' Amella soothed, trying to get her maid to stand. 'However, things won't seem any better until we get you inside and you change into dry clothes.'

Filthy and soaked to the skin, Rudessa reluctantly pulled herself to her feet. Her eyes were still shining with distress and she clung helplessly to her mistress, the unmistakable odour of fish wafting from her wet, soiled dress and Amella couldn't help but cover her nose from the stench.

The Satyr walked by and Amella called to him, asking him to wait a moment.

'I am overwhelmed by your bravery,' Amella told the Satyr with genuine gratitude shining in her eyes. 'I really don't know what we would have done if you hadn't been here to save us this day.'

'You may call me Selnus, Your Highness,' said the Satyr, bowing his head in respect, 'and I wish you to know, it is my duty to protect you whilst you are staying in the White Tower.'

Amella felt a swift arrow of sorrow penetrate her heart at the thought of her incarceration and was unable to pull it out of the chasm. The gloom of the tower danced inside her mind and thoughts of misjudged kings and queens filled her with a deep despair. She had no way of knowing how long she would be made to stay in this terrible place and she thought herself stupid to have let them take her so easily.

'Lord Taurion, Master Fangfoss,' she called out in a weak rasp, 'can you shed any light as to how long I must stay in this dreadful place?'

Lord Taurion's characteristic smirk seemed to reappear all too soon and he shrugged his shoulders to show her he was unable to answer her question.

'We will have no idea until your trial,' he told her, pulling at his dripping wet shirt with open distaste. 'Unfortunately, the Order of the Guild did not specify a time limit to your confinement, but I'm sure they will set a date as soon as possible.'

The Satyr interrupted their conversation when he saw the look of bewilderment spreading over the Queen's face and he indicated it was time for them to start climbing the mountain of steps.

'You must get inside and out of your wet things,' he said, pulling at his own damp robe. 'We are rather unfortunate out here because we don't have a healer close by so it is imperative that you should try to stay healthy and not catch a chill.'

Selnus was the first to attempt the steep climb with the chime key fixed firmly in his grasp and with each bold step he took a pale light shone beneath his feet. Amella and Rudessa reluctantly followed, climbing the stairway one step at a time until they finally reached the top, weak with exhaustion. Amella couldn't help but sigh when Rudessa started to cry yet again, her patience wearing a little thin, her own anguish forced behind a hard exterior. The maid's wailing was growing louder by the minute and her sobs were drifting far out to sea. Her misery echoed for miles and miles and whilst Amella helped her maid inside, she prayed someone would hear her mournful cries and, finding pity in their heart, would come and take them away from this desolate place forever.

Chapter 19

When Crystal and Clump finally entered the Valley of the Green Witch they thought the afternoon breeze carried the distinct aroma of rich, sweet grass. Still riding the horse which had been given to her by Bruis, Crystal played 'I spy' with her close companion, insisting on amusing Clump as he walked beside her and she laughed happily when he participated with far too much enthusiasm.

Very soon, they found themselves on a dirt track, heading downhill and deeper into the valley. The ground grew soft and yielding and Kyte grunted when his hooves slipped in the newly formed mud. They continued until they reached a gully and a small path could be seen going upstream. The ground was still soft and covered in a barricade of twisted brambles, their leaves having withered with seasonal decay and Kyte snorted unhappily when his tail got caught in their thorns.

Clump reached out and touched the side of Kyte's neck and Crystal pulled gently at his mane to make him stand still.

'What is it?' she asked, tugging a little harder when Kyte chose to ignore her command with a light toss of his head.

'We're not far from the mine,' Clump said, and a frown appeared on his face. He glanced towards the distant hills and Crystal followed his gaze from between the horse's ears.

'This track is far narrower than I would have liked and Kyte isn't going to relish finding his footing along this trail,' Crystal said, turning to watch Kyte flick his tail free with an impatient swish.

'He'll manage alright,' said Clump, with a shrug, 'and if we're lucky we should arrive at the mine well before nightfall. However, from here on we must be more alert because this is the place where fire-breathing dragons are known to roam. Over the next ridge is a place called Green Crag and in the caves that you're

186

about to see, many young baby dragons who have not long since hatched are waiting for a tasty meal. The Crag has been known to house over a hundred new baby dragons at any one time, weaned by a clan of rather overprotective parents so it's best that we don't draw attention to ourselves, unless you wish to become a light snack.'

Crystal slid a curious look at Clump and then nudged the stallion forward; her eyes were keen to examine the seemingly sleepy landscape and a wisp of intrigue floated somewhere behind them.

'What species of dragon is born here?' she asked, watching Clump take the lead and she glanced towards the sky in the hope of spotting something red flying overhead. Clump turned towards her and a scowl was set upon his face.

'This part of the valley is known to house the Ice Dragons and these creatures are the most beautiful dragons you will ever feast your eyes upon, but be aware, they are also the most deadly.'

Crystal couldn't contain her enthusiasm any longer and her eyes widened with tell-tale signs of excitement.

'Ice Dragons! Wow, how fantastic! Are you telling me that they're actually made of ice?' she gasped, already captivated by the mere thought of seeing whimsical, melting dragons.

'No, of course not,' Clump huffed. 'These creatures are not made of ice, but they look like ice, to be more precise they look like gigantic ice sculptures and they are able to live in very severe and adverse weather conditions. Their whole bodies can turn completely transparent like water and this is how they got their name. But don't be fooled, ice by name, ice by nature. These dragons shoot fire first and ask questions later and they are known to have very, very bad tempers!'

'Oh, that's a shame,' Crystal sniffed, letting out an exaggerated whine. 'I thought I was about to meet something that I could tell my grandchildren about when I'm old and grey.' Clump looked up at her in bewilderment, clearly unable to understand her train of thought for he knew it would be at least a couple of hundred years before the first grey hair dared to sprout from her young head and he hoped she would have something much more exciting to tell them by then.

Crystal suddenly jumped down from the horse, leading him towards the brook for a drink and a moment to rest. The water babbled a pretty tune when they grew close, tinkering playfully over the uneven stones and misshapen pebbles, calming both the princess and the beast. She closed her eyes and the wintry sun tried to penetrate her skin. She felt the tension from the last few days leave her shoulders and she stretched her back and arms, trying to unwind. She then turned towards Clump, feeling his eyes burrowing deep into her back.

'Best not to linger,' he said, his voice low, fearful of drawing unwanted attention and he stepped away from her, his eyes darting towards the soft, billowing trees, just up ahead. His jaw clenched with expectation and Crystal's tension returned. She tilted her head, listening for whispering signs of danger, but instead found a rush of old images, sweet memories of home flying to the forefront of her mind and her shoulders wilted like dead flowers. Clump saw her eyes fill with sorrow, but before he could say anything remotely comforting, she was clambering back onto the horse and offering out her hand for him to join her.

The sun was low when they arrived at Green Crag and they had perhaps covered no more than a few miles when they came across a huge dragon's corpse lying on the ground. The lingering stench of death filled Crystal's nostrils and she screwed up her nose when the putrid smell made her gag. The rotting carcass had been surrounded by large vultures who squawked their disappointment at being disturbed and a few hairy scavengers scuttled away when the horse approached; Kyte whinnied dutifully, being careful where he placed his hooves.

Clump's body suddenly stiffened.

'We need to get out of here,' the Windigo whispered in her ear and her body gave an unexpected shiver when she heard the urgency in his voice and so she spurred Kyte on with a low cry and a push, heading towards a spectacular array of dark caverns, looming in the foreground like an ancient Stone Age monument.

Crystal had never seen so many open-mouthed caves carved inside one piece of gigantic rock. The entranceway was enormous, the rock towering some sixty feet above sea level and the caves themselves looked to house a network of long, dark chambers which were hidden deep inside. It all seemed strategically planned and at every cave's mouth an abundance of hardy trees and wild bushes grew, keeping the vast holes partly protected from the raw elements of nature, creating a place which looked, in her opinion, like something from a gothic fairy tale.

Crystal eyed her surroundings and noticed a thick river of black, slimy gunk trickling down the outer sides of the rock as though someone had thrown large buckets of melted tar over its surface, but in a flash she realised she was looking at the excrement and waste matter of the dragons and she shuddered, suddenly repulsed.

'We mustn't get any closer,' Clump warned, reaching out to pull at Kyte's mane. 'Just keep to the trail and get Kyte to move as quickly as he can,' he urged, sounding agitated. Crystal nodded, feeling a trickle of cold sweat run down the back of her neck. Although she was curious enough to want to glimpse an Ice Dragon, she was no fool as to what they would do to her if they caught her on their territory and as they rode by, several of those dark, dreary caves lit up with red-gold light and long bursts of smoke bellowed out into the air as though let loose from a foundry furnace. Kyte soon became spooked and when a loud roar filled the air, his graceful trot turned into a canter and he ran along the thin, grassy path as though a dragon was hot on his heels.

When the sun disappeared from the sky, Crystal and her companion finally reached the Stannary Mines. Clump busied himself making camp just inside one of the broken mouths, giving Crystal both adequate shelter and a fair vantage point should anyone try to sneak up and try to take her by surprise. He soon became edgy and rather jumpy and Crystal realised he would shortly have to leave her to live his night as a ferocious timber wolf.

'I'll be fine on my own,' she insisted, trying to ease his tension when she saw he was dithering with anxiety. 'My father taught me a really cool spell which wraps me in an invisible force field and lasts until the sun rises. He told me he found it very useful when he was in the forest once.'

Crystal was unable to lift his black mood, even after she helped him make a fire and he had produced some kind of flowery stew. He sat beside her pushing his fat fingers through his matted hair, clearly unsettled and he stared into the flames with his mournful eyes, refusing to eat a thing.

'I will not be too far from you this night,' he told her, throwing more wood onto the fire. 'But you know I cannot stay with you in case I bring you harm and this makes me so angry with myself.'

Crystal looked into his clouded eyes and wished she could put him at ease. She sensed his heavy burden and pity filled her heart. He soon got up from the fire and then started toing and froing with restlessness, acting like a caged animal and the bright shadows from the firelight danced on his dark, hairy skin, making him look a little wild.

Crystal felt a moment of unease so called for him to stop whatever it was he was doing and opened her arms towards him, like a mother to her child. Clump stopped dead in his tracks as his brain engaged and she saw him falter. He brought his fingers to his mouth suddenly unsure of himself and then he was running to her with zeal shining in his eyes as he accepted her warm embrace. She hugged him tight, feeling his wet nose tickle her neck and this caused a rush of love for the dear Windigo to fill her heart.

'Dearest Clump, you have to understand you can't change who you are no matter how much you want to,' she whispered in his ear and she stroked his back to soothe him. 'You know, you just have to learn to live with what life throws at you, after all that's all any of us can do.'

She felt Clump stiffen, a clear indication that he didn't agree with her logic and then he was falling to his knees, sobbing.

'What is it, Clump?' she asked, her eyes filled with concern. She knelt beside him, lifting his chin with her finger so she could wipe the stream of tears away.

Clump sounded choked with sorrow.

'I don't want to leave you here all alone and vulnerable,' he blubbered, clutching her jacket as though he never wanted to let go. She hugged him tight once again, understanding his dilemma at leaving her in such a dangerous and lonely place, but she gave him words of encouragement, telling her she would be fine, until his tears finally subsided and his body no longer shuddered with despair.

The darkness fell upon them all too soon and when the moon rose high in the sky Clump jumped up, seemingly startled and without looking back, he left the warm sanctuary of her arms, rushing instead towards the cold kiss of night.

Chapter 20

The Wanderer sat alone in the canyon and he was afraid. After the scene at the river he knew he'd failed his master and therefore worried himself stupid over what consequences awaited him. He had stolen away like a scolded cat, his cloak swinging around his body in dark disarray, much like his senses and he constantly looked over his shoulder, convinced that Bridgemear would be close on his heels.

Reaching for his horse he snatched the hemp bag from off his saddle and pulled it to his chest. He glanced about, his sharp eyes searching the distance for any signs which told him someone was approaching and, once satisfied he was alone, reached inside to locate Elveria's spells. He cast the bottles carefully along the stony ground and felt a darkening frustration grow inside his gut. He picked up each vial in turn, pondering over what was held inside until confusion clouded his judgement and he put them back in the bag, unable to figure out what to do next.

He returned to his horse, disheartened, strapping the bag once again to his saddle and felt a blustery wind blow against his cheek, causing him to wince when a few specks of dust flew in his eye. He rubbed at his lids and he caught sight of a spiral of leaves and particles of dirt billowing up from the ground. A mere second passed and a miniature tornado evolved and the freak of nature caught his immediate attention. The wind suddenly dropped, but the leaves continued to spin, twisting together until the dying foliage and bits of earth levitated in the air, forming what he could only describe later as an ugly death mask, which moulded itself into the harrowing face of Elveria.

The face floated closer and its eyes crinkled at the corners with displeasure.

192

'You have failed me!' said the downturned mouth which was placed in its centre and the Wanderer shrank back in alarm.

'F-f-forgive me, my lord,' the elf stuttered, clearly shaken. 'I did not mean for the spell not to work but the magicians weave strong magic and the warrior Amadeus wielded the Sword of Truth.'

Elveria's face appeared to crease as he pondered over the Wanderer's words, the leaves around his eyes disintegrating when his brow furrowed and his lips crunched down with bitterness.

'I hope it is clear to you that I am not content with what happened today, but I am willing to give you a second chance, but realise this, you will get no more. I want Bridgemear dead and as for the others, I wish for you to follow them until you find out where they are headed. Now, you must somehow get Bridgemear to stop for the night and stay in one place until dawn. When you have managed to do this, open the dark red vial which I have given you and pour out what you find inside in a thin line along the ground and when dawn breaks perhaps then we will witness Bridgemear's demise once and for all.'

The Wanderer simply nodded, staring intently into the lifeless eyes of the wizard. Dead leaves drifted from his face like flecks of rust and when Elveria spoke, tiny, brown specks floated away from his decaying mouth.

'Do not fail me again,' the wizard warned and before the Wanderer could answer him, the wind pierced through the mask and scattered his face like a billowing cloud of dandelion seeds. The Wanderer took a moment to recompose himself having lost his nerve, but Elveria's cold warning was ringing loudly inside his head. He took a deep breath, watching the last remnants of the mask blow along the breeze and then he turned and mounted his horse. He racked his brains for a cunning plan, his mind in turmoil and he looked down at his hands and saw that they were shaking. He grabbed the reins, his brain, like his horse, restless, and there he sat pale and still, until a thread of an idea started to spin from somewhere at the back of his mind. The vein in his temple pulsed as he started to gather his thoughts for he wanted rid of Elveria so badly it was like a fever, burning him. He toyed with a few variations until he was stuck by desperation. A cold twitch touched his mouth when he finally realised what he must do, it was bordering on crazy, suicide even, but then if he was lucky, perhaps his plan might just work ...

*

Later on that day Bridgemear rode into the canyon. It wasn't much of a place but at least it meant he had only one more day's ride until he reached the Valley of the Green Witch. He rode his horse fiercely and the poor beast grunted from tiredness just like the other horses but the decision had already been made by the group that they would ride throughout the night.

Darkness was descending when Arhdel suddenly gave out a warning cry.

'Look! Over there, there's something dangling between the trees!'

His companions turned in their saddles to look to where he was frantically pointing and Bridgemear shot his arm up into the sky and projected a halo of light towards the scanty trees. What he saw there made him drop from his saddle and run with the others, his sword outstretched because in-between two thinning branches, a bloodied figure was hanging limply by its arms.

Arhdel was the first to cross the dry earth and reach the unconscious soul.

'Help me cut him down!' he shouted to Amadeus, already slicing his sword through the thick rope. 'It looks like he's been here for hours.'

'Grab him!' Amadeus gasped, when his side of the rope snapped and within seconds he was helping Arhdel ease the poor creature gently to the ground. They made him as comfortable as possible and Amadeus used his own cloak as a misshapen pillow. Both looked grim when they saw the amount of blood lost and it was Bridgemear and Niculmus who looked on with stricken faces.

'What on earth is a solitary elf doing out here all alone?' Niculmus asked, bending down to get a closer look at his wounds. He noted his head suffered an open gash as though he'd been hit by a rock from behind. His shirt was torn almost to his navel and there were obvious signs of an animal attack. Long jagged claw marks travelled down from his neck to his abdomen, his left arm had been mauled and he was missing several fingers.

'These look like the bite marks of a wolf,' said Niculmus, recognising the tell-tale signs. 'I've seen wounds like these on the homestead when our animals were taken, but wolves aren't able to hit their victims with a rock and then string them up whilst they are still alive.'

'It may have been a Windigo,' said Arhdel, scanning the surrounding trees for a glimpse of the predator.

'Look, there!' he cried, pointing to several claw marks etched across a large tree trunk, 'it may be just as I suspected.'

They each stared at the bark of the tree which had been stripped away to reveal the soft pulp inside and it was Niculmus who dashed over to touch the splintered wood with his inquisitive fingertips. The wood was so ingrained he could push his fingers deep inside. The claw marks were vicious and he stole a wary glance at the others before pulling his hand away.

'Will you be able to save the elf?' Arhdel asked Bridgemear, looking as though he already knew the answer and Bridgemear felt the wind blow over him and touch the back of his neck like a cold hand.

'I don't give him much chance to be honest. Why, he must be crazy to be out here alone, but still, I will at least try to do what I can. Will you make camp whilst I tend to his wounds? I fear as well as you that we have found him a little too late.'

Arhdel nodded gravely.

'At least we can say we didn't just leave him to die,' he sighed, his face turning morose. 'I only hope we don't have the added task of digging a fresh grave this night.'

Bridgemear shook his head, raising a blonde eyebrow when he looked down at the deathly figure already turning grey.

'I must hurry,' he said, gesturing to Niculmus to come and help him. 'I will need whatever power I can muster if we have any chance of saving this poor creature.'

Niculmus was by his side in an instant and Arhdel made his way to Amadeus to help build a fire. Bridgemear grabbed his staff and then held it at arm's length, pushing the rod towards the broken body which lay motionless before him.

'Niculmus,' he bellowed, forcing sleeping birds to awaken and shriek into the night from fright, 'raise your wand towards mine.'

Niculmus immediately pulled his wand from his belt, pointing it towards the tip of his master's stave. A spark of white light surged from his wand and connected with the sphere fixed to the head of Bridgemear's staff. The magician turned, striking the earth with the rod as soon as he felt the connection and a ball of shimmering light manifested before him. Bridgemear flung the tip of the staff towards the crumpled body and the ghostly glow hit the chest cavity of the elf and then vanished.

The wounded figure opened his eyes.

'He's alive!' cried Niculmus in delight, but Bridgemear stopped him from uttering another word.

'The bleeding has stopped that's all. I must go and find ingredients to make a healing salve,' he said, turning his attention away from him and hurtling towards the nearest spindly bush. His fingers inspected the few frail leaves growing on its branches and then he was snapping them off with a sharp tug and inspecting them more closely.

'It's so damn barren out here,' he hissed, drawing from the shadows when he realised they were of no use, 'there's hardly anything growing here that's useful.'

Arhdel and Amadeus continued busying themselves by feeding the horses and Bridgemear was seen rushing from one thinning bush to the next. The air crackled with apprehension and the horses became jittery when Bridgemear's frustration finally filtered in their direction.

The wounded figure began trembling and a deep groan left his lips when dark embers of fire ignited behind his eyes. The elf held his hand to his chest when the pain became too much to bear and he blanched before throwing up all over the ground. He gave an unexpected wail and started squealing in agony.

Bridgemear's head snapped back when he realised what was happening and he rushed to the elf's side, his hands cupped with just a few meagre berries.

'Quick, Niculmus,' he shouted, unable to find an adequate spot to throw down his ingredients so he could use his sceptre, 'cast a sleeping spell.'

Niculmus pulled out his wand and did as he was told, making the elf fall into a deep trance.

Bridgemear's mouth grew thin with concern, but he heaved a thankful sigh towards his apprentice.

'You have done well. Now I can concentrate on making a salve,' he explained, looking a little relieved.

'Can I give you a hand?' Niculmus asked, believing he had just been tested, 'for I have recently learned how to make such balms from the healer Sawbones.'

Bridgemear tipped his head and pondered for a moment.

'No,' he said, thoughtfully. 'I would prefer for you to stay at his side, he may awaken at any moment and one of us must be here to send him back to sleep if that should happen.' Niculmus accepted Bridgemear's command with a nod of his blonde head and he looked up to see Arhdel place a warm blanket over the stranger's body.

'Go and grab a bite to eat,' Arhdel insisted, pointing to where Amadeus was pulling something edible from out of his saddlebag.

'Go on, I'll keep watch.'

Niculmus was eternally grateful and smiled to show his gratitude. He pulled his cloak close around his shoulders as he left, shivering when the chill in the night air started to tease his skin. Arhdel stood on guard, his eyes alert and his sword clasped firmly in his hand as Niculmus walked away.

It took much longer than planned but eventually Bridgemear returned with enough ingredients to make the salve. He wriggled his fingers and a bowl appeared before him, then he mashed berries and wild flowers together with a long, flat stone. Once the dull paste was ready, the magician bent over the elf and smeared it carefully over his wounds. The night fell silent as he worked his magic and the fire crackled and hissed as though to remind them all of its existence.

'Now, we can only wait,' Bridgemear told Arhdel when the job was done. 'However, we have no choice but to stay until dawn. If he survives then we must take him with us even though he will slow us down but should he die, well, you know what to do.'

Tossing his head like a fly-stung horse, Bridgemear moved towards the fire, his mouth set in an unintentional scowl. Arhdel followed him and Niculmus, who had long since finished eating, was now asleep, the point of his wand visible underneath his thin blanket.

Bridgemear sensed Arhdel's eyes were upon him and he looked up, catching his stare. They looked intently at one other for a second longer until Arhdel dropped his gaze.

'Do not worry sire, I'm sure we will find her,' said the warrior, trying to sound confident.

Bridgemear turned towards him and his eyes were filled with anguish.

'I fear we are no closer to finding her now than when we first set out,' he rasped, and he looked up towards the moon, watching the clouds smother its silver light. 'We have found nothing on our travels that will help us find my daughter, indeed all we have come across in the desolate place is a half-eaten elf!'

Amadeus came and joined them but soon they all fell silent, locked within their own deep thoughts and when Bridgemear's frustration grew too much for him to bear he stomped away, kicking violently at any small stones which were in his path. He made his way over to his horse to place his staff through the lance holes on his saddle and tripped over something which had got caught on the heel of his boot. Suddenly he gave a tremendous cry of excitement and Arhdel immediately drew his sword.

'Sire,' Amadeus cried, running to his side, unable to comprehend the look of joy on the mage's softening features, 'what has gotten into you?'

'Look what I've found,' said Bridgemear beaming from ear to ear. He was holding up a circular object that was glistening against the light of the dancing flames.

'What is it?' asked Arhdel, screwing up his eyes and trying to focus better. 'Have you found a bit of fool's gold?'

'No, you idiot, it's an Elvin bangle,' Bridgemear cried, almost dancing on the spot. 'It's a memory bracelet and more importantly, it belongs to Crystal!'

Both Amadeus and Arhdel looked at one another in shocked silence until Amadeus managed to find his voice.

'How can you be so sure?' he asked, looking perplexed. 'For it looks common enough to me.'

Bridgemear flashed a look of hurt pride, before regaining his composure and explaining to them how he had made the bangle when he was still a lowly apprentice.

Amadeus's cheeks flared red.

'Forgive my ignorance,' he blushed, staring down at his feet, 'I did not mean to appear rude.'

The mage held no grudge and instructed him instead to awaken Niculmus. The warrior did as he was told with a bow of his head and immediately ran over and shook Niculmus's shoulder, watching him with some amusement when he jumped up confused and disorientated from being startled awake.

Niculmus stared into Amadeus's smiling face.

'Get up and join us,' he said, with a grin. 'Since you went to sleep Bridgemear has found Crystal's memory bracelet.' Niculmus rubbed his eyes and then glanced over to the magician. Shadows and light danced wildly on his face but he saw hope burning deep inside the mage's brilliant blue eyes. Racing across the ground Niculmus rushed to his master's side and saw the pretty bangle in his hand. As he drew close, he watched Bridgemear breathe over the centre stone, causing them all to catch their own, their eyes bright with expectancy. His breath melted away only to be replaced by a triangle of bright, purple light which shot from the stone. The light intensified and a gamut of colours exploded above his hand to form a moving picture.

The stone revealed the image of Crystal. She was standing in the mouth of a dark cave and each one of them let out a sincere sigh of relief when they saw she had not been harmed. The spell inside the bangle, however, only created moving images and not a sound came from Crystal's lips when she tried to relay a message to her father. Frustration soon wiped away Bridgemear's earlier euphoria, but he replayed the memory over and over again, watching her mouth pronounce silent words in the hope he could grasp what she was so desperately trying to tell him. His eyes focused on her lips and then a cry left his own and he turned to the others, a look of victory shining like stars in his ice blue eyes.

'She's telling me she's going to the Stannary Mines,' he yelled in triumph. 'We were going in the right direction all along.'

Bridgemear's laughter broke the sick elf's slumber and he sat up, his face filled with confusion. The dawn was breaking and mist was seen to snake between the trees like white, velvety ghosts.

'It's alright, you're safe with us,' said Niculmus, running over and putting a firm hand on his shoulder.

'My name is Niculmus. I am an apprentice at the Palace of Nine Winters, so tell me friend, what's yours?' He felt his companion tense and his confusion appeared to deepen.

'My name?' the sickly elf mouthed, looking along the ground as though he would find it written there. 'Yes, what is your name?' Niculmus repeated, 'can you remember who you are?' Two piercing eyes stared into his own showing only flashes of doubt. The elf eventually shook his head and lowered his gaze, a heavy sigh escaping his lips.

'It is of no importance,' Niculmus said, trying to reassure him. 'Please do not fret, I'm sure your memory will return in due course, however, we must try and get you on your feet for we must soon be on our way.'

A horn blasted somewhere in the distance and everyone froze and then, out of the thickening mist, several shrieking shadows ran from the dawn light, wielding silver swords high above their heads.

Amadeus ran past shouting, 'Ready yourself Niculmus, we are under attack,' and he raced to the horses, untying the reins and slapping their flanks to make them run for cover. He heard the sound of a sword cutting the air behind him and he roared with an explosion of fury, spinning on his heels, his sword raised above his head. He struck his attacker, splitting his shield and slicing his arm, and the man went down in an instant. Amadeus hissed like a viper when his attacker lifted his sword and a clash of steel rang through the air when they connected. Amadeus was a skilled warrior and he thrust his sword straight through his assailant's heart, piecing his chest cavity as though it was nothing more than ripe fruit. His attacker stared blindly as the blood poured from his fatal wound until he fell against the dirt – dead.

'We are being attacked by dragon masters!' Amadeus yelled, when he saw a large tattoo of a dragon's head on the side of his victim's neck. His voice turned thick with disbelief and he looked up towards the sky and saw the heavens turning blood red.

'Prepare yourselves for fire too!' he shouted towards the others whilst running to the aid of Arhdel. 'Beware! Savage beasts are almost upon us.' Arhdel, Amadeus and Bridgemear began fighting the group of dragon masters whilst Niculmus stayed at the injured elf's side, his sword raised to protect him. He watched the others fight, showing their masterful skill at arms and he was surprised when one of the dragon masters broke free and ran towards the approaching mass which was flying right towards him.

The dragon master raised his hands heavenwards, bellowing a command towards the sky. A huge fireball exploded in the air and the dragons roared in answer to their master's call.

Bridgemear watched the creatures gathering overhead in disbelief. Running to his horse, he grabbed his staff and hurled himself towards the dragon master, shooting a missile of fire from its centre whilst he ran. The flame hit the warrior clean in the face and he rocked from the blow, his feet taking three steps back and two forward and Bridgemear was more than a little surprised to see he was still standing. He shot another fiery projectile and then another, but the dragon master simply raised the palms of his hands to shield himself from the balls of white, forcing them to the ground. Laughing like a mad man and looking smug, he pointed his fingers to the sky and then he was flying as straight as an arrow until he landed on the back of his very own fire-breathing dragon.

'Run for your lives!' Bridgemear shouted, watching ten huge wings pin back ready to dive. 'I will try to hold them off whilst you all find cover. There are some huge rocks over there by those trees, if you can make it, you may stand a chance of survival.'

'Sire, we cannot leave without you,' Amadeus cried, watching Arhdel help Niculmus to carry their recently acquired comrade to one of the horses.

'You have no choice!' Bridgemear snapped, his eyes gleaming, 'only my magic and a miracle can save us now.'

'But, sire!'

'Enough, Amadeus, do not think to defy me; you must go quickly before it's too late.'

Amadeus hung his head like a docile hound before running to catch his horse.

Once the elf was safe Niculmus ran to his master.

'Please, my lord, let me stay by your side and fight,' he pleaded, his eyes burning with hope.

'Yes, very well,' said Bridgemear, without contemplation. 'I will need you here to help me for this attack will not be over anytime soon. However, I just can't believe this is happening. Never in a thousand years have the dragon masters turned against us. It is a clear indication of how things are getting way out of hand and whoever is plotting against us seems willing to go to great lengths to see us all dead.'

Niculmus nodded, a look of pride still glowing on his young face, but then an almighty roar filled his ears and fire shot along the ground, and he looked up to see the dragons heading straight towards them.

Bridgemear stretched out his arm and drew a circle in the air; a large shield appeared in his hand.

'Niculmus, you must do as I do,' he instructed, and bending his knees he placed his shield above his head, kneeling like a Roman centurion.

'Make your shield as thick as you can, it must be able to withstand immense heat and protect you from the flames,' Bridgemear urged his apprentice.

Niculmus obeyed, circling his wand above his head, listening to the angry roar of the approaching dragons grow closer.

Bridgemear pointed his staff at the descending clan before turning his attention back to Niculmus.

'Now we must create a barrier to protect us from their line of fire,' he said, allowing a sceptical smile to touch his lips. 'When I give you the signal create a blocking spell, we cannot stop the dragons, but we can stop the flames reaching us.'

A blood-curdling shriek penetrated Niculmus's ears and he glanced upwards to see the clan break their assembly, only to re-form seconds later.

'They are ready,' shouted Bridgemear his eyes growing wide with expectancy, 'now, after three, one, two ...'

Chapter 21

Stifling a yawn, Amella slid her arms into her dress with the help of her faithful maid, Rudessa. She moved to her makeshift dressing table and allowed the sunlight to bathe her in gold whilst she braided her long, auburn hair. She hated the tiny, cramped room she had slept in for two nights situated at the very top of the tower, unable to accept her new surroundings as anything but bleak. This morning it seemed was just like any other except Lord Taurion and Master Fangfoss had found their courage and fled from the tower with the help of Selnus in the early hours. Racing to the shore at breakneck speed Selnus rowed his boat until the Guild member's feet were firmly back on dry land and far from the clutches of the terrifying goblins.

Amella heard a commotion downstairs which made her knot her hair swiftly and run to the top of the stairs; she looked down to see Selnus dragging a large wooden trunk along the stone floor. He'd carried it up some eighty flights of stairs and the exertion caused him to snort from sheer effort. Amella clapped her hands with excitement when she espied her trunk, grinning like a young girl when she realised she would finally be able to have her own personal belongings around her. Like a nimble cat she descended to the lower floor, patting Selnus on one of his powerful shoulders in gratitude as she flew by, his once repulsive features seemingly now a thing of the past.

'Selnus, I can't believe my things are actually here,' she cried, showing her obvious delight. The Satyr reared his head and took a deep breath, clearly exhausted from the climb, refusing to speak until his lungs were once again filled with sweet air. Once he caught his breath, Selnus said, 'My lady, Professor Valentino had your things waiting at the quay when I arrived with Lord Taurion and Master Fangfoss this very morning. However, I found it unusually heavy to carry and my boat almost sunk from its weight.'

Amella chuckled and her eyes sparkled with imminent pleasure. 'You're teasing me,' she said with a light smile dancing at the corners of her mouth. 'I'm quite sure a few of my dresses and a handful of shoes would not be enough to sink your wee boat.'

Selnus huffed, unconvinced, forcing a cloud of hot breath to billow from his two enormous nostrils and he stomped about in protest.

Amella didn't notice his bad mood, staring instead at the dark wooden trunk on the floor and she reached down and allowed her fingers to trace over the metal clasp that held some of her most precious possessions inside. She was so pleased her clothes had finally arrived that she felt a lump rise in her throat. She glanced up, smiling brightly when she glimpsed the look of discontent brewing in Selnus's eyes. He caught her stare and saw there were tears of happiness shining in her own, unshed, and he drew back, realising she would want to enjoy a moment of privacy when she opened the lid to her trunk. He took his leave with a bow of his head and marched off down the many stairs and was soon out of sight.

Rudessa descended the stairway and made her way towards the Queen.

'Who would have thought something as hideous as a Satyr could turn out to be such a considerate creature,' she mused, moving even closer to her mistress's side. Amella nodded, admitting to thinking the same and, with a swirl of her skirts, sat on the floor next to the trunk.

She sighed quietly, tapping the lid with her fingers.

'I feel like I've waited a whole lifetime for these,' she said, finally lifting the lid and peeking at the mountain of rich, satin robes. Rudessa grew impatient wishing for the clothes to be out of the trunk and hanging in the makeshift closet but Amella had a different idea, stroking each garment as though it was the first time she had ever set eyes on it. The colours were so vivid compared to the drab walls that surrounded her that her eyes savoured the luscious reds, deep purples and vivid greens of her dresses. She rested her hands on a long, black gown made of silver silk. The kirtle and foresleeves were decorated with a stream of sea pearls and black diamond pouches and she found she couldn't hide her immense pleasure when her fingers glided over the precious stones. Her hands delved deeper inside the chest and her fingers brushed against something cold and unexpected. Puzzled, she pushed her silks to one side to reveal a dark, rounded stone.

She immediately reared up onto her knees, allowing interest and surprise to ignite behind her emerald-green eyes. She lifted the stone from its hiding place and placed it carefully on the floor. The circular stone was rather ordinary, except for the dark ring in its centre, which looked as though it had been placed there by some kind of branding iron. However, Amella recognised the symbol that was embossed in its centre immediately and the secret of the stone sent a spark of excitement rippling down her spine.

She thought of Professor Valentino who must have placed it there and felt only acute appreciation towards the magician who willingly risked everything to try and free her from this terrible place. This was the answer she had been waiting for: the Ring-stone would get her out of the White Tower, if only for a short time. Amella heard Rudessa's soft footsteps behind her and she turned to reveal the hidden treasure. Rudessa gave an unconscious sniff when she caught sight of it.

'What are you doing with a stone in your trunk?' she exclaimed, sounding exasperated. Amella's eyes rounded and she placed a finger to her full lips to quieten her maid. She kept her gaze fixed on Rudessa as she pointed to the stone.

'This is a Ring-stone,' she hissed, pulling her close, 'are you not aware of the magic they hold?' Rudessa shook her head, her wide eyes filled with ignorance and Amella gave a deep sigh of frustration.

'It is very simple to use for if I were to place the stone against my heart it will stop beating and I would turn to stone.'

'But what good will that do you?' gasped Rudessa, throwing her hands up into the air and Amella looked as though she was about to lose her patience.

'It means I can turn into rock and as a solid substance I will be able to travel through any naturally hard surface and go anywhere I wish. However, as soon as the Ring-stone is taken away from my chest I will return to my body and re-morph into my human form.'

'I-I-I still don't understand what you're saying,' stammered Rudessa, becoming flustered and she began folding a satin scarf to keep her trembling fingers busy.

Amella clasped hold of her hands.

'Rudessa, if I do this I will be able to leave this place, if only for a short time. I can then use the time wisely and see if I can find Elveria as I believe he is the culprit who has made me a prisoner here. We must work quickly though. I will pretend to fall with a fever and take to my bed. Selnus will not dare to enter my chamber until he grows suspicious. However, the moment he demands to see me, you must remove the Ring-stone from my heart and hide it some place safe. I will immediately return to my body and hopefully by then I will have some of the answers I seek to regain my freedom.'

Rudessa turned a ghastly shade of white, clearly unconvinced.

'Mistress, I am frightened of this magic. If what you tell me is true then you will turn to stone before my eyes and I fear you may not turn back when I remove it.'

Amella stood firm, refusing to listen to her maid.

'Look, Rudessa, you must do what I tell you or we will never be free from here. I have no choice, I must use the Ring-stone and you must be the one to help me.'

Heavy footsteps were heard approaching and Amella grabbed the stone and ran up the few stairs that led to her bed. Without a moment to lose she hid it under the wooden frame close to where she laid her head and then she was back at Rudessa's side, happily folding the last of her underclothes, much to the embarrassment of a rather modest Satyr when he entered a few seconds later.

'I have a surprise for you when you are ready for breakfast,' Selnus said, once the trunk was empty of her things and he had pushed it out of sight.

Amella looked outwardly calm but her legs were shaking like jelly.

'Oh, really? What would that be?' she asked, descending down several flights of stairs towards the small hovel they called the kitchen. The Satyr swiftly followed, chatting to her as she stepped through the shabby kitchen doorway and into the rather neglected

206

back room. He gave a swift snort, moving away from her and going instead to the small grated fire which acted as a stove.

'I have made you some sun biscuits,' he said proudly, bringing a plateful of bright golden crackers to her side and placing them on the small slab which acted as her breakfast table. The rich aroma of melted butter and cinnamon wafted in the air, making her mouth water.

'My, you have been a busy bee this morning,' she said, reaching out and taking a nibble. She felt the buttery ingredients melt on her tongue and then an orangey glow broke out on her skin and she giggled girlishly, unable to stifle the pleasure in her throat.

'I haven't had these since I was a child,' she beamed, pushing the plate towards Rudessa. 'Selnus, you are far too thoughtful for your own good,' she teased, and the Satyr smiled back, his thick, shiny lips revealing a set of monstrously huge teeth.

Once breakfast was over Amella returned to her bed chamber and told Rudessa to tell Selnus she had developed a severe headache and was suffering a mild fever and would therefore have to stay in her bed until it passed. Although she didn't like deceiving the kindly Satyr, she realised if she was to escape at all, she had no choice but to lie to him.

*

As soon as she reached her bed, Amella reclaimed the stone and then lay on top of her covers, belly up. She passed the stone to Rudessa whilst she settled herself and then placed her hands behind her head so that her fingers could touch the stone wall behind her. Amella ignored the look of panic in her maid's eyes and commanded her instead to place the stone above her heart.

Rudessa almost cried out when her quivering hands did as they were told and Amella took a sharp gasp of breath when the heavy stone was placed on her chest, its weight almost crushing her. An icy coldness melted through her skin and down to her heart, making her stifle an agonising cry and her lips immediately turned blue. Her heartbeat grew weak, the rhythm less regular and her pulse dropped to next to nothing. Amella struggled for one last breath and then her body stiffened and her flesh turned silver-grey and she turned into stone before Rudessa's tearful eyes.

Amella felt her transformation and it was as though she was simply a mere drop of water added to the vast pool of life. To her amazement she found she was able to move through the stone walls of the tower like a gentle ripple in the sand, pushing herself with little effort through the solid block and she headed straight towards the seabed. She moved like lightning through the rock formation beneath the sea until she made it to the shore. In minutes she was snaking between the shingle and layers of sandstone, heading further inland and on her way she found a maze of underground tunnels and secret passageways that she never knew existed and made a mental note of these new locations deep inside her brain. Miles and miles she travelled, through limestone, sandstone, molten rock and feldspar. Under rivers and through forests she travelled until she came upon an unknown group of mountains. Trying to save herself time and to avoid going around them, she flew through the outer surface and a cold voice, a voice she recognised, brushed her senses, forcing her to turn away from the mountains and head in a completely different direction. She moved downwards deep under the earth until she came across a tunnel and she tried to step through it, her foot protruding, but found she could not 'bodily' leave the stone.

She heard someone approaching and quickly pulled herself back to safety, camouflaged once again inside the rock, only her eyes could be seen and so she closed them tight, feeling her eyelids flutter like butterflies. When the footsteps stopped, she eventually found the courage to take a peek and saw Elveria standing only a few feet away from her. She held her breath, grateful he had not felt her presence and when he moved on to the next chamber she quickly followed.

Amella stared, mystified, when she saw a labyrinth of dark, lonely passageways standing in front of her. She wasn't sure where Elveria had gone and she swiftly manoeuvred through the dark walls of his chambers in a desperate bid to find him. She rushed through the stone, exhaling in relief when she came across him in an enormous cavern which was filled with treasures beyond anything she could have ever imagined. Spells and incantations roamed the air and ghostly figures of lost magicians from the days of the Elvin Bards were chained like prisoners to the dark, cold walls.

Amella crept closer, peering down at an assortment of stolen ledgers, ancient parchments and legal documents and she grew very afraid. She saw his huge collection of dark magic mingled alongside his treasured possessions and she shuddered, aware Elveria had enough power in this one room alone to blow her out of existence. She snaked along the soft contours of stone without a sound and in a corner by a group of lighted candles she saw a newly prepared document and her curiosity dragged her eyes to rest on the finest quality ink. She reached out, her hands forming like those seen on a marble statue and her somewhat stiffened fingers pulled the document a little closer. Her frightened eyes grew wide with disbelief when she saw what was inscribed upon the manuscript. The document stated it had been created by the Order of the Guild and, to her horror, saw a thousand influential names written upon it. It was a list of those in high power who allegedly damned her new constitution, enough it seemed for them to hope that she would be banished from her kingdom forever. Her worry grew tenfold as she dissected each name in turn, her mind racing ahead as she thought of the terrible consequences awaiting her should this 'Deed of Eradication' be proven in court. She felt herself tremble, aware that if Elveria released the document and had proof of the allegations set against her, then she could effectively be removed as Queen. She gasped aloud and then quickly shut her mouth when she realised Elveria had heard her, moving further back into the safety of the stone when Elveria turned abruptly and eyed the room with suspicion.

When he eventually turned away and carried on with what he was doing, Amella thought of Crystal and the power she possessed, knowing she could easily eliminate Elveria with a little push in the right direction. A stab of disgust immediately filled her heart when she likened herself to her father, having thought of using her daughter's magical abilities to help her free her realm of her betrayer of magic and she shook the thought aside.

With rising trepidation, Amella stole closer to Elveria. She was intrigued to see that he was holding something that looked like a common glass snow globe and she thought it strange for him to have something so ordinary in his huge treasury. Her eyes never left the back of his neck until she was standing only a few feet away from him and her nerves were as taut as piano strings when she finally paused, fearful he would hear her breathing. It took her a moment to find the courage to lean forward and take a peek at the globe, believing her stone face would be protruding from the wall, close behind him. She pushed herself forward and found she couldn't see very well for the light from the candles was bouncing against the glass and making it impossible and so she strained her neck a little further, bobbing to the left and then to the right, until she saw he was not holding a snow globe at all, but a black witch's crystal ball.

She watched Elveria draw his hand above the ball and a substance that looked similar to watery ink floated inside the glass like coiled smoke. She heard his robe rustle and he mumbled a spell, a whisper tottering on the edge of his tongue and then a multitude of colours rose up and mingled together like a paintbrush mixed with water. The swirls spun together, creating a kaleidoscope of colour and then they melted away and a human image was left painted inside. The picture was so very clear, so vivid, that Amella could not say later that she might have been mistaken or imagined it, causing her to almost choke in despair for the image Elveria had blended together was none other than her new apprentice, Niculmus DeGrunt.

Chapter 22

Crystal was wrapped in a cocoon of darkness as the night shifted closer to dawn. Kyte had long since departed, being a mystical creature he'd no need for food or shelter and had ventured deep into the valley for the night and would return first thing in the morning.

She tried to look out over the dark forest path and felt only the stirrings of loneliness and because of this the night appeared to pass so slowly. She knew that Clump had been given no choice but to leave her at midnight and so for the few solitary hours he was away she busied herself keeping the fire alight. The invisible force field covering the entranceway gave her much-needed courage to make it through the night but the glow from the flickering flames revealed shadows around her blue eyes, which looked dark with strain whilst she refused to fall asleep.

The mouth of the mine was protected on both sides by a wall of pebbled stone. The roof was no longer visible having been hidden by a thick layer of rotting wood and dense flowery mosses twisted together to create an evergreen curtain, concealing part of the entranceway. She inspected her surroundings, taking a peek inside the mine and felt her senses tingle when the draught of a cold breeze blew from deep inside, dusty, dark and creepy. She shivered, aware that Clump believed the mine shaft to be at least a thousand feet long and she turned back, anxious to get away from what might be crawling about deep inside.

An owl hooted somewhere in the trees, causing her to remember the time when she'd been lost in Forusian's forest. Afraid, she peered out into the looming darkness, the fire crackling at her feet and then she recalled the moment when Amella had found her hidden in a dark hollow of a tree and she closed her eyes, wishing with all her might that her mother would appear from the lengthening shadows and she flung her eyes open, staring towards the distant trees in hope, until they stung with longing.

A twig snapped and a bush shook only a few feet away from her and then something rushed through the undergrowth and her heart skipped a beat. She stood stock still, feeling excited at the thought of her mother having found her but then she saw a flash of white and heard heavy panting and she soon realised that whatever was out there was not her mother. Green leaves shimmered from the bright light of the moon and then they became so still that Crystal felt a moment of sheer panic.

'Who's out there?' she challenged the darkness and her voice crackled with fear. For the first time since Clump left her she felt her vulnerability and Crystal found herself to be openly trembling.

A bush parted and two amber eyes with the white of the moon shining inside them stared at her and she was convinced she had never seen an animal look so menacing. The wolf had a face of pure white with speckles of grey peppered over his forehead and down between his ears. His coat was so thick and luxurious that she had to fight a sudden urge to reach out and wrap her fingers through his wonderful coloured mane. His neck was black and fawn unlike the tips of his feet which were white like the first flakes of snow, matching his long, bushy tail.

The wolf dropped his head and trotted closer, sniffing the air as though he was picking up a scent. Crystal never moved, aware that the wolf could probably see her but was unable to draw comfort from the knowledge that she was safe behind the force field. Then the wolf stopped and lifted its head. Closing his mouth he let out a deep, low-throated growl which sent shock waves down her spine. A moment later a howl pierced through the darkness and another wolf, bigger than the first, nosed his way through the dense leaves and headed straight towards her. Its coat was jet-black and could hardly be seen through the dark of night but its eyes blazed red, like hell-fire. The grey-white timber wolf turned and raised its hackles and a deep snarl escaped its mouth as it challenged the intruder.

The black wolf snarled back, its lips curling and its long white fangs dripping with saliva and in a flash the animal pounced. The wolves connected with such force that they almost bounced off one another and then their teeth were flashing white against the darkness. Biting and ripping at each other's fur they bayed for one another's blood and within seconds the black wolf had the grey-white wolf pinned to the ground. Crystal gasped in horror when his powerful jaws clamped around the grey wolf's throat, threatening to rip it apart. There came a low whimper, a pleading whine and just when Crystal thought the black wolf was about to taste victory the underdog relaxed his neck muscles, causing the black wolf to loosen his grip. In a flash the roles were reversed and the grey-white wolf had the upper hand, his teeth sinking deep into the black wolf's flesh, the hairs on his haunches stiff and spiky as he fought to stay alive. The black wolf refused to be beaten and retaliated by biting his opponent's legs, trying to force the smaller wolf off his feet but the timber wolf was extraordinarily nimble and continued to rip at the black wolf's throat until blood gushed like wine from his enemy's neck and then the black wolf was trying to scramble to his feet, the victor standing firm. A howl of surrender left the black wolf's stricken mouth and the grey timber wolf snarled down at him, blood dripping from his jowls and he stood back to allow the loser of the fight to turn and run, his tail very firmly between his legs.

As soon as his enemy was out of the sight, the timber wolf dropped to the ground from sheer exhaustion. His breathing was laboured as he gasped for air and he licked his bloodied lips with his long, lolling tongue. He lay close to where Crystal was standing, watching him from behind the force field and she fell to her knees, retracting the spell which protected her from harm.

'Clump!' she cried when she saw he'd been hurt, 'what the hell were you thinking?'

The wolf made a noise in the back of his throat as though he was trying to speak and then panted, closing his eyes, feigning sleep. Crystal felt no fear when she bent over him and stroked his head, feeling the softness of his coat against her skin and for a moment she wished she could snuggle down next to him and hug him tight. She knew he had been lucky to outfox the deathly black wolf and a shiver ran down her spine. She sat next to him, stroking his fur until she noticed the first rays of morning creep along the ground and to her relief the wolf transmuted before her very eyes and became, once again, her beloved Windigo. She dropped her head and kissed the top of Clump's forehead, thankful he was alive and would, therefore, live to fight another day.

*

A distinct cry filled the mine shaft whilst Clump wailed like a baby when Crystal busied herself trying to tend his superficial wounds. Dark bruising around his neck and shoulders was visible and several deep puncture marks on his legs were beginning to crust over with dried blood.

'Hold still,' Crystal insisted, when he continued to whine like a frightened puppy, yet in her heart she knew he was lucky to be alive. Clump sniffed with stubbornness, dodging her hands each time she tried to see to him, his eyes looking troubled. Crystal huffed and puffed in frustration when she realised she wasn't getting anywhere but then a strange sensation filled her right hand and she automatically reached out to touch his injured face, stroking the contours of each bloodied graze and indented tooth mark with her glowing fingertips.

At that moment Clump was actually sitting still and Crystal saw the swelling ease at her touch and so she moved to his neck and shoulders and watched in awe when every bruise and scratch healed itself, like water evaporating in the heat of the midday sun.

She gasped, her bright eyes sparkling with unexpected delight and she immediately bent down and touched his legs, radiating happiness when all his wounds simply melted away.

'I've never been able to do that before,' she whispered, still in awe of the magic held inside her. 'I just can't get my head around the fact that I just somehow healed you with my fingers.'

Clump stared at her, his mouth set in a confused line but his eyes were dancing with pride.

'I've always thought you were different,' he teased, shaking his head and allowing a light smirk to form at the corners of his lips. 'Who knows? Perhaps it might just sink in one day just how special you really are,' he added, tapping the side of her forehead with a podgy finger. Crystal fell shy, not sure what to say to him and so she quickly changed the subject instead. Rising to her feet, Crystal asked, 'Who was it who tried to kill you last night?'

Clump stole a look towards the trees before he clambered to his feet. He looked down at her and she noticed his eyes were no longer shining with pride but instead held something much darker.

'I'm afraid to say it was the alpha male of my pack!' he hissed, with sudden venom. 'The black wolf who came here was none other than my father and it was not me he came here to kill, it was you.'

Crystal spun mid-step to face him, unable to stop staring at his face as though he had just told a big, fat lie.

'Why would your father want to hurt me?' she asked in astonishment. 'I mean he doesn't even know me and I wouldn't have thought he could smell me when I was behind the force field.'

The Windigo gave her a look of perplexity.

'My father would have been able to smell you the minute you entered the Valley of the Green Witch,' he explained, his voice turning sour. 'It is within his power to smell any living human within a hundred miles of here.'

'But, I'm not human,' she insisted, 'I'm an immortal.'

Clump almost laughed in her face.

'You were raised as a human, therefore you smell as such and being immortal doesn't make you any less tasty to eat!'

Confusion clouded Crystal's mind, her thoughts rushing once again to Forusian and how close he had come to killing her and because the sun was heralding a new wintry day she blamed it for her shivering.

'It's time we stopped dawdling and entered the mine,' she said, pulling her pelts closer, unable to shake the cold from her bones. Clump nodded his agreement, but he reached out and grabbed her by the shoulder, a look of concern displayed in his piggy, black eyes.

'Look, please don't worry; my father will not come back for you now.'

Crystal eyed him suspiciously.

'How can you be so sure?'

'Because I know he has never been beaten in a fight before and because of this he will have lost his honour,' and Crystal saw a flash of triumph shoot behind his eyes.

'Yes, you were very brave last night,' she acknowledged, picking up his bag and flinging it towards him, 'either that or very stupid,' she added with a slight grin. Her smile broadened when Clump began to giggle and she reached out and extracted the firebird's tail feather from inside his bag.

She rubbed the quill between her thumb and forefinger and a dazzling light fizzed against the stone and the feather glowed in her hand as bright as twenty lanterns. Clump pressed his back against the ragged walls, momentarily blinded by the light and he covered his eyes with the back of his hand. Crystal shielded her own until she grew accustomed to the startling white glare.

'Sorry, Clump,' she said, holding the feather above her head, 'but we need the feather to see where we are going.' Clump nodded, still trying to protect his delicate retinas and he ran in front, his fat legs sounding cumbersome as they hit solid ground.

In Crystal's opinion the inside of the mine looked rickety and rather dangerous. She frowned, finding the dirt under her feet to be like fine grey powder and she screwed up her nose when the rising dust rose, filling her nostrils.

'Clump, where exactly are we going?' she spluttered, waving her hands in front of her face, already missing the feeling of cool, fresh air on her skin, but Clump couldn't hear her for he was running way ahead. He finally stopped in his tracks when he heard the echo of her voice and called out for her to hurry and catch him up.

'It looks as though we have reached the lower shaft,' Clump explained, when she finally caught up with him. Crystal looked down and saw only a curtain of black staring back at her.

'Do we really have to go down there?' she asked, when tendrils of cold air wrapped around her body and an army of goosebumps marched up and down her spine.

Clump turned serious.

'Yes, I'm afraid we do,' he said, looking grim. 'We must travel at least five hundred acres below this mine, that's just less than a square mile to me and you.'

Crystal felt herself take a deep breath.

'Isn't there any another way?' she whined, overcome with a mountain of despair.

Clump shook his head and Crystal watched him lick his lips, a clear sign he was growing nervous.

'We must try and find the Demon's Altar and if we are lucky, we will find the Book of Souls resting beneath it.'

'What are you talking about?' Crystal cried, sounding horrified. 'You never mentioned anything before about a demon's altar, you only told me about finding this mine which is part of The Lost Trinity.'

'I know,' said Clump lowering his head, 'but I thought that if you knew too much too soon, you would not come here with me.'

'Too bloody right!' Crystal snapped, becoming angry. 'You deceived me and I trusted you, why I never thought you were capable of such a thing.'

Clump looked crestfallen, clearly ashamed. 'I'm really, really sorry,' he bleated, 'I was only trying to protect you.'

Crystal gave a heavier sigh.

'I know,' she said, begrudgingly, 'but you should have told me the truth from the very beginning. Look, let's just get down there, the sooner we find the altar the sooner we can leave this horrible place.' Clump reached out and grabbed her arm, drawing her swiftly to him and taking her by surprise.

'No, not so quick,' he rasped, looking very serious. 'You see, The Lost Trinity is where three of the most treasured artefacts in our world were once held and the Book of Souls is only one of those treasures.'

'So what are the other two?' Crystal asked, feeling her mouth go dry at his revelation and not really wanting to know the answer.

Clumps eyes filled with untold knowledge.

'Well, I'm told that the first treasure your mother wears around her neck. She was given the Wheel of the Lost Trinity, a magic pendant, forged deep within the mine by those who wished for a counterbalance of good to come from this place. But the dark side had a different idea and when the Book of Souls vanished beneath the earth, it created the Demon's Altar to try and stop anyone from attempting to raise it from the ground. The third part of the trinity comes in the form of three Lodestones; these stones have immense power, bringing folk who wish to find untold treasure directly to this place. However, it is all a lie, a trick of the darkness

217

for if the one who carries the stones is foolish enough to enter here, he will unknowingly unlock the altar and the day of reckoning will fall upon us.'

Crystal felt herself suck in her breath.

'So, let me get this straight, are you telling me we have to unleash the dark side to get to the Book of Souls?'

Clump quickly shook his head and let her go.

'Oh no, I hope not. We must try and retract the book without awakening the demons. If the Lodestones were here we would be in serious peril, but thankfully they have been lost for over a century and for that we can count our blessings.'

Crystal felt a moment of eternal despair and her throat ached from it.

'We won't succeed,' she said, looking deep into his eyes. 'We will never get the Book of Souls without awakening the demons, any fool can see that.'

Clump looked away, refusing to listen.

'No, that's not true, we have a chance no matter how slim of bringing the Book of Souls back into the light,' Clump insisted, reaching out for the ladder which led to the lower shaft and grabbing it firmly within his huge hands. 'We just need a bit of luck and a little magic to find it, that's all.'

Before she could argue, Clump mounted the rickety steps and swiftly made his descent into the darkened abyss.

Crystal took a deep breath and then turned and kicked the wall behind her, furious at herself for being so naive. A shower of filth and small shards of stone hit her on her head as though trying to knock some sense into her and she coughed and spluttered when the dust threatened to choke her. She brushed the damp and mouldy debris from her auburn curls and then started to fret over Clump's safety when she saw he had completely disappeared from sight.

'Damn you, you crazy fool!' she cried out, furious with herself because she knew she had no choice but to follow him. Grabbing the ladder she stepped onto the first rung before heading down to the belly of darkness and as she descended she had the most horrible thought that she may never see the light of day ever again.

Chapter 23

The devastation to the canyon was phenomenal. Fire burned continuously for many hours causing an inferno of flames to whip towards the blackened sky, suffocating any innocent animals and birds that tried unsuccessfully to flee. The swirling flames fired from the dragons' mouths turned everything they touched into floating clouds of black ash and those who were lucky to still be alive prayed they would not become charcoal effigies when it became clear of the dragons' intentions to destroy everything in their path.

The three elves were sheltering from the raging fires, hidden behind an inadequate piece of rock. The horses were there too, scared witless, whinnying and dragging at their reins as they tried to escape the horror, but the warriors held on tight, petrified of the potential danger awaiting them should they break free. The air around them was thick and acrid, forcing those on the ground to cough and splutter as they tried to draw breath. The venom of the dragons' rage continued to pour from their angry mouths, targeting the main area which housed the Prince Regent and his faithful apprentice, Niculmus.

The dragons gave a blood-curdling howl each time they descended from the skies, making those on land who heard their wailing almost weep with fear. The dragons' scarlet bodies soared through the sky, blocking out the bright morning rays with their extraordinary long wings. Made from a stretched membrane of toughened skin and pure muscle, the wings stretched from their legs to a dramatically lengthened fourth toe. They swept the air gracefully, swooping and diving in a natural dance until they were so close the warriors could almost see the madness in their eyes. The dragon's faces were sharp and predatory, almost bordering on the facial features of the pterodactyl and their strong jaws were made to strip away raw flesh from bone. Their tails, reaching at least thirty to forty feet long, bore little resemblance to the better known, smaller, Western dragons that were known to be rather docile and easy to ride.

Fire oozed from the dragons' mouths until the canyon became nothing more than a baked inferno. The flames ripped into the ground until it was charred, black with death with golden clouds of burning heat billowing high up towards the sky. The few trees that were left were still ablaze and the brushwood and shrivelled cacti continued to smoulder, looking like little grey-black headstones resting along the desert floor.

Time and time again the beasts sent huge blasts of fire down from the heavens to burn along the ground and towards the two magicians. The dragons wreaked havoc, their vicious mouths determined to eradicate them where they stood, but each time the fire subsided and the dragons flew close they were shocked to see the magicians were still standing firm, their shields scorched and stained with blackened soot but still able to protect them against their barrage of fire.

A piercing shriek from somewhere in the distance caused Bridgemear to squint his eyes and focus on the bleary horizon and he saw through the haze of smoke and filtering ash a dragon break from the ranks and disappear somewhere overhead. In a flash Bridgemear raised his staff, pointing it steadily behind him and waited for the assaulting dragon to reappear. Seconds passed and then the beast was looming before him, opening its long jaws as it grew close.

The magician shouted an enchantment when the first flames looked imminent and he used a pulse of energy to form a projectile, creating a huge jet of cold, icy water to gush like a river from his stave. It rose in the air, aiming straight towards the dragon, before connecting with the blaze which exploded from its mouth. The torrent swirled and twisted against the flames, crystal blue fought with yellow and red, until the fire fizzled out and turned to steam, evaporating in the atmosphere and producing a sudden dampness in the air. The dragon fled like a trapped bluebottle in a jam jar, zigzagging and spinning from one place to the next, trying desperately to flee from the cascade of water which followed him. Before it had a chance to escape, however, the water found a way into its long beaky mouth and gushed down the beast's throat and a choking sound filled the air as the dragon gasped for breath. It struggled when its stomach filled with so much water it almost drowned and, under its own heavy weight, fell like a bloodied stone from the sky, the vibration as it hit the ground forcing a shock wave to ripple straight through the earth.

A cry of fury rang out from the rest of the clan and their reign of terror intensified. Niculmus spared enough breath to shout, 'Bridgemear ... look out ... over there, by the cliff ... there are two more heading straight towards you!'

The mage bolted upright, shooting his stave at the two assaulting dragons and the stream of water it produced split down its centre like a vicious viper's tongue.

The water collided with the two dragons and they both instantly retreated and with more than their flames dampened they headed back to their clan, their red, horned-back tails flicking and thrashing the air as they fled.

Niculmus grinned, his teeth pearly white against his blackened face, causing Bridgemear to grin back when he caught his impish smile. However, Niculmus thought Bridgemear was starting to look fatigued but the mage remained steadfast until the dragons turned unexpectedly in mid-air and flew in a group towards him like burning missiles in the sky, pinning back their large wings and Bridgemear gasped, raising his staff once again and forcing his globe to glow white with power.

The spirit, Adlanniel, was seen to rush to the forefront of his stave, but her eyes soon filled with fear when she saw the multitude of dragons descending towards her and a piercing scream left her ruby-red lips when a line of fire roared straight towards her. The flames were so intense that they somehow penetrated the wizard's magic and the sound of splintering glass filled the air. Adlanniel was seen to spiral up towards the sky until she was finally able to gain some control and then she looked down at her magician, her face contorted with terror, and in the blink of an eye she vanished.

To Bridgemear's horror his staff flew from his hands, landing in the outstretched palm of the dragon master's and the magician's mouth dropped wide in shocked surprise. The dragon master's laughter filled the air, his cat-slit eyes burning with victory and a high-pitched screech left his dragon's mouth when he commanded his beast to withdraw for it was obvious the creatures were exhausted. Bridgemear stared after them like a gormless idiot. His power as a mage had never been challenged to such a degree and the thought of the dragon master stealing his staff made his blood run cold. After several minutes he was still unable to digest what had just occurred and, numb with disbelief, stared at the sky long after the dragons vanished from sight.

Niculmus called out to his master but found himself choking on the thick particles of ash which floated through the air and was unable to clear his throat. The smell of cooked horsemeat stung his nostrils and a wail of distress was ringing out from the terrified animals. Niculmus heard the sound of his comrades coughing and spluttering and then the two warriors staggered past him, having left the safety of the rocks, the sick elf holding onto Amadeus's belt like the blind leading the blind.

The smoke was beginning to change from black to smouldering grey, but the orange-gold flames were still burning ferociously along the ground. Niculmus scanned the immediate area and felt a dark dread fill his heart when he saw the devastation lying before him. For a moment there was an eerie silence that caused him to feel a moment of dread and then a sickening noise invaded his ears, forcing him to recognise the piercing cry of agony and he fled, diving into the cover of thick cloud.

He ran to where he thought the source of the sound was coming from, his eyes watering from the dense smoke which stung them and through the blur of tears he eventually saw something that made his heart almost burst from his chest. Lying before him, a black horse was burnt so badly it was screaming. Niculmus stepped forward and somehow tripped over the horse's feet and accidentally dropped his wand. He fell to his knees, grappling in the dirt and he became filled with panic when he couldn't find it.

The other horses were neighing hysterically and he could sense their huge eyes rounding with fear for he could hear their hooves dancing over the hot earth, their minds seemingly dizzy with trauma. Niculmus began fretting that if he wasn't quick enough they would soon break his wand. His fingers grappled in the dirt until he felt the touch of metal and he reached out and curled his fingers around his wand. He placed his free hand on the dying horse's abdomen and tears of sadness fell down his face but he quickly wiped them away with a scorched shirtsleeve and then mouthed a spell that he thought he would never have to use in his lifetime. He closed his eyes tight, squeezing away the blinding tears when the dying horse closed her own and he dropped his wand to his side once the spell had been cast and sobbed aloud when the horse took her final, shuddering breath.

The black cob rested peaceful in death but Niculmus found he was unable to stem the flow of his tears which poured like a river down his face. He cried over what had been his mother's horse and was unable to push the huge lump of grief which rose in his throat back to where it came from. The stench of burnt flesh turned his stomach sick and he was unable to stop the retch that rose from inside him, and he turned his head away and violently threw up last night's supper. He had never seen an animal suffer in such a terrible way before and he vowed he would never witness such an atrocity again.

Bridgemear suddenly appeared through the dark, trailing smoke, and he looked down at his apprentice, his face hard and solemn. His blonde plaited hair looked like dirty, old rope and his handsome face was smeared with streaks of black, making his ice-blue eyes look dazzling. He cast them down towards the smouldering body of the horse lying on the ground and he saw the new corpse was already stiffening and immediately ground his teeth in anger.

'How dare they!' he rasped, his voice sounding hoarse with disgust. 'Tell me, Niculmus, what have they achieved by all this?'

Niculmus shook his head, pulling himself to his feet, clearly numb with grief and he simply wiped the smoke and tears away from his eyes until his legs buckled and a large hand came out of nowhere and held him fast. Niculmus blinked in surprise, realising someone other than his master was holding him firm. A cup of water was thrust under his nose and he quickly reached out and took it, guzzling the clear liquid as though he'd been deprived for years. He was thankful when the burning sensation eventually left his dry throat and once his thirst was quenched, he turned to see the serious face of Arhdel standing beside him, his own face streaked with black.

'You did extremely well, my boy,' said the warrior slapping him sharply on the back. 'I have to say I think I may well have misjudged you and for that I am truly sorry.'

Niculmus tried to hide the look of open surprise but could not save himself from the sad smile which immediately split from his lips. He nodded his appreciation to the warrior, handing back the water when Amadeus appeared at his side. The injured elf was with him and Niculmus thought it seemed odd that he looked strangely happy. His face still held the scars of ill health and his fingers were all but stumps but he threw his good hand out to Niculmus and tried to shake his hand.

'I have remembered something,' he said, a little too brightly and Niculmus looked at him in confusion.

'I'm sorry, I'm not grasping what you mean?' he replied, still a little dazed.

The elf looked him straight in the eye and the darkness behind his thick, droopy eyelids appeared to melt. He was wearing a borrowed cloak which was far too long for him and his pale face made his lips look tinged with blue.

'My name, of course. I think my parents may have called me Merrow,' he burst, looking pleased. 'I mean, I know it was such a long time ago ... and my memory could well be playing tricks on me, but this name keeps rolling about inside my head, so I am guessing this is who I am.'

Niculmus raised an eyebrow at his unexpected revelation.

'Well, Merrow, it's a start at least, perhaps your memory is finally returning?'

'Yes, and I have remembered something else,' Merrow added, but the smile on his face suddenly slipped away.

'Oh, what is that?' asked Niculmus, forcing a weak smile, 'have you remembered who hurt you?'

'Sadly, no,' said Merrow softly. 'I have in fact remembered that I have no family of my own.'

Niculmus's smile fell from his lips and Merrow dropped his hand and turned to face the wizard Bridgemear.

'My lord, may I say with all due respect that I have never known such courage from a magician before. Even after everything you have done for me, of which I am eternally grateful, I find I cannot believe there are still those with power who fight only for the common good.'

Bridgemear looked as though he didn't trust himself to speak and he stared down at the elf, his eyes unfathomable.

'Then it is obvious you have not known the magicians from Raven's Rainbow,' he said, wiping dark sweat from off his brow. 'My brothers and I have fought for many years for a cause that will eventually bring us a world that is right and just.'

The elf looked doubtful but was wise enough to remain silent, turning instead away from the magician and heading for a blackened rock on which to sit and ponder his thoughts for a while. Niculmus's gaze slipped from Merrow to his master. He thought Bridgemear was looking extremely tired and he stood aghast when the Prince Regent suddenly collapsed, causing the two warriors to run to his aid and pull Bridgemear back onto his feet.

'There is nowhere for him to rest,' called out Amadeus, dragging his master to where his horse was tethered and trying to hide his look of despair. 'And I think we should leave at once,' he encouraged, securing the magician in the saddle and then gesturing to Niculmus to jump on behind and take hold of the reins.

'The battle was too long and the energy and power Bridgemear must have used has seen him suffer acute exhaustion,' added Arhdel in frustration. 'I am afraid he will not be able to recover here.'

Niculmus nodded and gripped his master's mount tighter when the horse reared his head, kicking his hooves with impatience, wishing only to leave this godforsaken place.

'We must not lose sight of our quest,' Niculmus announced, twisting his neck to watch Arhdel draw close. 'We cannot stop until we get to the Stannary Mines, the prince will have to rest as we travel; I can see no other way we can do this.'

'Nor can I,' Amadeus agreed, pulling Merrow up behind him and making sure he was sitting securely. 'No, we cannot stop again, not until we reach our final destination.'

With the burning fires still fizzling behind them, they rode out of the canyon and headed for the Valley of the Green Witch and once they entered her domain, continued on past Green Crag and then towards the Stannary Mines of the Lost Trinity. By mid-afternoon the following day, exhausted and weak, they finally reached their journey's end.

Chapter 24

The darkness was nothing more than terrifying. Never in a thousand nightmares had Crystal ever experienced such a desolate and bleak place than the inside of the mine, but she knew she had no choice but to enter into the bowels of darkness if she ever wanted to find the Book of Souls.

The mineshaft was extremely creepy with dull, eerie sounds echoing through its long, dark tunnels as though metal wheels were grinding somewhere in the distance, then the mine would fall quiet and Crystal's trepidation deepened with each reluctant step she took. In her hand she held the firebird's feather and it was proving to be a godsend as it chased away the lengthening shadows, but its bright light could not stop her sense of foreboding.

'We're going to be fine,' Clump told her when he turned and saw her face appear to turn paler with each cautious step. Crystal nodded and forced a weak smile, trying to show him she believed what he was telling her, but her obvious reluctance to continue down the dark and gloomy trail told Clump she was simply putting on a brave face and he noted she was becoming more and more subdued.

A thin, trickle of water trailed along the roofline, seeping through the tunnels' structure, followed by a cold draught which made the air feel damp and chilly. The dark, grey chambers simply rolled into one another in a labyrinth of isolation and nothing remotely resembling a demon's altar ever rose from within the gloom.

Clump tied a coil of rope which he'd found along the floor around his waist and then secured it around the princess. He explained to Crystal how this could help to keep her safe should the ground collapse unexpectedly beneath her feet and she felt herself break out into a sweat, unable to hide her bout of anxiety which was brought on by his tactless revelation.

Through narrow tunnels and partially blocked archways they trekked until they reached a point where two old, rusty wagons, filled with long-forgotten loads of stone, lay abandoned. The steel girders which they had once been wheeled along had long since been removed, giving them a somewhat stranded appearance. They sat like two ghostly bookends, sitting there side by side, and Crystal couldn't help drift closer to take a peek.

A gasp left her lips when two bright eyes peered back at her from within one of the dusty piles of stone, causing her to almost jump out of her skin and she yelped aloud, bringing Clump to her side, who glared at her as though she had completely lost her marbles.

'What is it?' he asked, looking confused. He held on tightly to the rope, as though she was about to be dragged away to hell and Crystal turned and pointed to the wagon, her breathing somewhat erratic.

'In there, in-between the stones,' she wheezed, 'I just saw something move.'

Clump reached out and snatched the feather from her grasp and he drew the light towards the wagon to reveal two small, beady eyes peering from out of the darkness.

'Oh, it's a blasted mining troll,' he snapped, looking rather annoyed at finding one, 'why, these critters are known to get just about everywhere.'

As he spoke the troll's voice came out of the shadows, snappy and angry, and Crystal realised he was mumbling some kind of obscenity whilst he climbed out of the wagon.

'What are you two idiots doing down here?' he barked, when he dropped to the ground and walked boldly towards them. Crystal looked down in awe at the tiny fellow. He was dressed in a dirty-looking shirt, short cropped trousers held up by a pair of leather braces. On his feet were vibrant red boots that reminded her of the shoes in the fairy story, 'The Elves and the Shoemaker' for the toes curled upwards into a spiral of leather. He looked to her like a stunted dwarf, perhaps no more than two feet tall, but without the beard and friendly face. His skin was peppered with particles of dust but his eyes were sparklingly clear with emerald green irises that shone like polished gems.

'Cat got your tongue, eh?' asked the troll, placing his hands on his hips and looking insolent. Crystal flicked her gaze towards Clump in astonishment, she had never met anyone so openly rude before, and she shrugged her shoulders, not quite sure what to say. Clump cleared his throat and immediately grabbed the troll's attention.

'Look, troll, we are searching for the Demon's Altar, we know it's here somewhere but don't actually know where, tell me, are you willing to help us find it?'

'For a start, my name is Elwid,' hissed the troll, turning his nose up in the air, 'and tell me, Windigo, what would you want with the altar? That place is of no concern of yours.'

'Oh, you're wrong,' Crystal butted in, 'for we both have to find what is buried beneath it.'

'So, you're looking for the Book of Souls,' said Elwid shooting her a crafty grin. 'Indeed, you are not the first to search for it and you won't be the last.'

Crystal looked stung.

'Stop being so nasty!' she snapped. 'Don't you realise we have travelled a very long way to get here and we are not leaving this place without it.' The troll looked unperturbed and shook his head.

'No, I will not help you find the Book of Souls for as far as I'm concerned, you were foolish to have ever entered the mine.' He headed towards the wagon and gave it a slight push. 'Look, if you want to take my advice, just go home whilst you still have the chance.'

To Crystal's surprise the wagon began to roll away and the troll gave a hysterical laugh as he jumped inside.

'Quick,' she shouted to Clump, 'He's getting away!'

Without thinking, Crystal lunged towards the wagon, her fingers somehow managing to grasp the outer casing and Clump, who had rammed the feather inside his mouth, struggled to stay by her side. Elwid looked furious that they thought to follow him and immediately tried to prise Crystal's fingers off the wagon and loosen her grip.

'Leave this place,' the troll insisted, furious that he was unable to force her to let go, 'believe me when I tell you there's nothing here for you but trouble.'

Crystal ignored his cries and managed to hold on. Her legs ached, her body felt battered but she still found the strength to climb aboard. Once inside she grabbed the rope that was still attached to Clump and knotted it around her hands, reeling him in like a large, plump trout. His fat legs were going ten to the dozen as he tried to keep up and she screamed at him to run even faster when he almost stumbled. A moment later Clump was holding onto the wagon as though his life depended on it, much to Elwid's despair. With his tunic flapping wildly, he eventually pulled himself inside and, weak with exhaustion, fell at Elwid's feet.

'Why did you have to do that!' Elwid spat childishly, 'this is my wagon and you're not welcome in it.'

'Oh, shut up!' Crystal snapped, unable to keep a lid on her patience a moment longer. 'Don't you care that we could have both been killed?' She grabbed the feather from Clump's mouth and watched in amazement when the walls continued to whizz past her face until she had no reference to time or space.

Elwid remained bitterly silent as they travelled, his back resting against one of the large white stones but eventually he could hold his tongue no longer.

'So, tell me why you want the Book of Souls so badly?'

'It's a long story,' Crystal told him flatly, noticing how the wagon was beginning to slow and not too sure what she should tell him, especially when she saw the fury burning in his eyes.

Elwid clenched his jaw.

'Tell me your reason or I will not allow you to go another step,' he spat, pointing a bony finger at her.

'Look here, Elwid, you're not going to stop me,' Crystal cried, swinging round and facing the angry little troll.

'I need the Book of Souls and that's all you need to know, but you must tell me if you are from the dark side of magic or not.'

Elwid stared at her and then sniffed. He shifted his weight onto one of his curled-up shoes and almost made her deaf when he shouted at her.

'I'm not telling you!'

Crystal was so angry that she wanted to smack his smug little face but she saw Clump raise his hairy eyebrows heavenwards and so she bit her lip instead, trying to keep a lid on her mounting frustration.

Unable to do so, she opened her mouth, ready to give the troll a piece of her mind but just then the wagon ground to a halt, spinning like a teacup on a fairground ride, spilling its precious cargo all over the floor. Crystal lifted the feather and glanced around to see they were no longer in a place that resembled anything like a mine shaft.

'Where are we?' she asked, pushing herself up off her knees and rising to her feet. She glanced around, noting there were strange paintings of what looked like human sacrifices on the pale walls, with cryptic symbols inscribed along its centre, filling the atmosphere with an unexpected zap of apprehension. Crystal caught her breath when she saw several ugly gargoyles staring down at her with twisted mouths and cold, stony eyes and wondered if the troll had been right to warn them not to come here after all.

'You are in a place called the Dead's Temple,' said Elwid, brushing the grey dust from off his trouser legs and then staring at her as though she should have known this fact already. Clump and Crystal glanced at one another in dismay, and then Clump looked away, searching in his bag for a handkerchief so he could mop his sweaty brow.

'I told you not to come here,' Elwid reiterated, 'I warned you this is not a place for your kind, but you insisted on coming down here.'

'It's okay,' said Crystal, bringing up her hand and showing him her palm as though this gesture would soothe him. 'It's fine, really, but tell me Elwid, will you take us to the altar or not?' Elwid's body appeared to twitch and his small, green eyes, both sharp and alive, grew shrewd.

'Why should I take you?' he muttered almost to himself. 'Tell me, what's in it for me?'

It was Crystal's turn to raise an eyebrow, but Clump quickly intervened. He grappled once again inside his bag, his huge fingers pushing the contents aside until he pulled out two thin, glass bottles.

'Buttermead!' yelled the troll when he clapped eyes on the distinctive bottles. He started rubbing his hands together in sheer delight and then added, 'go on, tell me how you knew that's my favourite drink?'

'Hmmm, err, well it has been noted in the past how trolls enjoy a little mead from time to time,' said Clump looking slightly shifty. 'I thought I would bring some along, just in case it was needed.'

'Oh, well, that changes everything and if you're willing to give me both, it's a deal,' said Elwid, his hands already outstretched. Clump nodded and reluctantly handed them over and Elwid was quick to hug them to his chest as though they were his precious children.

'I will take one bottle for taking you to the altar and one bottle for bringing you back, but hear me good and loud. The dark ones live deep below the ground and you will never live to see the sun rise again if you awaken them by accident. The Book of Souls is buried on the north side of the altar, but if you dig too deep, you will get more than you bargained for.' He sniffed the air like a tracker dog before running to a darkened corner to hide his bottles in a deepened recess.

'They will be safe there until I return,' he explained, glancing longingly at where they lay hidden. 'Now, let's get going. The altar is closer than you think,' said Elwid, wagging a finger, 'in fact it is just behind this wall,' he added, stroking the stone like some kind of pet.

The little troll moved several inches away and Crystal looked about for some sort of hidden doorway. She noticed the walls were very smooth and no matter how hard she tried she could not see the outline of an entranceway moulded into the stone. Unexpectedly, the troll began to sing a rather strange song and began dancing about, kicking his shins together and then hopping on one leg. It was a most peculiar spectacle to watch and Crystal pulled her lips tight to try and stifle a giggle.

His singing was rather sweet and alluring, his dancing was bordering on a casual folk dance which one might see in some place like Ireland, but whilst he sang the temple grew bright and from the ground a shuddering erupted and the wall melted away and moments later Crystal found herself to be surrounded by a splendid group of ancient trees which had the reddest leaves she'd ever seen. The branches on the trees were heavy with their rich, vibrant colour and they swayed and rustled as she approached, yet there was no breeze to make them dance to and fro. Crystal pushed a sweeping branch out of the way and there, deep within the hub of trees, sat the infamous Demon's Altar.

The altar was made of pure shiny gold and it glistened so brightly that Clump had to shield his eyes. It was moulded into the shape of a long pointed cone, decorated with crescent moons and intricate sun symbols and at its base ancient runes were inscribed upon it. The light around them grew dazzling, yet there was no sun or bright lights to cast the brilliant glow. Crystal thought it all looked like a mystical mirage, a trick of the mind and she wandered towards the altar until she was close enough to touch the precious metal with her fingertips.

The moment she touched the Demon's Altar the precious stone held in its centre of her amulet glowed golden and both Clump and Elwid stopped dead in their tracks when the glow swept over Crystal's body.

'That's never happened before,' said Elwid, quite openly flummoxed, 'the altar should not respond to anyone's magical persona.'

'What are you talking about?' asked Crystal, removing her hands and noticing her amulet was still shining bright. 'What does this mean?'

'I'm guessing you cannot be harmed,' said Elwid, shaking his head and throwing his hands high in the air, 'I really don't know, my job is to simply bring those who are foolish enough to want to come here down to the altar, whether it be someone filled with good or bad magic, the demons do not care, but I have never witnessed anything like this happening before.'

'So, you are the guardian of the altar so to speak?' Crystal asked, with creeping suspicion.

'No, not really,' said Elwid, still shaking his head. 'I am not here to protect anyone or anything, I'm here only as a guide.'

Crystal's brow furrowed.

'So, are you telling me that all that back there, when you said you wouldn't take us to the altar, that was just a ploy? Your intention was to bring us here anyway?'

'Aye, young pup, it was, and may I say it seems you have a lot to learn about the mountain folk,' Elwid openly sniggered.

233

'Why, you're nothing more than a despicable liar!' Crystal accused. 'You should be ashamed of yourself taking those bottles of buttermead under false pretences. But then again, you're not the first to lie to me.'

Clump cleared his throat.

'The mountain folk are renowned for their trickery and deceit,' Clump said, staring at the troll, 'it's what they do to survive, but please remember not all of us will stoop as low as a troll.'

Crystal turned to see the sadness in his eyes and felt a stab of guilt.

'Oh, Clump, you know I didn't mean you,' she said, throwing her hands down in despair. 'It's just that no one is what they seem in this world and sometimes that makes me so confused!'

Clump shifted from her side, untying the rope from around his waist and gesturing for her to do the same.

'Now look what you've done,' she snapped at Elwid, her blue eyes burning with simmering rage, 'I really hope you're satisfied now.'

Clump knelt down at the feet of the altar and pushed his thick, dark hair from his eyes, enabling him to search inside his bag for something to help him dig.

'Wait!' said Crystal, letting the rope fall, 'we must make sure we only dig on the north side of the altar.'

Clump shook his head and said, 'since when did you trust what a troll tells you? You of all people should have learnt by now not to believe a single word that's uttered from his mean lips.'

Crystal turned and saw Elwid's sagging cheeks become as red as his curly shoes. She hated admitting she had been taken in by the evil little sod, but accepting she had got it wrong made her feel rather foolish.

Giving Clump an encouraging smile, she said, 'You're right Clump, but tell me, what have you got inside your bag that can help us?' Elwid swore under his breath and went to sit under the nearest tree. Crystal noticed his shoes were the same shade of red as the vibrant leaves and this made her wonder if the shoes were what connected him to this place.

Clump did an exaggerated cough and Crystal turned to see him holding a small shovel in his large, hairy hands and her eyes widened in surprise.

'Don't try and tell me you've been carrying that all this way in your bag because I won't believe you,' she said, sounding incredulous. Clump couldn't help but chuckle.

'No, of course not, silly,' he said, pointing towards a hollow tree, 'this spade was resting inside there.'

'Mmm, that makes things a little too easy,' said Crystal, trying to understand the logic, 'I think the demons are hoping you will wake them and so they are giving you a shovel in anticipation – what do you think, Clump?'

Clump nodded, 'Sounds plausible to me!' he said, throwing the spade into the dirt and shovelling the rich earth to one side. 'But seeing that we know what we are doing, perhaps we will gain the upper hand.'

'Be careful,' Crystal warned, clearly doubtful, 'just humour me on this one and take it easy.' Clump shrugged his shoulders, but carried on regardless. He dug roughly three feet and huffed a little to himself when he found nothing but earthworms and a colony of centipedes. He flicked the bugs from off his bare feet, trampling the ground from whence they came and with an uncontrollable shiver, moved away.

'How far down do you think you can go?' asked Crystal when he started digging once again and she became a little more afraid with each shovelful of dirt he produced.

'I really don't know,' said Clump wiping his brow with the back of his hand when the sweat started pouring like rain, 'but if we don't find it soon, we will have to look at leaving for I am worried I will transmute before we manage to get out of here.'

Crystal felt the hairs on the back of her neck rise at the thought.

'Let's just keep trying for a little longer,' she urged, biting her lip once again, 'for I'm sure if we keep going we'll find it soon enough.'

As she spoke Clump hit something hard and he took a gasp inwards.

'I think I've found it,' he shouted, sounding somewhat surprised, 'I think we've got what we came for.'

'That didn't take too long,' said Crystal throwing him a worried look, 'I've got a sneaky suspicion we are heading for some kind of trap.'

'No, I don't think so,' Clump said, shaking his head and frowning. 'Remember, there have not been many folk over the years who have tried to find the book for fear of the repercussions and perhaps those who have come before us were simply digging in the wrong place.'

'You mean the north side?' Crystal said, with a shiver.

'Yes, exactly,' said Clump, bending down and retrieving a large, leather-bound book. He pulled the ancient tome from its dark hiding place and Crystal felt her eyes wander over the filthy cover. Clump brushed the dirt away with his huge hands, the hairs on his fingers acting like a sweeping brush to reveal the sorcerer Merguld's long-lost spell book.

'Wow!' Crystal mouthed, her eyes shining like stars, 'that's just incredible!' The book was bound with a leather clasp and Crystal tried to open it without much success. She glanced over to Elwid and she was disappointed to see he had fallen asleep, having suffered the urge to gloat, and so her attention swiftly returned to the book.

'Can you open it?' she asked, reaching out to try and take it from the Windigo's grasp, but Clump was having none of it and pulled it from her fingers and she pouted like a spoilt teenager.

Clump bent down and placed the book by her feet and then he brought her attention to his bag.

'Crystal, I have something I need to show you which I have been carrying with me and I don't want you to freak out when I do.'

He hesitated, his hand already delving inside, and then pulled out a small, ceremonial knife and Crystal shrank back in alarm.

'What the hell is that?' she croaked, her eyes fixed only on the brown and yellow sheath.

Clump looked very serious, his face set in a stern expression.

'This is a blood knife, they are very rare and are only used to open wizards' spell books. You see, the only way to open a book like this is by dripping fresh blood onto its cover.'

Crystal looked appalled and turned white, frightened by his revelation.

'Now, just wait a minute, you never said anything about needing any blood and furthermore, whose blood exactly do you think you will be using?'

'We need your blood,' Clump whispered so softly she had to strain to hear him. 'I'm sorry it has to be this way, I would happily donate my own, but mine is of no consequence down here.'

'How do you know all this?' she fumed, turning angry. 'You know, I'm starting to believe that you haven't told me one grain of truth since we got here.'

Clump winced and looked hurt.

'That's simply not true,' he said, turning defensive. 'Just because I know how to open the book doesn't mean I've been lying to you at all. It has been known for a thousand years that only another magician can open another's grimoire and blood is the tool all of you must use.'

'What's a grimoire?' Crystal asked, jutting out her chin, 'I've never heard that word before.'

Clump looked mystified, 'Why a grimoire is simply a sorcerer's spell book. Usually a magician will hold all his notes for spells and potions inside something like this, but the magician Merguld held something much more valuable in his, as well you know.'

'So why do you have to use my blood?' Crystal bleated, still feeling afraid. The glow from her amulet had finally died but this did nothing but make her feel more insecure.

'Well, isn't it obvious? It's because you are part magician, you have special magic flowing in your veins, enough to awaken the fourth mage, without you we are lost and your family left in serious peril.' The mere mention of her parents brought the memory flooding back of her premonition and the dark rider. With her eyes still brooding over the dagger she inched closer, feeling like a lamb walking up the slaughter house steps, and held out her arm towards him.

'Okay, go on, get it over and done with,' she squirmed, closing her eyes, unable to look. She pressed her mouth into a hard line and offered her wrist. In a flash, the knife was raised and before she had chance to pull away, the flicker of steel sliced down her arm just below her wrist and she opened her eyes when she felt a sting and watched in shocked horror when bright red blood oozed to the surface. The cut was probably no longer than an inch and as soon as she dropped her hand, the wound began to heal.

'Oh no, that's not what I expected,' Clump declared, looking down at the small incision in despair. 'We need enough blood before the wound closes or we won't have enough to force the magic spell which binds the pages together to deactivate.'

Crystal couldn't believe her eyes when Clump started trying to squeeze the blood from her veins and she watched almost mesmerised when the last few drops landed onto the cover with a splash. Her bright red blood began seeping through the thick cover and eventually soaked its dark surface like a sponge.

'I think that might be enough,' Clump said, when the cover changed colour from a dirty old brown to a rich vibrant red and as soon as he spoke, a slight breeze blew through the trees and the branches trilled with the force, stirring a few strands of Crystal's red hair. She pushed the strands aside with the tips of her fingers and she watched the leaves flutter from the branches and then drift to the ground, as though autumn had arrived early. Clump picked up the grimoire and walked over to the altar, placing the book at its feet and it was then when he noticed how the leaves appeared to be forming a line in the earth, snaking their way towards the grimoire and he quickly walked back to Crystal's side.

Suddenly, the book flew open, bursting with a bright shimmering light and Clump saw Elwid was startled awake. The troll jumped to his feet, his eyes seemingly burning from the sudden blinding glare and he gasped aloud, his small frame stiffening with acute apprehension. He tried to run towards them but it looked as though his feet were stuck fast and then something invisible grabbed his ankles and he was being dragged along the earth, right towards the grimoire. He fell to the floor, his hands grappling in the dirt, desperate to find something to grab hold of and when Clump realised what was happening he ran to help, but before he could reached him, the Windigo was flipped off his feet and propelled with such force, straight up into the air.

Crystal let out a scream, her eyes filling with fright when she saw the Windigo bounce against a tree and then land, winded, against the trunk of another. She dashed to his side, her mouth dropping open and she did her best to drag him to his feet. When his breath returned they both looked back towards the spell book and watched in horror as the troll was sucked inside. A look of helplessness was shining in his eyes as he fought desperately to hold onto a few trailing vines and that made Crystal almost choke with despair. A flash of fire burst from the pages, blue flame fought with spiralling green, until the troll was totally devoured and then Elwid was gone.

Crystal stared in disbelief, tears falling uncontrollably down her face, unable to digest what had just happened and whilst she tried to deal with what she had just witnessed, the procession of leaves began to encircle the spell book, nudging themselves underneath its heavy cover until they formed a small, raised platform in which to hold it. The leaves rose heavenwards as still more dropped from the billowing branches and headed in a blustery stream towards the grimoire, until they created a kind of woodland reading lectern.

Then a menacing voice shouted at them from somewhere within the trees.

'Who dares to come here and delve inside my book of magic?' it demanded.

Crystal almost jumped into Clump's long arms in fright. Seconds ticked slowly by and when nothing happened she eventually found the courage to let go of him and she took a reluctant step forward.

'Err, my name is Crystal and I come in peace!' she shouted out loud, pronouncing her words as though she was talking to some kind of alien. 'I am the daughter of Bridgemear, a wizard from Oakwood and husband to my mother, Amella, Queen of Nine Winters, and I'm here to ask you to please release the fourth mage from your grimoire.'

Crystal felt her tongue go dry and her knees shook as she waited for a reply. A crackle in the atmosphere was followed by a swish of magic and then the magician Merguld was standing before them, a menacing ghost returning from his dark resting place.

Crystal froze on the spot.

The magician was levitating just a few inches from the ground and he drifted closer, his long, green robe swirling around his body like waves of the sea. He wore a traditional wizard's hat, the colour of sky and his white beard floated way, way, down towards his large, bare feet.

He flew to where Crystal stood waiting, standing there like a stone statue, her terrified eyes rounding when she scanned his face for a sign of what he was about to do next. The magician's own eyes narrowed when he approached and his mouth turned down into a thin, bitter line and Crystal felt an icy claw close around her heart.

'You have tricked me,' he hissed, reaching out a hand to command the book to go to him. The book flew up in the air and landed in the magician's open palm. He allowed the sweeping pages to fall open and he tipped the book towards her so she could see words inscribed in red rise to the surface.

'What is this!' he cried out in fury. 'My grimoire tells me the fourth mage has already been released!'

Crystal looked at him as though he had gone completely mad and she shifted her gaze to Clump and saw he was just as dumbfounded.

The magician closed is eyes, snapping the book shut with a loud bang.

'You're no better than thieves,' he hissed, re-opening his eyes and glaring dangerously at her.

'I, I swear I don't know what you're talking about,' Crystal stammered, trying her best to deny the absurd allegation. 'Surely I wouldn't stand here like some kind of idiot asking for him to be released if I had somehow already done so?'

Merguld refused to listen and he hastily glided towards the altar with the book still firmly in his grasp.

'How dare you lie to me!' he rasped, refusing to believe a word, 'I can see you have somehow taken him from his resting place without my knowledge, why, take a look amongst the pages, for his soul is nowhere to be found.'

Merguld shot out his arm, a whoosh filled the air and the grimoire was there, floating right under her nose. She stared blankly at the magician and he nodded for her to take the book and to do as she was told. Timidly, she reached out and felt the book drop into her hands and she almost buckled under its weight. The pages flew open, showing her a tiny glimpse of what was written inside and illustrations of the three mages were soon there for her to feast her eyes upon, but there was no image of a fourth mage to be seen anywhere at all.

Crystal felt a pulling sensation around her waist and she turned to see Clump urging her to retreat and she took an involuntary step back.

'Stop where you are!' commanded Merguld, pointing a warning finger, his wizard's hat slipping down, over his face. 'I haven't done with you two yet.'

A disturbance, a type of scuffling noise broke her concentration and she looked through the trees that were almost bare of leaves and to her astonishment she saw Bridgemear appear with Arhdel and Amadeus by his side.

'I can't believe it, my father's here!' she suddenly declared, dropping the grimoire to the floor and running with open arms straight into his embrace. Bridgemear ran towards her when he saw a rush of red hair, throwing a suspicious glare over to the Windigo when he espied him in the background. He hugged his daughter for what seemed like an age, his happiness at finding her alive was clearly obvious in his bright blue eyes. He was still weak but he would gain strength and momentum in the knowledge his daughter was safe from harm.

'How did you know where to find me?' Crystal asked, noticing how his eyes crinkled when he smiled down at her.

'I found the bangle you left me,' Bridgemear confessed, lifting it up for her to see, 'in the canyon; I almost broke my neck falling over it.' Crystal beamed broadly, remembering when the firebird had disintegrated in the canyon and how she'd stuffed the bangle under a small stone when picking up Clump's bag.

'I knew you'd find it!' she grinned, holding him at arm's length, 'but how did you get all the way down here?'

Before Bridgemear could explain, someone tapped her lightly on the shoulder and she turned to see Niculmus standing before her and the light dancing in his eyes told her he was also pleased to see her and, without thinking, she let go of her father and hugged him tight.

'Our new friend, Merrow, is full of surprises,' Niculmus rasped when she threatened to suffocate him where he stood, her arms wrapped so tight around his neck he thought she might damage his windpipe.

'He was found to be carrying some kind of Lodestones in his pocket and they miraculously brought us right to you.'

Merrow wandered to her side and gave her a low bow. His skin was grey and Crystal shuddered, caused not by his deathly pallor but by a sneaking suspicion that she had seen him somewhere before. The elf pushed his robe aside and then opened his hand towards her, to show her his secret treasures. The second he revealed his sweaty palm, the stones flew from his hand and headed straight towards the altar, causing Merguld to snigger out loud, a wicked glint forming in his rheumy eyes.

'It is all so very touching that you have found each other once again, but now it is time for you to pay for your stupidity. You should never have released the fourth mage without my permission and for that I allow the demons below the altar to rise up and the day of reckoning to finally be upon you!'

'Oh no, by all that is magical, this can't be true!' shouted Clump, wiping at his eyes as though they were deceiving him when the stones slid down the centre of the cone.

'Quickly, everyone, get out of here whilst you still can for the stupid fool was carrying the Lodestones of the Lost Trinity!'

Before anyone could catch their breath, the altar gave a mind-shuddering rumble and then burst into a thousand jagged fragments, sending potentially lethal shrapnel flying through the air only narrowly missing Crystal's stricken face.

'Get down!' Niculmus bellowed towards her, dragging her to the ground and throwing himself on top when the dangerous remnants sailed through the air. 'The Windigo is right! We must get out of here, before it's too late!'

Chapter 25

'I demand to see Queen Amella at once!'

Rudessa stood in the Queen's doorway, trying to hold her temper, but the Satyr's next words gave her cause for alarm.

'If you do not allow me to see her in the next few minutes, I will be forced to take matters into my own hands!' he snorted, his eyes showing a keenness she hadn't seen before. She chewed her fingernails, fighting her conscience and found she had terror in her heart. Quickly, she threw her hands behind her back and a heavy sigh left her lips. She looked up at his broad physique and rippling muscles and knew he could knock her to the ground like a feather with one swift swipe from his hand. It was becoming obvious that she would not be able to keep him at bay for much longer, but she knew she had to at least try and do her best to delay him from entering the Queen's chamber.

'The Queen is still not well,' she sniffed, noticing her feet were starting to become fidgety and she dropped her eyes down to her toes before flicking her gaze towards him. 'Tell me, Satyr, will you not let her sleep in peace until the morrow?'

The Satyr's eyes were guarded and when he spoke his voice was low and rumbling.

'It has been several hours since I have seen the Queen and I am growing anxious,' he told the maid, placing both hands firmly on his hips. 'Now, I will not repeat myself again.'

Rudessa attempted a reassuring smile, but the panic in her eyes destroyed the effort she was making.

The last of the twilight was closing in like grey steel when Rudessa rushed up the stairs towards the silver stone figure lying stiff and cold on a bed of soft covers. The Queen's striking features, smooth and polished, were embedded deep in the rock but Rudessa had no time to admire the special effects of the spell. She had to confess though that she was both surprised and annoyed that the Satyr had grown suspicious much sooner than they had both first anticipated and with him bellowing to enter the Queen's bedchamber, she reached out her trembling fingers and removed the Ring-stone from Amella's heart.

The moment the stone was pulled from her chest the Queen was dragged away from Elveria's hidden sanctuary and with startling speed drawn through the earth in the reverse order of which she had travelled, unable to stop herself. Everywhere she had visited flew past her face at breakneck speed until she was flung back in her own body, staring with open confusion into the startled eyes of her faithful maid.

Without warning, the Satyr was heard to be climbing the wooden steps, his hoofed feet clattering clumsily against the hard wooden panels and Rudessa, on hearing him coming, panicked, flinging the Ring-stone straight out of the stone bay window, just by her head.

'Quick! Selnus is here,' she rasped, pulling the bedcovers over Amella's body and flicking the tousled corners down. Still flustered, she tried to regain her composure when the Satyr approached the Queen's bedside by quickly smoothing down her skirts. Her sweaty palms slid down the fabric with ease and she raised them to her hair, beginning to fiddle with her hairpins as he moved closer. She stole a sideward glance at him and saw his eyes were filled with creeping suspicion, showing her he was not fully convinced. Amella was quick to react to the situation, sitting up and shifting her long auburn hair away from her face.

'What are you doing in here,' she snapped, trying to push back the blankets so she could swing her legs over the side of the bed. She found her arms to be bound and she looked down and realised Rudessa had placed a thin cotton gown over her. She pushed her arms inside the short sleeves and tried to look outwardly calm.

'You have no right to come in my chamber,' Amella continued, pulling at the bedding to cover her modesty. 'Tell me Selnus, what would the Guild have to say if they knew you entered my chamber without permission?' The Satyr looked a little less confident and his face filled with doubt. He turned to Rudessa, giving her a puzzled frown.

'It appears the Queen no longer suffers from a headache,' he stammered, his suspicion changing to embarrassment. 'My sincere apologies, Your Highness, however, I must tell you that after several hours of you lying in bed without a word, I thought for some strange reason you were playing me for a fool.'

Amella feigned astonishment, looking at Rudessa as though she would never think of doing such a terrible thing.

'My dear Selnus, if I didn't know better, I would think you'd suffered too much sun today,' she told him with bright eyes.

The Satyr attempted a weak smile.

'Again, I'm very sorry for the unexpected intrusion, but I'm sure you can understand my position.'

'No, actually, I cannot,' stated Amella, standing tall and allowing Rudessa to help pull on her fine green robe, 'for I have no reason to play you for a fool, it's not like I can escape this place or go anywhere I shouldn't now, is it?'

'Indeed,' gasped Selnus, bowing low, 'but may I just add that I have prepared you a little supper in the kitchen for when you are ready to eat.'

'Selnus, that is a very kind gesture, however, I'm afraid I have little appetite after suffering such a migraine and I think it would be better for me to go without food until morning,' said Amella, pulling her lips into a tight line.

'Very well,' Selnus replied, turning on his heels and leaving the chamber as quickly as he had entered. 'I will bid you goodnight and see you both in the morning.'

'By all the heavens, I have to say that was too damn close,' hissed Rudessa when Selnus was heard tripping noisily down the long, spiral staircase to his own quarters. 'I simply cannot believe he got so suspicious so quickly.'

Amella walked away without answering and she moved so fast Rudessa found herself chasing after her. She flew down the few steps, her feet pounding the wooden planks that led to the lower landing and almost leapt onto the main floor. The makeshift dressing room seemed cold and uninviting and Rudessa lit the sconces which were placed on the back wall, bringing the room alive with the flickering golden light and therefore illuminating Amella's shimmering, pale skin.

'What is it?' she asked her mistress when she was brave enough to speak, 'tell me, what has happened since you left this place?'

Amella pulled a stray, auburn curl behind a pointed ear and turned to face her maid, her facial features taut with anguish. The last threads of daylight were piercing through the small window, flooding the room with weak light and Amella drew closer to the sconces, not wishing the darkness to wash the day away.

'I'm not really sure,' she confessed, wrapping her arms around her waist for added warmth. 'When I left you, I travelled for many miles through hill and dale and I somehow managed to stumble on Elveria, hidden beside the Lagoona Mountains. He has made an underground domain close by and it is one of the largest dens I have ever seen. I followed him into each new cavity and travelled through the rock and into his secret inner chamber where he has many outlawed spells and stolen artefacts hidden away from view, possessions which, until now, have been deemed lost. But there is something more sinister that I must tell you.

'Within his piles of stolen relics, he has the rarest of crystal balls and whilst I observed him using it, he commanded the ball to show him the facial image of one of my apprentices. Indeed, I see no sense to it at all. Tell me, why would he hold the likeness of a young boy such as Niculmus DeGrunt inside it?

I have been trying to scratch my brain to figure out why he would know this apprentice and I have come to the conclusion that Niculmus is somehow in collusion with Elveria, for all that has happened to my daughter is all too much to be just a mere coincidence. Indeed, as I gazed into the crystal ball it all became clearer.

Niculmus upset Crystal at the Grand Meadow, creeping up behind her and scaring her half witless. I have no doubt in my mind now that he was planning to abduct her that very night. And then he was there, at Minerva Lake, when Crystal was taken by the dreadful firebird and yet he stood before me looking lost and afraid when he told me he was unable to save her, which I believed, accepting his explanation without question, for he was a newly appointed apprentice and very inexperienced within the art of magic. Now I see things from a very different angle and a clearer eye, Niculmus DeGrunt is a traitor to the realm and I need to find him, fast!'

Rudessa nodded encouragingly at Amella's shocking revelation, but found she was unable to come up with any immediate answers that might give comfort to her distraught Queen. She brushed her hand against her mistress's back and saw Amella's eyes well with tears.

'I must use the Ring-stone again,' Amella declared, holding back a sob. 'I must travel through these few dark hours and try to find my daughter before Niculmus gets his hands on her. As you are aware, the apprentice is travelling with her father and if Bridgemear finds her, which I'm sure in time he will, he may be inadvertently leading Niculmus right to her.'

At the Queen's words Rudessa blanched, her eyes filling with dread and she opened her mouth, her arms outstretched as her lips tried unsuccessfully to form words.

'What's wrong with you?' asked Amella, taking hold of Rudessa's hand when she noticed they were shaking, 'tell me, have you become ill?'

Rudessa shook her head, and her own frustration caused her to snatch her hand away from Amella's grasp, unable to stop the twinge of guilt that wormed straight through her gut. She headed for the window, wringing her hands like an old washer woman and she hesitated for another heartbeat until she was able to blurt out the ludicrous statement from her reluctant mouth.

'Oh my, Your Highness, I fear there is a bit of a problem with you using the Ring-stone again, because I have done something really stupid and, err, without thinking, kind of threw it out of the window!'

Chapter 26

Elveria watched the swordmaster pick up the scroll and caught his narrowing eyes.

'Bring the Queen back to me at once,' he ordered, wagging his finger with purpose, 'I want her here before the morrow, do I make myself perfectly clear?'

The swordmaster nodded, bowing and taking his leave, then out of the darkened shadows, Lord Taurion and Master Fangfoss emerged, their hands clutching a silver goblet filled to the brim with a strong, amber liquid.

'My lord, it's good to see you back amongst the living,' Lord Taurion smirked, pulling his associate a little closer. Elveria lifted his eyelids and watched them approach, his expression bordering on smug.

'Yes, indeed my friends,' he urged with a flourish of his hand, 'you're right; I'm back in my rightful place and out of the woodwork, so to speak. It has been a very dangerous time, but now the Queen is ready for trial and the evidence against her is set in stone, I no longer need to hide away. The evidence I have in my possession is damning enough, she never stood a chance against me and we have much celebrating to do this night for I am where I belong and wish to enjoy my moment of glory.'

Both Lord Taurion and Master Fangfoss's eyes burned with cunning and they raised their goblets heavenwards, each grinning from ear to ear and it was Lord Taurion who was the first to congratulate the mage on his overwhelming victory.

'You are very clever, my lord, and it is good to hear the trial against Amella is now underway,' he said, his smile broadening. 'Tell me, is it true the council will sit in two moons' time?'

Elveria's light chuckle turned into a sadistic roar, his usual stark features creased with lines of amusement, lines seldom seen in public.

'Yes, indeed, it is all true,' Elveria answered, with a nod. 'As you've just heard, I have sent for the Queen by order of the Guild and by the time the next full moon rises, she will have been executed and the future of Nine Winters thrown into disarray.'

Lord Taurion's smile instantly dropped from his face at Elveria's unexpected revelation and the wizard's dark eyes saw the change in his comrade's demeanour.

'Come, come brother, what ails you?' Elveria asked, placing his goblet on the lacquered table which was used by the honourable Guild members. 'Tell me, Taurion, you are not losing your nerve already?'

Lord Taurion blanched, hearing the sharp edge in Elveria's voice and he also placed his cup on the table, the urge to smash the goblet against the wall crushed with Elveria's dark presence.

'With all due respect, my lord, I ask that you don't talk such nonsense. I have been your humble servant for many a year, however, I have to say that I did not expect the Queen's demise in all this.'

'Then you are a fool,' hissed Elveria, flinging his long, black cloak over his shoulder, his own eyes hardening like flint. 'If she does not die then she will simply return to reclaim her throne at a much later date. Don't you see, we must squash this maggot straight into the ground whilst we have the chance, making sure she will never again resurface.'

Lord Taurion stared at him aghast, unable to comprehend his reasoning.

'But, my lord, to have her murdered!'

'Well, I did try to make it look like a simple accident but that dratted Satyr took his role a little too seriously.'

'What, that was you who summoned the goblin sharks? Why, we were all nearly killed!'

'Not quite, more's the pity,' said Elveria, his mouth turning to a sneer.

Lord Taurion swung round to face Master Fangfoss and saw his eyes warning him to keep his mouth shut. He watched Fangfoss

249

guzzle the malt like some common street merchant, wiping his chin dry with the back of his hand when he dribbled his drink like a simpleton.

Lord Taurion stood rigid, his mind unable to accept that Elveria would have happily seen him drown or, worse, eaten by the dreaded goblin sharks. He hesitated for a fraction too long before heading to where a fire flickered bright and golden in the hearth. The flames tried to warm the chill which seemingly swept around him and he stiffened when he felt the elder mage's hand clutch hold of his shoulder.

'Do not lose sleep over her,' Elveria advised, patting him like a sniffling hound. 'You know as well as I that she has brought all this on herself. She could have played this all so differently but her ignorance and foolishness alone has put her in this terrible predicament. However, when she is dead, Bridgemear will no longer be Prince Regent and therefore he will go back to being a mere wizard. On her demise, he will leave her kingdom seeking solitude and inner peace, a luxury he will never be afforded. With Amella gone, his world will fall apart and his daughter will once again be abandoned, forcing her to return to the ordinary world and everything will be how I want it.'

Taurion noticed the room smelt of strong, male masculinity and betrayal. The dark walls were filled with decorative banners from long ago and ancient swords belonging to dead kings were hanging like trophies high above the fireplace. Sections of tracery were joined together with carved wooden pegs and the fine patterns of the seven emblems of the Guild were embossed within the ceiling, looking down on his head like treacherous spies.

'You appear to have thought of everything,' Lord Taurion snapped, trying to shrug Elveria's hand from his shoulder, a sickness spilling into his gut when he felt the magician's fingers dig into his flesh. He snatched his shoulder from his grasp and almost stumbled when he shifted towards the tall, lancet windows, bile rising unexpectedly in his throat and he grappled with the stiff hasp until he managed to force it open, pushing the glass pane wide enough to let a sudden coldness blow against his skin.

He filled his lungs with fresh air, his shoulders rounding a little less. His thoughts filled with the Queen, realising he had never truly expected to see her dead. The sun was high in the sky and the noise of heavy boots crossing the stone courtyard below brought him back to reality.

Master Fangfoss coughed uncomfortably, unable to ignore his partner's disposition, and took to sitting in one of the great armchairs situated close to the fireside. The tension inside the room heightened with the flames and when Taurion finally turned away from the window, Fangfoss gestured for him to come and join him. The atmosphere was oppressive and Lord Taurion shifted from his spot with some reluctance. He felt Elveria's dark eyes watch his every move, causing him to sweep his own cloak around his shoulders before he made his way back to the fireside.

'Are you feeling a little better?' Elveria asked in a shrewd voice. 'Perhaps it is the malt, I think it may not agree with you?'

Taurion shook his head, still dazed and his mouth turned dry at the thought of the blood soon to be spilled by Elveria's hand.

'Tell me, my lord, what is to happen to the elf woman who is pregnant by the poorer land dwarf?'

Elveria's eyes shifted to where his stave was laid to rest.

'There was never any pregnancy, it was all a lie,' he stated, walking over and grabbing it firmly in his hand.

'But why?' pressed Taurion, sounding inclined to disbelieve the wizard. 'None of this is making sense anymore.' Elveria's eyes turned cold, his face shimmering with grey and he watched Lord Taurion sink awkwardly into his chair.

'Because, you idiot, I want the Guild to believe that the abomination against our ways has already begun. I needed them to think that mixed breeding had already started and I merely gave them a push in the right direction. Don't you see, if we are to get rid of Amella then the evidence must be overwhelming.' Elveria's voice was a low, serious growl and Lord Taurion looked stung by his words and he brought his hand to his face to hide the disgust that welled in his eyes.

'So, you think this is the only way you can become the ruler of Nine Winters, by killing Amella? Are you telling me you want this, no matter what the cost to others?' Taurion asked, unable to hide his despair.

'Indeed, I do,' said Elveria, closing the double doors and sealing the antechamber, 'no matter what the cost to others.'

Master Fangfoss started quivering in his chair, the light in his eyes seemingly fading and he snivelled like a terrified child when he realised the magician was growing angry. Elveria suddenly pointed his stave towards Taurion's chest.

'I fear you have become a royal sympathiser, something I had not expected of you, my how the tide turns so quickly and more's the pity, for now I have no choice but to end this stunted conversation.'

Lord Taurion jumped from his seat in alarm; hurtling forward he collided with something that wasn't there, causing him to fall back onto the chair, momentarily stunned. Elveria stood stock still when a light breeze flared from within the room and his robes and beard blew with a gentle grace. His eyes glowed black with wickedness and he brought his stave in front of him, allowing a crackle of power to hit the atmosphere and before Taurion could retaliate, the magician threw his hand towards the fire, pulling the flames directly from the hearth and sending them in a burning trail straight towards the Lord.

There was a piercing scream and then the room erupted with huge, burning flames, causing Master Fangfoss to squeal like a slaughterhouse pig, diving behind the magician's robes, petrified it would be his turn next.

He stared in terror as Lord Taurion danced and wriggled in agony when giant flames licked hungrily at his flesh. In seconds he was totally consumed by fire and in less than a minute he fell dead at the wicked magician's feet. Smoke rose from his body in trails of black, the smell of cooked flesh repugnant. The magician flicked his stave when the carcass fell, throwing the flames back into the hearth from whence they came.

'I've always warned you of the dangers of playing with fire,' Elveria said sardonically, looking down at the charred remains of Lord Taurion. 'It's a shame you never took my advice.' His attention then turned to Master Fangfoss. Cursing under his breath, he bent down and grabbed him by the scruff of the neck, pulling him swiftly to his feet.

'If you value your life, when the guards come in here, you will tell them this was all a terrible accident,' he hissed in Fangfoss's pointed ear. You are a witness to what happened here today, you saw with your own eyes my attempt to save Lord Taurion, but I arrived too late.'

Master Fangfoss shook with fear, the web of lies spun by Elveria already falling into place.

'Lord Taurion is no more and if you want to live, you will serve me as I see fit,' hissed Elveria.

The elf simply nodded.

Elveria relaxed his grip, allowing the elf back on his feet and then he dusted his robe with the back of his hand, removing the small, delicate pieces of ash which were trying to settle on his clothing.

'Amella *will* die,' he whispered just before the doors flew open and three guardsmen entered. 'And so will you, Fangfoss, if you ever breathe a single word of what really happened here to anyone.'

Chapter 27

Spears of light crashed in blinding bolts inside Merguld's burning temple, causing those inside to huddle together and shield themselves from the sparks of burning fire. Clump was the first to see a bat-like creature pull itself from the earth, glowing red and snarling its way towards the surface from where the altar had once stood and he felt himself shudder.

His eyes darted around the temple in the hope of finding a way out and it was then that he noticed Merguld was now nowhere to be seen. A high-pitched screech left the demon's mouth, and the decibel was so intense that his ears began to ring. Against his own wishes, his eyes were drawn back to the monster and Clump watched in awe as it continued to claw at the dirt. The demon turned and raised its ugly head, hissing its displeasure at seeing the Windigo lying there. Then, when the monster was halfway out of its earthy grave, it gave a howl, calling for its mate to follow whilst it uncurled two, huge wings.

Clump wiped the dust from his eyes and went to stand but found he was unable to move. He had been thrown to the floor in the blast, but now he saw his legs were lodged under a heap of shiny metal and no matter how much he wriggled and pushed, he couldn't break free. Pain burned his flesh and he closed his eyes, his adrenalin pumping and then he pulled himself together and started grabbing at the chunks of debris which lay diagonally across his legs. Even with his great strength he couldn't move them all and so he tried to bum shuffle his way out. He found it was no use he was stuck fast and a numbness was creeping from his toes and spreading way up to his knees, bringing a cold that he'd never before experienced. He shuddered, turning to scan the inside of the temple in the hope of finding someone willing to help him and when

Arhdel extended his hand, Clump gratefully took hold, allowing the warrior to pull at him with all his might.

'It's no use, my legs are trapped!' shouted Clump, when Arhdel's attempts to free him appeared utterly fruitless. 'Go, leave me here and take care of the princess instead,' he rasped, letting go of Arhdel's firm grip. Arhdel looked down at the Windigo and gave him such a scowl that said he would do no such thing, but Clump was pushing Arhdel's outstretched hand away and gesturing for him to leave. Another high-pitched squeal came from the depth of the earth and Clump felt another shudder run down his spine. He turned and saw there, right in front of him, yet another demon pulling itself from the earth and he watched it shake free large clods of dirt which clung to its folded wings and then he heard the demon hiss like a venomous viper.

'Get her out of here whilst you still can!' Clump shouted at the warrior. Arhdel wavered when he saw the second demon flex its vicious talons, blood pumping through its veins, strengthening its long, taut limbs. The monster looked up and scanned the temple and spotted Clump lying defenceless on the floor and with yet another spiteful hiss, began crawling towards him. The demon opened its huge mouth to reveal a long, thin tongue which snaked between a set of yellow, pointed teeth, their incisors wide enough to rip through his flesh in one easy bite.

Arhdel saw the creature heading towards them and couldn't stop himself from cursing aloud, making the scar along his cheek wrinkle as he did so.

'I don't understand why I cannot move you!' he gasped, grabbing hold of Clump's arm yet again and giving him one last tug. 'But, you're right, it's useless, I need to get Amadeus here to help me shift this debris and I need to do it fast, before that demon reaches you.'

Clump shook his head fiercely and started shouting and insisting the warrior leave him behind, but Arhdel ignored his ranting and ran instead to where Amadeus stood with his sword drawn to protect the magician and his daughter. He saw that Bridgemear's arm was around Crystal's shoulders to protect her and both Niculmus and Amadeus were standing with their backs towards the princess. He ran to Amadeus's side but was immediately intercepted by Merrow.

'We are all doomed! None of us can get out of here!' wailed the elf, grabbing hold of Arhdel and staring at the warrior like some kind of frightened animal. 'Look, the demons are sealing the tunnel; we are all going to die!'

Arhdel glanced over to where they had entered and sure enough the tunnel was being sealed by a river of gold that ran from the altar. The liquid was like a slick stream, pouring along the ground until it reached their only exit and before his very eyes the golden mass raised itself up, instantly solidifying and making the entranceway impenetrable.

'Then we have no choice, we must work quickly and kill the demons,' Arhdel hissed, shrugging the elf's hand away, 'for it's clear to me that if we don't act soon, we will be picked off like flies where we stand.'

Bridgemear overheard their conversation and left Crystal's side to face the warrior, his facial muscles becoming as taut as piano strings.

'All I needed was my staff,' he said bitterly, raising the Sword of Truth in one of his mighty hands. Shadows of light glistened against the blade, making Bridgemear's eyes appear to flash with menace and he swung the blade savagely in the air. 'Enough of this madness!' he growled, 'for I have killed far bigger fish than these in my lifetime and so it is time I ended this charade. However, I must tell you that I fear for the Windigo. Crystal has told me he has become a close friend, but I don't think we will be able to save him.'

'You must!' Crystal shouted, on hearing his damning words, and the magician turned to see her eyes fill with tears. She rushed forward, her mouth set firm.

'Please, father,' she begged, holding him fast, 'I just know you can save him.'

Bridgemear's jaw tightened and he glanced at the two warriors, but their faces looked as doubtful as his own and so he patted her hand affectionately as though she was merely a small child to be pacified. His attention was stolen by Niculmus, who moved with a swiftness that he had not expected and he watched the apprentice circle his arms around Crystal in a gentle, yet protective, embrace. He saw Crystal look down in surprise when his hands snaked unexpectedly around her waist, but Bridgemear felt only intrigue when she didn't pull away from his touch and his eyes rounded with his own surprise.

'Niculmus, stay with the princess no matter what happens and keep her safe,' he suddenly ordered in a definitive, stern voice. Niculmus nodded and the fire blazing in his eyes told the mage he would not let him down and without another word passing his lips, Bridgemear ran forward to attack the demons.

Wielding his sword high above his head, he jumped straight over the Windigo and aimed his blade at the first winged monster that was only inches away from where Clump lay trapped. In a blurring vision of honed-edged determination, Bridgemear lunged himself at the monster. The creature, although taken by surprise, was quick to react, flinging its huge wings around its body for protection and enabling a sharpened claw to catch the bottom of Bridgemear's boot, knocking him down to the ground, his sword narrowly missing its target and flying free from his grasp.

Before he had time to gather his senses, the demon was upon him and Bridgemear flexed his hand towards the monster and a long, thin spear of magic shot from his palm, immediately penetrating inside the demon's belly. Writhing and twisting the demon contorted in what looked like an agonising dance. A pure white flame was burning deep within its abdomen like fire licking straw, but then from its gut something wriggled and broke free, pulling itself from the stomach of its mother and Bridgemear blanched, turning pale when he saw a new demon had been birthed from the power of his magic.

'Damn you!' Bridgemear cursed in frustration. The newly formed monster turned its head towards him, the look of hatred already sculpted on its ugly, bat-like face, but then Amadeus and Arhdel were standing before him with their own swords outstretched, the flash of cold steel shining like silver against the red projected from the monster's evil eyes.

The three demons started to draw alongside one another, screaming and hissing their displeasure, growing impatient to be freed into the outside world. With their slimy bodies taut, the larger male came to the forefront and in a flash its thick, powerful arm struck out and knocked the two warriors crashing to the ground. They rolled across the floor like plastic skittles severely winded and they took several seconds to recover. In the growing darkness it was hard to see what was really happening, but the demon's eyes were ablaze with fire.

In a flash, it was Bridgemear who was seen staggering to his feet and running to retrieve his sword, but the new-born demon was much, much faster and it kicked the sword from his grasp.

There came a piercing cry and Bridgemear bore witness to Arhdel hitting the demon so hard with the hilt of his sword he somehow broke its wing. The monster howled in agony, already cowering away into a darkened corner to finger the damaged limb, squealing with rage when the wing remained limp and lifeless. Bridgemear grinned from the distraction until a sharp burning sensation pierced through his shoulder and a heavy force pinned him to the ground. He gasped for breath, realising one of the demons was using a pincer-like claw to drag him along the floor and then an overwhelming heat washed over him, when another claw ripped into both of his legs. He screamed in terrifying agony, his blonde hair soaked with sweat in a matter of seconds and he clenched his teeth to stop himself screaming again.

'You have slain too many of our kind,' the demon hissed close to his face, its sour breath turning his stomach. 'Now it is time to slay you and when you're dead, your world will be ours for the taking.' Suddenly a firm hand rested on Bridgemear's good shoulder and he looked up with blurred vision to see the white face of Niculmus looking down at him. The apprentice crouched onto his bended knees, his wand raised high in an attempt to intimidate the monster.

'No, Niculmus! What the hell do you think you're doing? You know your magic isn't powerful enough to win over something of this magnitude!' Bridgemear cried, blanching and trying to clear his head by shaking it. 'Your magic is far too weak against such evil, go back you fool and save the princess like I told you!'

The creature lashed out and Niculmus ducked, his wand still secure in the palm of his hand. The demon hissed with sudden fury and attacked once again, but Niculmus was busy muttering a spell and an array of dazzling stars and illuminating white bands started to float throughout the atmosphere and encircle each of the demons, catching their immediate attention. It lasted for only a few seconds and then the creatures were roaring once again when the glowing bands slipped over their heads and tightened around their middle, holding their winged arms fast and Niculmus was deemed by the elder mage to have totally lost his mind.

Niculmus closed his eyes and Bridgemear feared for his sanity, the wound through his shoulder was oozing a river of blood and his legs were so badly hurt he worried his inner strength would not be enough to allow him to walk again. He tried to drag his broken body along the floor, leaving a long, crimson trail behind him, but he was desperate to reach his sword and then he heard Niculmus shouting out, and he switched his attention to the apprentice, caused by the tone of his voice.

'For all the forefathers that have lived and died before us, for all the memories of the past we hold so dear, be gone demons from this life that you wish to fill with darkness and leave this place forever.' As Bridgemear listened, he thought Niculmus no longer seemed like a boy. The light from Niculmus's wand glared unmistakably bright when the demons broke their bonds and went for the attack, but then the apprentice's wand did something truly amazing. It flew from his hand and broke into several sharp pieces, floating in the air like the fragments of a shooting star, dazzling those who were unable to drag their eyes away, until the shards of light changed shape, turning into blinding deltoids of golden light. Shaped like arrowheads, they grew in size and then quadrupled and Bridgemear turned to see Crystal holding her necklace and assisting Niculmus by energising his transcendental magic.

The power within the room was so intense Bridgemear thought his head was about to explode. The atmosphere crackled with Niculmus's celestial magnetism and Bridgemear was baffled as to how the apprentice could suddenly turn so powerful. He remembered the scene at the river where he had only been able to hold the Challicums off for a matter of minutes and yet, when his magic faltered, Niculmus had held them back for considerably longer.

A hum, like a swarm of angry bees, filled the air and was abruptly followed by an undistinguishable commotion and then the ghosts of Bridgemear's forefathers, high lords and protectors from the past rallied together and congregated inside the temple. Ancient sorcerers, royal defenders and majestic kings from many, many centuries ago came up from the ground, from in-between rocks and down through the ceilings. White witches raced with Elvin Bards to be the first to reach the glowing deltoids and each and every one of the ghostly apparitions flew with purpose towards the arrowheads, grabbing the glowing spheres in their outstretched hands before hurtling them towards the demons. The deltoids shot from their fingers like bullets from a gun, hitting their targets with remarkable precision and the arrowheads burst the moment they pierced the demon's outer skin and a white combustion exploded inside their bodies, like fire ravishing paper.

Squeals of agony and desperate roars filled the smoky atmosphere when the demons turned to blackened dust, perishing instantaneously at the hands of such pure and intense magic.

Suddenly, Merguld's grimoire rose from within the ashes, its pages gleaming and the scattered remains of the altar rose from where they had fallen; the sealed entranceway melted away and the golden river ran once more along the ground, retracting to whence it once came, like a film rewound, the thick droplets of gold congealing together until the altar was moulded perfectly back into shape and Clump was no longer trapped beneath it.

A ghostly figure, larger and less transparent than the others, floated closer to Niculmus. The other phantoms, a thousand images of the past, shimmered with triumph at their unexpected victory but now no longer needed, lingered like forgotten memories, waiting to return to the graves from where they came. The grimoire floated over to the ghost leader's hand, the apparition, a magician, was smiling respectfully down towards the young apprentice.

'My lord, it is fair to say you have done very well,' the ghostly figure said, looking pleased. 'I see your soul has not lost any of its supremacy, even after so many centuries of having been locked underground.' The ghost chuckled lightly when a look of confusion spread like melted butter all over Niculmus's face.

'I don't quite understand what you're saying,' said the apprentice, looking more than a little perplexed. The ghost's features grew serious, but his eyes still danced with pride.

'Why, my dear boy, the truth is that you have the soul of the fourth mage. Without you being here today your ancestors would not have been called upon to assist you with ridding this place of those terrifying monsters and our once good civilisation would have been taken over by the dark side.'

Niculmus heard Crystal gasp and he flicked his gaze towards her, a look of bewilderment displayed upon his handsome face.

'What! You're the fourth mage!' she rasped, incredulously.

'You've heard of me?' Niculmus asked, bringing his hand to his chest, clearly shaken.

'Why, yes, of course, you're the reason why I was taken by the firebird and why I was sent on this quest in the first place. I was supposed to come here and awaken the fourth mage to save my family from persecution and all the time you were by my side. But I don't understand, why did I have to go to all this trouble to find you and end up awakening the demons if you were already in Nine Winters?'

The ghost chuckled again but this time it was through his years of knowledge.

'Things never happen quite the way they should,' he told them, floating a little closer. 'Indeed, no one knew that the fourth mage was no longer trapped within this book, so you had no choice but to seek Merguld's spell book and try to release him. However, Merguld is not as clever as he thinks and obviously the fourth mage conjured his own spell, a spell which would bring him back to his kingdom should the need arise. You see, Princess, the day you were born is the day Niculmus was also born. In a way you two are linked together for he also needed to make this journey, for he must learn how to use his gifts well. It's just unfortunate that no one knew this 'til now, otherwise we may have been able to avert today's harrowing experience for everyone; however, this story doesn't end here. There is still evil amongst your kind and I sense Princess Crystal that your mother is in great danger. Go back to your homeland with much haste and greater speed and perhaps Niculmus can help stop a catastrophe that is inevitably waiting to happen.'

Crystal and Niculmus stared at each other in wide-eyed wonder and then Crystal spotted Merrow out of the corner of her eye trying to haul Clump to his feet. He had made a tourniquet from the bottom of his cloak and with his bare hands tightened it around the top of Clump's thigh to help stem the flow of blood. Merrow then half dragged, half carried Clump to where the group was starting to congregate.

Clump tried to grin at Crystal when he saw the worry in her eyes, but failed miserably when the overwhelming pain became too much for him to bear and she ran over to him, throwing out her arms so she could press her fluttering hands directly over the gaping wound.

'Thank god you're safe,' she declared, pressing a little harder and watching the colour creep back into his face. 'Did you hear that we no longer have to worry about releasing the fourth mage?'

Two furry caterpillars which were his eyebrows rose.

'Yes, I heard,' he said, looking more than a little surprised. 'I guess none of this has worked out quite like we planned.' Clump broke her gaze and Crystal was confused by his doleful attitude and opened her mouth to say something, but a low moaning penetrated her concentration instead and she turned to stare into the shocking bloodstained face of her father. He looked ghastly. His face had suffered two deep cuts to his right cheek and his left eye was so swollen it was a mere slit. His clothing was so badly torn there was nothing left except tatters, revealing the gaping wound to his shoulder, and his legs could not be seen for blood. He had been hoisted to his feet by Arhdel and Amadeus, but it was obvious he needed immediate medical attention.

'You heard what the ghost said, we must leave immediately,' Bridgemear whispered, when she rushed over to him. She looked down and saw his legs were slashed like threads of ribbon and his shoulder a mass of raw meat on bone. She gasped outwardly, momentarily shocked at the severity of his wounds and when Arhdel and Amadeus laid him flat on the ground at her command, she crouched down beside him and immediately set to work on his broken body.

'I will self-heal,' he told her when she started fussing over him. 'Only it might take a little longer than usual, that's all,' he added, wincing in pain.

'Hold still!' she ordered, trying to hide the shock from her voice. 'Why these wounds are way too deep and you don't have enough time to self-heal before you bleed to death,' she cried, unsure where to start first.

262

Bridgemear unconsciously caught his breath. He saw Crystal touching the deep lacerations to both of his legs and although the pain was excruciating he could already feel a warm tingling sensation coursing through his lower body. He felt Crystal press on his wounds and then she was pulling at what was left of the skin on his upper thigh and, although he tried, he was unable to stop himself from crying out.

'I'm so, so sorry,' she whispered, her eyes filling with tears, 'but there is no other way I can do this,' she added, brushing her hands over his face and pressing his eyelids closed.

As she worked, Crystal noticed how the temple had turned still and quiet and she glanced up from what she was doing to see the ghosts floating away, perhaps, she thought, back to their graves or to seek their final resting places once again. Although grateful for their help she quickly lost interest, concentrating on healing her father, working her magic whilst the others watched in awe when a red-golden glow wrapped Bridgemear in a shroud of light and a few of his bones were distinctly heard snapping back into place. The minutes ticked slowly by and with every second that passed, Bridgemear started to look much better.

'How is this possible?' the mage gasped, when a consuming white fire raged through his body, refuelling his inner strength at an astounding rate. 'Why, my legs feel as good as new!'

He suddenly jumped to his feet, astonished, his fingers probing his shoulder and finding only a new, fresh scar. He grabbed Crystal's hands, feeling the heat that lingered in her fingertips, and his eyes widened with wonder. She remained silent, breaking her father's incessant stare and he let her hands drop, still shocked at her ability to heal him so quickly. She watched him turn to both Amadeus and Arhdel and saw their own eyes wide with wonder.

'We must leave for Nine Winters,' Crystal stated, cutting short a conversation that was just about to start between the warriors and her father.

'Look, over there, the entranceway is clear so let's get out of here and hope we make it home in time,' she added.

Someone scurried to her side and Crystal spun round to see Clump staring at her, his own eyes looking troubled.

'This is where we have to say goodbye, Princess,' he said, taking a deep breath and pulling his lips tight. Crystal's eyes widened with confusion and she looked at the others as though they would tell her what he was talking about.

'What do you mean?' she asked, searching his face. 'You know fully well we have to leave for Nine Winters immediately.'

Clump broke her gaze and started counting the tips of his fingers, playing for time, and Crystal reached out and tried to cover his hands with her own. Clump looked as though he was about to cry and she watched him bite his lip.

'I'm afraid my part in all this is over now you have found the fourth mage, so I must leave you and go back to my homeland,' Clump explained, but the sadness which crept in his voice made it obvious to her that it was not what he wanted to do at all.

'No! You can't leave me,' Crystal said, sounding mortified. 'Why, you've become one of my best friends, I'd be lost in this world without you and I insist that you come back to the palace with me at once.'

It was clear to everyone that Clump was struggling with his emotions and he blanched, his small, rounded eyes appearing to darken at the very edges.

'I'm sorry, Princess, there's nothing I'd like more but to come with you, but you know that's not possible. I'm a Windigo, a terrifying timber wolf, and your people would fear me to the point where they would hound me out until they saw me dead.'

'No! I won't let them!' she cried, her eyes filling with despair.

'I'm afraid there would be nothing you could do,' Clump argued weakly, 'for everyone fears what they do not understand.'

The temple turned cold and Crystal heard herself sob.

'Please, Clump, don't leave me,' she pleaded, suddenly finding tears spilling down her cheeks. 'I need you here with me.'

'I have no choice, I have to leave,' Clump croaked, his own tears breaking from his eyes and he sniffed loudly, trying to keep himself together. 'My role here is now complete and I must go back to where I belong. Those who sent me here will wish for me to return, but please remember you're the best friend I ever had and I will never forget your kindness or the time we have spent together.'

He howled, a deep, low-throated howl, taking Crystal by complete surprise and when Arhdel drew his sword, Clump ran from her side and straight towards the entranceway. Crystal ran after him and she stretched out her arms as if to try to stop him but he was far too quick and her fingers only brushed the mountain of thick hair covering his shoulder as he rushed by. He had gotten no more than perhaps forty feet from her when he transmuted right before her eyes, his back stiffening as he fought to remain in his half-human state, and then he was on all fours, crouching and foaming at the mouth like a rabid dog, his melanoid colouring mingling with so much white, and then he was lifting a paw, his golden eyes bright with life, looking at her with such longing it hurt to see it lingering there, but before she could reach him, Clump was bounding down the tunnel and lost forever inside a pit of darkness.

Chapter 28

The court was full to the brim when a shout from the Lord High Chamberlain declared an unexpected witness was to enter the assembly, bringing new and vital evidence to the witness stand. Crystal sat next to her father, having returned from the Stannary Mines just in time for the trial of her mother to begin and many of her parents' closest allies were sitting by her side in the royal gallery.

Amafar, Voleton and Mordorma had also returned to Nine Winters and were sat behind her father but it was Niculmus who was sat by her side. Ever since their reacquaintance at the mine, the apprentice's demeanour had changed towards her and now wherever she went, he followed.

From where she was sitting, Crystal had a clear view of the entire courtroom and she spotted Professor Valentino and Magician Phin pulling their robes close and getting themselves comfortable in the public gallery. She was surprised to see them there for they were both held in high regard and had the right to sit in the royal gallery and she scanned the room further and noted that Merrow was sat, a little squashed, in-between Arhdel and Amadeus.

Puzzled, she was about to say something to her father but then she heard the Inquisitor demand silence and a hush rose throughout the courtroom and her lips automatically closed. The trial was in fact in its second day and the evidence which the Guild had already seen fit to produce was in the form of the Deed of Eradication. Amella's future was looking extremely bleak and the Queen was seated all alone in the dock, her beautiful face set in a harrowing stare and her eyes defied her by showing their uncertainty.

A sudden noise filtered from the back of the court and everyone turned in their seats, their curiosity ignited and Crystal, along with the rest of the royal gallery, watched with growing anticipation when a lone figure dressed in common robes made its way towards the Order of the Guild.

The council members turned in their seats when gentle footsteps made their way across the hard, stone floor and their cold, hard eyes narrowed. The footfall appeared to grow hesitant when it finally reached the forefront of the court and then an elf woman threw back her blackened hood to reveal herself and it was Niculmus who took an unexpected gulp of air, jumping from his seat and grabbing hold of the golden rail which prevented him from falling into the lower courtroom.

'No, this cannot be!' he rasped under his breath, yet his voice travelled and the woman spun on her heels, her face turning aghast when she caught his bewildered stare.

Crystal saw the woman's worried eyes lock with Niculmus's and then her dark lashes closed and silent tears rolled down her pale cheeks. Crystal was stunned to see the elf was almost the mirror image of her handsome, young companion. Her long blonde hair fell down to her waist in a wave of thick tresses and her chocolate-coloured eyes were the darkest Crystal had ever seen. Her ruby-red lips parted when the tears continued to flow and she was seen to take a shuddering breath. After a moment her composure returned but her attention was towards the Queen, her eyes now refusing to look in Niculmus's direction.

'Your Majesty,' the elf mumbled, giving a low curtsey. 'I have come here today to tell you and this council a terrible truth, a truth that will cause great distress to my family but, alas, a truth that I believe will settle these crimes against you once and for all.'

Amella remained silent, her eyes clearly troubled, but the Elders started clucking like a group of overgrown hens at her unexpected revelation, and it was the Inquisitor who finally bade her to draw closer to the council before gesturing to the excited crowd to hush or be prepared for the consequences.

'Please, take a seat,' interrupted the Lord High Chamberlain, directing her with a wave of his hand to an appropriate chair. She nodded her thanks and took her place, trying to force herself to look a little more comfortable and less ill at ease. The room was eerily silent whilst she fiddled with her clothing and the tension in the room worked up a notch or two.

'When you are ready, please tell us who you are and why you are here,' said a stuffy little elf dressed in expensive robes and wearing his officially appointed hat. He eyed her suspiciously like so many before her, adding, 'and please speak up, so everyone can hear you at the back.'

The elf woman nodded and cleared her throat.

'My lords, Your Highness. My name is Serquin and I am the mother of the royal apprentice, Niculmus DeGrunt.' There came a rush of noise from the chosen assembly before the Inquisitor made it plain that he demanded order by striking his staff against the solid, stone floor. Shock waves left the magic stave and those closest shuddered from the velocity and quickly fell silent.

'Tell us why you are here,' the Lord High Chamberlain insisted, glaring at the council as though they were nothing more than silly children. 'There appears to be some confusion as to what part you play in all this.'

Serquin eyed the room like a cornered mouse, her eyes darting into every corner as though planning her escape, looking anxious and very unsettled. Her mysterious, dark eyes appeared to deepen as she grew accustomed to her surroundings, her gaze eventually resting on the many members of the Guild. She eyed each one individually, their unknown faces seemingly becoming etched inside her mind, until she reached someone whose features she instantly recognised.

'Many years ago,' she suddenly whispered, unable to drag her eyes away from his face. 'I came upon a magician who was both charming and gentle. I had no elf man of my own back then and I therefore found his attention towards me to be extremely flattering. Of course I knew nothing would ever come of it as love between us was forbidden back then, but he appeared insistent and wouldn't take no for an answer when I tried to tell him that we could never be more than friends.'

'What are you saying?' piped up the Inquisitor, looking rather shocked. 'Are you asking us to believe you had relations with a magician?'

Serquin's strong exterior appeared to weaken at his cold stare and she shrank back, suffering a moment of fear when his sneering mouth twisted mockingly at her and she struggled to keep hold of what was left of her crumbling composure.

'Let the elf continue,' ordered the Lord High Chamberlain, giving the Inquisitor a dressing down with a warning glare, 'this memory must be very painful for her to relive, especially with her son being here, in this courtroom.'

At his words, Serquin's eyes searched out her only child. She could see the look of bewilderment mixed with disbelief displayed on Niculmus's young face, yet she knew she had no choice but to tell the truth, no matter what the consequences might be.

Serquin coughed lightly before she continued and her lips trembled.

'Over many months the magician continued to pursue me. I spurned his advances several times, yet he ignored my wishes and sent me special gifts instead, weakening my resolve. You see, you have to understand that both myself and my family were very poor and his generosity made our lives much more bearable, sending us presents such as fresh meat, fine clothing and exquisite pieces of jewellery, enabling us to live a much better life, a life that would have otherwise been insufferable.'

A gasp was heard to come from the royal galley but this time Serquin would not look upwards and she shifted uncomfortably in her seat, the dark shadow of shame flitting somewhere behind her troubled eyes.

'Then one night I had a vision of white come to me in my sleep, a heralding messenger. The vision told me I would do something that I knew was forbidden that very night, but told me I must be strong and live with the consequences until the day of judgement came and I would, in turn, be blessed for what I allowed to happen. That same night the magician came to me in my bed …'

There came a huge roar of outrage from the council members and when Serquin found the courage to look at her son, she saw Niculmus had turned scarily white. A sudden cry from the Lord High Chamberlain made her falter and she looked up to see him cast his angry stare towards the horrified crowd.

'Silence!' he bellowed, his face turning red. 'Let the witness speak or I will have you all thrown out for contempt of court!'

Serquin waited, dry mouthed, for the tremor of noise to die down and as she waited, she fiddled with the hem of her sleeve to distract herself and help keep her nerves under control.

'Please, proceed,' ordered the Lord High Chamberlain, when the council gave a wave that they were willing to tolerate her a little longer and Serquin's voice was almost a whisper when she said, 'that night I allowed the magician into my bed and we shared the night as an intimate couple. It only happened the once. After that, I never saw or heard from him ever again.' Her eyes were shining like shards of broken glass until she took a breath and then a stream of tears fell from her long, dark lashes.

'Little did I know it, but the magician left me with child that night,' she sobbed, jumping from her chair and pointing an accusing finger directly into the Order of the Guild, her troubled eyes resting on one irate looking magician in particular.

'Elveria is the father of my only son, Niculmus DeGrunt!' she declared.

Shock, mixed with disbelief, exploded inside the hall and Elveria jumped to his feet, his own face ashen.

'This is simply preposterous!' he yelled over the continuing roar, 'why, I have never seen this elf before in my entire life!'

Serquin dropped back into her chair, the reality of her allegation hitting her harder than expected and Elveria openly condemned her as though she was completely insane. Then, through the chaos and growing disorder, another less familiar body stole through the crowd and down towards the assembly. A loud cackle broke from the approaching figure, causing the gathering to stop their high-pitched cries and turn instead to see who had the misfortune to enter the court at such an inappropriate moment.

'Lilura!' yelled Niculmus, when he spotted the old crone. 'What on earth are you doing here?'

The witch cackled again at seeing her young protégé and gave him a wide, toothless grin. It had been many months since she had practiced magic with him and she was pleased to hear he was using his ability wisely.

Crystal looked utterly confused until Niculmus turned to her and explained how Lilura was the witch who helped him to learn magic as a small child, but Bridgemear looked shaken and Crystal reached out and touched his hand in the hope it would somehow calm him.

The witch ignored the loud shouts of protest which hung in the air like a bad smell and she drew closer to the assembly instead, sensing their fear of her. With slow, calculated steps the witch made her way to Elveria's twitching side.

'One drop of blood is all we need,' she hissed when a wicked glint appeared in her eye. 'Surely, Elveria, that's not too much to ask to prove your innocence?'

Elveria's gaze held hers a moment too long.

'I will do no such thing,' he spat with contempt. 'Why, this is all complete nonsense,' he added, allowing his nostrils to flare and his mouth to droop in disgust. 'Witch, I order you to stop your ranting for I have nothing to prove this day or any other day for that matter. This is a conspiracy against me of which I will have no part; I will not be caught up in this pathetic web of lies which you see fit to weave against me.'

Lilura hissed like an angry cat, her old, piercing eyes closing to mere slits.

'You're not going to get out of this mess quite so easily,' she persisted, when he tried to produce an authoritative glare. 'After everything you put the royal family through both this day and in the past, why, how dare you have the audacity to stand here claiming you are innocent! All those years ago when Crystal was born you knew you also had a child, a son, yet you argued with the Guild for Bridgemear to pay dearly for his crimes against the realm and ultimately planned on making his child leave this world forever for reasons which will soon become much, much clearer. However, you made one grave mistake.'

'You see, unbeknown to you, the child you produced was blessed with the gift of the soul of the fourth mage; the good and wise sorcerer came back from the grave on the day of Crystal's birth. He was released from the Book of Souls the very moment she was born, yet you thought that by taking Bridgemear and Amella's child away from these lands, you would be able to have the power you have craved for so long. You planned to harvest your son's powers for your own gain and when you heard the disastrous news of Amella's pregnancy you did everything possible to try and destroy

271

them all. However, the fourth mage was always one step ahead of you and his knowledge showed Niculmus his ability in magic at an early age, to the point where he was taken under my wing to learn his true art. You see, I already knew of Crystal's existence and also recognised the unconventional powers displayed by Niculmus, and so I encouraged him to make a new life within his rightful place of the Supreme Circle of Mages.'

'Why, this trial is nothing more than a theatrical farce, made by your own hand Elveria, for your intentions are as clear as the waters that run through these lands. All this is staged, for all you want is to see the Queen dead, Bridgemear banished and the princess to be so traumatised at the loss of her parents that she willingly leaves us to go back to the awaiting arms of the ordinary world. My, how people call me wicked, yet you, Elveria, you are truly poison.'

There came a loud gasp from the gallery, but Lilura hadn't finished with Elveria just yet.

'You may think you are clever, Elveria, but a few were privy to what you had planned and so I took the liberty of taking matters into my own hands and to protect the princess I created a mere diversion and sent her to look for the fourth mage with the help of a trusted Windigo. Unfortunately, I did not realise the Lodestones of the Lost Trinity had been found and my plan almost backfired but, thanks to the intervention of the fourth mage, I am pleased to see the princess is here, safe and well. You thought you could destroy the Queen and monopolise the Elders to make them hide Crystal away like a dirty little secret, but I was there from the beginning, I saw it all and I will see this out until the bitter end.'

'You have no proof of this wild accusation!' Elveria hissed, turning to face the council and throwing his head like an insufferable mare.

'Oh, indeed I do,' cackled the witch, looking rather pleased with herself. She drew closer to the mage, her long robes, stained with dirt, rustled along the cold, stone floor behind her. 'You see, you took the Wanderer under your wing. What, you think I didn't know? Of course I knew and did you really believe the smithy would keep his mouth shut when you took his best horse for such small a coin? However, yet again your plan was foiled when the stupid elf enticed a dark, vicious Windigo to wound him in the hope it would be enough to stop Bridgemear in his tracks when he came across him in the canyon. The Wanderer hoped that, on seeing his wounds, Bridgemear would tend to him and when the spell cast on Elveria's behalf awoke the dragon masters at dawn it would be enough to see him dead. His plan almost worked too, but the Wanderer underestimated the viciousness of a Windigo and got himself so badly injured that, along with losing a few of his fingers and almost his life, he suffered amnesia.'

The witch suddenly turned around and pointed a bony finger in Merrow's direction, causing triumph to flare upon her face when she saw his first connection with the truth ignite behind his eyes. Reality hit Merrow hard, like a slap in the face and he blanched and, overcome with shock, started grasping for breath and his pale face turned whiter than snow. Lilura immediately tapped into his mind portal. She watched him play the graphic scene inside his twisted head, the Windigo tying him between the branches of the trees so he couldn't escape and then transmuting when the evening turned pitch into a huge, black wolf, attacking him within an inch of his life, until he was unexpectedly disturbed by four approaching riders and instinctively ran for cover.

Lilura chuckled, the last piece of the jigsaw finally fitting into place and so she turned her attention back to Elveria, clearly amused at the Wanderer's misfortune.

'Merrow, or should I say 'the Wanderer', is all the proof I need, for you told him everything and now that his memory has returned there will be no holding him back. I also have the added bonus of your son being here in this court and so it seems that I have enough evidence against you to see *you* sitting in Amella's place instead. You see, for all your years of knowledge and power, you never could get anything right, Elveria, that's why you're not High King of Raven's Rainbow. However, whilst I still have breath in my body I will protect our kind from the likes of you. Crystal and Niculmus are our future and the likes of me do not fear it.'

To Elveria's surprise, the Lord High Chamberlain sent a signal to the guards and the mage couldn't help but gasp in astonishment when they pushed their way past Master Fangfoss and grabbed the elder mage by his arms. He looked up, aghast, and saw the look of victory spreading over Lilura's wrinkled face like water soaking paper and her toothless grin widened when they clasped his wrists in chains.

Nevertheless, Elveria was not to be taken so easily and in a flash he vanished into thin air, the manacles crashing to the floor, the noise of iron hitting stone sending a wave of uncertainty to rush through the shocked assembly. But Lilura had anticipated Elveria's reaction and just before he disappeared, a long, clawed nail shot out and sliced across his leathery, old face. The look of shocked surprise stayed in Lilura's vision long after the magician was gone, and his blood, crimson against her yellowing skin, trickled down the length of her sharpened nail, until she wiped her finger clean with a piece of torn cloth, offered to her by the Lord High Chamberlain.

'Come to me,' Lilura said, lifting her head and gazing at Niculmus. 'Do not be afraid, my child, for I wish you no harm.' The whole courtroom held its breath and watched the apprentice rise from his seat. The witch beckoned towards him with a bony finger and Serquin nodded her head in encouragement before her eyes shifted back to the witch.

Niculmus turned to Crystal and, reaching out, he crushed her hands in his. His eyes held hers for what seemed like an eternity and she saw the look of uncertainty flare inside his eyes and without thinking she pulled him close. He wavered, feeling warm and secure in her arms but then he let her go and with slow, calculated steps, Niculmus made his way down towards the witch.

His face was set firm with cold apprehension as he entered the courtroom and he stretched out his arm, already turning up his shirtsleeve and baring his skin, aware of the test of which the witch intended to do. Lilura held his wrist with a tenderness he had not expected and then she turned her attention to the Lord High Chamberlain and the deep lines around her eyes crinkled like paper.

'If Niculmus is truly Elveria's child, when the bloods are mixed together the secret of father and son will be revealed by the helix of their entwined magic becoming one unity.'

The old crone scratched his flesh with yet another of her sharpened nails and a dozen, tiny pinpricks of blood raced to the surface and she dabbed them clean with the already bloodied cloth.

His life's blood seeped over the darkening red stain left by Elveria and Lilura suddenly dropped the cloth onto the floor as though it had just burnt her fingers. A hush fell over the entire court and everyone, including the Queen, strained their necks and held their breath as they waited to see what would happen next ...

A red mist lifted from the cloth and it hung in the air whilst the sound of tinkering bells rang inside everybody's heads until they shook the noise clear. The mist rose higher and soon became two twisted coils representing Elveria and Niculmus's blood and a second later several ghostly chains appeared. The helix was being driven by their magical genes and the crowd watched in awe when the genetic chains reached out and struck one another as if in battle and then to everyone's amazement, the links fused together, making them whole.

'Why, Lilura, it appears you speak the truth,' declared the Inquisitor, shaking his head in disbelief, clearly flabbergasted. The witch sniggered, turning her attention to the courtroom to watch Merrow being led away by two elf guards, and she gave a high-pitched cackle, her eyes flashing with contentment.

'Don't look so surprised!' she hissed, shifting towards the assembly of Guild members and grinning so widely they could see the dark spaces where her teeth should have been. 'Can't you see that even the likes of me must make sure that our future is secure.'

At that point it appeared Serquin could no longer cope with the current situation and a strange sound left her throat, as though she was being strangled, causing Niculmus to rush over to her in alarm.

'Mother, are you alright?' he asked, when she put her hand in his and he looked down and saw she was trembling.

'I pray you will find it in your heart to forgive me one day,' she whispered, fearing he blamed her. 'Please believe me when I tell you it was never my intention to humiliate you in this way.'

Before Niculmus could reply, Bridgemear was jumping down from the galley and he landed sure footed, right next to him.

'Set the Queen free!' he ordered, pointing to Amella who was still sitting in the dock and a cry of support rang out amongst the royal gallery until the noise was so intense the Inquisitor had no choice but to intervene and he hit the ground so hard with his stave that he made everyone's teeth rattle.

The Lord High Chamberlain looked on with a face set in stone whilst many of the members of the Guild, both ashamed and embarrassed, refused to look him in the eye. He cleared his throat and called for order, and silence eventually swept across the courtroom.

'I think it is clear to all of us in this royal court that a plot has been set against the Queen of Nine Winters, a plot that has been foiled by those who are loyal to the crown and who have seen fit for justice to prevail. From this moment on, let it be known that Elveria is no longer an honorary member of the Guild and a bounty is to be placed upon his head. Although it will be the Queen's personal decision as to his punishment when he is finally caught, Elveria is deemed wanted, and if anyone should harbour such a criminal, then they should be aware of the price they will ultimately pay once he is caught.'

A gaggle of noise burst from the room and Crystal was seen rushing to her mother's side. Amella's face was as white as a ghost's but she smiled down at her daughter with a confidence that comes with winning an injustice.

'It's all over!' Bridgemear cried out, throwing his arms around his wife and pulling her so tight he almost crushed her and Crystal threw her arms around them both, locking them together in an emotional embrace.

Eventually an exaggerated cough was enough to interrupt their tearful embrace and both Amella and Crystal pulled away from one another to see Professor Valentino looking rather glassy eyed towards the Queen.

'It's time for you to return to the palace,' the old magician said, trying to hide the emotion in his voice, 'my Queen, your carriage awaits.' Amella dried her eyes with a handkerchief given to her by her daughter before nodding her sincere thanks to the mage. Amella turned to leave but saw that both Niculmus and his mother were shifting further into the shadows and she called out and gestured for them to come to her side.

'You saved my life,' she told them both, trying hard not to lose her composure which was hanging by a thread, 'and for that, I am eternally in your debt.' She reached out and gently pushed the hair away from the side of Niculmus's face and she gasped when she saw that his ear was not pointed.

'I had no idea,' she said, in hushed tones, 'I never thought for a second that you could be Elveria's son.' She eyed Serquin with compassion and Serquin dropped her gaze and curtsied, the shame of what she had done all those years ago still plainly obvious on her face.

'Your Majesty, you owe us nothing,' she said respectfully, 'I'm just thankful that you have been set free and that justice has, for once, prevailed.'

The Queen nodded, returning her attention back towards Niculmus.

'I am very pleased to say I was completely wrong about you. You see, I thought you wanted to hurt Crystal and when I found Elveria hiding inside his den and saw he had a crystal ball which held your image, I put two and two together and got five. I'm so sorry I misjudged you, Niculmus, however, I hope you realise this chain of events changes everything. Because of what has happened, you can no longer be an apprentice to the Palace of Nine Winters.'

Niculmus outwardly gasped, his eyes turning round with shock and he stared at the Queen as though she had just physically slapped him.

'But, Your Majesty, it's all I've ever wanted,' he reasoned, trying to make her see sense, 'without the apprenticeship I can never become a royal sorcerer.'

'That is true,' Amella acknowledged, noticing Professor Valentino was gesturing that it was time to leave, 'which is why you are to be tutored by the Prince Regent, personally, from this day forth as an equal.'

The look on his face turned to one of confusion and Crystal couldn't help throw her arms around his neck to give him a great, big hug. Amella lowered her lashes and walked away and when Crystal went to pull away she found Niculmus wouldn't let her go. Instead, she felt him drawing his strong arms around her waist and she looked up into his dark, penetrating stare and saw the hunger for her burning deep inside them.

'I thought for a moment I was never going to see you again,' he choked, stroking her hair with the back of his hand. His eyes were bright with genuine relief and Crystal shuddered, feeling her mouth go dry when she realised she was staring at his parted lips, suddenly longing to be kissed by them.

'I'm sorry to interrupt, but your parents are waiting,' said the professor, sounding slightly awkward, 'I think it's time you headed home.'

A sudden hysterical laugh caused disruption in the courtroom and then a whoosh filled the air and Lilura flew by, clutching tightly to her ancient broomstick.

'Farewell, Niculmus!' she howled, her long black robe flapping in the stirring air, 'until we meet again, my young mage.'

The assembly ducked in their seats when the witch's broom bolted for the door, her dark presence still hanging in the air long after she'd gone.

'This is all very surreal,' said Crystal when Niculmus placed a cape over her shoulders and then tied it gently around her throat. Niculmus nodded and his eyebrows lifted a little.

'Yes, I know what you mean,' he said, walking her to the carriage, 'and I have to say it's been one of the strangest days of my life.'

The journey home was not as content as Crystal had expected and both her parents appeared to be locked deep within their own thoughts, allowing tension to trickle through the air. Once they arrived at the palace, Bridgemear ushered her down the marble corridors and straight towards their personal chambers and once the doors were closed, Amella broke her wall of silence.

'Elveria will stop at nothing to kill us,' she told her family and Bridgemear's eyes were seen to dim. Amella moved to where a fire burned in the hearth and after untying her cloak her attention turned to Crystal.

'My darling, we have no choice, for your own safety I must send you back to the ordinary world until Elveria is caught and brought to justice.'

'Never!' Crystal immediately cried, overwhelmed by what her mother's words meant, 'I won't leave Nine Winters ever again!'

Bridgemear jumped from where he had been sitting, his jaw flexed.

'Your mother's right, we have no choice,' he said with a deep sigh. 'Elveria will stop at nothing until we are all dead and the only place where we know you will be safe is back with Matt and Beatrice.'

Crystal saw Amella flinch at the mere mention of her mortal mother's name and Crystal ran to her side, clutching her hand, begging her to reconsider.

'Don't make me leave,' she whimpered, refusing to let go of her hand. 'You know as well as I do that this is where I belong.'

Amella looked at breaking point and her eyes shone like broken stars, but it was Bridgemear who pulled Crystal from her mother's grasp, holding her at arm's length and looking deep into her eyes, willing her to understand their terrible dilemma.

'It's not forever,' he promised, 'it's just until this idiot's caught and then we will come for you.'

Crystal started crying and then a sharp hammering at the door startled her from her tears.

'Who the hell is that?' demanded Bridgemear, furious that someone had the audacity to interrupt them at such a private moment. He rushed to the door, his eyes burning with rage and he flung the door wide.

'Niculmus!' he said in stunned surprise, his anger deflating and in its place sat only confusion. 'How did you get past the guards?'

'Err, I'm really very sorry to disturb you,' Niculmus said, ignoring his question and looking rather sheepish, 'it's just I wondered if I could have a quick word with the princess.'

'No, this is not the right time,' Bridgemear insisted, taking a step closer, but Crystal was already pushing him aside, running towards the apprentice and Niculmus pulled her straight into his arms. He immediately took a few steps back into the darkness and pressed her body against the wall.

His voice turned into a low whisper.

'I can guess what they're thinking of doing,' he told her, lifting her chin and looking deep into her eyes, 'and much as I loathe saying it, I think it is the right thing to do.'

Crystal crumpled like paper in his arms and he struggled to keep her on her feet. He pulled her to her full height and when he saw the sorrow in her eyes he couldn't help bending to kiss her tears away. Crystal responded to his touch and her swollen lips sought his own. His body was warm and his chest hard and he smelt so incredibly male that she found herself melting. Niculmus pulled back, clearly at odds with himself, especially with her parents being so close.

'This is not our time,' he whispered throatily, stroking her cheek with the tip of his finger, 'but I promise you that when you return, things will be very different between us because, I think I've fallen in love with you.'

Crystal looked stunned but then a thin smile split from her trembling lips. His soft voice awoke something deep inside her, stirring feelings which she had denied for too long and she wrapped her arms around him, feeling his hot breath tickle her neck and she heard him inhaling her scent and she shuddered with sexual awakening.

'It is decided, you will leave on the morrow,' Bridgemear interrupted, causing them to split from one another as though a spear of lightning had shocked them apart. Niculmus looked slightly awkward, but he held out his hand and Crystal took it and he drew her away from the shadows and back into the light.

'We will be together, I promise,' he said, glancing at the prince in the hope he would not be against such a match. The mage looked openly confused until he realised what the apprentice was implying and then he reached out and pulled Crystal from Niculmus's grasp, leading her back into her mother's care.

Crystal flew into her mother's arms and allowed her to guide her back towards the fire, her head feeling light and dizzy. The door was closing behind them, but she caught a final glimpse of Niculmus who was blowing her a kiss and she suffered another flutter of excitement, suddenly able to cope with her current dire situation.

'I'll come back to you,' she promised him under her breath, 'and when I do, things *will* be very different.' She turned her attention to her parents, her mind focusing on her uncertain future and with her determination reignited, Crystal realised she would do as they asked and return immediately to the ordinary world.

Epilogue

Somewhere in the distance a church bell tolled the hour of midnight. Crystal listened to the silence that followed with a heavy heart and then folded back the crisp, clean sheet to her bed. She was relieved to finally be back in the ordinary world however, because of the circumstances surrounding her return she felt like it was nothing more than a bitter pill she was having to swallow.

The landing light suddenly shone under her bedroom door and then the toilet flushed and a moment later Beatrice was tapping lightly on her door. Crystal dived under the covers, grabbing Hercules in mid-flight, her heart fluttering with panic and she quickly thumped her pillow into place, just as Beatrice popped her head around the door.

'Night, love,' her mortal mother said, pushing the door a little wider when she saw her daughter was still awake, 'I think it's time you turned your light out and got some well-earned sleep.'

Crystal looked up and saw her mother's caring face and felt a wave of love rush straight through her heart. She was so pleased to see Beatrice again that she immediately jumped from her bed and ran straight into her mother's un-prepared arms. Somewhat startled, Beatrice almost keeled over when Crystal nearly knocked her off her feet and she took a step back in surprise when her daughter broke out into floods of tears, and for a moment Beatrice was clearly lost for words.

'What on earth's the matter?' Beatrice finally rasped, unable to hide the surprise from her voice and instantly hugged her daughter to her bosom. 'Tell me, dear, has something happened today that you think I should know about?'

Crystal immediately stiffened and pulled away from her embrace and she watched her mother pull her dressing gown tight around

281

her middle as though to ready herself for the drama she thought her daughter was about to display.

'What is it, child?' her mother pressed, unable to read the message in her daughter's watery eyes, 'what's wrong? Darling, tell me what's troubling you so?'

Crystal wiped her nose with the sleeve of her pyjamas and then reached out, a little late, for a paper hanky.

'My life's a complete mess!' she snivelled, blowing her nose noisily and trying to fake a smile.

'What would make you say that?' Beatrice asked, rolling her eyes with a sigh. 'Of course it isn't, in fact I'd go as far as to say it's quite the contrary, my dear.'

Crystal made her way back to her bed and Beatrice swiftly followed, and once Crystal was tucked between the sheet and duvet she smoothed down the covers and then sat beside her. Beatrice clasped her hands together and her expression softened, her grey eyes pooling with wisdom.

'I know life seems so complicated once you hit your teens, but I promise you that by the time you leave university you will have a glowing future all mapped out for you.'

Crystal gave her a look that told her she doubted that very much, but she didn't say the words that were dangling on the tip of her tongue and instead reached out and lightly trailed her fingers over her mother's hand. Her skin felt so warm and soft that Crystal grabbed hold of her fingers and pressed them gently against her cheek.

'I don't think my life is ever going to be quite that simple,' she said, letting her mother's hand drop and Beatrice smiled and brushed her daughter's hair away from her beautiful, blue eyes.

'Life is never easy, my dear, no matter who you are. Now enough of this doom and gloom. Let's see you off to sleep and we can talk more about what's bothering you in the morning,' she coaxed, reaching out and patting Hercules on the head as if he was a real dog.

Crystal nodded, grabbing him by the leg and tucking him under her arm before snuggling down for the night.

'I promise that everything will look much better in the morning,' Beatrice soothed, pulling the duvet up to her daughter's chin and then squashing the covers around her body for good measure.

Crystal yawned sleepily and so Beatrice stood up and switched off the bedside light. Her slippered footsteps were muffled by the deep, shagpile carpet but then Crystal heard her bedroom door close and the landing light immediately went out, leaving her alone with only her tangled thoughts to keep her awake. She closed her eyes, praying for sleep, but her mind wouldn't empty because all she could think about were her immortal parents, along with Clump and Niculmus. She missed them all so much already and the tedious minutes turned into long, monotonous hours until she finally managed to drift off to sleep. But then something startled her from her doze and she sat up, staring blindly out of the window, unsure what had woken her and when the darkness revealed nothing but light clouds and bright, shining stars, she curled up in her bed and pulled Hercules even closer.

The thought of Elveria finding her rattled about inside her brain but she was comforted by the thought that apart from her parents, only Tremlon knew of her exact location. She had placed the force field outside her window at her father's request, but had to admit it gave her little peace. Her mind drifted back to Nine Winters and she felt an ache fill her heart that was so painful it almost made her cry out.

When dawn finally broke she drifted off into a restless sleep and only a few hours later she heard her mother calling her for breakfast. Tired, Crystal pulled herself with some reluctance from her warm covers. Hercules was seemingly lying abandoned on the floor and she stepped over him, pulling on her dressing gown and slippers and making her way downstairs towards the kitchen and the smell of hot, buttered toast.

The doorbell rang out the minute she entered the hallway and Beatrice called out for her to answer it. She protested loudly, knowing she was looking messy and suffering severe bed head but when her mother insisted, stating it was probably only the postman, she relented and meekly answered the door.

'Hey, good to see you up so bright and early,' Matt said, pushing a bunch of bright yellow flowers into her hand and looking rather pleased with himself. 'Anyway, I thought I would pop over and say hi after yesterday. You see, I had a good, hard think about what you said and I've come to the conclusion that you would never leave this world without me. I mean, I know it's tough being here without Amella and Bridgemear but I don't believe that's enough of a reason for you to go back to Nine Winters without me by your side.'

'Oh, so that's your conclusion in a nutshell is it?' Crystal asked, beaming brightly and opening the door a little wider so she could accept the flowers graciously. She was so very pleased to see him and wanted to give him a great big hug, but she daren't do such a thing in case he became suspicious and she somehow gave the game away. She pulled the door towards her to let him in and once inside, led him away from the kitchen whilst under her breath she added, 'if only you knew the truth of it Matt, if only you knew what I'd really been up to!'

He turned to her then as though he had heard her and a dark shadow shifted somewhere behind his eyes.

'You went without me, didn't you?' he suddenly asked, his eyes accusing and Crystal looked totally stunned.

'Is it so obvious?' she heard herself saying and Matt turned pale at her reply. She felt herself redden at his penetrating glare and she rushed him into the living room, closing the door swiftly behind her.

'Matt, I think you had better sit down,' she said, her eyes turning hesitant once they were alone, 'if you really want to know the truth, then yes, you're right, I have been back to my kingdom and there's something else I think you need to know.' She stopped then and pulled her dressing gown a little tighter, mimicking her mother's earlier reaction to surviving a crisis.

'Matt, I'm really sorry, but I need to tell you that I've met someone else ...'

Coming Soon…

Defenders of Magic

Lightning Source UK Ltd.
Milton Keynes UK
UKOW05f0650190813

215585UK00001B/14/P